Liz Fielding was borr [...] Zambia before her twe [...] her own special hero [...] way, lived in Botsw [...] pauses for sightseeing pretty much everywhere in between. She now lives in the west of England, close to the Regency grandeur of Bath and the ancient mystery of Stonehenge, and these days leaves her pen to do the travelling. For news of upcoming books visit Liz's website: lizfielding.com

A prolific author of more than one hundred books, **Diana Palmer** got her start as a newspaper reporter. A *New York Times* bestselling author and voted one of the top ten romance writers in America, she has a gift for telling the most sensual tales with charm and humour. Diana lives with her family in Cornelia, Georgia. Visit her website at dianapalmer.com

Discover more at millsandboon.co.uk

CHRISTMAS REUNION IN PARIS

LIZ FIELDING

TEXAS PROUD

DIANA PALMER

MILLS & BOON

First Published in Great Britain 2020
by Mills & Boon, an imprint of HarperCollinsPublishers,
1 London Bridge Street, London, SE1 9GF

Christmas Reunion in Paris © 2020 Harlequin Books S.A.
Texas Proud © 2020 Diana Palmer

Special thanks and acknowledgement are given to Liz Fielding for her contribution to the *Christmas at the Harrington Park Hotel* series.

ISBN: 978-0-263-27898-9

1020

MIX
Paper from
responsible sources
FSC™ C007454

FSC
www.fsc.org

This book is produced from independently certified FSC™ paper to ensure responsible forest management.

For more information visit: www.harpercollins.co.uk/green

Printed and bound in Spain
by CPI, Barcelona

CHRISTMAS REUNION
IN PARIS

LIZ FIELDING

Writing a series with authors you love is a joy.

Thank you Kandy Shepherd and Susan Meier for sharing the Christmas at the Harrington Park Hotel experience with me.

And thank you to my editor, Bryony Green, who never once nagged, but waited patiently for me to get my act together and deliver the book!

CHAPTER ONE

City Diary, London Evening Post, 28th September

> *Following a meeting with creditors of the Harrington Park Hotel, the owner, Nicholas Wolfe, announced today that he has filed for bankruptcy.*
>
> *Once a name breathed with a sigh of pleasure, the hotel was considered a home away from home by those wealthy enough to enjoy the Harrington experience. But the hotel began to lose its way following the death of Rupert Harrington two decades ago.*
>
> *Katherine, his widow, handed ownership of the hotel to her second husband, American businessman Nicholas Wolfe, in order to concentrate on her young family. Wolfe lacked the magic Harrington touch, however, and under his stewardship the brand lost its sparkle. Following Katherine's death in a road accident the hotel's decline, while slow, was terminal.*
>
> *Rumour has it that James Harrington, owner of the Michelin-starred restaurant L'Étranger, and the younger son of Katherine and Rupert Harrington, has teamed up with his interior designer twin, Sally Harrington, to put together a bid, hoping to restore this iconic London hotel to its former glory.*

CHLOE WAS RUNNING LATE. She should be on her way to another job, but an outbreak of flu had left the hotel short-handed and when the head of Housekeeping had asked her to extend her shift, refusal had not been an option.

The double shift had left her exhausted, her legs, feet, head were aching, but this was the last guestroom. The room had been booked for a late arrival, but she was running out of time.

Always uneasy about being upstairs when guests were beginning to return from shopping or sightseeing, she worked fast, but it had to be perfect. She needed this job and mentally ticked off a checklist, ensuring that everything was exactly as a guest who was staying in a luxurious boutique hotel in the heart of Paris would expect.

The small fridge was fully stocked. The flowers perfect, the fruit without a blemish. A bottle of mineral water stood beside a gleaming glass. A small pink-lidded box containing two light-as-air *macarons* was on the tray beside the coffee machine.

She took a breath, momentarily swept back to the taste of raspberry and rose petals melting in her mouth. A long-ago treat from the boy she loved…

She'd spent too long daydreaming and the click of the key in the lock brought her back to reality with the arrival of *madame* to check the room.

'J'ai terminé…'

'Prends ton temps, madame…' The man's tone was reassuring, not *madame*, but the guest telling her to take her time as he dropped his bag and crossed to the window.

He spoke in French and his accent was good, but he was English and her hand trembled as she smoothed back the cover.

A complaint would have been bad, but far worse was the risk that she would come face to face with someone who might recognise her. Someone who had attended the same exclusive private boarding school.

News of where she was, what she was doing—in mocking tones of scandalised amusement—would be flashed around social media within hours. She would have to leave Paris, start again somewhere else. That would cost money, put her dream further out of reach.

The possibility, she told herself, was vanishingly small. She took a breath, reminded herself that staff were invisible. Even if she did come face to face with someone with whom she'd been at school, someone who knew her parents, they would only see the white shirt, the black waistcoat and skirt.

The uniform, not the person.

She straightened from her task, took one last glance around. The man was staring out at Paris, already ablaze with lights for the Christmas season, but she didn't see the view, only the face mirrored in the glass.

Chloe gasped his name.

'James…'

It was no more than a whispered breath, but his gaze flickered from the lights of the city to her own image mirrored alongside him.

For a moment, as they looked into the reflection of each other's eyes, her heart stood still. Would he recognise her? Remember her?

The thought had barely formed before he spun around so fast that, as if he had disturbed the earth's rotation, the room rocked.

She flung out a hand as her world tilted, throwing her off balance, but there was only air to grasp until strong fingers clasped hers, his body steadying her world as he stepped into her, supporting her, holding her, saying her name.

Not a ghost, but the living man with whom, a lifetime ago, she had shared an intense, passionate teenage love.

A doomed romance that had brought disaster down on both their heads but, in his arms, she had forgotten reality, naively blanked from her mind the future planned for her by ambitious parents.

For a few short months, lying spooned against his body, feeling the slow, steady thud of his heart beating against her ribs, the softness of his sleeping breath against her neck, anything had seemed possible.

Now, unbelievably, he was here, grown into the promise of the youth whose every kiss, every touch had stolen her senses, his fingers entwined in her own, a hand at her back, holding her safe against the breadth of wide shoulders, their bodies touching close. Looking at her as if he could not believe what he was seeing.

His eyes were still that thrilling swirl of grey and green that, for years, had haunted her dreams. To look at his wide, sensuous mouth was to feel his lips angled against hers, feel the heat of his need echoed in the desire pounding through her veins and for a moment, weakly, she leaned into him.

'Chloe…' He breathed her name into her hair, as uncertain as the first time he'd kissed her, as the first time they had made love. The same thrilling tremor rippled through her and for a heartbeat, maybe two, she was that girl again, in his arms, lifting her face to him, inviting more.

And then he said her name again, not with that first rare wonder, but with disbelief written into the frown puckering his forehead.

She was clinging to him, waiting for his kiss, while he was attempting to relate the glossy princess of the sixth form with whom he had fallen in love to the maid turning down his bed.

His confusion brought her to her senses.

James Harrington was living his dream, the one they had shared in grabbed moments of privacy, in the precious, never to be forgotten, stolen half-term week that her parents had thought she was spending with an aristocratic school friend. He'd rented a cottage on the coast. They'd swum in the cold sea, eaten luscious food in the middle of the night, made love in front of the fire, totally consumed by their passion.

Blissful, precious days when they hadn't had to hide, but had lived their dream, planning the life they would have together one day in Paris. A fantasy world where, for a few short days, nothing could touch them.

And then the stick had turned blue.

James had done his best to convince her that he could take care of her and their baby, that they would be together no matter what. She'd wanted to believe him, but that fantasy had died with morning sickness. That was something you couldn't keep secret in the hothouse atmosphere of school. Someone had heard her and ratted her out to matron.

'Chloe?' James kept her hand in his as she took a step back, attempting to reclaim a little dignity.

'No...'

Rage, despair, long hours working three jobs had taken their toll and she was no longer that Chloe. *His* Chloe.

She couldn't bear for him to see her like this and she wrenched her hand away, throwing it up to keep him back as she stepped back towards the door.

'No!' she repeated more forcefully as he took a step towards her.

The fierceness of her rejection stopped him, giving her time to wrench open the door.

'Chloe, wait!'

The uncertainty was gone, now. All doubt.

Ten years older, without the dewy freshness, the gloss,

of the girl he'd known, pretending not to know him, to only speak French—he might have hesitated, been left with that disturbed feeling you had when you saw a stranger who looked like someone you once knew.

That might have given her enough time to escape.

But he'd always been Jay to everyone.

James, soft and sweet, was the name she'd used when they were on their own. A stranger would not have clung to him, lips parted, inviting a kiss. No maid would abandon her trolley and run, and she knew that he would come after her, demanding answers that she did not have.

He'd grown up in a hotel, knew his way around behind the scenes; there would be no hiding place and she didn't wait to explain, to change. She just grabbed her coat, bag, boots and made her escape down the narrow lane at the rear of the hotel, the thin soles of her flats slithering on the icy cobbles.

Once in the street, she was quickly swallowed up by the Christmas-shopping crowds laden with glossy carrier bags from the designer stores on the Rue Saint-Honoré, but she didn't slow.

She kept running until she was below ground in the safety of the Metro where she boarded the first train to arrive, pushing into the crush, heart pounding, shivering more with shock than cold, gasping for breath, as the train sped through the dark.

It was early evening and the train had the steamy heat of transport packed with people wanting only to get home to their families, food and warmth after a hard day.

Chloe didn't see them, hear the coughs, the grumbles.

She was lost in the memory of the last time she'd woken in James's arms. His repeated promise that they would be together, that he would be there for her, always. The brief stolen kiss when he'd received a text telling him that he'd been picked to join the cricket team for a grudge match with a rival school on the other side of the county.

It had never occurred to either of them to be suspicious.

There had been no hint of anything other than an ordinary school day until she'd been called to the head's office.

The head wasn't there. Her parents were alone and so, she'd realised, was she. Matron had pretended to believe her diet story, but it was clear that she had not been fooled.

While she had been listening to Miss Kent drone on about Hardy, someone had packed her belongings and within ten minutes of being delivered into the hands of her mother and father she had been driven away from school.

She had been cut off from the moment she'd left the classroom; there had been no way for her to leave a note, a message.

James had known where she lived but even if he'd come after her, he wouldn't have found her. They hadn't taken the road towards their Hampshire estate, or the motorway into London.

Frightened, she had asked her mother where they were going. Her only response had been to hand her a tissue and turn away.

James Harrington, stunned, scarcely able to believe his eyes, his ears, remained rooted to the spot.

He had barely noticed the woman turning down his bed. He was still coming to terms with the sudden turn of events in London. The reappearance of his older brother after seventeen years of silence, the announcement that Hugo was the new owner of the Harrington Park Hotel.

Once he'd recovered from the shock, heard his story, he'd been thrilled that his estranged older brother, Hugo, wanted both him and Sally to be involved in wiping out the bad years when their stepfather Nick Wolfe had been in control. Excited that he wanted them both to help him restore the hotel to the icon it had once been. But his return had dredged up brutal memories. That ghastly Christmas morning when he and Sally had woken up to discover that Hugo was gone, and no one would tell them where he was or when he'd be home.

Their mother had done her best to fill the gap left by his absence, to be there for them. She had even signed the hotel over to Nick, no doubt convinced by him that it would give her more time to spend with her remaining children. The man was an ace manipulator.

The car crash in which she'd died had shattered them both, and Nick Wolfe had been quick to rid himself of the burden of a couple of stepchildren.

It had hit Sally especially hard and her reaction when Hugo had turned up out of the blue had been a release of all that anger, all the pain that had been bottled up inside her.

He'd understood her inability to accept that Hugo had been forced to stay away, to empathise with what he'd been through, but it had been emotionally draining, his nights disturbed by the return of exhausting dream searches down endless corridors for those lost.

His parents.

Hugo.

Chloe and the baby they had made.

She had vanished off the face of the earth ten years ago and when he'd seen her reflection in the window beside him, he had thought for a moment that he was imagining it. That she was a phantom dredged up by those dreams.

Then their eyes had met.

He'd caught her as she'd swayed, felt her breath on his cheek, his lips. Could still feel the warmth of her hand where he'd grasped her fingers. Still, in his mind, feel the warmth of lips that had, for just a moment, been his to take.

Instead, scarcely able to believe his eyes, he had hesitated, unsure, and she had run.

Did she believe that he had rejected her?

'Never!'

Jerking himself out of shocked immobility, he wrenched open the door but wasted seconds had given Chloe time to disappear.

She wouldn't have waited for the lift and he raced to the staff stairs, which led straight down to a part of the hotel that guests never saw. He was down two flights before reality brought him crashing to a halt.

If he burst into Housekeeping, chasing a woman who'd run from him, he knew exactly what they'd think. Bad enough, but he'd won a major television show, was the youngest chef ever to win a Michelin star for L'Étranger, the restaurant he'd founded on the back of his television fame.

His face had been on the cover of enough lifestyle and food magazines to make him recognisable, especially here in Paris where food was a religion.

He didn't care what they said about him, but speculation would be all over social media by morning.

Until he knew why Chloe was working here, in Housekeeping, he needed to exercise discretion because something was wrong. Badly wrong.

The Forbes Scotts were old money. The kind of people who lived behind a security cordon on their estate when they were in the country. In a penthouse apartment accessible only from a private lift in the city. Who spent their vacations on the private islands owned by their friends.

Powerful, rich as Croesus, they could, as he'd discovered when he'd tried to contact Chloe, throw up a wall of silence as impenetrable as their security systems.

He hadn't seen or heard from her since she'd been whisked away while he'd been on the other side of the county, bored out of his mind, sitting out the game as twelfth man on the sidelines of the pitch.

After all the publicity about the Michelin star he had, for a while, lived in hope that Chloe might walk into L'Étranger one day; take in the clubby atmosphere of the ground floor, order a cocktail, ask to meet the chef. Or maybe arrive for the fine dining on the floor above with friends, a partner...

At least send him a card offering her congratulations.

Something. Anything.

Pie in the sky.

She might have smiled to see his success, perhaps remembered a doomed, youthful passion, but she would have moved on, married someone approved by her parents.

She would definitely not want to have her life complicated by him turning up and demanding answers.

Clearly, whatever had happened in the years since she'd disappeared from school, it couldn't have been that.

Did she marry someone her parents disapproved of? That wouldn't be difficult. She'd warned him how it would be. Money spoke to money and anyone short of a multi-millionaire would have been viewed as a fortune hunter.

Did she have a family now?

He leaned back against the wall, swept up in the memory of the anger, the pain of the young man he'd been. He'd had no illusions about the likely outcome of a youthful pregnancy caused by the urgency of their need for one another. His ineptitude.

He pounded a fist into the wall.

Did she think that he'd blame her? She'd warned him what her parents were like, how controlling they were, but with the arrogance of youth he'd dismissed her fears. He'd had the money his father had left him. A pittance compared to her family's wealth, but enough to live the life they had talked about.

He'd promised he would take care of her and their baby. Promised that they would be a family.

He swore as his phone pinged a warning that it was time to leave for his meeting with the chef he hoped to recruit for Harrington's. He turned to walk back up the stairs and paused as something glinted on the steps above him.

He reached out and picked up a piece of crushed silver. It was, or had been, an art deco silver hairpin. He knew that because he'd bought it for Chloe's seventeenth birthday, and it seemed likely that he'd stood on it on his rush down the stairs.

He did not want to leave but Chloe was, for the moment, beyond his reach and time was short if Hugo was to have the hotel open for Christmas Eve.

Louis Joubert was an old friend, but even so it was going to be a hard sell and he had the dramatic temperament to match his flair. He had squeezed in this meeting before starting service and keeping him waiting would not be a good start.

James slipped the piece of silver into his pocket to deal with later.

It was a crazy busy time of year for everyone and he should be in London, in his own kitchen, but he wasn't leaving Paris until he'd talked to Chloe.

CHAPTER TWO

Sally, I've just arrived in Paris and I've seen Chloe! She's working at my hotel as a housekeeper. She ran away when I recognised her. I couldn't follow her and now I have to meet Louis before he starts work. I'll find her tomorrow, try and talk to her then, but I had to tell you. How is Singapore? J x

OMG! What on earth is she doing working as a maid in a hotel? Her family is minted. I'm not surprised she ran. She must have been mortified to have you see her like that. Do be careful, Jay. You'll be ripping a plaster off an old wound for both of you. S x

THERE WAS A second text a few moments later.

Singapore is a lot warmer than Paris, btw. And totally inspiring.

Sally had added a smiley face to her second text, which suggested that she at least was enjoying the break, which after the last few weeks was a relief. But his twin knew Chloe, knew what her disappearance had done to him.

Losing people had been a big part of their lives. It had defined them. Made them into the people they were.

'Jay! I'm sorry to be late. The traffic…'

Lost in the memory of the week that he and Chloe had stolen to be together, Jay was jerked back to the present by Louis's apologetic arrival but it took a moment to gather himself before he stood and greeted his old friend with a hug.

Chloe had told her parents that she would be staying with a school friend for the summer half-term break. No one had cared where he was.

It had been blissfully hot that week and her skin had been silky gold as they'd swum naked in the sea on their last evening, unaware that the clock had already been ticking down on their last moments together.

'No problem, Louis. It's good to see you.'

'Is it? You were far away, my friend,' he said, sitting down. 'I had to say your name twice. Or maybe you are now so grand that you only answer to James?'

'No,' he said quickly. Only two people had ever called him that. His mother and Chloe… 'It's still Jay.' He shook his head. 'I've a lot on my mind. It's a crazy time of year in this business.'

'In any business,' Louis replied, 'but forgive me for doubting that you were contemplating the deconstruction of a figgy pudding for your Christmas menu. That depth of introspection usually involves a woman.'

Jay managed a smile. 'You have rather more experience in that department than I.'

Louis lifted his hands in a wordless gesture before proving Jay's point by reducing the waitress to a blushing mess with no more than a lift of an eyebrow to gain her attention.

'So? Who is she?' Louis asked, after ordering coffee.

Jay shook his head, but said, 'A girl I knew a long time ago. It was a shock to see her in Paris.'

'A pleasant one?'

'Pleasant?' That was far too bland a word. 'It was something of a bombshell if I'm honest.' He was still struggling to believe it... 'It was a long time ago. We were very young.'

'The bittersweet memory of first love?' Louis's shrug was a masterpiece of Gallic appreciation. 'Your heart is broken, but you become a man.'

'How very French.'

Louis grinned. 'What can I say? The world is full of beautiful women and food is the most seductive of life's pleasures. It gives to all the senses. Scent, taste, touch... Well, I do not need to spell it out for someone who is the master of his art,' he said, his grin fading as he remembered some past pleasure of his own, or maybe pain.

'No...' And Jay was the one reliving that moment when he'd held out a spoon for Chloe to taste some treat he'd made for her. Eyes closed, she had sighed with pleasure as she'd licked it, then melted as he had kissed it off her tongue.

'Why are you wasting time talking to me when you could be with her?' Louis asked, after a long moment when they were both lost in the memory of that first—and for Jay only—love.

'It's complicated,' he said, forcing himself to focus on the reason he was in Paris. 'And pinning you down to this meeting was too difficult—' too important '—for me to bail at the last minute.'

London might be the hottest place to eat right now but Louis was French to his marrow and the Harrington Park Hotel had been on the slide for years.

He'd promised Hugo he would find him a chef capable of bringing one of the fabled Michelin stars to the restaurant. He'd worked with Louis in Paris when they were both at the bottom of the ladder, fighting to be noticed, and he was top of a very short list, but James had no illusions that persuading him to take the necessary leap of faith was going to be a piece of patisserie.

Tomorrow he would find Chloe, talk to her, find out what had happened all those years ago. Find out why she was working as a maid in a hotel. Why she had never contacted him.

He scarcely dared believe that she would be free. Had there been a ring on her finger?

That brief touch was seared into his brain and, despite Sally's warning, he was clinging to the edge of hope.

Aware that Louis was regarding him thoughtfully, he launched into details of Hugo's experience in running a highly successful chain of boutique hotels in New York, before outlining his brother's ambitious plans for the Harrington Park Hotel.

'So, what is your vision for the restaurant?'

Louis's very casual question did not fool Jay. As he'd hoped, the chef's entire body language had sharpened at the mention of a New York connection. The possibility that London might be the stepping stone to even bigger things.

He'd cast his line, now he needed to give it a little tug.

'It won't be my vision, Louis,' he said. 'It will be yours.'

'I would have total control?' he asked, finally losing the casual pose. 'Surely you will be Chef Patron at your family hotel?'

'The hotel is Hugo's passion, Louis. I'm delighted that it's back in family hands and I'm happy to help where I can, but I have my own ambitions.'

'More restaurants?'

'I'm working on a couple of ideas,' he admitted, 'but in the immediate future I'm going to be writing a food column for one of the lifestyle magazines and I'm working with a publisher on a book adapted from the blog I've been writing since the beginning of my journey.'

'Your blog…' Louis raised a hand in admiration. 'It reads like a love letter to food.'

Close… He'd begun the blog that first winter in Paris, after he'd fled London. It had been a way of talking to Chloe, telling her where he was, what he was doing without invoking the wrath of her family.

'You are going to be very busy, my friend.'

He'd spent two years in the city before getting his break on a television show. His shrug, as Gallic as anything Louis could throw at him, suggested that time was not a problem, but he wasn't about to confess to the total lack of a social life.

It wasn't for the lack of opportunity. He was driven to succeed, to show the world, to show Nick Wolfe, Chloe's parents—as if they cared—that he was worthy of their respect.

Hugo and Sally were equally compelled. It was their legacy.

Taking the hint, Louis moved back to the purpose of their meeting. 'Who else are you seeing while you're in Paris?'

It was time to reel him in.

'I told Hugo I would find him a *chef de cuisine* who would give him a star within twelve months. The competition in London is red hot right now but I believe you are the man for the job, Louis. The question is, are you up for that challenge?'

He didn't wait for an answer but swiftly laid out the terms of the very generous package Hugo was offering and, while Louis was still taking that in, said, 'When can you be in London to start recruiting your team?'

'You are that sure I'll say yes?' Jay didn't respond. 'It's a big step, leaving everything here.' When he still said nothing, Louis said, 'You did it when you were far younger than me.'

'I had nothing to lose, everything to gain.' For him the move had been an escape, a chance to leave behind everything that reminded him of the people he'd lost. 'This is a rare opportunity, Louis. A chance to make your mark internationally, but time is of the essence and I will need an answer by tomorrow.'

'I'll have to give notice.'

'Speaking from experience, I think you'll find that a chef with his mind elsewhere will not be encouraged to linger.' He relaxed a little, sure now that he had his man. 'Don't you have a *sous chef* stepping on your heels? Someone who is always coming up with ideas for new dishes, encouraging you to take a day off? Go on vacation?'

Louis responded with a rueful smile. 'A precociously talented brat who reminds me of you. I feel his hot breath on my neck every day.'

'Then this is his big moment as well as yours.'

'Maybe. He'll be cheaper than me and times are tough. I'll talk to my boss after service. Whatever happens, I'll call you tomorrow with my answer.'

'By midday.' He was reassured by the fact that Louis wasn't prepared to walk out on his commitments, but there was a time pressure. 'Hugo plans to open the hotel with a party on Christmas Eve. He's going to recreate what was always a special event for guests, staff, family…'

He could still see his father lifting Sally up so that she could hang her new decoration high on the huge tree in the entrance hall. Could still feel the prickle, the smell of the pine as he hung his own ornament. His mother's smiling face as she watched Hugo do the same before the switch was thrown and the tree was lit up in a shimmer of a thousand tiny white lights…

'That's pushing it, Jay. Creating and testing an entirely new menu takes time.'

'What? Oh, yes, but you won't be on your own. My staff will offer you every assistance until you've had the time to recruit your own team.' The Harrington siblings were reclaiming part of their lives they had thought lost for ever and it had to be a success. 'But if you're half the chef I believe you to be, you'll have a notebook full of ideas.'

'Thank you, Jay.' Louis stood up and offered his hand. 'I know that this is a huge opportunity and I appreciate your faith in me. If I'm released, I won't let you down.'

'How long will you need to wrap up things here?'

'There is nothing to keep me. My mother will take care of subletting my flat.'

'You can stay at the hotel until you've had time to find somewhere,' he said, leaving cash on the table and walking with Louis to the door. 'You've met Sally?'

'She came to visit when you were working here. You are twins, yes?'

Jay nodded. Twins, but she had been so much more fragile, battered by a series of devastating losses. It had been down to him to take care of her when their stepfather had shown his true colours, changing their status at St Mary's from day pupils to boarders when the ink was barely dry on their mother's death certificate.

And then he'd left her, too, walking out of school when he'd discovered that Chloe was gone.

There had only been staff at Chloe's family estate in Hampshire, at the flat in London, none of whom had been talking. He hadn't known if he would have been allowed to return to school. He hadn't gone back, but instead had begged a job in the kitchen of a hotelier who had known his father while he'd continued to search for her.

He was just minutes older than his sister, but at times it felt like years.

'Sally is an interior designer now,' he said. 'Very talented. Hugo has asked her to take on the restyling of the hotel and she's in Singapore seeking inspiration. No doubt you will want to work with her so that the dining room and menu are a match.'

'You're thinking fusion?' Louis asked, with a frown.

'I'm thinking international with inspiring vegetarian and vegan dishes. Will that be a problem?'

'It is the way the world is moving,' Louis agreed. 'I have a great many ideas that I haven't been able to introduce to a restaurant serving classic French cuisine. Many inspired by you. How long are you staying in Paris?'

That had always depended on whether Louis accepted the offer. It was a busy time of year and he was needed in his own kitchen, but he wouldn't leave until he'd talked to Chloe.

'I'll take the chance to look at a few restaurants while I'm here,' he said. 'Is there anywhere interesting that you would recommend?'

They paused in the doorway, while Louis suggested several places, then put a hand on his arm. 'Life is more than work, Jay. Forgive me, but you look like a man who needs a holiday. Paris is a city made for love. Find your girl, revisit old times.'

Jay watched him stride away. Louis was right. He was tired, drained by an excess of emotional angst, late-night meetings with Hugo and Sally, but he knew he wouldn't sleep. Instead of returning to the hotel, he began to walk, oblivious to the cold, pausing only to watch the lights dancing on the Eiffel Tower as a bell in a nearby church tower chimed the hour.

Chloe stirred as the train stopped, looked up and, realising where she was, pushed through the crush to get off. There were messages on her phone from Augustin, who owned the bistro where she worked in the evening, pleading with her to come in as soon as she could.

Her head was pounding and all she wanted to do was go home, curl up in bed and pull the covers over her head but Augustin had been good to her and she couldn't let him down. Besides, there was no time to think when she was serving; force of habit kept a smile on her face and just now she needed anything that would keep her from thinking about all she'd lost.

James. Their baby…

Seeing him brought back all that pain and for a moment she was so overwhelmed by grief that she clung to the stair rail while people pushed by.

Someone stopped to ask if she needed help, but she shook her head, forced her legs to move.

Back on the pavement, out of the shelter of the Metro, she was caught by a fit of shivering. Shock as much as the cold stinging her eyes that were wet with rare tears. She blinked them away as she reached the bistro, grateful for the warmth and the relieved welcome of Augustin who, rushed off his feet, didn't care that she was late, only that she had arrived.

She swallowed a couple of painkillers for her head, dealt with hair that had come loose in her haste and realised that she'd lost the silver pin that kept it in place. The silver pin that James had bought her for her seventeenth birthday.

That was the moment that she gave into the tears, sinking onto the floor as they ran, unchecked, down her face.

'Chloe? Are you okay?' There was a tap on the door and when she didn't answer, Augustin opened it. '*Chérie…* what is it?'

She scrambled to her feet, dashing away the tears. 'Nothing. I'm upset because I lost something precious. Stupid. I'll be right there…'

He looked doubtful.

'Really. Just give me a minute.'

He nodded and a couple of minutes later she was in her apron, apologising as she took orders from impatient diners. This was what she did now. What she was.

The money wasn't great, but she worked hard for the tips, saving every cent, hoping one day to create a future for herself. A life where no one could dictate what she did, what she thought, who she loved.

But she was on edge; every time the door opened behind her she twitched, half expecting to hear a familiar voice.

'*Mademoiselle…?*'

Recalled to attention by a diner, she forced a smile. '*Poulet fermier,*' she said, repeating the last item, just to prove that she had been listening, took the rest of the order and then went to the bar to collect their drinks.

'Are you okay, Chloe?' the barman asked as he removed the cap from a bottle of beer.

'It's been a long day.' She stretched her aching neck. 'We're short-staffed at the hotel. It's not just here that I'm doing the work of two.'

But not tomorrow. Tomorrow was Sunday and the bistro was closed. And as for the hotel…

She didn't know how long James would be staying, but he would be waiting for her and she wasn't going anywhere near it until she was sure that he'd checked out.

* * *

Jay gave up on sleep long before it was light, but there was already a text from Louis confirming that he would take the job and, in view of the urgency, would be leaving for London that morning.

He responded with pleasure and not a little relief and, despite the early hour, called Hugo to give him the good news.

'Thanks, Jay. That's a big item crossed off the list. Are you catching the early Eurostar?'

He should get back to London, but his own *sous chef* was more than capable of holding the fort and he couldn't leave until he'd found Chloe, talked to her.

'There are a few things I need to do here,' he said, 'but tell Louis to call my office if he needs help in recruiting staff. We have a waiting list of really good people I'd give a job to in a heartbeat if I had an opening.'

There was a moment of silence while Hugo digested that, but all he said was, 'Thanks. I'll see you when you get back.'

He wasn't leaving the room until he'd seen Chloe so, after a quick shower, he ordered croissants and coffee from room service. It was still early, but he hung a 'make up my room' sign on the door, took his laptop to the desk, out of sight of the door, and settled down to wait.

It was late afternoon before there was a tap on the door, a call of, 'Housekeeping.' It wasn't Chloe. Not exactly a surprise.

He'd hoped she might, once she'd thought about it, decide to face him, but if that was the case, she wouldn't have come here. She would have called him through the hotel switchboard and arranged to meet somewhere neutral.

She hadn't done that, and someone else was working her floor, so she had to be avoiding him.

The housekeeper seemed surprised to see him there, but

with a wave of his hand he indicated that she should carry on, waiting until she was pulling back the bed before, very casually, asking, 'Where's Chloe today?'

'Chloe?' Her expression was blank.

'The English girl who was working this floor yesterday. She was at school with my sister,' he said, which was perfectly true.

'Oh?' Her cautious response suggested doubt, but he pressed on, as if he hadn't noticed.

'Is it her day off?'

She shrugged. 'No. She called in sick today. Everyone has the flu.'

'I'm sorry to hear that. I hoped to catch her before I leave.' The girl stopped fussing with the pillow and waited. He noted the name on her staff badge and said, 'I'm in Paris recruiting staff for my family hotel in London, Julianne. After I saw Chloe, I texted my sister—' which was also true '—and she wants to offer her a job.' Not true, but he didn't have time to mess around with complicated explanations. 'I don't suppose you have her telephone number? Or, better still, her address?' She was unlikely to answer a call from a number she didn't know. 'If she's sick, Sally would want me to make sure she's okay.'

'They'll have it in the office,' Julianne pointed out.

He pulled a face. 'A bit awkward asking them for it. Under the circumstances.'

Another shrug, but this time there was only one meaning. A fifty-euro note found its way into her hand and a minute later he had what he wanted.

Aware that he had run the risk of exposure, he shouldered the backpack that contained his laptop and change of clothes, asked the receptionist to call him a taxi to take him to the Gare du Nord, and checked out.

At the railway station he bought flowers and took the

Metro to the outskirts of Paris. It was getting dark by the time he reached the shabby cobbled street where Chloe lived. Her apartment was at the top of the house and, heart sinking, he climbed five flights of cold, cheerless stairs with damp running down walls that looked as if they hadn't seen a lick of paint in half a century.

There was no response to his knock, but a chink of light showed under a large gap at the bottom of the door.

'Chloe!' he called, knocking again.

Nothing.

Angry now, he raised his voice. 'Come on, Chloe. I'm not leaving, so you might as well let me in.'

CHAPTER THREE

CHLOE LEANED AGAINST the door, fighting the desperate urge to open it. To see James one more time.

She had done everything to try and shut down her brain but, ever since she'd seen him reflected in that window, her memory had been running a loop of the time they had been together, replaying every moment she had spent with him.

She had come close to calling the hotel to speak to him more than half a dozen times, telling herself that it had been cowardly to run, that he would have questions.

Or maybe not.

James had been shocked to see her but, unlike her, he'd achieved what he'd talked about, dreamed about. He had an exciting and successful career. She doubted that he had more than a fleeting memory of a youthful infatuation and, as she'd watched his rise, she'd told herself that she was content. That she wanted him to be fulfilled, happy.

Seeing him so unexpectedly had shattered that image of selflessness. She was furious with him for being the guest in a luxury hotel, while she was the one making his bed.

Alone in her miserable one-room apartment, she wanted to lash out, scream at him, tell him what she'd suffered, but with him standing on the other side of the door all she could think about was that spring and summer when, for the briefest moment, she had been happy.

'Please, Chloe…' This time he was begging and, unable to help herself, she turned the key and opened the door.

James straightened as if he had been leaning against it until he heard the key turn. There were dark shadows beneath his eyes as if, like her, a sleepless night had been spent remembering…

For a moment they just stood in silence, looking at each other. Then he reached out, grazed her cheek with his cold fingers and, without thinking, she leaned into his hand like a kitten seeking comfort.

He drew her close, so that her head was against his chest, against his beating heart, and her arms, with nothing else to do, encircled a chest broader than she remembered.

He took a step forward, taking her with him as he kicked the door shut. The flowers he'd been holding hit the floor, a bag slipped from his shoulder and they were in each other's arms without a word being spoken, clinging to one another as if they would never let go.

After for ever, he leaned back, cradling her face between his hands as he looked at her. As she looked at him.

He brushed a tear from her cheek with the pad of his thumb, kissed away another, then she was tasting the salt as his lips found hers.

It had been a long time since she'd been kissed, felt desired, beautiful. She'd dreamed of this moment, imagined how it would be when the lost years fell away and she'd be that girl on the cusp of her seventeenth birthday, melting in the arms of a boy who made her feel like a princess.

This was nothing like that fantasy.

They had spent nearly a year getting to know one another in the most intimate of ways. James knew all the sweet spots, and she groaned with pleasure as he deepened the kiss, her limbs liquefying as cold fingers stroked the back of her neck, slid beneath her sweater to cup her breast, teasing her already rigid nipple with the tip of his thumb.

There was nothing but hot, desperate need as he stoked the heat and she was with him every step of the way as, shedding clothes with every step, he backed her across the room until she was pinned against the wall. Abandoning her lips, he took her breast, the nipple now achingly hard against her bra, into his mouth.

She cried out as he sucked hard, a shout of triumph that could have been heard over the bells of Notre Dame, urging him on as his hand breached leggings, underwear, to seek out the hot silky ache between her legs.

Desperate, weak with longing, she dug her fingers into his shoulders as he raised his head and looked straight into her eyes as he stroked her to a peak of pleasure. Watched as she fell apart beneath his touch until, at the perfect moment, he drove his fingers deep inside her to deliver a shattering release.

Still shaking with the aftershock, she grabbed handfuls of his tee shirt and pulled it over his head. She wanted to touch him, taste him, feel his skin next to hers. Give him what he'd just given her and more.

She pressed her lips, her tongue, against his chest, tasting him, her hands busy with button and zip as she backed him towards the bed and he tumbled across it.

What followed was raw, brutally intense, utterly consuming and afterwards Chloe lay with her heart pounding, her breasts crushed against a rock-hard chest that was hairier than she remembered, their legs entangled in the intimate confines of her narrow bed, as she came down from the high of a tumultuous climax.

Only one word had been spoken since James had walked through the door. 'Wait…' as he had grabbed his trousers from her hands. Protecting her. Protecting them both.

A hard lesson learned.

Now the only sound was of them catching their breath as they looked at each other with the dazed expression of two people who'd just had the sky fall in on them. As the reality of what had just happened began to dawn on them.

On her.

She had just had rip-your-clothes-off sex with a man she hadn't seen for ten years. She didn't do that. Ever…

Well, not since the time when, despite all the plans they had made, she had, deep down, known that their future would never happen and, in a moment of desperation, despair, had thrown herself at him.

As a teenager it had been stupid. And they had both paid a price for that.

As an adult that total loss of control was embarrassment on the Richter scale even with the protection.

What had she been thinking?

She looked across the broad chest, to the stubble of beard that was new. The easy answer was that she hadn't been thinking, but that would be wrong. She'd been thinking and thinking and remembering for the best part of twenty-four hours.

Thinking about every moment, every touch, her body vibrating from thoughts that refused to be shut out. The sight of him had lit the blue touchpaper and, when she'd touched him, it had gone off like New Year's Eve.

At least it was the same man—the *only* man.

She could console herself with the fact that it was about him rather than simple lust. But what did you say after ten years?

James turned his head and said, 'Hello.'

That was it. It was that simple?

Not simple.

She had to force her response through a throat constricted by a mangle of emotions. Not the embarrassment, the awkwardness, but joy, wonder, to know everything she had clung to was real, true; that her passion for James was as intense, immediate, overwhelming as it had been when she was seventeen.

'Hello.' The word was barely audible, but James smiled and shifted his arm so that he could put it around her shoulders, pull her closer and for a moment she could close her eyes and imagine that she was a teenager again and in love.

Then, James said, 'We're going to need a bigger bed.'

In spite of the emotional turmoil whirling around her head, she let out a shout of laughter.

He'd said the exact same words one evening when they were supposed to be revising for a biology exam and had opted for the practical.

'You remembered,' he said, grinning.

'How could I forget? *Jaws* was your favourite movie and when I didn't get the reference, you insisted I watch it with you. It scared me so much I…' She stopped as she remembered exactly what she'd done to make him turn off the movie. 'So, what's your favourite film now you're a famous chef with a Michelin star?' she asked, before he could go there.

'It will always be *Jaws*…' He raised a hand to briefly cradle her cheek. 'Are you hungry?'

She had been starving it seemed, but not for food. The mention of it, however, brought her crashing back to reality and she yelped as she caught sight of the clock.

'I'm going to be late for work!' she said, wriggling free of his legs, his arms as she tumbled out of bed.

'Work?'

He sat up, combing his fingers through hair she had so thoroughly tousled. She dragged her eyes away, opened drawers looking for clean underwear but the bed squeaked as he stood up. The room was small; all it took was a step and she could feel the heat of his body at her back.

'I thought you called in sick today.'

'No…' She turned to face him. 'I said it was a family emergency, but I work evenings as a waitress at a bistro.'

James looked around, taking in the tiny studio apartment. The kitchen scarcely more than a cupboard. The place in the corner where the rain had come through the roof and the wallpaper she'd put up to make it feel more like home was stained and peeling away.

'It takes two jobs to live like this?'

'Three. I do some cleaning work when I can get it. Paris is expensive and I won't be paid for the day I missed at the hotel.'

'They can't do that,' he protested.

'It's agency work. They can do whatever they like.'

'I'll cover it…' The words died in his mouth as he realised how that must sound. 'We have to talk, Chloe.'

'There's nothing to talk about.' She needed to take a shower but, as she turned away, church bells began to ring. 'Oh… It's Sunday…'

'All day.'

'I…' She shook her head. 'I don't know whether I'm coming or going.'

'I think we both know the answer to that,' he said. 'Loud enough for the neighbours to hear.'

Blushing furiously, she ducked around him and shut herself in the shower. The pressure was abysmal and the water lukewarm or she'd have stayed under it until he gave up and left.

Fat chance of that. He wasn't going anywhere until he had answers to all the questions that must have been burning a hole in his brain for years.

She was going to have to talk to him and the sooner it was done, the sooner she could get back to reality.

When she emerged, still a bit damp around the edges, but dressed, the kettle was on and James was fastening the buttons on his shirt. One was hanging on a thread. As he attempted to fasten it, it came away in his hand and he looked at it for a moment, and they were both remembering the moment when she'd tugged at it in the frantic race to get out of their clothes.

'Give it to me,' she said. 'I'll sew it back on for you.' Because if he didn't stop looking at her like that there was only one hunger that would be satisfied. If they were going to talk, they needed to get out of this room. 'And in answer to your question, yes, I'm hungry.'

'I've got a few recommendations. I'll see if I can get a table somewhere,' he said, putting the button in her hand and shrugging out of his shirt.

The boy she'd loved had been a slender, graceful youth but the years had given his body strength, power, maturity. He was everything she had loved and more and it took every ounce of self-control not to wrap herself around him, fall back into bed and let the world go hang.

Self-control was something she'd learned the hard way. She'd had years to work on blocking those memories. Keeping those feelings at arm's length. Easily resisting the temptation to accept temporary relief when it had been offered. Or so she'd imagined.

Easy to resist when there was only one man who could give her what she wanted. The barriers had come tumbling down when it was that man standing in front of her.

Once, one time...

She'd spent the few minutes in the shower reminding herself of all the reasons that it could not happen again.

Shoring up the barriers. Even so, it was a relief when he pulled on his sweater while she sewed on the button.

He was cold, not taking pity on her, she told herself as she hooked her sewing basket out from under the bed and searched for a needle and matching thread.

'Tea or coffee?' he asked as the kettle boiled.

'T-tea, please,' she replied, sitting on the edge of the bed, concentrating hard to thread the needle with hands that were not quite steady.

His hand fastened over hers, stilling the shake before he took the needle from her and threaded it.

He handed it back without a word, made tea in two mugs, set them on the bedside table and sat beside her.

'How long will it take you to pack?' he asked.

'Pack?' She jabbed herself with the needle, leaving a tiny spot of blood on his shirt.

He took her hand, looked at it, and said, 'You'll live, but I'm not sure you're up to that.'

He took the shirt from her, swiftly stitched the button in place, and by the time he'd returned the needle to the spool and pulled the shirt back on, she had almost regained control over her breathing.

'I'm not going anywhere,' she said.

'You can't stay here.'

Yes… Yes, she could. She had to send him on his way. Convince him somehow that what happened was not important. She took a breath…

'I'm sorry, James. That was a fun trip down memory lane but don't let's get carried away.'

'Look at me, Chloe.'

His voice was low, cobweb soft, but it had an undeniable force and she obeyed without considering the foolishness of such a move. She was shivering and his warmth was tempting her to lean into him, press her lips in the curve of his neck where it met his shoulder. Trembling with the need to put her arms around him, slide her hands down his body, feel the contraction of his muscles, the leap of his response to her touch.

She lowered her lashes so as not to be drawn in by the intensity of his grey-green eyes, but his voice was insistent.

'Look me in the eyes, Chloe, and tell me again that was just a bit of fun. That it's something you do every time a man knocks on your door with a bunch of flowers in his hand.'

She whimpered, a wordless denial that betrayed her and he reached out, lifted her chin so that she was looking directly into his eyes.

'Do you think I didn't look for you?' he asked. 'That I didn't climb the walls of your family estate? Try every way to get past the security at the London penthouse? Contact all of your friends in an effort to find you?'

She swallowed down the ache in her throat, knowing how that would have gone.

'I had dogs set on me, a beating from security guards—'

'They hurt you?'

'They made their point quite thoroughly, but that wasn't the worst.' She closed her eyes as if she could blot out whatever was coming. 'The worst was the summons to Nick Wolfe's office where a solicitor informed me that if I didn't stop "harassing" you, your family and friends, they would go to court and take out a restraining order. Can you imagine how much my stepfather enjoyed being a witness to that humiliation?'

'You weren't harassing me!'

'I was harassing everyone in pursuit of you.'

'I'm so sorry…'

'I don't want your pity. I want you, Chloe. I've never

stopped wanting you and what just happened, happened to both of us. Come back to London with me.'

'London?' She shook her head. 'No...'

His hand opened to cradle her cheek. She had longed for this moment, yearned for the moment when he would hold her, tell her that the nightmare was over and that they would be together.

It was wrong, she knew that it was never going to be over but, weakly, she surrendered to the warmth of his arms and he drew her close.

'I never stopped believing that one day you would get in touch, Chloe. I understood that you couldn't be with me. I just wanted to know that you were okay.'

This was okay. Being held close, being loved...

'Where have you been all this time?' he asked.

'I was sick for a long time, in a clinic—'

He stiffened, drew back to look at her. 'Sick?'

'In my head. After they took our baby.'

And this time, when his arms tightened around her, he held her so close that she could scarcely breathe. She knew that pain; a stab through the heart that no words could ever heal.

'I knew,' he said. 'I always knew they would insist on a termination, but somewhere, deep down, I carried an image of you together.'

She pulled back, looked up at him. His cheeks were wet and, as she wiped her fingers across them, he shivered. For a moment she was tempted to tell him what had really happened, but then he would be burdened with her pain, too.

'I'm sorry, James.'

'Don't apologise to me. I'm the one who messed up. I should have been with you.'

'There was nothing you could have done.'

'I could have tried. If I'd known where you were, I would have come for you. Done anything...'

'Do you think I didn't want to tell you, James? To call your voicemail just to hear your voice? When I was free—'

'Free?'

'Better. When I had recovered,' she corrected herself carefully, 'the situation was made very clear to me. A reputation is a fragile thing, James. If I tried to contact you in any way it would not just be your life in the crusher, but Sally's too, and she had suffered enough.'

'Your parents were that afraid of us being together?'

'We were too young to know what we were doing.' She heard herself trot out words that had been repeated over and over. Gently, coaxingly, with increasing irritation at her stubbornness. Hated them but knew in her heart that they were true.

'Maybe we were,' he said, with an angry gesture at their surroundings, 'but I think we would have done better than this.'

'Would we? Seventeen years old with a baby? Would you be where you are now?' she demanded, feeding off his anger. 'My parents had plans for me, and they didn't include a boy with no family.'

Anger was easier. It was the glue that had held her together, kept her putting one foot in front of the other as she'd refused the soft words, the temptation to accept a comfortable life in return for becoming a coroneted breeding cow...

His body snapped away from hers and cold air filled the gap as he took a long slow look around the apartment, lingering on the crumbling ceiling where the rain regularly came through, and then back at her.

'I may not have a family that can trace its ancestors back to Adam, but some people are more interested in creating something new than looking back at the past.'

'I'm not condoning—' she began, but he wasn't done.

'We may not have had wealth or status in the way your family see it, but there was a trust set up by our grandfather to pay for our education, a substantial inheritance from my grandmother. We would have been young, with a baby, and I'm not fooling myself that it would have been easy, but we wouldn't have been living in a cold room with a leaking roof.'

'You don't understand—'

'What's to understand, Chloe?'

'That it was never about the money.' She sank onto the bed. 'It was about ambition. Much to Father's irritation he could never find a link to the Stuarts so he couldn't actually trace his family back to Adam and hence God—'

'Well, that must have been a blow.'

'But it does go back to one of the barons that came over with the Conqueror.'

'You're serious...' He sat beside her, denting the mattress so that she was tipped towards him. She should move, but the struggle to escape the tilt of the mattress would just make things worse so she stayed very still. 'So why doesn't your father have a title?'

She shrugged. Her shoulder rubbed against his, soaking in his warmth... 'The family straddled both sides in the civil war,' she said quickly. 'The older brother was a Royalist and lost everything. The younger had been close to Cromwell and was lucky to keep his head at the Restoration.'

'And yet they have prospered.'

'They were fast learners. Keep out of politics. Follow the money...

'My father was offered a knighthood for services to charity but considered it beneath him. A bauble for actors and pop stars. He wanted his grandson to have a real title.'

'A real title? How did he imagine that was going to happen?'

'You've heard the expression "a marriage has been arranged…"?'

'What?' He frowned, shook his head. 'No.' Then, when she didn't say anything and he realised that she was serious, 'You have got to be kidding. That's medieval.'

'Not even close. It was still very much part of the deal at the end of the nineteenth century when the British aristocracy was saved from penury by the arrival of American heiresses in search of a title.'

'We've moved on from *Downton Abbey*, Chloe.'

'Not as far as you'd think. I was signed up for the gig when I was still in my pram. The present earl went to school with my father. That's what schools like St Mary's and Eton are for, James. Making useful friendships. Connections with influence and money.'

'I don't believe I'm hearing this.'

'Believe it. The earl was invited to be my godfather. It may have started out as one of those half-joking "Wouldn't it be perfect?" conversations over the font—"My lad, your girl" sort of thing—but the seed was sown and when the earl made some bad financial choices, I became the bail-out option.'

'The boy had no say in this?'

'I imagine he saw it as his duty. The upkeep of a stately pile costs money and marrying it is the family business.'

'Did you know about that? Before we…?' His gesture filled in the gap.

'Theoretically,' she admitted, 'but it was like some pantomime story that had nothing to do with me.'

'Pantomime is right, and it's been ten years, Chloe. I doubt your aristocrat is still hanging onto the glass slipper.'

She shook her head, desperately trying to make him

see. 'My family thinks in centuries and you'd be amazed how patient a man can be when there's a fortune at stake.'

'He's still hoping you'll go back?'

'I have no idea what he thinks, but he hasn't married. I have no doubt that my family know where I am, how I live, and are hoping that a really bad winter will finally bring me to my senses.'

James let out a huff of frustration. 'What kind of man is that entitled? And I'm not talking about a coronet. You're an adult, Chloe. No one can force you into a marriage that you don't want.'

'There is no force. The pressures are more subtle than that.' She managed a shrug. 'It's all about duty to the family.'

She raised an eyebrow at his emphatic response.

'I'm sorry, but duty? Really? What about their duty to you? What about love?'

'In their eyes they were doing what was best for me, James. I'd have been the envy of every girl at St Mary's, including your sister.'

He shook his head. 'I'm astonished, under the circumstances, that you were allowed to go to a mixed boarding school.'

'My mother was a boarder at St Mary's. She told my father that the connections, the friendships, I made there would set me up for the future. That was something my father understood. Their marriage was...'

'Arranged?'

'"Carefully managed" was the phrase she used. People with a lot of money tend to be cautious about letting outsiders near enough to get their hands on it. Maybe she wanted to give me the chance to have a little fun before I settled down to duty.'

'Was that all I was?' he asked. 'Your bit of "fun"?'

'No!' She shrugged. 'Maybe. We were very young. If I hadn't become pregnant…' The denial died on her lips and her fingers twitched, wanting to touch him just one more time.

'It might have burned itself out?'

She dug her nails into her palms. 'Yes,' she lied.

'Then I'm to blame for this.' A sweep of his arm took in the room, while his eyes didn't leave her.

'No!' She took a slow, steadying breath and forced herself to look straight into his eyes. 'No, James. We were both there that day. Bad things happened but they were not your fault. I walked away from my family and now I'm asking you to leave and forget you ever saw me.'

'You think I could forget this?' he demanded, standing up without warning so that she had to grab onto the edge of the bed to stop herself from tumbling sideways. 'Do you think I could forget anything that happened between us? I know you were scared but I would have taken care of you.' When she didn't answer, he said, 'Maybe a termination was easier—'

'No!' The denial brought her to her feet.

She'd always thought that it would be easier for him to believe that there had been no baby, that what she'd done was a burden she had to bear alone, but he had a right to know the truth. 'Never… My parents wanted it, but she was all I had…'

'She?'

The silence was thick in the room and she was struggling to breathe.

'She?' he rapped out.

'There was no termination. We had a little girl, James. I called her Eloise…'

CHAPTER FOUR

THE COLOUR DRAINED from James's face. 'A little girl?' he repeated. 'We have a daughter?'

'I held her for a few minutes after she was born. She had a mop of brown hair just like yours, big eyes. She was so beautiful.'

'Was!'

'Is…' she said quickly. 'I imagine her some days.'

Every day, every waking hour…

'I see this bright, happy little girl who looks a lot like Sally, with parents who love her, who will always put her first, listen to her dreams…'

He grasped her arms, bringing her back from her fantasy.

'Where is she, Chloe?'

She shook her head. 'I don't know. My father finally agreed to let me have my baby but only if I signed adoption papers before she was born.'

'Agreed? That wasn't his decision to make.' He dragged fingers through his hair. 'Is what he did even legal?'

'I don't know. I was alone, isolated from anyone I knew, and I would have agreed to anything to save our little girl.' There were tears pouring down her own cheeks now. 'I didn't believe, once she was born, once they'd seen her, held her, that they would force me to go through with it.

That they would be able to go through with it.' She swallowed. 'My mother might have weakened but my father sent her away before Eloise was born. He never had any intention of letting emotion get in the way of his plans. I was holding her, but I fell asleep and when I woke, our daughter was gone.'

James opened his mouth, closed it again, unable to speak.

'Afterwards, once I understood that I would never see our baby again, I had a kind of breakdown.'

'How did they explain that to the earl?'

'As far as the world was concerned, I was at a finishing school here in France.'

'But you were in a clinic?' His eyes continued to drill into her brain for long seconds until she shivered and he pulled off his sweater, dropped it over her head and, taking her arms one at a time, fed them into the sleeves as if she were a child, before tugging it down over her body.

She wanted him to hold her, to warm her, to tell her that he understood, but instead he took a phone from his trouser pocket.

'I have to get you out of here,' he said, scrolling through his contacts, his own hand shaking. 'Start packing.'

'No. I can't go to London with you,' she said, turning away to rescue the flowers that had dropped, unheeded, to the floor, abandoned in their frantic need for each other.

Her heart turned over as she saw that they were white roses. The same gorgeous fat buds that had been delivered to her on her seventeenth birthday. Red would have raised eyebrows, and questions, but the staff had assumed that they were from her mother...

She had long ago learned to wall up her feelings, memories, but that survival technique had been obliterated in the heat of passion and now, as she breathed in the scent of the roses, it took every ounce of that hard-won self-control to force down an emotional torrent that threatened to over-whelm her.

Every instinct was to bury her face in the blooms, to tell James that she loved him, just as she had when the world was new, and anything had seemed possible.

She had given him her heart, along with everything else, unreservedly when they were young. She had just done it again, but he must never know that because this wasn't a new beginning.

She had known what her parents had planned for her and she should never have allowed herself to become involved with him. To put him at risk.

There could never be a new beginning.

James had moved on, was living the life he had planned, and this had to be an end.

The goodbye they'd never had a chance to say.

She drew on all her strength and, saving the self-indul-gent pity party for later, she put the flowers in a jug, added water and set them on a table under the window.

'Thank you for these,' she said, with the professionally bright voice she used with customers at the bistro. 'They are lovely.'

Jay watched as she riffled the petals of one of the roses, just as she had when he'd bought them for her once before. Nothing had changed. The heat, the passion. Nothing, and yet everything, and he understood that she was distanc-ing herself from him, sending him away. Doing what she thought was best for him.

There were so many questions he wanted to ask her. Questions he'd blocked out in the hours of practising basic kitchen skills, soaking up knowledge, honing a natural gift until he'd got his big break on a television competition for young professional chefs.

Questions that had been running through his head ever since Chloe had run from his hotel room.

They had been wiped from his mind, ceased to matter as they'd reached for one another, reconnecting, filling the emotional and physical void as, for one shining moment, she'd come into his arms and ten missing years had been blown away in an explosion of passion.

And then, while he was still floating in a state of blissful delusion that the world was, finally, the right way up, the barrier had come back up and she was running again. Not from him, but to protect him. When he should be protecting her.

She had chosen to live in a cold, damp walk-up that was too small to swing a cat in—that no self-respecting cat would tolerate—rather than live in comfort with parents who, not content with stealing their daughter from him, had threatened him and his family. Because that kind of adoption could not be legal. One of his colleagues had adopted and she had been on tenterhooks for months, in case the mother changed her mind…

They had recognised the threat. Young as he was, determined as he'd been to find her, they had been afraid that if he found out what they'd done he would have talked to a lawyer.

That was what the threats had been about.

He was safe enough, but Chloe was different.

She was living well below the radar, but it was hard to hide these days, especially from people with friends in high places and a bottomless purse, and she was an heiress on a grand scale.

Her father might have disinherited her, but it wasn't that easy. She was their daughter and would have a legal claim on their estate, as would any children she might bear to some man who did not have the Forbes Scott seal of approval.

She might refuse to play by their rules, but they would want to know where she was, what she was doing and who she was doing it with.

His reappearance would be their worst nightmare.

It wasn't the cold draught whistling through the gaps around the window that sent the shiver up his spine. Her parents had been coldly ruthless with Chloe when they had discovered she was pregnant.

It was clear, from the little she'd said, that the loss had come close to destroying her, that she had been confined to some kind of sanatorium for months, maybe longer.

He had been unable to help her, protect her back then, but guilt for her suffering was his, too.

'Louis…' he said, turning away and dropping his voice as the chef picked up.

'Checking up on me, Jay? I'm in a taxi on my way to the hotel right now.'

'That's brilliant but I'm calling about something else. You mentioned subletting your apartment. Can I take it? Just for a few weeks until your *maman* can find someone long term?'

'You've found your girl?'

'I have, but it's complicated,' he said. 'I'd rather you didn't mention it to anyone.'

'Not even your family?' And when he confirmed that he meant exactly that, Louis said, 'Don't get into any trouble, my friend. Angry husbands are unpredictable.'

'It's not that kind of complicated. It's her family that are the problem.'

'So long as you know what you're doing.'

'Who of us ever knows that?'

Louis laughed. 'Mama will be happy to be spared a trip into Paris in this cold weather. You've stayed before and you know where everything is. There are towels in the air-ing cupboard, wine in the cooler, the basics in the fridge. You're welcome to whatever you can find. The cleaning service comes early on Saturday and I was saying a fond goodbye to a friend last night, so there are clean sheets on the bed, and everything is dust free.'

'Thanks. Let me know what you need in the way of rent and I'll sort it.'

'No one will be moving in for at least a couple of weeks. Take it with my compliments.' Louis gave him the keycode, then said, 'I appear to have arrived at the Harrington Park Hotel. It's…impressive.'

'It was,' Jay said, 'and it will be again with your help. I owe you, Louis. Call me if you need anything.'

He ended the call, took a notebook and pen from his coat pocket and made a note of the keycode, then said, 'It's all fixed.'

'What?'

'I've found somewhere for us to stay while we sort things out.'

'What things? There's nothing to sort out. Please, James, don't make this any harder than it has to be. You've found me and you have your answers. Go back to London, to your restaurant, your life.'

'It's not just my life, Chloe. We have a little girl and I'm going to find her if it's the last thing I do. For that I need your help.'

'I can't…' She shook her head.

'Can't?' It wasn't this appalling room that was giving him the shivers. 'Can't or won't?' he demanded.

'Can't. No one can help you find her, James. It was a closed adoption.'

Closed? The word sounded doom-laden.

'What does that mean?'

'It means that the papers are sealed. I have no idea who

adopted Eloise or where she is. It will be up to her, once she's eighteen, to choose whether or not to trace me.'

'Not me?'

'Your name isn't on the original birth certificate.' She was struggling to speak, he realised. This was a lot harder for her than she wanted him to see. 'We were not married so you would have had to be there. When she was registered.'

'I'm so sorry,' he said, wanting to hold her, show her how sorry he was, but she was holding herself stiffly, away from him as if afraid that if she let go, she would break... 'I'm so sorry to have to put you through this. To force you to remember.'

'Do you think I could ever forget?' she said fiercely. 'Even for one moment?'

'No. Of course not.'

She reached out and took his hand. 'I'm sorry, James. I'm sorry I wasn't stronger.'

'No,' he said. 'You saved her. Gave her life...'

'And if, some day in the future, she decides to find me, ask me what happened, why I let her go, I'll tell her about a long-ago spring and a lovely boy. A special man... I'll tell her where to find you.' She was smiling through the tears filming her eyes. 'I'll be fine.'

'If you don't die of pneumonia first,' he said, struggling to keep the intense emotion from his voice. 'You really can't stay here, Chloe.'

'James...'

'I'm serious. Can you imagine what the press would do to me if they found out that I'd left the mother of my child living in a freezing room where the walls were running with damp?'

'How would they find out? Any of it?'

'I asked the girl who came to clean my room for your address, Chloe.'

'Oh,' she said. 'That's not good.'

'I was desperate and when she said you were off with the flu, I told her that you'd gone to school with my sister and that Sally would want me to make sure you were okay.'

'And she believed you?'

'Fifty euros dealt with any doubts she might have had.'

'Confirmed them more likely. She'll be telling everyone that I've been flirting with one of the guests.'

'I don't think she recognised me, but it wouldn't take a moment for someone to check who was staying in that room.'

'No matter how careful the management are, there will always be someone who's a stringer for the tabloids. It's just the kind of tip-off they thrive on. Even if it was nothing, they could come up with a headline that would make it seem sordid.'

'And it's not nothing.'

'No.' And it was Chloe's turn to let slip an expletive. 'This is my fault. If I hadn't run away—'

'If it's anyone's fault, it's mine, Chloe. I was so desperate to find you that I didn't think through the consequences. The most incompetent researcher is going to find out that both Sally and I were at St Mary's. A little more digging would turn up the fact that you and I left school mid-term in the same week—'

'You were expelled?'

'No.' He shrugged. 'Maybe. I didn't wait to find out. I just wanted to find you.'

'You walked out of school?'

'I knew what I wanted to do,' he said, 'and I didn't need starred A levels or a degree for that.'

She groaned. 'They'll go after Sally, won't they?' Chloe's concern for his sister, so evidently real, warmed him. Gave him hope.

'I'm afraid so. She won't say anything, but they'll have my family history. The hotel is already in the news. And then there's the fact that while your family could give Croesus a run for his money, you are living here.'

'It's not that bad!' she protested.

'Imagine the pictures in the tabloids,' he said. 'They won't focus on the furniture that you've painted, the herbs on the windowsill, the fabrics you've used to make the place more comfortable.'

'Oh, dear Lord…' She looked up at him. 'There will have been gossip at the time and people will swarm out of the woodwork with stories.'

'It's the reality of being in the public eye.'

Her hand tightened around his and for a moment neither of them spoke until the silence was broken by the blasting of a car horn in the street below and a stream of invective from an outraged driver that was clearly audible through the ill-fitting window.

'What are we going to do, James?'

His first instinct had been to go back to London and take Chloe with him. The passion, the desire was as urgent as it had ever been, but they were no longer a couple of teens and the minute he was home, he'd be sucked into pre-Christmas preparations at the restaurant, peace-making between Sally and Hugo, his publication deadline.

She was right. Bad things had happened. They needed time to work through them, to talk, rebuild their relationship.

Right now, nothing was more important than that.

'First things first. You are going to pack—don't leave anything personal behind. Check your rubbish to make sure there's nothing that can lead to you. When you're done, I'll call a taxi and then you are going to disappear.'

'I can't! I have a job!'

'Agency work, you said. Call them and tell them you won't be available until further notice.'

'They'll be annoyed.'

'What can they do? Fire you?'

'But—'

'We are going to the apartment of the chef I've just hired for Harrington's. An informal arrangement with no names on a lease. No paper trail.'

'But…'

'There's a sofa bed in the living room.'

'That's not what's bothering me.' She lifted her shoulders, blushing just a little. 'And my job can be done by anyone, but how can you leave your restaurant?'

'I'm about to give my very talented *sous chef* an early Christmas present by appointing her *chef de cuisine*.'

'But what about your star? Don't they take one away if the *chef de cuisine* leaves?'

'How do you know that?'

'This is France, James. Food is a way of life. I'm right, though.'

He grinned. 'Yes, but I'm not going anywhere. I've been taking on more work, thinking about a second restaurant so I'm less hands-on in the kitchen these days. If I formalise my role to that of executive chef, I think that will cover it. Do you need a hand packing?'

'Um, no… I don't have much,' she said.

She stood up, peeled off his sweater, handed it to him and then stretched up and pulled a holdall from the top shelf of a small wardrobe. She began by lifting the neatly folded contents of her drawers into it. She was right, she didn't have much.

Paris was an expensive place to live, but she was working long hours at two jobs and part time at a third. She should have more than this.

Jay watched her for a moment, the lithe movements of her limbs, the play of light on her skin as she moved to the wardrobe and folded the few garments hanging there and added them to her bag, along with shoe bags, a small box and a folder.

He really hoped she meant it when she said she wasn't bothered about the sofa bed…

She glanced across and caught him staring. 'Can you straighten the bed while I get my stuff from the bathroom?'

'Of course.'

He straightened it out, smoothed the pillows, took the mugs of tea, long gone cold, to the sink and by the time he'd washed them, hung them on their hooks, Chloe had zipped up her bag.

'I'm ready.'

'That's it?'

'Well, the towels and bedlinen are mine. Will we need them?'

She thought she would be coming back here at some point, he realised, but he didn't want that argument now. He just wanted to get her out of there.

'Not unless there's something special you'll want in the next week or two. Is there anyone you need to tell that you won't be here?' he asked. 'Friends who will worry if you disappear?'

Chloe turned from scanning the flat for anything she might have forgotten and looked at him.

'A man, you mean?'

Of course a man. Chloe was a lovely young woman. It was inconceivable that she hadn't been involved with anyone in all this time.

'The woman at the hotel knows where you live,' he said quickly. 'I thought she might be a friend.'

'A friend wouldn't have handed over my address for

fifty euros. Not without asking me first,' she pointed out, then gave a little sigh. 'One of the women at the hotel was looking for somewhere to live. There was a studio vacant on the second floor, so I wrote down the address and the number of the landlord. She was already fixed up, but she pinned it to the noticeboard in case anyone else needed a place. Anyone could have seen it.'

'What about neighbours?'

'We're all out at work. I rarely see anyone. Shall we go?' she said, reaching for her coat. 'No need to call a taxi. It'll be quicker on the Metro.' She wound a scarf around her neck. 'And that won't leave a trail.'

'Am I being paranoid?' he asked.

'Probably,' she said, 'but we've been hiding our relationship since we spent the entire end-of-term Christmas disco at opposite ends of the hall trying not to look at one another. Why change things now?'

'You danced with George McKinnon.'

'Poor George. You took him down in the rugby match the next day.'

'It's all part of the game.'

'You were on the same team! And you danced all evening, too. I didn't lose it when Lydia Grafton produced a piece of mistletoe and kissed you.'

'Why not?' he asked, reaching for his coat, buttoning it.

'I felt sorry for her.' She lifted her shoulders in an awkward little shrug, clearly wishing she hadn't got into this. 'You were top of her Christmas list, James, but I knew that Santa wasn't going to deliver. You'd already given yourself to me.'

'*Plus ça change, plus c'est même chose*, Chloe,' he said, shouldering his backpack and picking up her bag.

Plus ça change...

CHAPTER FIVE

'THIS IS A lovely apartment…'

Jay followed Chloe as she explored her new surroundings, running her fingers along the arm of a soft leather sofa. Glancing out of the tall windows to the street below.

The apartment was one floor above a pretty courtyard in the Latin Quarter, with its Left Bank vibe, and he could well understand why his friend would want to hang onto it, no matter where in the world he was based.

She opened the door to the bedroom and paused, just for a moment, before glancing back at him. 'What was that you said about a bigger bed?'

It wasn't just bigger, it was enormous.

'Chloe, what happened…the sex…' He raked a hand through his hair, a nervous gesture he'd long grown out of. 'It wasn't… I didn't mean to…'

'I was there, James. It happened to both of us,' she said, when he stumbled to a halt. 'It always did.'

'Yes…' His throat was so dry he could hardly speak. 'But I just wanted to make it clear that whatever happens is your decision. This is your place, your rules. I've slept on the sofa before.'

She nodded, giving him no clue to her thoughts, and when she went to check out the bathroom he didn't follow. He'd stayed with Louis one New Year and he knew that it had a roomy walk-in shower and a tub large enough for two. He didn't need that image in his head right now.

'Are you hungry?' he asked, when she'd explored the bathroom and was fidgeting around the apartment. Looking but not looking.

'To be honest I don't know what I am. Everything happened so fast. You've yanked me out of my home, my job, my world,' she said, with a gesture that took in her surroundings, but not owning them. 'I understand why, but what happens next? How am I going to live, James? What am I going to do?'

Her words brought him up short. Even without the possibility of paparazzi interest, getting her out of that ghastly room had been the right thing to do, but he'd turned up out of the blue, taken over her life and the sex had seriously complicated things.

He'd backed off pushing the physical side of their relationship, but he hadn't given much thought to the future beyond getting her back to London and into his life.

He wanted to take her hand, hold her, reassure her that it was all going to be okay, but she'd suffered in ways he couldn't begin to imagine and it was clear that she needed some time, space to make sense of everything that had happened.

Maybe they both did.

'When was the last time you had a holiday?' he asked.

'I, um… I haven't…' He waited. 'If you mean a real holiday, then it was the week we spent at the cottage.'

'That makes two of us,' he said. 'Maybe this is the moment for us both to take time out of our real worlds and have some fun. Leave the future to take care of itself for a couple of weeks?'

'Fun?'

'That wasn't a euphemism for sex, Chloe. I was thinking

that we could take a ride up the Eiffel Tower, have dinner on a Bateau Mouche, take a trip on a tour bus.' They were the first things that came to mind but there had to be a lot more. 'All those things that you don't bother to do when you live in Paris because they're always there.'

'It's not exactly the weather for a ride on an open-topped bus.'

She was still struggling, but she hadn't responded with a flat-out no.

'We'll just have to wrap up warm and take a flask of coffee laced with brandy.'

Even as he said it, he was remembering a freezing night when they'd thawed out in a warm, candlelit bath and, as their eyes met, a flush of pink stained her cheeks and he knew she was remembering it, too.

'We can queue for bread straight from the oven,' he said, seizing the moment. 'Shop in the markets like real Parisiens and pay a visit to Dehillerin. I need new copper pans for the restaurant, and you can help me choose.'

'Not all fun, then?' Chloe said, shaking her head, but she was smiling now.

'When you're a kid you take your pocket money to Hamleys in Regent Street,' he said. 'When you're a chef, you take it to the Paris emporium founded by Eugene de Hillerin a century ago. It will make a great blog post.'

'I'm sure it will,' she said, 'but if that backpack contains everything that you brought with you, I think your first stop had better be for some spare clothes.'

He groaned. 'I hate shopping for clothes.'

She rolled her eyes at him. 'Do you want me to come and hold your hand?' she asked, and he felt the tension seep out of him.

'I'll treat you to breakfast at Café de Flore before we face the ordeal,' he said. 'Why don't you unpack and think about what else you'd like to do while I make a couple of calls and then we'll find somewhere interesting to eat?'

'James…' He waited, but she shook her head. 'Nothing.'

Chloe left James to his phone calls. She didn't have much to unpack and once that was done, she lay back on the gorgeous bed, stretching out limbs heavy with the delicious lassitude that followed vigorous sex.

It felt like coming alive after a long dark winter.

Her Sleeping Beauty moment…

She groaned at the cliché of James climbing the castle wall to wake her with a kiss. It suggested that she had been a passive recipient, when in reality it had been a wholly mutual body slam and one that her body, so long deprived, was eager to repeat.

Her brain, on the other hand, was sending out confused messages.

Its pleasure centre had been jolted out of stasis. Long undisturbed parts of her body were throbbing out a demand for more while health and safety central, the area that had guided every step since she'd chosen freedom over comfort, was frantically flashing a red light.

A warning that this could only end in tears.

James, certain that they could pick up where they left off and carry on as if nothing had happened, reminded her so much of the boy she'd fallen in love with. Eager, full of plans and, when she'd told him that she was pregnant, so sure of their future together as a family. He'd brushed aside her anxieties, ready to confront her parents and, despite his youth, be a man.

And he had been all of that.

He'd been strong, fought tooth and nail to find her and when his efforts had been blocked by lawyers, he hadn't crawled away into a hole. He'd had no family to support him, but he'd done all the things he'd talked about and made a success of his life.

She was the one who'd been weak, crumbled under pressure.

Maybe this would all end in tears but, with James or without him, this was a wake-up call.

It was time to stop running and take hold of her life. Remember her dreams.

Jay chose a bottle of a fine Pouilly-Fuissé from the wine chiller, opened it, poured two glasses and then settled down on the sofa to call Sally and let her know what had happened.

When it went straight to voicemail, and he realised that with the seven-hour time difference it would be close to three a.m. in the Far East, he didn't bother to leave a message, and instead called Freya, his talented *sous chef*.

'Chef?'

'Freya, a personal matter has come up here in Paris. I'll have to stay on for a while.'

'We will manage, chef.'

'I know you will,' he said, 'which is why I'm appointing you *chef de cuisine* at L'Étranger.'

'As a temporary measure?'

Freya was the epitome of Scandi cool, but she hadn't been able to contain the audible gulp before she asked the question.

'No, not temporary. We both know that I've been doing less hands-on work in the kitchen in recent months. With so many new projects demanding my attention that isn't going to change so it makes sense for me to move to the role of executive chef. We'll discuss the financial implications and any changes you might want to make to the menu when I return. You can call me at any time.'

'Yes, chef. Thank you, chef.' She cleared her throat. 'Jay?'

'Freya?'

'Is everything okay?'

He smiled at her unexpected concern. 'Everything' was a long way from certain, but then Chloe appeared in the doorway, causing the same life-changing hitch in his breath that he'd experienced the very first time he'd noticed her, and he said, 'Yes, chef.'

He disconnected, tossed the phone on the table.

A simple little black dress clung to her body; her fair curls had been brushed out around her shoulders. Just looking at her gave him goose bumps but, unlike earlier, when they'd been wordlessly drawn to one another, the silence felt like a force field that was holding them apart.

'Are you finished with your calls?' she asked, when the silence had gone on for far too long.

'Yes… I'd hoped to speak to Sally. She'll want to know that I found you,' he said, rushing on to fill the void, 'but I forgot about the time difference.'

'Time difference? Where is she?'

'Singapore. A lot has happened in the last few weeks. It's why I'm in Paris. But I've sorted out things at the restaurant. No one is expecting me back…' He took a breath, picked up the glasses and handed her one. 'You look…very French.'

'Do I?' She smoothed the cloth across her stomach in a self-conscious gesture. 'Frenchwomen buy classic, keep their clothes for a long time and have no hang-ups about being seen wearing the same thing many times. So well spotted.'

'I'm not sure if I've paid you a compliment or not,' he said uncertainly. Chloe didn't help him out and he struggled on. 'If you have a dress you love, that looks fabulous on you, why wouldn't you want to wear it more than once?'

'It beats me,' she said, clinking her glass against his,

'but I'll drink to fabulous.' They both took a mouthful of the very fine wine. 'And fun.'

Something had changed while he was talking to Freya.

Chloe had been through horrors he could not begin to imagine and today she had not only relived that nightmare for him, but once again, because of him, she had been forced to leave everything she knew.

He'd spent years planning what he'd say if he ever saw her again, but at that moment the words were all wrong, overblown, ridiculous...

'To fun,' he repeated.

They just stood for a long moment, looking at one another until he drained his glass and said, 'Drink up. We need to get out of here.'

James took her arm as they wandered through streets thronged with tourists seeking out the Left Bank vibe, the haunts of writers such as Hemingway and Sartre.

The evening was cold, but the air was filled with the rich spicy scent of food from all parts of the world. Couples were clinging to each other, and not just the young. Stores were lit up with Christmas lights and it should have been magical, but it wasn't and Chloe dug the heels of her boots into the pavement, bringing them to a halt.

'Pardon,' he said, apologising to people behind them who were forced to swerve around them and didn't hesitate to voice their feelings. 'Are you okay, Chloe?'

'No,' she said, pulling her arm free. 'This isn't going to work.'

'I don't understand.'

She raised an eyebrow. 'Really? We know one another more intimately than anyone else on earth and yet you're holding my arm as gingerly as if I was an elderly great-aunt with an uncertain temper. One who will lash out with her stick if you get too close.'

He laughed, but without conviction.

'Don't!' she said, and he lifted a hand in silent apology. 'If you feel awkward, I can handle it, but you don't have to pretend just because we had sex.'

A couple of passers-by whistled, and James looked around a little desperately. 'Could you lower your voice just a little?'

'I've had more contact with a stranger on the Metro,' she hissed and walked on, forcing him to follow her. 'Because that's what you are. It's above the door of your restaurant. L'Étranger. Which is weird, by the way. You don't eat with strangers.'

'It doesn't just mean "stranger",' he said. 'It also means "outsider".'

Outsider? 'Is that how you see yourself?' she asked, shocked.

'It's how everyone else saw me when I came to work in Paris. I'd lost pretty much everyone, everything I was ever close to. My parents, Hugo, my home, you and our baby. It was a recurring theme and I was done with it. If I didn't get close to anyone, I couldn't lose them.'

'Oh, James. I'm sorry. That's such a dark place...' Aware that he was looking at her, she said, 'My breakdown was postnatal depression brought on by grief.'

'Your father should be horsewhipped.'

'And what would that achieve? The damage is done.' She shook her head. 'I had nothing, James, but you were able to focus all those feelings, all your heart, on your career. On the dishes you create.'

'Assemble the best ingredients, treat them with respect and they will always deliver.'

Unlike people. He didn't say it. He didn't need to.

For a moment they just looked at one another as people swerved around them, then she took his arm, tucked it firmly beneath hers and said, 'Come on. Enough with the navel-gazing. Let's eat.'

There were no shortages of places to choose from, but James led the way down a narrow alleyway to a small restaurant. It was busy but when he told the *maître d'* that it had been recommended by Louis Joubert, they were immediately shown to a table by the window.

'What would you like to drink?'

'I'm regretting the expensive glass of wine I didn't finish when you rushed me out of the flat,' she said, smiling at the waiter as he handed her a menu.

'Blame our hasty exit on your dress.'

'Really?' She turned to look at him. 'If I'd known that was the problem, I'd have taken it off.'

'Chloe…'

'I dreamed about this, James. How, one day, you would walk back into my life.'

'Oh? How did it go?'

'The usual way. Like one of those perfect, soft-focus movie moments. The last scene of *Sleepless in Seattle*…'

He looked baffled. 'I don't know that movie.'

She rolled her eyes. 'It does lack a woman-eating shark…' She shook her head. 'It doesn't matter. It was never going to happen, not like that.'

'But we did meet.'

'Yes, but it was more like one of those dreams where you're caught naked in public.'

He frowned. 'You ran away because you were embarrassed because you were working as a maid?'

'About as embarrassed as you'd have been if I'd seen you taking out the rubbish in a burger joint,' she said, but it had been more than that. She'd run from the uncertainty, the fear of rejection... 'Be honest, James, what did you think?'

'Think? I don't know. I was too shocked for anything coherent...'

'That's reality for you. Real life isn't a soft-focus dream and sometimes, no matter how great the ingredients, the sauce curdles.'

'I came after you,' he protested. 'I was halfway down the back stairs when I realised how it would look if I burst into the staffroom in pursuit of a maid.' He sighed. 'I was thinking too much by then. I should have just kept going and to hell with what anyone thought.'

'You wouldn't have found me. I was out of the door and gone.'

'I did find something.' He went to his coat and returned with something that gleamed silver in the candlelight.

Chloe gave a little gasp as she recognised the distorted Celtic swirl of the hair pin James had bought her for her seventeenth birthday.

'It my hairpin,' she said, automatically lifting her hand to where it would normally be tucked into the bun she wore when she was working.

'You must have lost it in your haste and I'm afraid I crushed it as I pounded down the stairs after you.'

'I shouldn't have worn something so precious to work, but some days I needed it.'

She reached out to take it, but he returned it to his pocket. 'I'll have it fixed.'

'It will cost more than it's worth.'

'The fact that it's precious to you, that you wanted to wear it, makes it worth any amount of money to restore it.'

She had to swallow hard to shift the lump in her throat before she could thank him.

'You weren't the only one who dreamed, Chloe. I dreamed, too.'

'In soft focus?'

He shook his head. 'I dreamed about what I would say to you.'

'Hello was a good start.'

'It went downhill from there.'

'It was a bit of a bumpy ride,' she agreed, 'but there were some good bits.'

'Well, that's encouraging. Are you going to give me a clue?'

'I think we need to decide what we're going to eat,' she said, turning to the menu. 'Now, are you going to get all cheffy and insist on talking me through it, or can I just go ahead and order the butternut squash soup and the tagine?'

He ordered the soup for both of them, the tagine for Chloe and fish skewers with ginger served with a risotto for himself and took the waiter's recommendation for a wine robust enough to cope with the spices.

'Your French is very good, James. How did you end up working in Paris?'

'Someone I worked for in the school holidays, an old friend of my father, gave me a job after I walked out of school and, later, he organised a placement for me at one of the big Paris hotels. It's where I met Louis Joubert, the man whose apartment we're camping in.'

'Where is he? Louis?'

'He's in London. At the Harrington Park Hotel. Nick Wolfe finally drove it to bankruptcy. Sally and I were going to make an offer to the creditors, but before we could get all the finances in place it was bought from under us. By Hugo.'

'Hugo?' She thought for a moment. 'Your older brother who disappeared?' James hadn't talked about his brother at school. As far as anyone there knew, he and Sally had no other family. But he'd opened his heart to her... 'He's back?'

'We had a message that the new owner wanted to talk to the Harrington twins. We thought that maybe they wanted to involve us in some way, make capital out of the family connection, but when we walked into the lawyer's office Hugo was waiting for us.'

'That's incredible!' She sat back in her chair. 'That must have been such a shock. Like seeing a ghost.'

'Apparently it's the season for it.'

She waved that away. 'Where has he been all this time?'

Over the food he told her Hugo's story, his plans to restore the hotel, his desire to involve them both.

'That's...' She shook her head because there were no words. 'You must be overjoyed to have him back.'

'I... Yes. After the initial shock. When I'd heard his story. Sally is finding it harder. She can't get her head around why he stayed away for so long. Why he never sent so much as a postcard. He didn't even know, until he got to London, that our mother had been killed in a car accident.'

She swallowed. She didn't have to imagine how it felt to have someone disappear from your life. To have no idea where they were or if they were alive.

She knew.

'Do you understand?' she asked.

He nodded. 'Mum turned her back on him. That's hard to forgive but she was vulnerable, and Nick Wolfe was an accomplished manipulator...'

'Poor Hugo. Poor Sally.'

'She's struggling to forgive him, but she'll get there. She has agreed to handle the design brief for the hotel, which is a start.'

'And you came to Paris to find Hugo a chef?'

'Job done. I already had Louis at the top of the list I'd drawn up in the event that we managed to get the hotel ourselves. I thought it would be a tough sell, but Louis was ripe for a move.'

'And now you've found me. Your list of the lost is getting shorter. And the hotel, your home, is back in your family.'

He nodded, but his mouth tightened, and she knew that he was thinking of their daughter.

She put her hand over his. 'How many years was Hugo lost to you, James? How many years since we were together?'

'Too long,' he said.

'But we endured the dark times,' she said. 'We survived, carried on living and Eloise will be eighteen in just over eight years. If she needs us, she will find us.'

His hand turned and he grasped hers. 'And if she doesn't?'

He sounded despairing but she had lived with that thought a long time and had an answer.

'We will know that she doesn't need us, James. That she's happy, with a family who love her.'

CHAPTER SIX

JAMES NODDED HIS acceptance of what she'd said and, as the waiter arrived with their food, released her hand and sat back.

The soup was rich, unctuous, warming with a hint of fish stock and a cluster of large prawns.

'That has to be the best thing I've eaten in for ever,' she said. 'Was there some chilli in there? I feel warmed to my boots.'

'Just enough for a little heat, not enough to get in the way of the flavour. Perfectly balanced.'

Food took them away from the fraught discussion of the past. James told her about the places he'd worked, some good, some ghastly. About the television show that had given him his big break. About the ups and downs of starting his own restaurant.

They were finally able to relax, laugh and when, a couple of hours later, they walked back out into the street, James took her hand as if it was the most natural thing in the world.

'Thank you, James. It's a long time since I ate in a good restaurant.'

'Food is one of the most important constituents of a holiday. Besides, I don't often have the chance to do this. It's important to get out there, see what good food is on offer.'

'A bit of a busman's holiday, then. Can a chef ever just enjoy a meal without analysing it?' she asked.

'Identifying some subtle ingredient is half the fun, but it's possible. Can you ever look at a bed without wanting to straighten the corners?' he asked.

He was grinning and she laughed as she shook her head, said, 'Thanks for reminding me about the day job. You are going to have to cheer me up by describing the best dish you've ever tasted.'

'Oh, that's a tough one…'

She suggested a few classics, but he shook his head. 'I've tasted some of the greatest dishes, prepared by world-famous chefs,' he said, 'but the magic comes from more than what's on the plate in front of you.'

'Don't tell the food bloggers that!'

'Believe me, I'm not going to discourage them,' he assured her. 'They're good for business and a restaurant dish has to have eye appeal as well as the perfect blend of flavours.'

'But?' She glanced at him. 'There was definitely a lingering "but" hanging around the end of that sentence.'

He pulled her hand beneath his arm, drawing her close. 'The temperature has dropped like a stone. Add hats and gloves to the shopping list,' he said.

'Hats and gloves,' she repeated. 'But?'

He paused at a crossing, watching the traffic, waiting for it to come to a halt before they could cross the road. For a moment she thought he wasn't going to respond to the prompt, and she left it as they turned the corner in the courtyard, but as he punched in the keycode, he said, 'You're right about the "but". Eating is about more than a pretty dish. It's an emotional experience.'

'So not what I expected.'

'It's not about how trendy the restaurant is, or the number of Michelin stars it can boast,' he said. 'It's who you're with that makes food memorable.'

He opened the door, stood back to let her lead the way.

Inside, the flat was warm, and he shed his coat, not looking at her, because it wasn't some dish he was remembering, she realised. It was about who he'd been with when he ate it. Someone else…

She took a breath, wishing she'd never gone down this path, but knowing that she couldn't stop. 'Are you going to tell me?'

'If I tell you,' he said, turning to look at her, his face expressionless, 'my reputation will be entirely in your hands.'

For a moment she was taken in, then she cuffed his arm as she realised that he was teasing. 'You still do that!'

'And you still fall for it.'

She unbuttoned her coat, and he took it from her, giving her a moment to catch her breath while he hung it with his in the lobby. Loving that he was still, deep down, the boy she'd fallen in love with. Afraid of the rush of pleasure it gave her.

'Tea, coffee?' he asked, picking up the wine glasses as he headed for the kitchen.

'There's tea?'

'Herbal stuff. Camomile, spiced ginger, mint? We'll go to Galeries Lafayette and pick up the real thing in the morning. Or there's chocolate?'

'No, I'm fine.'

She could hear him moving about in the kitchen, water running as he washed the glasses. 'Have you guessed yet?' he called after a few moments.

She sank into the soft leather of the sofa, stretched out her legs and cast her mind back.

'It has to be comfort food of some kind?' He didn't answer and she tried to think of the best/worst comfort food she knew. 'A chip butty?'

'Are you referring to the perfection that is a soft bap, split open, filled with chunky fries and covered with curry sauce?'

'That was the rugby-team version. I prefer mine dipped in mayonnaise.'

'You don't know what you're missing,' he said. 'Try again.'

The kitchen on their floor at school had been equipped with a toaster but it had so much use that it was always breaking down, so James had brought in his own and kept it in his room. And a camping gas ring that broke every rule.

She remembered toasted muffins with raspberry jam that tasted of summer. He'd had the biggest pot of Marmite you could buy and on cold winter nights he would heat up tomato soup out of a tin...

When she looked up, he was leaning against the door, watching her, waiting for the penny to drop. And finally, it did.

It was not something they'd eaten at school but late one night in the little cottage by the sea and her heart turned over at the memory of that day, that moment...

'It's a fried-egg sandwich.' Before she could draw one shaky breath, he was beside her, taking her hand. She laughed a little shakily and said, 'But not just any fried-egg sandwich.'

'The eggs have to be free range,' he said, 'bought at the farm gate. They have to be fried in butter...'

They were so close that she could feel his breath on her ear, her cheek...

'...and generously dolloped with brown sauce, squished between slices of thick white bread. And the yolk has to be runny enough to spill out over your fingers when you bite into it.'

The image was so real that she could almost feel the yolk, taste the sharpness of the sauce...

'Licking your fingers is half the fun,' she said.

'Licking someone else's is the other half...'

'It was the last Friday in May,' she said, because someone should keep talking or they were going to do something stupid and she was so determined not to do that stupid thing...

'We'd been on the beach hunting for fossils.'

The sun had been shining, but the sky was streaked with mare's tails from a storm that had passed in the night. And right now, her heart was pounding, her lips burning...

'You found an ammonite.'

'A big one. I don't know what happened to it.'

'You left it in my room. I still have it. That, and a book of poetry that you gave me, the photographs of you on my phone and the clothes I stood up in, were all I took away from school.'

She turned to look at him. 'Sonnets from the Portuguese. "I thought once how Theocritus had sung... Of the sweet years, the dear and wished for years..."'

For a long moment they looked at one another and then James said, 'We had to leave the next morning and you insisted on going for a swim even though the water was freezing. Afterwards you were shivering so much that I ran you a bath so that you could warm up...'

'My fingers were so cold I couldn't manage the buttons. You did them up all wrong,' she said.

He grinned. 'I undid them all right.'

'You were always good at that part.'

'You had sand in your hair, sticking to your skin...'

'I was cold and sore where it had rubbed.' The breath

was being squeezed out of her body and the touch of her clothes against her skin was torture.

'Sand gets everywhere.'

His breath was on her lips, warming her as he had that day, his soapy hands sliding over her breasts, her thighs, between her toes—any place where a grain of sand might cling...

Did her lips touch his first or did he move to close the space between them? It didn't matter. All that mattered was that they were together, that she was melting into a kiss so sweet, so mesmerisingly slow that she barely noticed the moment that she opened her mouth to the sensuously sweet dance of his tongue.

This was her soft-focus dream moment and she drew back just long enough to say, 'The sandwich was epic, James, but let's skip it and go straight to the bath.'

Chloe stirred, stretched.

Jay had been watching her for a while, completely blown away by the unexpected way she had opened up to him last night, become again the seventeen-year-old girl who had thrown away every last vestige of reserve.

Wondering if she would be happy about it in the cold light of day.

She'd been up and down, all evening. Flirty and distant in turn. He'd understood. She'd been through so much and talking to him had clearly brought back painful memories.

Despite that first explosive moment, he'd had no intention of pushing her into an intimate relationship. He'd waited years for this and wasn't about to ruin things by pushing her into something she'd regret.

In the end he hadn't had to push. All it had taken was a throwaway remark, to spark the memory of a special moment when they'd been happy, for her to fall, taking him with her.

The cottage had given them so much freedom. They hadn't had to hide their feelings from disapproving teachers, gossipy girls.

They'd held hands as they'd walked to the beach, laughed a lot, done their bit to save water by sharing showers, been as noisy as they liked when they'd made love.

But that day had been different. What had started as a problem with buttons had built into a no-holds-barred, sensually devastating experience in which Chloe had given everything, demanded everything, with consequences that had changed both their lives. Hers, far more than his.

He bent and gently kissed her lovely mouth. 'Wake up, sleeping beauty.'

'I'm not asleep.' She opened her eyes and what he was seeing was not regret.

'I've been lying here afraid that I was dreaming and that if I opened my eyes, this would all vanish and I'd have to dash to my freezing bathroom, cram into the Metro and spend the entire day making beds and cleaning hotel rooms.'

'It's not going to happen. You're on holiday and so am I.'

'We're on holiday and we're lying in bed wasting the day?'

'Who said anything about wasting it?' Confident now, he propped himself up on his elbow, ran the back of a finger along the curve of her shoulder. 'You look positively edible lying on that pillow.'

'Edible?' She raised an eyebrow. 'Is that what chefs say to a woman when they want to—?'

He put a finger to her lips.

'You are the only woman I've ever said it to, Chloe. I've been too busy building a career, building a business, to waste time indulging in casual sex.'

'Why would it be casual?' She frowned. 'There was no one?'

'There was always someone, Chloe. Just because she wasn't there, I couldn't see her, touch her, didn't change that.'

Lost for words as she took in the enormity of what he'd just said, she reached up, took his face between her hands and said, 'Ditto.'

'That's from one of your movies. There was a song you loved...' But she was kissing him, and he lost the thread.

They shopped in designer outlets in the Marais district. James topped up his wardrobe, bought a scarf. Chloe tried on a bright red coat. She needed a new coat and she was tired of wearing black.

James wanted to buy it for her, but although she wasn't working, she insisted on paying for it herself. She thought he was going to argue, but maybe something in her stance warned him not to push it. Instead he bought her a white faux-fur hat.

'I look ridiculous,' she said. 'And I never wear hats.'

'You look gorgeous and you're going to need it when we go on the bus tour.'

They ate *soupe du jour* in a bistro, which turned out to be leek and potato, but nothing like the way they had made it at school. Afterwards, while they had coffee, James checked his phone.

'Problems?' she asked, when he'd been busy on it for a few minutes.

He looked up. 'Sorry... I didn't mean to ignore you.'

'It's okay. You must have stuff that needs your attention.'

'I do, but my attention was totally focussed on booking dinner on a Bateau Mouche for this evening.'

'Oh.'

'Was that a happy "oh"? Or a *That is such a tourist thing to do* "oh"?'

It had been a surprised, *It would have been nice to talk about it or to have been asked first* 'oh', but he had wanted to give her a treat so she said, 'You did say we were going to behave like total tourists so it was a surprised, happy, *How lovely! I've lived in Paris for years and never done that* "oh".'

He grinned. 'I can't believe the things I never did when I was living here. I haven't even seen the Mona Lisa.'

'I am shocked.'

'You go to see her regularly, I assume.'

'Every week and twice on Sundays.' Then, grinning, she shook her head. 'It's been a while,' she admitted. 'It takes more than a moody portrait to impress a teenage girl.'

'A moody portrait?' He shook his head in disbelief. 'What about the enigmatic smile that everyone raves about?'

'If you must know, I gave her four out of ten for effort. I swear that if she'd been wearing a watch, she'd have been sneaking a glance and wondering how much longer Leonardo was going to take.'

He laughed. 'That's harsh.'

'Maybe I was projecting my own feelings onto her,' she admitted. 'The adults were droning on endlessly about the pictures, the sculptures and a ceiling that they stared at for what seemed like hours.'

'You really didn't have a good time.'

'You want the truth?'

'Will I be able to handle it?'

'I was thirteen. It was Paris Fashion Week and instead of

having a sneaky sip of champagne at Dior with my mother, my father insisted that I accompany him on a tour of the Louvre.'

'A sulky teenager? I'll bet he regretted that.'

She sighed. 'I knew better than to show my feelings. I was very polite to the *directeur* and his guests, smiled in all the appropriate places, even asked a question or two. I knew how to make Papa proud.' She shrugged. 'Until I didn't.'

'I'm so sorry, Chloe.'

She reached out, took his hand. 'Don't be, James. Don't ever be sorry. I've never, for one moment, regretted what happened between us.'

'Ditto...' He drew back, aware that wasn't an appropriate response but couldn't have said why. 'But let's give the Louvre a miss.' He called for the bill, then said, 'It's not fashion week, but we could find a Dior boutique?'

She shook her head, touched that he would be so thoughtful. 'We're doing the tourist trail, it's on every sightseer's bucket list and it's long past time that I gave the old girl another chance.'

They took their purchases back to the flat, Chloe changed into her new coat and they caught the bus from the Sorbonne to the Pont des Arts and walked across the bridge.

'This isn't good. I should have booked a skip-the-queue ticket,' James said as he saw the mass of people waiting to clear security.

'No need.' Chloe tugged him away. 'We'll go in through the Carrousel du Louvre.'

She led the way through the underground shopping precinct, followed the signs and ten minutes later they were inside the museum.

'The Mona Lisa is in Italian Renaissance next to the Salle Denon, but there is a lot of other really fabulous stuff you have to see.'

He'd been downloading the museum app to his phone, but now he looked up, clearly surprised that she'd remembered. 'How long ago did you say you were here?'

'My father was a patron.' She gave an awkward little shrug. 'He probably still is… He considered the appreciation of fine art to be preparation for the life I would live. There was more than one private visit.'

He frowned. 'I didn't have the slightest clue just how different your life was from the rest of us, did I?'

'No,' she said, putting an arm through his to hold him close, 'but that means it's your lucky day. I have a retentive memory so forget the app. You are about to get the advantage of my privileged lifestyle for the price of two tickets.'

He didn't move, just looked at her.

'It's a bargain,' she prompted.

He took a breath. 'Yes, sorry… Where do we start?'

'With Canova's Psyche and Cupid.'

They stood in front of the exquisite marble sculpture while Chloe gave him a potted history of Canova and its subject. 'Their story is one of forbidden love and, after many trials, redemption.'

'Is redemption the same as happy ever after?' he asked,

'Well, it's a Greek myth, so it's not quite that simple.'

He turned from the sculpture to look at her. 'Like life, then.'

She nodded. 'Just like life.'

'That was incredible,' Jay said, a couple of hours later, as they walked through the Christmas fair in the Tuileries, looking at the craft stalls.

'I have to admit that it was a lot more fun with you than my father.'

'I'm relieved to hear it. And fun is what we're about.'

He bought mulled wine and then stopped to look at some

hand-blown glass Christmas ornaments. 'As children, we all used to choose a new ornament each year and hang it on the tree set up in the reception area of the Harrington Park,' he said.

'You're not children any more,' she said. 'And Hugo might not want a tree with all those memories attached to it.'

'We're all children at Christmas,' he said. 'And the tree is part of Harrington history. Which would you choose?'

He watched as Chloe looked at the ornaments, occasionally picking one up. 'The glass bell is very pretty...'

'But?'

'A bit safe. If it were up to me, I'd choose the flamingo.'

'The flamingo it is. And I'll take Cupid.' He nodded to the stallholder. 'It will remind me of our visit to the Louvre.' And because Chloe would be there to hang her own ornament on the tree. 'You weren't kidding about your memory, were you? By the time we reached that ceiling—which was truly amazing, by the way—you had quite an audience. Several people asked if they could book you for a private tour.'

'What a pity I didn't have a card for you to hand out. I could set up my own private tour service.'

He paused at a stall selling cheese to cover his shock at what she'd just said. 'Why would you want to be a tour guide?'

'The tips are good.'

Not going to happen. This was a pause, a little time out, while they reconnected. After an uncertain start, it had been going so well and it was just a matter of time before she returned to London with him and they restarted the clock on their lives.

He'd handed over the kitchen to Freya, and he could write anywhere, but he had other commitments. An awards dinner where he was booked to present one of the prizes. Meetings that couldn't be cancelled...

'I'm sure they are,' he said, 'but do you think your life would be better with four jobs?'

He accepted a sliver of sheep's cheese from the stall-holder. It might as well have been cardboard.

'I could give up the cleaning,' she said, oblivious to the edge in his voice, or deliberately ignoring it as she tried a blue-veined cheese. 'Oh, I like that...' She held out a taster for him to try. 'It's really good, James. Creamy, salty...'

He took it, tasted nothing, but she was waiting for a re-action. 'Yes, it's very good.'

Maybe he lacked conviction, because she sighed and finally stopped avoiding his question.

'I may have rejected my family, James, but the spirit of entrepreneurship is imprinted in the Forbes Scott genes. It's why I work three jobs and save every cent so that when the right moment comes, I'll be ready.'

He frowned. Ready for what?

'This is your moment, Chloe. There's going to be a book in the spring, more television and I'm in talks with a major hotel about establishing an on-site afternoon-tea service. L'Étranger is going to be a brand. I want you to be a part of that.'

He'd hoped to impress her with his own drive, antici-pated some enthusiasm, but she frowned. 'Won't Hugo be offended if you go to a rival?'

Hugo? He shook his head. 'I've already talked to him. He's fine about it.'

'Are you sure?'

She turned to the stallholder to ask him for a hundred and fifty grams of the blue cheese and the only thing he was sure about was that she hadn't responded to his expectation that she would return to London with him. To working with him. Being with him.

'It's possible that he's accepted your decision because he wants to keep you happy,' she said.

'Hugo and I are fine.' She raised an eyebrow. 'We are,' he insisted.

'I hope you're right, but the fracture in your family is complicated. You were split apart by the appalling deceit of one man and, despite the fact that you were children, it's inevitable that you will feel guilt for not having seen the truth.'

What?

'That's crazy,' he protested.

She didn't argue. 'Isn't that why Sally is so angry with him? The reason you are keeping him at a distance?'

'No! I'm not...' The objection was automatic, too quick, and he pulled a face. 'I don't know.'

'You're both afraid that Hugo will disappear again. That's a perfectly natural response, James, and your brother clearly understands that it's going to take time to build trust and knit your family back together. He's not going to do anything to jeopardise that.'

'Is that how it is with us, Chloe?' he asked.

'You never knew why Hugo disappeared, James. That's like a death, but without a body to grieve over.' She took the cheese, paid for it while he was still trying to get his head around that. 'It was different for us. We both knew what had happened, why it happened. Our tragedy was that there was nothing we could do about it.'

'But it doesn't have to end there. Cupid and Psyche had their lives messed up by family—'

'My father is a powerful man, James. He is not a god,' she said, handing him the little paper carrier. 'This is for you. Cheese is very good for the bones.'

But whose bones? Unsure of the answer, he was disinclined to ask. But he would call Hugo later and talk to him. Really talk to him. Ask him how things were going, tell him about Chloe. Maybe broach the question of the afternoon-tea service again, but right now he didn't want to think about any of that.

'Cheese is one of life's great joys,' he said, 'but right now you have to make a really big decision.'

'James…'

'Are we going to take a ride on the Ferris wheel, or risk our bones on the ice rink?'

CHAPTER SEVEN

'DON'T!' CHLOE SHOOK her head as Jay held up his phone to take a video of her with the Eiffel Tower flashing behind her, 'Could you behave any more like a tourist?' she hissed.

'No one but a tourist would be coming on this cruise. Look around you, everyone is doing the same thing. I'm just going to send this to Sally and Hugo so that they can see that we're having a good time.'

He'd called Hugo while Chloe had gone out to buy a new lipstick, and over a long conversation had told him what had happened in the past. Why he was staying in Paris.

Hugo had asked one or two questions, but mostly he'd just listened.

For now, Jay was doing his best to forget about the things that were piling up in London, steering clear of the future and concentrating on the moment.

Chloe rolled her eyes, shook her head, but gave a little wave and said, '*Bonjour*, Sally! *Bonjour*, Hugo!'

He clicked away for a moment and then said, 'All done. The modern equivalent of the postcard.'

The boat began to pull away from the dock, the waitress topped up their glasses, they smiled for the boat's photographer when she stopped at their table.

Food arrived, scallops, duck, something frivolous in chocolate, all delicious but it wasn't about the food. It was about watching Chloe's reflection in the glass canopy as she gazed out at the river. About being with her.

She looked pensive, faraway and he suspected that she wasn't seeing the passing boats, the impressive floodlit buildings, the Ferris wheel from which they'd seen Paris lighting up beneath their feet earlier that evening.

She turned and saw him watching her. 'You're not looking.'

'Yes, I am,' he said. 'I'm looking and looking.'

She blushed, smiled. 'This is lovely. Thank you, James.'

'You say that as if this is over.'

'No… But holidays can't last for ever.'

'That is true. I have to be in London at the end of the week for an industry awards thing.'

'Are you up for something?'

He shook his head. 'Not me this year. I'm presenting an award and I need a date. Are you, by any chance, free on Friday, Miss Forbes Scott?'

'I…' She cleared her throat. 'You're a celebrity, James. There will be cameras there, interest in who you're with.'

'Interest in me is focussed on the hotel at the moment.' His inbox was full of emails from reporters wanting to know how he was feeling about it being back in family hands. 'The lifestyle magazines are full of archive photographs from its glory days. Pictures of film stars, politicians, aristocrats from around the world.'

'I think you'll find that the Forbes Scott name would trump that.'

'You could change it to Chloe Harrington.'

There was one of those moments that sometimes happened in crowded places, when, for a split second, everything fell silent.

Then someone laughed, the clink of crockery being

moved, the gentle pop of a cork and Chloe let out a breath that she hadn't been conscious of holding.

'That's a bit extreme, don't you think?' she managed. 'Just to go to a party.'

'I was thinking of something rather more long term.'

'There's no rush,' she said and, because she didn't want this to develop into a conversation that required an answer she wasn't ready to give, 'Why don't you take Hugo as your guest? It would not only show a united family front, but it would be a chance for him to meet industry professionals on this side of the Atlantic.'

'Yes...' James was no longer looking at her, but at the empty glass in his hand. 'I'll ask him,' he said, signalling the waiter, 'but right now I'm going to have a brandy. Would you like something?'

She shook her head. 'Shall we take the bus trip tomorrow?' she asked, changing the subject. 'And perhaps, afterwards, we could check out the *bouquinites*. It's been an age since I've rummaged for a book bargain.'

He thought about it for a moment then nodded and said, 'Why don't we go for it and top it off, literally, with an evening in the champagne bar at the top of the Eiffel Tower?'

'Not a chance.' The joke had been feeble, but they had moved safely on from name-changing talk. It wasn't just that it was too soon... 'That really is a tourist trap too far. And don't tell me that you've never been to the top of the tower, James Harrington, because I won't believe you.'

He held up his hands, found a smile. 'You've got me. Choose whatever you like for tomorrow evening and I'll do my best to deliver.'

'Truly?' She reached across the table and took his hand. 'Then I choose to stay in while you cook for me the way you used to. If that should happen to involve a glass of champagne, I would be extra happy.'

'Your happiness is all I care about,' he said, holding her with a long, steady look until the waitress arrived with the bill for the drinks and the photograph. He paid her, adding a tip, then picked up the photograph and looked at it.

They looked so ordinary as they'd smiled for the camera. Just another happy couple out on a date without a thing in the world to trouble them.

'One for the family album,' he said, sliding it into his pocket as the boat settled back against the pier.

'Let me give you another one, James.'

Chloe had been trying to find the right moment for this, aware that it was an emotional minefield, one she'd shied away from when they were alone. Now he'd given her the perfect opening and she fumbled with the clasp of her bag, finger shaking a little as she took out a small leather folder.

'I found these copies today; they're for you,' she said, offering it to him.

He looked at her for a long moment before he opened it.

On one side was a scan of their daughter at twenty weeks. On the other there was a close-up of their newborn infant, moments after she'd been placed in her arms.

'Eloise...'

He touched the precious images, looking at them for a long moment. Then he looked up and, as she saw the struggle he was having to hold back feelings that he couldn't allow to spill over, she wished she'd been braver.

Wished they were somewhere private so that she could hold him. So that he could let the tears fall.

'I'm sorry. I should have waited.'

He shook his head, stood up.

The cruise was over, the boat was emptying, and he helped her into her coat, hailed a taxi, walked her to the door of the apartment.

It wasn't that he didn't speak, just that the few words he

said to thank the staff as they left the boat, to tell the driver where to take them, had nothing to do with her. With them.

He keyed in the door code but when he didn't follow her inside, she said. 'Are you okay?'

'I'm fine, but I need to be on my own for a while.'

His touch to her arm was a gentle reassurance that it wasn't about anything she'd done, but as he walked away she wondered if she should follow him. As if sensing her hesitation, he turned, nodded. 'Go in. I won't be long.'

Jay walked to the river, bought coffee from a late-night stallholder and sat on a bench. Moments later an old homeless man shuffled along and sat beside him.

He asked him if he could buy him a cup of coffee, maybe a burger.

The stallholder shook his head, said, 'Don't give him any money, or he will drink it.'

Jay nodded, and they sat together for a while in silence until, unbidden, the old guy started to tell him how his wife had got cancer and died. How grief had driven him to drink, his son had been taken in foster care and he'd lost his house. A justification of how he'd ended up sleeping rough.

'What happened to you, son?' he asked, assuming he was on the same downward path.

'Nothing,' he said. Whether the old man was telling the truth scarcely mattered. Compared to him, he was the luckiest man alive. 'I'm absolutely fine.' He got up to leave. The temptation to take out his wallet and hand over some cash was inevitable, but bearing in mind the stallholder's warning he said, 'Is there anything you need?'

'I could use a coat.'

It was true, the one he was wearing was in rags, and Jay took his off, emptied the pockets into his jacket.

'He'll sell it,' the burger guy warned.

He didn't doubt it, but he handed it over anyway and walked back to the flat.

Chloe stirred, felt the cold emptiness in the bed beside her, heard the soft tapping of fingers on a keyboard.

She'd gone to bed but had stayed awake, fretting, until she heard James come in. He'd gone into the kitchen, switched on the kettle and, finally able to relax, she had drifted off.

It had only been a few days and already she missed being able to reach out and touch him, to know that he was beside her, and she eased herself up on the pillow so that she could see him.

He was sitting at the little table beneath the window, the light from the screen lighting up his face as he worked. He was spending all his time with her but there had to be things that he couldn't pass on to someone else. There was a blog with an army of followers, the book he was working on...

'"My candle burns at both ends, it will not last the night..."' she said.

He turned from the keyboard. There were dark hollows beneath his eyes, but he was smiling. 'I'm sorry. I didn't mean to wake you.'

'It wasn't the keyboard,' she said. 'It was your absence. The bed is cold without you. Where did you go?'

'Down by the river. I just needed a walk to clear my head.'

'Did it work?'

'Yes,' he said. 'It did. I'll take this through to the other room.'

'There's no need,' she said, swinging her legs out of the bed. 'I'm going to make a cup of tea. But just so you know, we don't have to gallivant all over Paris as if all the attractions will be gone in a fortnight. I'm perfectly happy staying in while you work.'

He looked as if he was about to say something about the world and how it had ended for them once before, but he let it go.

'I'm just about done here, but a cup of tea would be very welcome.'

She put the kettle on, cut brioche to make toast while it boiled, and added a pot of marmalade James had bought in the food hall at Galeries Lafayette to the tray.

He smiled appreciatively when she carried it through and joined her when she climbed back into the warmth of the bed.

'Midnight snacks. It's like being back at school.'

'More like four in the morning snacks. And you still have homework, apparently.'

'There's a saying, Chloe, that a man who loves his job never works a day in his life.'

'Confucius.'

'I'm sorry?'

'It was Confucius who said it.' She bit into the toast, relishing the mingled warmth of brioche, butter and the sharp orange tang of the conserve. 'I need to find something that I love that much.'

'Not bedmaking?' he teased. But then he said, 'I didn't realise it at the time, but you never talked about what career you had in mind after school, university. But maybe university wasn't in the plan?'

'I've no idea. It wasn't something I ever discussed with my father. I didn't actually go to school until I was eleven years old, when my mother insisted that I needed a social group.'

'I never knew that. I assumed you'd always been at St Mary's. You were a straight-A student.'

'I had tutors. My mother was brought up to run a country house, be the perfect hostess, but no one had cared much about her education and her ignorance used to irritate my father. He was determined that I would be able to hold my own in every aspect of life.'

'Hence the gallery tours,' he said, lifting the tray to the floor before rolling onto his side so that he was looking at her.

'Among other things. As my father's only heir, it would be my responsibility to keep his legacy intact. I had to account for every penny I spent from the moment I was given an allowance. He fined me if I couldn't balance my books.'

'Unbelievable.'

'It only happened once,' she said. 'I'm a fast learner. And I'm grateful for that lesson every day of my life.'

'You could have done anything, Chloe. You still can. You could take a degree now, as a mature student. I'd support you.'

'There's only one thing I want from you, James, and you don't have to do a thing.' She ostentatiously sucked a smear of marmalade off her thumb.

'A lady would have left that to me.'

'If I'd wanted to be a lady, I would have married the earl-in-waiting,' she said, pushing him onto his back and straddling him. 'Right now, all you have to do is lie back and think of England.'

'Where's your coat?' Chloe asked as they prepared to leave the apartment.

'Last night I gave it to a man who didn't have a home, let alone a coat.'

She raised an eyebrow. 'You gave a homeless man your cashmere coat?'

'It only takes one thing to throw us off balance, a single missed step.'

'And you thought how easily it could have been you?' she asked. Then, 'No. Me. You thought it could be me.'

'We're all one step away from the park bench.'

'That was a seriously head-clearing walk.'

'I take it your father would not approve?'

'He has a charitable foundation, but I imagine he would have thought such a gesture quixotic.'

'Quixotic?'

'Romantic, then.'

'A coat is just a coat, Chloe, and I promise you, my head was never clearer.'

She linked her arm with his. 'I'm fine with romantic. It was a good thing to do but we are going to have to make a stop and replace it or you are going to freeze to death on top of that bus.'

Half an hour later, suitably coated, scarfed and gloved, they were waiting for the hop-on/hop-off bus at the stop near the Sorbonne.

'Are we crazy doing this?' Chloe asked, stamping her feet and looking up at the low clouds. Then, realising that James was engrossed in something on his phone, she made an irritated growling noise. 'I'm sorry. Am I disturbing you?'

'What?' He looked up. 'How do you feel about getting out of Paris for a day or two, Chloe?'

'Somewhere warm?' she asked, hopefully.

'No warmer than here but, since you're getting picky about the more obvious tourist venues, I thought we could hire a car tomorrow and take a trip out to Thoiry to see the light show at the zoo.'

'Oh…' She'd thought he was working, but he'd been looking at places to take her.

'Oh, great? Or, oh, that's the dumbest idea I've heard this week?' he asked.

'Oh, this holiday thing could get addictive.' This James thing could get dangerously addictive…

'So that's a yes?' he prompted, when her head was stuck on that thought…

'Yes, please. I've heard it's absolutely magical.'

'Right answer. I've booked tickets for tomorrow evening and a suite in a nearby château, so we won't have to drive back at night.'

Once again only asking her after he'd gone ahead and booked, but before she could say anything, he showed her the picture of a hotel suite furnished in French provincial style.

'Ohmigod, that's gorgeous.'

'Again, right answer.' He smiled, thoroughly pleased with himself. 'The place even has its own vineyard.'

'Er… You do know it's the wrong time of year to visit a vineyard?'

'But not to talk to the *vigneron* or taste the wine. If it lives up to the notes on their website and you like it, I might buy some for the restaurant.'

'What does my opinion have to do with anything?'

He frowned. 'Your opinion has to do with everything. You are part of my life, Chloe.'

She wanted to be part of his life but a cold spot in the pit of her stomach warned her that this was going way too fast.

She wanted to say hold on, wait, but the bus appeared, and they climbed aboard.

James flashed the ticket on his phone over the scanner while she grabbed a couple of earpieces and by the time he joined her on the top deck she was plugging them in, finding the right language, adjusting the sound.

'Do we need these?' he asked.

She ignored his frown. 'Totally. If I'm doing the tour I want to know who did what and when.'

They toured the Île de la Cité, sighed over the damage to Notre Dame, took selfies of themselves with the Arc de Triomphe in the background, but neither of them mentioned the family album.

There was a brief flurry of snow as they reached the high spot at the Trocadero. The few people who'd braved the top of the bus with them scrambled off at that point, to go and take photographs of the Eiffel Tower.

Alone, they abandoned the headphones and held out for a few more stops before Chloe said, 'I can't feel my cheeks.'

'I can,' James said, holding his gloved hands, still warm from the cup he'd been holding, against them. Thawing her lips with a lingering kiss that heated her in a way that the brandy-laced coffee had signally failed to do. She clutched at his coat, wanting to hold onto the moment, but then a couple of hardy souls joined them on the top deck and James pulled back a little and she laughed.

'What?'

'Your hair...' It was dusted with snowflakes that, as a shaft of sunlight broke through the clouds, sparkled like diamonds and she took a snap before, self-consciously, he raised a hand and vigorously brushed it over his head. It came away wet.

'You were right, *chérie*. I should have bought a hat.'

'No. It was perfect, but right now I'm done with this. I need soup. Something spicy with beans,' she said. 'Actually, make that anything as long as it's steaming hot.'

'Good call.'

Later, thoroughly defrosted, they wandered along the Seine near Notre Dame, browsing the *bouquinites*. The booksellers had been a feature of the area since the middle of the sixteenth century, but had taken up permanent residence, with their green boxes, in the late nineteenth century and now, as well as vintage books, sold prints and magnets to the tourists.

'What are you looking for?' Chloe asked.

'I collect old cookery books, but I'm also hoping to find something for Sally for Christmas.'

A chat with one of the stallholders produced an early copy of *The Memoirs of Alexis Soyer* that he was excited to find and, while he was haggling over that, Chloe found a beautiful book with colour plates of art deco interiors and handed it to him.

'That's perfect,' he said. 'Sally will love it.'

'What about Hugo?' she asked, putting down a print before he noticed her interest.

'I have no idea. He's my brother but I was just a kid when he disappeared,' he said as they moved on. 'I know he's been a hugely successful hotelier in the States, but I have no idea what interests him.'

'Give it time, James.'

'Time is the one thing we never have. He's been so wrapped up in restoring the hotel, and I have so much on myself. There hasn't been much time to get close.'

'You should organise something that you can do together. Is he into sport?'

'He used to play cricket at school, but they don't play a lot of that in New York.'

'Or in the winter in England. What about football? Can you get tickets to a match?'

'I could, but actually he and Dad were big rugby fans. I remember Dad taking him to watch England play France just before he died. Mum tried to persuade Nick to take him to a match, but it never happened.'

'It sounds as if you've found, not only the perfect gift, but a chance to connect outside work.'

'That is a brilliant idea. I'll get tickets for one of the Six Nations matches at Twickenham.' He checked the fixture list on his phone. 'There is nothing like the sound of fifty thousand voices singing "Swing Low Sweet Chariot" to remind a man that he's English.' He removed his gloves, propped his elbows on the Pont Neuf bridge and clicked away for a minute. 'All done.'

'Wonderful. You'll have a lovely day.'

'It'll be better if England win, but I heard what you said about talking to him, Chloe.' He turned and leaned back against the curve of the ancient stone. 'I called him yesterday and opened up to him about what happened to us.' He glanced at her. 'I hope that's okay?'

'Of course it is. It's your story, too… What did he say?'

'Not much, to be honest. He just listened.'

'I like the sound of Hugo. The world needs more people who know how to listen,' she said, straightening and signalling to a taxi that was dropping people off. 'You'll get there, but right now I think it's time for a little fun.'

He opened the car door. 'Fun?'

'You can wipe that smile off your face, James Harrington,' she said, ducking into the warmth of the cab. 'We're going to be out of Paris for a couple of days and after that you have to go back to London.' The cab driver looked back. 'Rue Coquillière,' she told him. 'DeHillerin.'

'Oh, kitchen fun!' The grin splitting James's face was so wide that he looked exactly like the boy she'd fallen in love with. The boy who'd treated food as if he were an artist, his ingredients the palette he used to create his masterpieces.

Not that they had all been masterpieces. There had been some spectacular disasters, but his passion, his enthusiasm had never been dented by failure. He'd gone for it one hundred per cent.

'Have I said how much I love you?'

'What you're feeling isn't love,' she told him. 'It's anticipation of the culinary equivalent of a trip to Disney.'

'We should do that, too.' The grin, impossibly, widened. 'I'll wake you with a kiss in Sleeping Beauty's castle and we'll live happily ever after.' He reached across the seat to take her hand. 'What do you say, Chloe?'

'I'd say no, thank you, and if you'd read the original story, you might not be so keen on that scenario, either.'

'Is it one of the gruesome ones?'

'They are all pretty gruesome. That one is just plain nasty.' Right down to the stolen babies.

She shivered and James, assuming that she was cold, put an arm around her. Clearly he hadn't heard the clear no, and she felt guilty as she leaned into him, accepting the comfort.

CHAPTER EIGHT

'IT'S NOT GOING to snow,' Jay said.

They were headed out of Paris on the A14, planning to book into the château first, have lunch and then head out to the zoo later for the light show.

'The forecast says snow.'

'The forecast said that any snow is going to fall east of Paris. We're heading west.'

'The sky says different.'

Jay looked across at her, not bothering to hide his amusement. 'Are we having our first argument over the weather forecast?'

'I'm not arguing,' she said. 'I'm merely stating the obvious.'

'I'd forgotten how stubborn you can be,' he said.'

'Only when I'm right.'

'Okay,' he said, 'you may have a point, but this is a major road and we're not in England where half an inch of snow brings the country to a halt and you know what?'

'Never met him.'

He grimaced. 'I can imagine a lot worse things than being snowed in with you, Smarty-Pants, but for now the road is dry and we should soon be at the turning for the château. Forget the weather and look out for that.'

'Yes, sir.' She threw a mock salute and, when he rolled

his eyes, she said, 'I haven't forgotten how bossy you can be.'

Before he could object, they reached the turning and, since it was a while since he'd driven on the right-hand side of the road, he had to concentrate on exiting the dual carriageway.

'This is so pretty,' Chloe said as the road narrowed, and they travelled through countryside dotted with small vineyards. Twisting and turning to look at the farmhouses they passed until they reached the outskirts of a large village.

He edged the car through the busy square where a market was in progress.

'Oh, look, it's a *brocante*, James. Can we stop?'

It wasn't what he'd planned, and he had no idea what she thought she'd find in a village flea market, but until now he was the one coming up with all the suggestions. This was the first time she'd asked him for anything.

'Of course we can stop, just promise not to buy anything that won't fit in the car.'

'Spoilsport.'

'Okay, you can buy whatever you like, but you're going to have to figure out how to get it home.'

Home. The word brought a smile to his face. He was living in a one-bedroomed flat on top of the restaurant. It would do as a temporary measure, but he'd find somewhere bigger for them as soon as they were married. Somewhere with a garden.

He found a place to park on the edge of the village and as they walked back, hand in hand, he felt as if they were finally putting the tensions left over from the past behind them. Moving on.

It was a Christmas *brocante*, with a lot of decorations on sale. Willow wreaths, hand-made wooden and felt tree decorations. Boxes of old glass baubles—the kind that smashed if you dropped them.

On one stall he found a snow globe with some age to it.

'My mother had one of these,' he said. 'I wonder if it's still at the house, or if Nick got rid of everything.'

'I'm surprised he didn't sell it. The house.'

'It's in the hotel grounds. It would have been the estate manager's house in the days when the hotel was a private mansion. I assume that Hugo will live there. Or maybe a manager if he decides to put one in. The chances are he'll go back to New York.'

'You, Sally and Hugo should get together and go through everything. There will be photographs, old school reports, birthday cards and maybe even your mother's snow globe.'

'Maybe, but I'll buy this anyway.' He gave it a shake so that the snow swirled around the wintry scene. 'I'll keep it on my desk to remind me of the day it didn't snow.' He held out his hand as if to demonstrate. 'Oh, look, I think that's the sun,' he said, looking up at the sky where there was a glimmer of light behind the clouds.

'Barely,' she said, before turning to examine a huge old mirror in a gilded frame that had seen better days. 'If I had a mantelpiece, I'd buy this.'

'It would have to be a big mantelpiece,' he said, 'and I'd need a bigger hire car.'

'True. This is more my size,' she said, picking up an old art deco cup and saucer and examining the pottery mark stamped on the bottom.

'What use is one cup?' he asked.

'It's pretty and vintage cups and saucers are collectible, James. This is probably the last of a set that has been in someone's family for generations. They would only have been brought out on special occasions.'

She haggled with the man running the stall and then, when it was safe in bubble wrap, she handed the bag to him.

'Give it to Sally. It will go with the book you bought her.'

About to protest that he should have paid for it, he had a better thought. 'You can give it to her yourself at the Christmas party.'

'I don't want to come to London, James.'

'Because your parents will be there?' He took her arm. 'It'll be all right,' he said. 'Once we're married, they won't be able to touch you.'

Her answer was drowned out by a brass band striking up close by them, playing carols. He put a note in the collecting tin and, as they wandered on, he began to see things through Chloe's eyes.

Not unwanted junk, but family history.

There was an overstuffed leather chair, worn on the arms where it had been rubbed by countless hands. Or one set of hands countless times through a long life.

'That definitely won't fit in the car, James,' Chloe said, when he sat down to check it for comfort.

'I could have it delivered.' He took a photograph with his phone and asked the seller for his card. 'It would look great in the ground-floor club bar at L'Étranger,' he said, when she looked askance at him.

He left Chloe turning over some old linens and wandered back to the mirror. They didn't have anywhere to put it now, but one day they would. A mantelpiece in a house with a garden…

He called a friend with a van to organise a pickup, sent him pictures of both items and then paid for the mirror and the chair.

He was looking at a small dark blue vase with a gilded panel of white roses when Chloe found him.

'I get it,' he said, showing it to her. 'It's all about the history. Who owned this? Who gave her the *I love you* flowers she put in it? A lover? A man she was married to for fifty years? Her children…?'

'You are such a romantic.'

'Guilty as charged, ma'am.'

The stallholder, sensing her moment, suggested a price that was undoubtedly more than the vase was worth, but he didn't haggle.

'Now our story is part of it, too,' he said, when she'd wrapped it and handed it to him. 'A memory of a day spent together in a French village that I will fill with white roses on the anniversary of this day every year.'

Chloe blinked. 'You'd better put a reminder in your phone.'

'I'm wounded that you have so little faith.'

'Okay,' she said. 'Here's a little test. When is my birthday?'

'Very soon. The twenty-eighth of November,' he said, without hesitation. 'I made you a cake.'

'It was in the shape of a book. And you sent me roses. Yours is in April. The twelfth. I made you a cake, too, but nothing fancy.'

'Lemon drizzle. And you gave me a first edition of Escoffier's *Guide Culinaire*.'

For a moment neither of them moved, then Chloe cleared her throat and said, 'There is so much pretty china here.'

'You see a lot in charity-shop windows. It's sad, but who uses cups and saucers in the age of the mug?'

'Only the Queen and hotels.' She looked at him. 'And tea rooms.'

She picked up a pink, white and gold cake stand and held it up for him to see. 'Is your afternoon-tea service going to be all spare, minimalist white china, or can you imagine using this?' she asked. 'Tables laid with beautiful vintage china, every person drinking their Darjeeling or Earl Grey out of something original. Individual.'

'It's a lovely idea,' he said, 'but is it dishwasher safe?'

'Not a chance,' she said, 'but who cares? You'll employ some very careful person to wash it.'

'And you think I'm a romantic.'

'This is romance with a USP. Imagine this cake stand filled with pretty little cakes, on your website header. Delicate cups and saucers as bullet points...'

'If I admit that it's a great idea and buy this,' he said, 'will you work with Sally on the design?'

'Me?' She frowned. 'No...'

'But it's perfect, Chloe. You're going to be part of my life and you have such a great imagination. I want you to hunt down the china, manage the tea service for me. You have all the skills for this...' He turned to the stallholder to pay for the cake stand, then said, 'This has been an unexpectedly productive morning. You are going to have so much fun with this.'

'I am not going to do anything of the kind,' she said. 'I am going to have lunch and any talk about tea rooms or business of any kind will give me indigestion.'

The entrance to the château was a couple of miles outside the village. Beyond the gate the lane became an unpaved track winding through woodland, but then they were clear of the trees and beyond a pair of majestic wrought-iron gates stood a pink and white château glowing against a slate sky.

Chloe put out a hand and grabbed James's arm. 'Stop!'

He pulled up between the gates and looked at her. 'What's the matter?'

'Absolutely nothing.' She looked at the wide sweep of the house, its pink walls, white stucco trim, the dormer windows in the roof and steps leading up to the front door and couldn't stop a smile spreading from somewhere deep inside until it consumed her entire body. 'This is the dream house I drew as a child.'

'As in a picture stuck to the fridge door with a magnet, drew?'

She nodded. Then pulled a face. 'Obviously not the fridge door, it was pinned to my cork board by my nanny, but yes, I drew it and coloured it in with crayons.'

'You must have seen a picture of it in one of your mother's magazines. They've been hosting weddings and events for years,' he suggested.

'Maybe,' she agreed, although she knew it had to have been in her nanny's copy of *Celebrity*, which featured weddings of even the marginally famous.

'I have to admit that from here it looks even better in real life than in the online photographs, which, in the age of digital enhancement, has to be a first,' James said. 'Can we go now?'

She nodded. 'But slowly.'

He continued along the drive at a snail's pace, giving her time to look around, take in an ancient cedar on the front lawn, catch a glimpse of the orangery and, beyond the trees, a small lake gleaming leaden under the grey sky.

By the time he'd pulled up at the front of the château, one of the double doors had been thrown open and a couple of French bulldogs were followed down the steps by a slightly flustered woman.

'Welcome to Château Bernier St-Fleury, Mr Harrington, Miss Forbes Scott. I'm Marie Bernier. Call me Marie...' She turned to the dogs. 'Beau, Felix—heel! I'm so sorry.'

They scampered around Chloe, sweet but clearly out of control.

'They were my mother-in-law's dogs,' Marie said. 'I'm afraid she spoiled them.'

Chloe bent to rub a silky ear and its owner immediately rolled over and presented her with his tummy. 'I can understand why. They're adorable.'

'They like you, Miss Forbes Scott. Do you have dogs of your own?'

'Chloe, please. I'd love to have a dog, Marie, but I live in a Paris flat and I'm out at work all day. It wouldn't be kind.'

'And you, Mr Harrington?' she asked as one of the dogs abandoned her for James and he offered him a hand to sniff before rubbing an ear.

'Everyone calls me Jay,' he said, 'and like Chloe I'm a city dweller with a job that keeps me busy for long hours. Maybe in the future,' he said. 'When we have a house with a garden.'

Marie smiled, nodded. 'Of course. But, please, come in out of the cold.'

'Your name is Bernier, like the château?' Chloe said, following her inside while James fetched their bags from the car. 'It was built by your family?'

'My husband's family built it as a summer retreat in the nineteenth century. When my father-in-law died, my husband had to take over the business here. That was nearly twenty years ago.'

'It's a magical place.'

Marie Bernier's smile was wry. 'Unfortunately, Chloe, there was no magic wand to repair the roof and there is so much of it…' She raised a hand in a gesture that took in the extent of it. 'The property market was in a shocking state after the bank crash and the family went into the hospitality and weddings business out of necessity. We hit the market just at the right moment and it has been a great success, but now it is just me.'

'I'm so sorry.'

She shrugged. 'We should be planning our retirement now, but Henri had a stroke and then a series of heart attacks. I know things are hard for the young these days, but I always say to my young couples that they should not take life for granted. No one ever died wishing he'd worked harder.'

She indicated the stairs that rose in an elegant curve from the polished wood floor of the hall.

'I'll take you up to your suite so that you can settle in. There's a fire in the morning room and everything you need to make yourself tea and coffee. We have just one other couple staying tonight but they won't be arriving until much later, so you'll have it to yourselves. Dinner will be served at eight. Just ring if you want anything.'

She opened a pair of doors and gave them a quick tour of the suite that James had shown her on his phone. There was the pretty blue and white bedroom furnished in the French style, a little sitting room through a curved archway and a huge claw-footed bath in a wonderfully romantic bathroom.

'Poor woman,' Chloe said, when Marie had left them alone. She was standing at the window looking out over the garden and James came up behind her and put his arms around her. 'I can't imagine how hard it must be to run this place on her own.'

'She's a strong woman,' he said.

'You're thinking about your mother,' she said.

'And my dad. After Mum died, when we found out what Nick was really like, I blamed her for rushing into a second marriage, but she hated the hotel, blamed the stress of running it for Dad's heart attack. Nick must have seemed like a gift.' He noticed her frown and shook his head. 'It's history. Nothing to be done...' Then something caught his eye and he said, 'Look, Chloe! A swan!'

They watched as it came in to land on the lake, skimming across the water before settling with a shimmy of its tail.

'Did you know that they mate for life?' she said.

'So do gibbons. And angelfish…'

She laughed. 'Angelfish?'

'It's true. Check it out.'

'I believe you,' she said, leaning back into him as he pressed a kiss into her neck.

He was so strong, so sure of himself, of his future. She could go back to London with him, sink into his life the way she was sinking into his arms and know that he'd take care of her. That she'd be safe.

'Are you cold?' he asked, when she shivered.

'A bit. Let's go and have some tea.'

'How were the lights?' Marie said, when they returned from Thoiry later that evening.

'Amazing!' Chloe said. 'Noah's Ark, an incredibly beautiful underwater world and an entire Renaissance procession from the court of Henri IV.'

'Ah, yes. He stayed at the Château de Thoiry. It's a lot older than this one,' she said, with wry smile. 'I'm afraid dinner may be a little late. My chef's wife had a fall and he had to take her to the hospital. She is his assistant and serves—'

James paused, one foot on the stairs. 'Can I help?'

'Help?' She shook her head. 'You are a guest,' she objected.

'I'm also a chef. Give me a minute and I'll be with you.' He didn't wait for an answer but bounded up the stairs.

'Really, he does not have to do this,' Marie said, clearly concerned about the reputation of her château.

'You needn't worry. He's really very good. He has a restaurant in London.'

'London…?' She repeated the word as if astonished that anyone in England could cook.

'He trained in Paris.'

'Oh… That is why he speaks such excellent French. As do you, Chloe.'

'Thank you, Marie. I spent a lot of my childhood in France and I've lived here for a long time.'

She smiled, but then remembered their conversation. 'It is kind of him, Chloe, but he'll be in the kitchen working, instead of in the dining room with you. No, I'll manage.'

'Show me,' Chloe said.

The dining room was a large and elegant room with French windows that in the warm weather would open out onto a terrace. A long, dark table with a magnificent silver epergne at its centre had been laid for four with heavy silverware and fine glasses that gleamed in the light from two chandeliers.

Unfortunately, despite the fire that had been lit in the hearth, it wasn't very warm.

'It's lovely in the spring and the summer,' Marie assured her. 'The windows open onto the terrace and the lake. Our other guests are here to look us over as a wedding venue…' The strain was beginning to show and Marie, despite her determination to soldier on, was close to tears. 'The rehearsal dinner in here. The reception in the orangery…'

'It's beautiful,' Chloe said, putting an arm around her. 'I can see how it will be in the spring and so will your other guests when you show them but, since there will only be four of us this evening, perhaps we could find somewhere a little cosier?'

She frowned. 'Cosier?'

'Is there a table in the kitchen?'

She bridled. 'We have a commercial kitchen for guests.'

'But you have a family kitchen?'

'Well, yes, but that isn't, I couldn't possibly...'

'Let me see.'

At her insistence, Marie led her through the hall to an old-fashioned family kitchen. On one wall was a huge dresser loaded with china and copper pans. There were herbs drying on a pot rack hanging from the ceiling and a range oven that was throwing out blissful warmth. And in the centre of the room stood a solid wooden table that looked as if it had been there for a hundred years.

'Marie, this is perfect. I'll just go and wash up and then I'll come and help you set up.'

She met James in the hall.

'I'm sorry. This was supposed to be the perfect romantic evening,' he said, 'but she was clearly about to crack.'

'I love that you stepped up. I love you.' Before he could even think of a response to that, she kissed him. 'The dining room is an ice box. We're cooking and eating in the family kitchen. I'll be down to help as soon as I've washed up.'

Jay, aware that he was grinning like a loon, watched Chloe run up the stairs but then, as headlights swept across the glass panels on either side of the door, Marie appeared, back in control and looking every inch the chatelaine.

'James... I am indebted to you. To you both.'

'On the contrary, Marie, believe me when I say I have every reason to be grateful to you. The kitchen is through here?'

'It is. The menu is on the blackboard. There are no special dietary requirements.'

'Then look after your guests and leave the food to me.'

He was checking the menu against the ingredients when

Chloe joined him. 'What have we got?' she asked, reaching for an apron and tying it around her waist.

'A soufflé *Suissesse*, smoked salmon pâté, duck with glazed parsnips, cheese, and then a tarte Tatin with quenelles of home-made vanilla ice cream. The pâté and the ice cream have been prepared.'

'That helps, but you don't have time to make a tarte Tatin from scratch. The pastry needs to rest for an hour.'

He smiled. 'Since when were you the expert?'

'I don't just wait tables in the bistro. I help out in the kitchen when I'm needed and tarte Tatin is a staple.'

He held her gaze for a moment, then said, 'Marie has already made the pastry, or we'd have had to improvise. Since you're such an expert I'll leave you to peel the apples and line the dish with the pastry while I make the caramel so that we can get it in the oven.'

'Yes, chef.'

Ten minutes later, the tarte was ready and, once it was in the oven, Chloe peeled parsnips while James made a start on the bechamel sauce for the soufflé.

Marie joined them and began setting up the table for four.

'You should eat with us, Marie,' James said.

'Impossible. You will need someone to serve.'

'You're on your own here?' Chloe asked, concerned.

'The bookings came in late and the girl who usually helps is away. I could have called someone else, but I thought with Claud and his wife here I could manage.'

'It's the butter-side-down law.'

Marie laughed. 'Always. I should have known that once the first thing went wrong today the rest would collapse like a house of cards. It is always the way.'

'Something else has gone wrong?' Chloe asked. It wasn't just the missing chef and his wife?

'A wedding cancellation. A bride with cold feet. Or maybe it was the groom.'

'I imagine you had already put a lot of work into the planning.'

'It's not about the work, and I keep the deposit in the event of a late cancellation,' she said, 'but it always makes me a little sad. All those hopes and dreams for a future that will never happen.'

'They might get back together,' James said, looking at her. 'People do.'

'Yes, they do…' She desperately wanted this to work, but he suffered from selective hearing… 'Lay another place, Marie. We'll eat like family. You can relax and talk to your guests about their wedding plans and we'll take our time between courses so that we can all eat together.'

'Is there anything I can do to help?' she asked.

'Open a bottle of your finest white wine?' James suggested.

She went through to the cold room and returned with a bottle that immediately dewed in the warmth of the kitchen, opened it and poured them each a glass.

'To rare and special guests.' She raised her own glass to them. 'Always welcome. *A vôtre santé!*'

CHAPTER NINE

CHLOE WAS AWARE that Fiona, the Scottish bride-to-be, had been looking at James all evening. She'd done her best to distract her but, finally, she said, 'Your face is so familiar, Jay. Have you ever been to Edinburgh?'

'Sadly, no,' he said. 'I just seem to have one of those faces. Can I tempt you to another slice of tarte Tatin?'

She held up a hand. 'Don't! I have a wedding dress to shrink into, but I have to say, Marie, that if Jay is your stand-in chef, I cannot imagine what the first division is like. That tarte has to be on our wedding menu.'

Marie looked at James, clearly embarrassed, and he said, 'I can take no credit for the wonderful pastry. The addition of the almonds was a lovely touch, Marie, and one I will borrow if I may?'

Marie blushed. 'It was my mother's recipe. I would be delighted to share it with you.'

'You are definitely having your wedding here, then?' Chloe asked, heading Fiona off before she could return to thoughts of where she might have seen James.

She looked questioningly at Sean. He shook his head, but his indulgent smile said yes. She threw her arms around him. 'You are my angel!'

Embarrassed, he disentangled himself. 'We came to

an event in the grounds here last spring and Fiona hasn't stopped talking about it since.'

'I know how she feels,' Chloe said. 'The château took my breath away when I saw it.'

'Is that why you're here?' Fiona asked, looking from her to James. 'To arrange your own wedding?'

'We haven't got around to a date yet,' James said, reaching out, taking her hand when the silence went on a moment too long, looking at her, holding her with the intensity of his gaze. 'And Chloe can choose whatever location she likes as long as it's soon.'

Fiona gave a happy little sigh. 'Wait until the spring,' she urged. 'You can't imagine how pretty it is here when the blossom is out. I just about died when I saw the wedding pictures on the website.'

'If you'd already seen the château, why have you come now?' Chloe asked, desperate to change the subject. 'It was dark when you arrived and you're leaving so early that you won't see it in daylight.'

'Sean was coming to Paris for a meeting and I begged for a night here so that I could see the inside of the château and take a look at the bridal suite. I wish we could stay longer, but we have to leave at a ridiculously early hour so that he can catch a flight to Frankfurt.' She rolled her eyes, whispered, 'He's a banker.'

'Which is why we must reluctantly leave such great company,' Sean said, getting to his feet. 'Thank you for a wonderful evening, Marie. If I had my way, we'd have our wedding breakfast in here.'

Fiona laughed. 'There's not enough room for eighty guests in here, darling.'

Clearly that was Sean's point, but he smiled. 'Only eighty?'

She gave a little shrug. 'That's the maximum number

Marie can seat in the orangery, but we'll have a bigger party in the evening.'

'Of course we will. I won't see you in the morning, Jay, Chloe.' He shook Jay's hand, kissed Chloe's cheek. 'Thank you both for an unforgettable meal.'

When they were gone, Chloe ignored Marie's objections and began to clear the table. James, the consummate professional, had cleaned down as he'd cooked, and the kitchen area only needed a final wipe.

'What time is breakfast?' Chloe asked.

'Whenever you want it,' Marie said. 'There is no one else booked into your room so you can stay as late as you like. And I will refund the cost of your stay.'

'Marie…'

'I mean it. Without you I would have lost that wedding booking.'

'She's right, Chloe. You were born to run a big house,' James said as they made their way upstairs. 'Marie was floundering, not just earlier, but several times during the evening. You kept her going.'

'Only after you had stepped in to save the day.'

'I imagine I volunteered about half a second before you did it for me.'

'Maybe.' Her smile faded. 'She's not managing, is she?'

'Honestly? If I were Sean, I'd be encouraging Fiona to look for somewhere else to hold my wedding but thanks to you they didn't notice that anything was wrong.'

Chloe glanced at him as they reached their room. 'Fiona certainly noticed you, though.'

'Yes. Thanks for the deflection,' he said, sliding his arms around her. 'We make a great team.'

'I can peel a great vegetable,' she agreed.

'It wasn't just the cooking,' he said, 'although that was so like the way it used to be with us.'

'Out of hours in the school kitchen with you putting out a hand and barking "spatula", or "ginger", and me following orders like a theatre nurse?'

'Like a *sous chef*,' he corrected, then frowned, belatedly catching something in her voice. 'It was good, wasn't it?'

'Yes,' she said, melting a little. 'It was good. And I really enjoyed this evening. It felt real.'

'Real?'

'Yes. Sightseeing, eating out…' She raised a hand in an effort to convey what was missing. 'They're great, but they aren't real life.'

He put his hands on her shoulders and looked down into her face. 'Holidays are part of life, Chloe, and I realised that you needed time to adjust. For us to get to know one another again.' She felt suddenly trapped, but as she pulled away James turned and headed for the bathroom. 'It's going to be perfect,' he called back. 'Just how it used to be.'

'We were children, James. And it wasn't perfect.'

He didn't answer and she followed him.

His hair was standing up in an untidy ruff where he'd pulled his tee shirt over his head and he had his toothbrush in his hand.

He looked at her through the mirror and it was obvious that he hadn't heard her. 'I've been thinking.'

'Steady,' she said, unnerved by his sudden gravity.

He didn't laugh.

'This is important, Chloe. I meant what I said earlier about getting married as quickly as possible. I checked with my lawyer. Once you're my wife, legally your father will have no power over you.' He turned to face her. 'He would never again be able to control you by shutting you away in some discreet private clinic…'

For a moment she couldn't breathe as he touched her deepest fear, but as he reached for her she turned away, bending over the bathtub to fix the plug in place, turning on the water until the gush of it drowned out the sound of a girl begging...

'Can we talk about this tomorrow? The only thing that I want right now is to wallow in this vast bath and wash away the smell of cooking.'

Steam was beginning to rise from the huge claw-footed bath, and she sprinkled in something that filled the room with the scent of a summer meadow—flowers, crushed herbs, new-mown grass—as it bubbled up.

'Will you wash my back?' she asked, turning to face him. 'Or are you too tired?'

He reached behind her and turned off the taps and for a moment she thought that he was going to insist on talking about marriage, London...

'It's not full,' she protested.

'We can top it up when we're ready.' He made a circular motion with his hand, indicating that she should turn around.

'We?'

He raised an eyebrow. 'If I'm going to wash your back thoroughly, I'm going to have to get in with you.'

Relief flooded through her. 'I was hoping you'd say that.'

'I know,' he said, 'and I'm happy to help, but first I'm going to have to undress you, so turn around.'

The absence of the lazy smile he wore when anticipating great sex was oddly disturbing and, as she obeyed him, she felt a flutter of panic beneath her breastbone. But then his breath whispered across the nape of her neck. His lips followed, planting soft, seductive kisses that brought something less than a moan, more than a sigh to her throat as he pulled loose the pin holding her hair so that it fell about her shoulders.

She had been leading this dance.

Since that first crazy time he had always been so careful to let her take the lead in their lovemaking. To show her
that whatever they did together was her choice. But the restraint had slipped and the shiver rippling through her was
more than desire, heat, lust as he followed the slow journey of her zip down her spine with his lips, pausing only
to unclip the roadblock of her bra.

This was deeper, darker, and as her dress, bra, slipped
to the floor she tried to turn to him.

'Be still,' he murmured against her ear, cupping her
breasts in his hands, teasing her nipples with the tips of his
thumbs as he held her against his chest, his arousal nudging
her. Then, as she moaned, 'Are you still in a hurry, my love?'

'You can take all the time in the world,' she gasped, 'as
long as you keep doing that.'

Because the physical connection between them was as
real, as powerful as it had been when they were teens exploring this exciting new world and each touch had been
a discovery.

It still was.

What had happened in those first explosive moments
after he'd found her was the release of the need, hunger, a
sexual energy that had been suppressed through all those
missing years. When they were close like this nothing else
mattered. It never had…

He didn't have to hold her, she was leaning back into
him, rubbing against him, whimpering, begging, building
up to a frustrated scream…

'Shh…' he whispered in her ear, one hand low against
her belly but tormentingly not low enough. 'You'll make
Fiona jealous.'

She swore then and he laughed, still tweaking one rock-
hard nipple while sliding his other hand lower, into her
tights, her underwear.

Her core was liquid, her legs barely able to hold her, but instead of the release she was begging for, bucking her hips to find his fingertips and achieve with or without him, he moved his hand away, abandoned her breast and began to slowly peel the clinging tights and pants over her hips.

He took his time, his hands spread over her buttocks, fingers, mouth finding every tender spot as he carried them down to her feet until he was on his knees and, at his bidding, she lifted each foot until she was naked.

'You can turn around now, Chloe.'

She turned to face him, quivering with the intensity of her need, her nails digging into his naked shoulders as she clung to him for support, feeling exposed as she never had before.

He leaned forward, placed a row of kisses along the base of her belly. Scarcely breathing, she waited for the touch of his tongue. It didn't come. Instead he looked up at her and said, 'Your turn.'

The bath grew cold as she subjected him to the same slow, agonisingly sweet torture. Arousing him with her fingers, her breasts, her tongue, as he had aroused her. Fighting to curb her own need, drawing out every second to give him the same intensity of sweet agony that he had given her.

His control was awesome, but there came a moment when, with a yell that, if the walls hadn't been a foot thick, would have woken the dead in the nearby churchyard, he picked her up and carried her to bed and, much later, every need satisfied, blissful oblivion.

Jay lay in the darkness and listened to Chloe breathe. He'd felt the exact moment when she'd slipped away into sleep, limbs heavy, utterly sated, wearing the same little smile he'd seen after the first time they'd made fumbling, first-time love. Admitting to feeling a little sore but delighted with herself.

It had been a long day and he should be exhausted but sex left him stimulated, his brain racing. If he'd been at home, charged up like this, he would have gone into the kitchen and started to play with ideas.

He could get on with the book, but the light, the sound of the keyboard, would disturb Chloe.

All he could do was lie in the dark, unable to shut down his mind as it replayed everything that Chloe had said. The things she hadn't said.

The missed moments when an answer would have been life changing but she had changed the subject or diverted him as she had done tonight.

Had she always done that?

Even when they were young, and he was running on about the future? Their life together? She would smile and kiss him, and they would make love, and he'd thought that was her answer. But she had known all along that it was never going to happen.

He hadn't noticed until tonight. But tonight, he'd used the marriage word and in her panic she'd been less than subtle in her attempt to avoid it.

He'd thought to punish her a little for that, keep her on the edge until she was begging him to release her. Take her to that place where she wouldn't have to think about a future that scared her. Give her *la petit mort*...the little death that followed orgasm.

She had begged but he was the one who'd lost, because she had given and given, and he was the one who had died a little.

'Feel free to tell me I told you so.'

Chloe stirred, rolled over. It was late, the room was

flooded with light, but not the light you got on a sunny morning, not even a sunny winter morning. It was the kind of light you only got in winter when…

'It's snowed!'

James, hair damp from the shower and already dressed, turned away from the window. 'According to Météo-France,' he said, 'the storm took an unexpected swerve to the west in the early hours.'

Grabbing the comforter from the bed, she wrapped it around her and went to join him.

'Oh, my…'

From their window, too far away to see the marks left by animals and birds, the scene stretched away in a sheet of unblemished glittering white across the lawn to the lake.

Every branch of every tree was a tracery of white against a blue sky. The silence was absolute, everything completely still until a wood pigeon took off from a branch in a flurry of snow, startling a whole load of other birds into flight.

'It's so beautiful,' she said, leaning against his shoulder. 'Thank you so much for bringing me here, James. I'll never forget it.'

'I'm not sure it was such a good idea.'

'Well, I did warn you that it was going to snow,' she said. 'I wonder if Fiona and Sean got away safely.'

'I heard them leave just after five this morning.'

'They woke you?'

'No. I heard their car. I'm not used to being idle,' he said, dismissing the sleepless night as if it were nothing. 'I had a million things going around in my head. Plans for us.'

He turned to look at her and in the brilliant light she could see the faint smudges beneath his eyes. 'Plans?'

'You're right, Chloe. These few days have given us a chance to reconnect, rediscover each other, but it's time to get real.'

She had known this was coming, but she wasn't ready...

'I may have been a little hasty,' she said. 'We should take a snow day.'

'The snow is pretty, but not very deep. Nothing short of a fallen tree across the lane is going to stop us from leaving today.'

She laughed. 'Am I that obvious?'

'You know that I'd happily stay another night if it would make you happy, Chloe, but I have to be in London tomorrow evening. I just hope the weather hasn't affected the trains.'

'Yes, I'm sorry. I'm being selfish...'

She rose on her toes, but her brief kiss became deeper, more intense, and for a moment, as he held her, London, the future, was forgotten. Being with him was all that mattered.

James was the one who pulled away, resting his forehead against the top of her head for a moment. 'It's not too late to change your mind and come with me, Chloe.'

'I thought we'd agreed that I'd just be a distraction,' she said. 'You'll have a much better time with Hugo.'

'I doubt that, but you don't have to come to the awards ceremony.' He lifted his head to look into her eyes, laid his hand against her cheek. 'There's just time for us to be married before Christmas but I need you with me so that we can sort out a civil ceremony. We can do the whole white dress, big party later. Here, in the spring, if you like.'

'If Marie is still in business. I'm not sure she's coping very well.'

'The château will still be here. I'll shut the restaurant and bring my own staff if necessary.' He wasn't smiling; he meant it. Wanted an answer. 'I bought a decoration for you to hang on the family tree, Chloe.'

'Did you? When?' she asked, grabbing any chance to delay this moment.

'At the Christmas fair. You chose the flamingo.'

'I thought you just wanted my opinion.' She was struggling to breathe; the walls were closing in… 'I hadn't realised you'd bought it for me to hang on your tree.'

'It's not my tree, Chloe. It's a family tradition and I want you to be part of my family. I thought, hoped, that it was what you wanted, too.'

Trapped, cornered into a conversation that she had been avoiding, she clutched at the comforter, holding it like a shield.

'I don't feel adequately dressed for this conversation.'

His thumb caressed her cheek. 'You don't need to be dressed if the answer is yes, Chloe.'

'It's complicated,' she said, through a throat that was suddenly stuffed with cobwebs. 'I'm complicated.'

'We can work through it. Just tell me what is bothering you.'

'You know I love you, James. Finding you, being with you, has been a joy. But moving to London, giving up my life here—'

'You have no life here.'

'Please, James, try to understand…' She took a step towards him, but he was already moving away, and she didn't know how to stop him. How to explain something she didn't understand herself. 'Can we talk about this later?' she pleaded.

'Of course. I'll leave you to get dressed. I have to make a few calls and the messages are piling up and it will be easier working at the table in the morning room.' He picked up his phone, slung his laptop bag over his shoulder but paused in the doorway and looked back. 'I'll have Marie send up a tray for you.'

Her mouth was open to say something, anything to stop

him leaving, but all that emerged was a whispered, 'No. Thank you. I'll come down. I need some air.'

And then she was looking at a door that had been closed very quietly.

Jay leaned back against the door he had just closed with such excessive care. Slamming it would serve no purpose, no matter how much he felt like it.

He didn't understand.

He'd been upfront, clear from the start about how he saw their future, and Chloe had seemed happy to go along with his plans. Okay, she hadn't shown any great enthusiasm about joining him in London, but his life was there.

She was fully engaged in their physical relationship. More than engaged. She'd taken the lead when he would have willingly waited, understanding that she might need time.

Maybe he should have waited, because she had shied like a spooked foal at the mention of marriage and if it wasn't to be that, what was it?

'Good morning, Jay.' Marie was regarding him intently. 'You slept well, I hope?'

He straightened. 'Yes, thank you, Marie. We were very comfortable.'

'Chloe is still sleeping?'

'I've left her taking a shower while I get a little work done.'

She lifted a despairing hand. 'Men. They are all the same.' She shook her head, sighed. 'You'll find breakfast laid out in the morning room,' she said, 'but find time to take a walk before you go. Fling a few snowballs. Be young.'

'I'll do my best,' he said, but then as she began to move away, 'Marie…' She waited. 'I have to go to London to-morrow, but I think Chloe might like to stay on here for a day or two. Would that be possible? You mentioned more problems yesterday? There was more than the chef and the cancelled wedding, I think.'

'You're right, but it's nothing that need concern you, Jay. I have no guests booked in until next weekend and I would welcome Chloe's company. She is welcome to stay.'

'You are alone here?'

'The cleaning staff come in every morning when we have guests. Less often between bookings, although it's vital to keep on top of the dust. My sons visit from Paris when they can, but they have important careers, children at school.'

'They must worry about you here on your own.'

'They have been urging me to sell the château and move near them.'

'And you?'

'It's not that easy when it has been your life, but my husband was the *vigneron*. It became his passion.' She smiled fondly at the thought of him, before bringing herself back to the moment. 'I have someone who has taken on the job, but a good vintage requires passion.'

'I understand. Perhaps I can talk to you about your wine before I leave? I was impressed with those you served last night, and I'd like to take some samples back for my sommelier to try.'

'Of course. Tell me when you're ready and I'll take you through to the cave, for a tasting.' She took a step, then paused again. 'I looked you up on the Internet this morning, Jay. Chloe told me that you had a restaurant in London—' she gave a little shrug '—to reassure me, you understand. I am honoured to have had you cook in my kitchen.'

'It was my pleasure, Marie. Cooking and eating in good company is always a pleasure. It was a most enjoyable evening.'

The morning after was anyone's guess.

CHAPTER TEN

CHLOE CLUTCHED THE comforter around her, staring out at the pristine landscape, aware that she'd hurt James, that she was behaving irrationally.

This had been her dream, so what was stopping her from jumping on the train to London? Grabbing the first available date at the register office? Hanging that damn flamingo on the Harrington Christmas tree?

She had to get outside and take a head-clearing walk. Work out what was wrong with her. Why, when her heart was so certain, was her head fighting commitment to the boy she'd never stop loving, to the man he'd become?

She blasted herself awake under the shower, dried her hair and wrapped herself up in her warmest clothes.

A cleaner, polishing the curved wooden handrail of the stairs, excused herself and moved to one side, but Chloe smiled to reassure her. She'd been there when she was meant to be invisible.

'Is Madame Bernier in the kitchen?' she asked.

'No, *madame*, she is giving a wine tasting to one of the guests in the cave.'

'Of course. Thank you.'

She didn't want to wait while coffee cooled, just drank some orange juice, grabbed a croissant and, followed by the dogs, walked across the lawn to the lake. They chased

ahead of her, nosed under the snow, begged for her croissant, which she surrendered without a fight. Once under
the trees where the snow was thinner, she found sticks that
she threw for them to chase.

Letting her head clear, letting go of everything as she
laughed at their antics.

A low sun was slanting through the clouds, gleaming
pale yellow on the glass front of the orangery, the lake was
still, disturbed only by ducks and dab chicks who took to
the water in a flurry of indignation when the dogs bounded
up, wanting to play.

A single majestic swan.

She brushed snow from a bench and sat down, with the
dogs panting from their exertions at her feet, and soaked
up the perfect peace.

Jay spent some time in the wine cave with Marie, tasting
wines, asking her about the grape variety, the number of
bottles produced, all the information his sommelier would
need. Marie was very knowledgeable, giving him a tour
of the cave.

It began as a distraction from his concern about Chloe
and where their relationship was going, but he found himself drawn in by the history of the vineyard, which predated
the château. By the process.

He chose half a dozen vintages to take back to London
with him but as they emerged he saw the tracks in the snow.

'Chloe has not waited for you, Jay.'

'No…' He took a breath, aware that the next hour would
change his life. 'I'll put these in the car and then I'll go
and find her.'

'I'll bring you some hot chocolate to warm her while you
talk. I suspect you could do with something more bracing,'
she said, 'but you will be driving.'

'Coffee will be fine. Thank you.'

She patted his arm and went inside while he put the wine in the car and let the silence settle around him, the peace calm him.

Chloe heard the crunch of snow long before James appeared, offering her a lidded carry-out mug.

'Marie thought you might be cold and sent you hot chocolate.'

'That was kind of her. Thank you.'

He swept the snow from the bench and sat beside her, looking out across the water.

'When do you want to leave?' she asked when he didn't speak.

'I'm ready to go, but you're not coming with me. I've arranged with Marie for you to stay on for a few days.'

Chloe fought down the giddy pleasure that thought gave her and turned to look at him. All she got was his unsmiling profile, the sun gilding the tips of his hair and the outline of his close-cropped beard.

'Why would you do that?' she asked, keeping very still.

'It makes sense,' he said. 'You love it here and I'll be in London.'

'I'll rephrase that,' she said, unable to keep the barest tremor from her voice. 'Why would you do that without talking to me first?'

Clearly taken aback by her tone, he said, 'I thought you'd be pleased.'

'That is beside the point.'

'Is it?' He turned to her. 'What is the point, Chloe? Tell me, because I really don't understand what's going on in your mind.'

But she did.

She finally understood.

'I love you, James, but I can't live with a man who wants to control me. Put me in a box. Make me into some version of me that fits in with his life.'

'What on earth are you talking about?'

His astonishment was real. He had no idea what he'd been doing, she realised, but then it had taken her a while to work out what was bothering her.

It seemed that he needed a demonstration, so she put her hand on his shoulder and in a slightly patronising tone, said, 'You don't have to worry about a thing, Chloe. I'm going to set up a tea room. It'll be the perfect little job to keep you busy while I concentrate on building my empire.'

She opened her hands, palms up in a gesture that invited him to contradict her.

He shook his head, clearly bewildered. 'I can't believe you're thinking like this. I love you, I only want what's best for you, Chloe, to take care of you, protect...'

His voice faltered as she rose to her feet and took a step away from the bench, distancing herself from him because this was hard. Really hard...

'They are the exact same words my father used,' she said, oddly calm as she shattered the dream she'd been cherishing for years. 'Over and over. When he took me out of school he said he was rescuing me...' She swallowed down the memory. 'Isn't that what you thought you were doing when you rushed me out of my apartment?'

'No,' he protested as he came to his feet, but something had clearly hit home. 'Maybe, but it's not the same.'

'He said them when he forced me to sign the adoption papers. When he'd taken our baby. When he took me to the clinic and left me there for months and months...'

'Chloe, please,' he said, reaching for her, 'this is nonsense...'

'You rushed me out of my flat, James,' she said, backing away, because to touch him, to let him touch her, would make it impossible for her to say the words. And she had to say them before this went any further... 'You rushed me out of my life. It wasn't a great life and I know you were doing what you thought was right. But so, in his twisted way, did he. I escaped that cage, James, and I will not step into another one, no matter how comfortable.'

He recoiled as if she'd hit him and she had to dig her nails into her palms to stop herself from reaching out to grab him, hold him...

'You didn't have to come with me,' he said, fighting to hold back his anger, because she had hurt him. Because he still wasn't hearing what she was saying. 'I didn't drag you kicking and screaming down the stairs. The only screaming I heard was you begging for more.'

'I asked you to leave,' she reminded him, 'but you stayed.'

'I couldn't leave you in that place!'

'It wasn't your choice.' Was that her speaking in that calm voice? She felt like an onlooker, someone listening to a woman she didn't know... 'I went with you, James, because I never stopped loving you. It was never a fun fling. It was real, to-the-ends-of-the-earth love. It always will be—'

'Then whatever I've done, or you think I've done, we can fix this!'

'But last night,' she continued, as if he hadn't spoken, 'when I tried to explain, you held my shoulders and spoke to me as if I were a wilful child.' She looked him in the eyes, her heart breaking at his bewilderment. 'He did that.'

'No! I am nothing like your father.' He dragged his hands through his hair, searching for the words to convince her. 'I held you because while you were pulling me so close physically, I could feel you slipping away from me and I was so scared of losing you again.'

'You never lost me. I was always yours.'

'So why was it that any time I mentioned London, or marriage, you changed the subject, or distracted me? You do a very good distraction, Chloe...'

'It was real, James. Every touch, every kiss...'

'Was it?' He shook his head. 'I finally realised what you were doing last night. I'd thought that here, away from Paris, you might begin to see our future...'

'Thinking for me,' she said.

'Thinking of you,' he said, 'but clearly you can't see that.' And this time it was James stepping back, his face the colour of stone. 'Your father is still controlling your life, Chloe. Until you confront that, deal with that, you will never have a future. With me. With anyone. You will always be alone, hiding in a damp, cold room, working as a maid.'

It was a cruel thing to say, meant to inflict pain and it did, but she understood his need to retaliate.

And he was right.

He'd appeared out of the blue like a knight in shining armour, lifting her clear of the rut she'd worn so deep that she'd lost sight of the horizon, of a future. Now it was there, shining before her...

'I won't go back to that,' she promised him. Promised herself. 'Thank you for finding me. For a wonderful week. I will never forget it, or you. But whatever happens next has to be my choice.'

She felt she should offer him her hand. A final gesture, but if he took it, she knew how hard it would be to let go. And if he rejected it...

'Drive carefully, James.'

He frowned. 'You are staying?'

'No, but I'll make my own way back to Paris.'

'That's stu—'

He caught himself, maybe imagining for himself how

it would be with the two of them sitting in silence on the drive back. So different from the teasing journey the day before. Exploring the *brocante*, sparking ideas off each other. Then there would be the awkwardness of another night in the same small apartment. Or of James insisting he move into a hotel.

'I'll arrange a car for you.'

'No, James. Thank you, but I can get back to Paris by myself.'

His mouth tightened at this further rejection, but he said, 'I am aware of that. You clearly weren't listening when I said that you could do anything. Be anything.' He took a breath. 'It's nothing to do with control. I brought you here and it's my responsibility to see you safely home.'

'You are the one not listening, James. If this was sex and I said no—'

'Stop!' He was white with anger. 'It is not the same.'

'I was making a point.'

'It's made,' he said. 'You want to make your own way back to Paris. Am I allowed to ask if you have money?'

'Yes, all I need,' she assured him. 'And I will contact Julianne at the hotel, thank her for giving you my address and tell her that I've been to London to talk to an old school friend about a job, but that I have decided to stay in Paris.'

Something that, if she'd been thinking more clearly, she could have done at the time, but maybe she'd wanted to believe James's concern about scandal. Wanted to be carried away. But life was not a prettied-up fairy tale.

'That's it, then,' James said and this time there was no lift on the last syllable, no suggestion of a question. 'Nothing more to be said. I'll go straight to the Gard du Nord and take the first available seat on the Eurostar this afternoon.'

'I'll text you when I've moved my things from Louis's apartment.'

She could see him fighting the need to tell her to stay for as long as she liked, and she died a little inside. She had never meant to hurt him like this…

'If you need anything, any time, you know where I am. But then you always did.' He raised a hand in a heartbreakingly helpless gesture and, his voice cracking, he said, 'I love you, Chloe.'

He didn't wait for her to respond, but as he walked quickly back across the snow she whispered, 'I love you, James Harrington. Always have. Always will.'

A few minutes later, Chloe heard the car driving away and, unwilling to return to the château, she began to walk around the lake. She had reached the orangery when Marie found her.

'You've been out here too long, *chérie*. You'll catch your death.'

'Unlikely in this clean fresh air,' she said, although the dogs had long ago deserted her for the warmth of the kitchen. 'Did James ask you to come and check on me?'

'He was very unhappy to leave you here, I think?'

'I'll take that as a yes.' She sighed, stopped walking. 'He's unhappy because I won't go to London with him, Marie.'

'Is there a reason for that?'

'Not one that he understands.'

She gave a little shrug. 'It is just a few days, yes? He has arranged for you to stay here until he returns.'

'He told me,' she said, 'but it's not possible. We've split up.' Saying the words out loud hit her with the reality of what she'd done, and hot tears began to run unchecked down her frozen cheeks. 'Sorry. So stupid…'

She scrambled in her pocket for a tissue and Marie put her arms around her, held her close, murmuring soft comforting words in French, until she pulled away, drew in a long shuddering breath and blew her nose.

'It was my decision,' she said. 'James is not to blame for what happened. He would have taken me back to Paris but…'

'It would have been an uncomfortable journey. But it's very sad. You seemed to be so close. When I saw you working together it was as if you were two parts that had found one another and together make a whole. And when he looked at you…' She sighed. 'You have been together long?'

'We met when we were very young. My parents did not approve and split us up.'

'But you found each other again.'

'By chance. I was working in a hotel. He was staying there…'

'That is so romantic!'

'Honestly? I took to my heels and ran away, but he found me.'

'Like a movie!'

Despite everything, Chloe laughed. 'Maybe. A bit. The love is still there, the passion is as strong as when we were teenagers. James wanted to whisk me off to London, to marry me before Christmas, but it seems that I have unresolved issues. Maybe we both do.'

'Can you resolve them?' Marie asked hopefully.

'This isn't a movie, Marie. Some things are not meant to be. Sadly, I will be leaving as soon as I can organise a taxi to the nearest railway station. Or maybe there's a bus?'

'You will go nowhere today, *chérie*,' she said firmly. 'I will make us something comforting for lunch and then you can put your feet up in front of the fire. You can weep, or sleep, or talk if you feel like it. Give your heart a little time to catch its beat. Tomorrow will be soon enough to pick yourself up and start again.'

'I can't afford—'

'As my guest,' Marie said, dismissing the notion that she should pay. 'I tried to refund Jay for last night after he stepped in so gallantly to help us, but he wouldn't hear of it. We spent such a good hour in the cave, where he tasted our best vintages, asked so many questions about the vineyard...' There was a wistfulness in her voice, then a wry smile as she said, 'He won't want to serve it in his restaurant and be reminded of this morning...'

'I doubt he'll let that cloud his judgement. He's always been driven. I don't think, until now, I realised how much.'

'His issues? It was clear that Fiona had recognised him from somewhere and a quick search on the Internet revealed him to be the youngest chef ever to be awarded a star...' She waved a hand, fanning her face. 'The embarrassment!'

'There's no need to be embarrassed. He could have been a short-order cook in a pub for all you knew.'

'You are both so kind... Please stay, Chloe. At least for tonight. A small enough thank you.'

The thought of travelling back to Paris, to the empty apartment, was not appealing and she surrendered to the temptation. 'Thank you, Marie, but can I take a rain check on the pity party? There has been too much weeping in my life. What I'd really like is to see the château. From cellar to attic.'

Marie gave her a long look, as if uncertain whether she would break down somewhere awkward, and Chloe turned to the orangery.

'Shall we start here? Tell me all about the weddings that have taken place here, the events...' Marie shrugged, produced a bunch of keys and opened the door. Explained how the room was set up for weddings, how each one was individually tailored to the couple's wishes.

'How much help do you have?' Chloe asked as they

walked back to the château. 'The detail you put into each wedding, each event, must involve a huge amount of work.'

'There is an army of young people who come in on the day, but I have to admit that the joints are stiffer these days. The recovery time from the pressure of weddings and events gets a little longer each time. And as I was telling James, my sons are eager for me to move to Paris to be nearer to them.'

'I can understand that. With this beautiful château and a solid business, you'll be inundated with offers.'

'Maybe. But my husband and I put our hearts and soul into making the château viable.' Marie paused to look up at the pretty pink and white facade, love for the place shining from every line in her face. 'I can only let it go when I'm sure I've found someone who will love it as I do. Someone who can see beyond the fantasy to the hard work it takes to maintain it. I thought I had, but they changed their mind.'

'You heard yesterday?'

Marie nodded as they reached the door to the mud room and kicked off their boots, hung up their coats.

'You said you worked in a hotel, Chloe. What do you do there?'

'Housekeeping. I wait tables and help out in the kitchen at a bistro. Cleaning work.'

'Odd jobs for one as expensively educated as you.'

'Expensively?'

'You have the poise, the accent and it was clear at dinner last night that you have a wide knowledge of the arts, Chloe.'

'Expensive but disjointed. Like my life. I have to go back to Paris, Marie, but when I've sorted things out there would you consider giving me a job? A sort of internship? You don't have to pay me. I'm not afraid of hard work and I'll do anything for my bed and board and the chance to learn everything about how this works.'

'You would like to buy the château?' she asked hopefully.

'I wish! I have a little money, but nowhere near what I'd need to buy somewhere like this, and no one is going to give an ex hotel housekeeper that kind of loan. But I can dream. Start small, work hard and, with a following wind and some luck, build up to something grander.'

'Jay! How are things? How is Chloe?' Sally said, swooping down on him before he could escape.

The awards evening had been a nightmare. Sally had been leaving him messages...

He'd had years of putting on a face, not letting his feelings show, smiling for the camera, but losing Chloe for a second time had been like forgetting how to breathe.

All he'd had from her was a brief text to let him know that she'd taken all her stuff from the flat, emptied the fridge, cleaned up but she hadn't said where she'd gone. Back to the horrible room he'd found her in, he had no doubt.

'I can't stop,' he said. 'I've got meetings.'

She caught his sleeve before he could dodge around her. 'Not so fast, Jay Harrington. Why have you been avoiding me?'

'I've been run off my feet since I got back from Paris.'

'Tell me about Paris.' She hooked an arm through his and steered him purposefully through the obstacle course of scaffolding, ladders and workmen to the quiet of a small alcove she'd temporarily commandeered for her drawing board. 'Where's Chloe? I assumed you'd bring her back with you.'

'She decided to stay in Paris.'

'As in permanently?'

'Yes.'

She muttered a profanity. 'I did warn you.'

'Don't blame Chloe. It was my fault. I messed up.'

'I find that hard to believe. You adore her and you're the sweetest, kindest man...' He gave a half-shake of his head. 'This has to be a mistake. What did you do?'

'She said I was behaving just like her father.'

'What? That's ridiculous.'

'Apparently not. And when you know everything that happened, you'll understand that there is no coming back from that.'

'Everything?' She took his hand. 'You look wrecked, Jay. Come around this evening.'

'I'm working—'

'It doesn't matter how late. I'm still running on Singapore time.'

'It suits you,' he said, finally looking at her. 'You have a sparkle.'

'And you look as if you haven't slept for days, but for all the wrong reasons.'

'Right first time, but there's nothing anyone can do about that.'

'I can listen.'

He managed a wry smile. 'Chloe told me that the world needs more people who know how to listen.'

'Did she?' She gave him a thoughtful look. 'That is interesting. Bring me something luscious from the restaurant and we'll see how that goes.'

'I'm not... I've passed the chef's hat to Freya. I've been working on a new project, one of the big hotels has asked if I'd be prepared to create a James Harrington afternoon-tea service, but something Chloe said is bothering me...' He shook his head. 'I need to talk to Hugo.'

'Don't we all!'

He gave her hand a reassuring squeeze. He had no confidence in her ability to help him with Chloe, but there were things he needed to say to her.

'I'll be with you at about nine and I'll cook for us but right now I really need to find Hugo.'

'Tell him...' He waited, but she held up her hands, backing off. 'It's okay, I'll tell him myself.'

As Chloe walked up the stairs to the room where James had found her, her neighbour on the top floor passed her.

'Hi, Chloe, have you been away?'

'Just for a few days. Has there been a problem? The snow...?'

'No, but the landlord came around to check the pipes and when he didn't get an answer, he let himself into your place. When I caught him coming out, he made an excuse about checking your heating, but he's bound to have gone through your stuff.'

'There was nothing for him to find, but thanks for the warning.'

Marie had been glad to offer her a job and she'd stayed on at the château for a few days but, as she'd promised James, she had wasted no time in calling Julianne.

The woman had been all innocent sweetness and saying sorry that she wasn't coming back.

She unlocked the door. After nearly two weeks shut up, it smelled of damp and, despite the cold, she dropped her bag, crossed to the window and threw it open. Then she saw the roses James had bought her.

The crisp white petals had softened and when she touched one of the flowers, they fell in a shower onto the table.

This was the moment to weep, but instead she felt a powerful surge of anger. Not with James, not even with her father.

With herself.

CHAPTER ELEVEN

'I'VE BROUGHT SCALLOPS,' Jay said, when Sally had buzzed him into her apartment.

'Fish? My neighbours will love you!'

'Sorry. I remembered how much you like them and, living above the restaurant, I don't have to think about food smells. If you've got some eggs, I'll make a soufflé omelette instead.'

'Help yourself, but just for you,' she said. 'I'm not hungry.'

He gave her a long look. 'Not hungry, or not eating?'

'Not hungry. Really,' she said when he didn't look convinced. 'Louis produced some wonderful veggie dish for us to taste at lunchtime, but to be honest my stomach doesn't know what time of the day it is.'

'If you need to sleep…'

'Oh, no,' she said, grabbing his arm as he made a move towards the door. 'You're not going anywhere until you've told me what happened in Paris. What would you like to drink?'

'If I'm going to face an inquisition it had better be Scotch with just a splash of water.'

'No inquisition.' She pushed him towards an armchair, poured a large measure of Scotch into a glass and handed it to him with a bottle of water, so that he could add his own.

She topped up her own glass from a bottle of tonic water then curled up on the sofa. 'Okay. Start at the beginning and tell me everything.'

He took a sip of the Scotch, sat on the edge of the arm-chair. 'Can I get something off my chest first?'

'That sounds ominous.'

'No...' He looked into the glass he was holding. He'd planned what he was going to say, but this wasn't a moment for a speech. 'You said, when I saw you at the hotel, that I was the sweetest, kindest man.'

'You are.'

'No, Sally. No one sweet or kind would have walked out of school without a thought for you. Not caring how you would cope.'

'Jay...'

'You were struggling with the loss of Mum, afraid of Nick. I knew that and I abandoned you. I want you to know that I'm sorry I did that. To tell you that if you should ever need me again, I won't let you down.'

When he looked up, Sally was wiping a finger beneath her eye, blinking furiously.

'Oh, sorry, I've made you cry.'

'No... Yes...' She shook her head, laughing a little as she contradicted herself. 'I love that you felt the need to say that.' She reached across and laid a hand over his. 'I'm not denying that it was painful. You had always been there, a second heartbeat, and I felt desperately alone. And at the time I was angry... But you had just been hit with the kind of blow that would have broken many men and you were just a boy.'

'I grew up very quickly.'

'And look at you now,' she said.

'Now... Now I feel exactly like that boy, Sally. Confused, lost.' He swallowed a mouthful of whisky. 'The difference is that this time I'm going to have to live without hope.'

'There is always hope. Tell me what happened,' she urged softly.

For a while the only sound was the faint buzz of traffic, then Jay began talking. Starting at the beginning, the moment he'd seen Chloe's reflection in the window. Each step until he was at her door and that first extraordinary, clothes-tearing sexual meltdown...

'Wow...' Sally said, pulling at her collar to let in a little air. 'Just wow.'

'I mistook it for more than it was. I thought she felt the same reconnection, the same till-death-us-do-part, second-chance joy.'

'I'm not sure that sex is ever that important.' He looked up and caught a look on her face. 'It sounds more as if you were both breaking a ten-year-long drought,' she continued briskly when she saw him watching her. 'Go on.'

He took the little leather folder from the pocket in his shirt, opened it and handed it to his sister. She looked at it, looked at him. 'Is this what I think it is? Chloe had the baby?'

'A girl. Chloe called her Eloise.'

'Oh, Jay...' She ran a hand lightly over the images then looked up, tears in her eyes. 'You have a little girl. I have a niece...'

'Yes, but the chances of us ever meeting are minimal. Chloe was forced to sign adoption papers.'

A hand flew to her mouth. 'She must have been heartbroken. How could they do that to her?' she said. 'Who cares about such things these days?'

'Thomas Forbes Scott cared. He had other plans for Chloe.' He told her the whole story. Their flight from her apartment...

'Why didn't you bring her straight back to London?'

'She flat out refused. I thought that she needed time to get her head around what had happened.'

Sally pulled a face.

'What?'

'A wee bit patronising.'

'Patronising?'

'You didn't need time,' she said. 'Ten minutes after incredible make-up sex, you were behaving like an alpha caveman. All that was missing was the club.'

'It wasn't like that,' he protested. 'I was happy to give her all the time in the world, but whenever I brought up moving to London, the future, she...' He shrugged.

Sally raised an eyebrow.

'She distracted me.'

'She wanted the sex but not the commitment?'

'She said she loved me, Sally.' He dragged a hand through his hair. 'I accepted her reasons for not wanting to go to the awards ceremony, but if she'd come home with me, there was time to book the registrar. We could have been married by Christmas.'

'Christmas! Are you completely mad? A woman wants more than a quick walk-through at the register office on one of the biggest days in her life.'

'It was just a formality. I said she could have the big-dress day later. At the château. Anywhere she chose.'

'*You* said. I'm getting a lot of what you said, Jay. What did Chloe say?'

'She said that she wasn't sure the château would still be in business. That she was worried about Marie. The woman who owns it.'

'Classic deflection technique. But what was the big hurry?'

'Chloe's father had shut her up in a private clinic once

before. She had some kind of breakdown after they took the baby from her.'

'I'm not surprised, but what's that have to do with anything?'

'She's the heiress to a huge fortune living in a ghastly walk-up, taking minimum-wage jobs. Her father would have had no trouble finding doctors willing to swear that she was behaving irrationally, that she needed protecting from herself.'

'I'm surprised he hadn't already gone there.'

'Maybe he thought that eventually she would come to her senses. Accept the marriage he'd arranged. If she was married to me—to anyone—he would lose that control and he would try to stop it.'

'Did you tell her that?'

'I told her that I loved her, that I only wanted the best for her, that I just wanted to take care of her, protect her...' He got up, helped himself to another Scotch, drank it down in one mouthful. 'That's when she informed me that they were the words her father used when he was taking her from school, taking away our baby to give to strangers. When he was shutting her away in a clinic.'

'And what did you say?'

'She compared me to her father, Sally!'

'What did you say?' she repeated.

'That she had unresolved issues and that until she dealt with them, she would never have a life or a future.' Angry, hurt, he'd said worse. A lot worse...

Sally got up, took the bottle from his hand before he could pour another drink and put her arms around him.

'What should I have said, Sal?'

'Nothing.'

He looked at her. 'Nothing?'

'Nothing is always the best option when the alternative

involves a very large foot in a wide-open mouth. Even if what you said is, I suspect, true.' She led him through to the kitchen and put on the kettle.

'You think I'm right?'

'Yes, but unfortunately being right is sometimes worse than being wrong. Always worse than just keeping quiet.'

She opened a cupboard, found a packet of camomile teabags and dropped one into a mug.

'I had such plans. I was talking to her about the tea service one of the big hotels wants me to set up for them. She had some great ideas. She even said that I needed to talk to Hugo first…'

'Hugo?'

'He'd said he had no problems with me setting up in a rival hotel, but she thought he was backing off to keep me happy. I wanted her to run it for me, Sally.'

'How did she feel about that?'

He thought about it. 'As I said, she was full of ideas,' he said. 'I thought she was eager to be part of it.'

'You thought?'

'Assumed,' he admitted.

'But you didn't ask her?'

'I didn't think I had to. I'd found her. We were going to get married. I even bought a big old mirror she liked.' His sister raised an eyebrow. 'She said that if she'd had a mantelpiece, she would have bought it.'

'And you were going to buy a house and give her the mantelpiece.'

'What's wrong with that?'

She rubbed a hand against his sleeve. 'You were full of plans for the future and you told her what her part was going to be in them.'

'I love her, Sally. I wanted her to see herself as part of my life. To be involved.'

'And what did she say?'

'It was getting late. She was hungry…' He shrugged. 'She said that talking about business gave her indigestion.'

She sighed. 'It must be a man thing.'

'What?'

'Not listening.'

'She fudged, Sally. She didn't say no. Not until she accused me of being like her father.'

'You did rather jump in with both feet. You knew exactly what you wanted, James. She needed you to ask what she wanted and when you didn't, I imagine she felt cornered. The difference is that this time she was strong enough to stand and fight.'

'Fight? I'm not her enemy.'

'No. Just carried away by a rush of excitement, energy, joy.'

She poured water onto the teabag, dunked it for a moment, then handed him the mug.

'I hate camomile tea, Sally.'

'I know, but it will help you sleep and when you've slept, you will go back to France, find Chloe and, on your knees, ask her what she wants. And listen to her.'

'She might not want to see me. Not after what she said.'

'You have to show her that you heard her. That you're listening.'

'After what I said.'

'I didn't say it would be easy. One final warning. Before you go you need to ask yourself one question.'

He took a sip of the tea, pulled a face. 'Go on.'

'What will you do if her plans, her dreams, are different from yours?'

'He's here, Chloe. Are you ready?'

Maître Bernier, the lawyer son of Marie, looked anxious. A second lawyer, who had travelled to this meeting from London, said nothing.

'Yes,' she said, rising to her feet. 'I'm ready.'

He nodded to his secretary, who returned a few moments later. 'Monsieur Thomas Forbes Scott,' she announced.

Chloe dug newly gelled nails into her palms, breathing carefully, forcing herself to remain calm as her father walked into the room. Not to betray by so much as a blink the slightest emotion. Deeply grateful for the boardroom table that stood between them so that he shouldn't see her knees knocking.

For a long moment he said nothing, just looked at her, absorbing every detail of her appearance.

He still had the arrogant command that had inspired both awe and a desperate need to please him when she was a child. As a girl. And later, fear.

His hair was streaked with silver these days, but his eyes were as dark and compelling as ever.

She remained statue-still under his scrutiny. Her hair had been cut and was hanging in a smooth bob over the classic camel blazer, silk shirt, casual trousers—a mix of charity and high-street bargains put together with French chic with the help of Marie's daughter-in-law, who had advised that nothing should look new.

The shoes had been an extravagance; her father would not be fooled by cheap shoes, but they had been very gently distressed, as if they were old and treasured friends.

The precious amber beads that had once belonged to her beloved maternal great-grandmother were the finishing touch. A message.

'Chloe,' he said, finally acknowledging her.

'Papa.'

'You asked for this meeting,' he said. 'Have you something to say to me?'

She had been thinking about what she'd say from the moment she'd asked for this meeting. There had been a hundred things. An entire essay of accusations to fling at him.

She wanted to look him in the face, challenge him to acknowledge the pain he had caused, but her father had studied law. A challenge invited a rebuttal and she would be forced to listen to him justifying every action with icy detachment.

They both knew what he'd done and if he had felt one jot of remorse, he would have sought her out long ago to beg her forgiveness.

She took a breath and, praying that her voice would not shake, she said, 'Maître Bernier, who is acting on my behalf, has obtained a copy of the will of Lady Alicia Gordon, my maternal great-grandmother. It appears that I inherited the bulk of her estate while a minor and which, as her executor, you have administered on my behalf.'

She managed to keep her voice even, level, despite the tremor beneath her ribcage. She was his daughter and she would show him how she had learned...

'Mr Peter Ward, who is a representative of Lady Alicia's solicitors, has come from London with documents for you to sign in order to release the estate to me.'

She indicated the documents lying on the table in front of him.

He didn't betray what he was thinking by so much as a flicker of an eyelash. No hint of regret that this meeting was not to be her surrender. Nor did he look at the papers.

'It was a very small estate but a great deal of money to be given to an unstable young woman. What do you intend to do with it?' he demanded.

'Play the tables at Monte Carlo?' she suggested. 'Or I might give it to a donkey sanctuary. Great-Grandma was very fond of donkeys.'

There was the slightest tightening of the muscles around her father's mouth as she baited him for lying to the lawyers about her mental health. It was only through Maître Bernier's careful diligence that she had discovered her inheritance. Her great-grandmother's solicitors had been astonished to learn that she had been living and working in Paris for years rather than confined to a clinic.

'Alternatively,' she said, 'I could hire a detective to discover the whereabouts of the baby you took from me in what Maître Bernier informs me was an illegal adoption.'

'You will never find her.'

The distinguished London solicitor, a man who had struggled to contain a smile at the mention of the donkey sanctuary, let slip a shocked breath.

'Are you sure, Papa? I have this photograph of her as a baby,' she said, sliding an enlarged picture of her holding the newborn Eloise from beneath the pile of documents. 'The hunt for the stolen Forbes Scott baby would be a sensation on social media and if I put it beside a photograph of me at the age she is now it's quite possible that someone will recognise her.'

'You would not do that.'

There wasn't a hint of uncertainty in that declaration; it was like fencing with a brick wall. But while it was true that she would never expose her daughter to the inevitable Internet frenzy, she had to protect her friends, Georges Bernier, herself, from any chance of retaliation for this day's work.

'I would,' she said, with equal conviction, 'should circumstances force me to it.'

She laid out the stark warning, holding those dark eyes for a long moment. His reputation, his status, his name, were everything to him and he had to believe the threat was real.

She'd thought it would be hard, but there was nothing left that he could do to hurt her. He finally recognised that too and when he looked away, she said, 'I think we're done here, Maître Bernier. Do you have a pen?'

Her father glared at him and then, as the Maître's secretary was hurriedly summoned to witness his signature, he produced the fountain pen he always carried with him from his inside jacket pocket.

He signed, the secretary signed and, when it was done, her father replaced the cap on his pen, returned it to his pocket and walked out of the office without a word to any of them.

There was a moment of awkward silence, then Mr Ward gathered up the papers, assuring her that the transfer of funds would be made within days.

'If you need any further assistance in anything that has arisen today, Miss Forbes Scott, we will be happy to assist.' Then, having shaken their hands, he left to catch his train back to London.

'You were magnificent, Chloe,' Georges Bernier said.

'I thought I would be terrified, but he was smaller than I remembered.'

'It is often the way with ogres. We build them up in our mind but, when we confront them, they are like the wizard in that old American movie.'

'Oz,' she said.

'Pardon?'

'The Wizard of Oz was all smoke and mirrors, Georges. My father is a lot more dangerous than that.'

'That is why you threatened to destroy his reputation?'

'He has intimidated people I love in the past and I wanted them, and you, to be safe.' Her one regret was that James had not been there to see him vanquished. To see her being strong… 'His name is the one thing he values.'

'Do you ever see your mother?' he asked as he saw her to the door.

'No.' She sagged a little. 'I hoped she might have come with him today. Seen me face him.'

'It's almost impossible for women to break free of controlling men, Chloe.'

'It happened to the mother of a friend of mine,' she said, thinking of James. 'The father of my baby.'

They had only been together for just under a week, but his absence was like the ache of a missing limb.

'Maybe, when your child is older,' he said, opening the door for her, 'she will search for you. And maybe, one day, your mother will find her own courage. It has to come from within.'

'But you need someone at your back.' Someone like James. 'Someone to show you the way.'

Georges took her red coat from the stand, held it for her.

'I'll be in touch when everything has been settled.' He gave her a long look as she dealt with the buttons. 'You *were* joking about Monte Carlo?'

'Yes, Georges. I was joking.' Then she grinned. 'But I quite like the idea of a donkey. Do you think Marie would mind?'

'A donkey would help keep the grass down in the paddock, but it will need a friend. Donkeys get lonely.'

'Do they?'

Why did she question that? Everyone got lonely…

'Two donkeys, then. And on the way home I am going to stop at Pierre Hermé and treat myself to raspberry and cream *macarons* to have with my coffee.'

Half an hour later she was climbing the stairs to her grotty little apartment when, as she neared the top, she found herself confronted by a pair of feet, crossed at the ankles and encased in a pair of familiar shoes.

'James…' He was sitting on the top step, blocking the way to her door. 'How was the awards evening?' she asked, since he appeared to have lost the ability to speak.

'Not great,' he admitted. 'My body was there. My heart was here. It made breathing tricky. If it hadn't been for Hugo, I'm not sure I'd have got through it.' He sighed. 'Sorry. I promised myself I wouldn't be pathetic.'

He got to his feet, moved to one side while she unlocked the door but waited for an invitation before he stepped inside.

'Don't stand in the doorway letting in the cold,' she said, aware how this had gone last time. How easily it could go the same way again, because she had been thinking about him as she'd bought the *macarons*. As she'd travelled back across Paris. Thinking about calling him, to tell him that he had been right. That because of him she had faced her demon and she was free.

But she had compared him to that demon, to the man he'd called a monster, and, like the words he'd used to hurt her, it contained a grain of truth.

'And I'll forgive the pathetic if you put on the kettle,' she said as she took off her coat. Keeping it snippy so that even if she was tempted to fling her arms around him, he would get the *Back off* message. 'Make a cup of tea and I'll share my *macarons.*'

'Pierre Hermé,' he said as she put the little carrier on the table and went to hang up her coat.

'A little treat,' she said. 'I was thinking of you earlier and how you used to sneak out of school and go to Covent Garden to buy them for me.'

'A visit to their café in the rue Bonaparte was on my list of things to do.'

'I'd have liked that,' she said. 'But we did a lot.'

'Yes…' He frowned. 'Have you got a new job?'

'I haven't got any kind of job at the moment,' she said. 'Thanks to you I am between jobs. Temporarily unemployed—'

'I'm sure your agency would find you something,' he said, a definite edge to his voice.

'The pathetic act didn't last very long.'

He shrugged. 'I have many faults, Chloe, but I keep my promises. Even the ridiculous ones I make to myself.'

'Yes, James.' She was forced to swallow down the lump in her throat. 'You always did. But you're right. I have no regrets about working in housekeeping but it's time to move on.'

'If you've been for an interview, I guarantee you've smashed it. You look amazing. As if you could take on the world.'

'Not an interview. And the look I was aiming for was chic Parisienne heiress with nothing to do but have lunch with her friends. But I'll take amazing.'

'Can I ask why?'

'Why are you here, James?'

He held up his hand. 'Sorry. You're right. It's none of my business what you do,' he said. 'I won't take a minute of your time. I just came to give you something.'

The vase he'd bought her, and which had still been in his car, along with their other purchases at the *brocante* when he'd left? Or the flamingo? Surely he wouldn't have returned to Paris to bring her a Christmas tree ornament?

'A courier would have been a lot cheaper than a ticket on the Eurostar.'

'The cost was not an issue. I came to give it to you in person so that I could apologise for being so dense. For not listening. For making you feel so bad that you compared me to your father.' He lifted his shoulders in an oddly awkward shrug. 'And I wasn't sure if you would still be here.'

He looked around at the boxes, packed and waiting to be moved. 'It looks as if I'm only just in time.'

'I'm not running away, James. Not hiding. Not from you. Not from anyone. I was going to let you know where I'll be. And also, to apologise. What I said to you was unforgivable.'

She wanted to go to him, put her arms around him, lay her head against his shoulder and beg him to forgive her, but he was holding himself at a distance. No doubt protecting himself from being hurt for a third time.

There was also the risk that, having once put her arms around him, she would not let go. And she had plans of her own.

'I won't deny that it was like a knife to the gut,' he said, 'but I understand why you said it. Finding you was like having the lights switched back on but even while you were in my arms you were somehow out of reach. It wasn't so much that I didn't listen to you,' he said. 'It was that I didn't want to hear what you were saying.'

'In your arms was the one place I was totally with you, James. There was nothing held back. Nothing that wasn't true.'

CHAPTER TWELVE

THERE WAS A moment when she thought he might have taken a step towards her, but instead he unzipped his backpack, took out a velvet-covered box and put it on the table beside her.

Definitely not the vase and far too fancy for a Christmas tree ornament.

She picked it up, ran her fingers over the silky surface, looked up at him, frowned. 'What is this?'

'A memento of a simpler time.'

'My hairpin...' she said as she opened the box to reveal the silver pin lying in a satin nest.

It had been restored, not just the damage where he'd crushed it with his foot, but all the little dinks and knocks of the years she'd worn it had been smoothed out and polished so that it looked like new.

'Thank you, James. This was, is, very precious to me,' she said, running a fingertip along the curves, around the heart at its centre, just as she had when she'd first seen it all those years ago. 'I will take more care of it in future.'

'No...'

She looked up.

'Don't put it away in its box, Chloe. You might lose it again, or damage it, but it's like life. Not to be kept for best, but to be worn every day.' He picked up his backpack and slung it over his shoulder. 'That's it. What I came for. I'll leave you to enjoy whatever life that outfit is taking you to.'

'Wait…!' He was half turned from her so that she only had his profile. 'You came from London just to give me this?'

'It's just a couple of hours on the train and I didn't want our relationship to end on harsh words.'

'It will never end, James. We have a daughter. We might never find her, never be there for the great moments in her life, but because of her we are joined for ever.'

She saw him swallow, momentarily unable to speak, and she took a step towards him.

'It's her birthday at the end of January. Maybe I could come over to London and we could have lunch together? Raise a glass in celebration of her life.'

'London? You'd come to London for the day?'

She smiled. 'It's just a couple of hours on the train.'

'Touché.'

'I'm not scoring points. I told you, James, I'm not running and I'm not hiding, and I have you to thank for that. You were absolutely right when you said my father was still controlling my life. Because of you I realised that I had to face him, or I would never be free. And now I have.'

Now she had his full attention. 'You've seen him?' he demanded. 'When?'

'This morning. Hence the disguise,' she said, indicating the outfit she was wearing. 'I had my hair trimmed and styled, my nails gelled, and I wore the amber necklace left to me by my great-grandmother,' she said, fingering the big round beads that lay next to her throat, 'because he'd recognise it and he'd know that, however low he imagined I'd sunk, I had never been reduced to selling it.'

'I should have been there…' he began, then caught himself, holding up his hands in a gesture of surrender. 'I get it. It was something you had to do on your own.'

'Who are you?' she said, laughing. 'And what have you done with the real James Harrington?'

And, finally, he was grinning, too. 'Okay, you've got me. How did it go?'

'Let me buy you lunch,' she said, 'and I'll tell you.'

Somewhere, out in the city, over the sound of traffic a bell was sounding the Angelus. A door slammed below them. And Jay hesitated.

His intention in coming back to Paris had been an attempt to take their relationship back to the moment in the doorway when they'd both lost it and start again. Only this time do it right. Take nothing for granted.

Wait to be invited in but accept Chloe's decision if she chose to keep him on the doorstep.

Give her the repaired pin. Accept her decision if she didn't want it.

Apologise for not hearing her. Listen to what she said in response.

With each step he would leave the next move to her.

No touching, no hanging around waiting for more than she was prepared to give.

They had been skating on the surface of the past with him attempting to drag her into a future that he had planned. If they were to have a future, they needed to build something new. Together.

The offer of lunch was unexpected. But it was on her terms and if he had to bite his tongue to stop himself from insisting on paying for it, then that was what he'd do.

'How are your plans going?' Chloe asked as they walked down the road.

His plans were unimportant. Pretty much non-existent,

if he was honest. He wanted to hear about the meeting with her father, but he curbed his curiosity.

'The book is with my editor,' he said, 'and a kitchen has been booked for a photographic session. I'm not looking forward to that.'

'And the tea service?'

'The hotel I was in talks with are not interested in the vintage theme.'

'It was only an idea, James.'

'I know, but it's one that I like too much to compromise on. It may fit the Harrington image, but Hugo and Sally appear to be at loggerheads over some design issue at the moment. It's not the moment to toss in another complication.'

He took her arm without thinking as they crossed the road. She didn't pull away but, remembering her comment about the elderly aunt with the walking stick, he let go as soon as they reached the other side.

'I always felt bad about the way I abandoned Sally when I walked out of school,' he told her, 'but we've talked. It's good.'

'Maybe I'll get a chance to see her when I come to London. How is your friend Louis settling in? It's a big change for him.'

'He's loving the creative freedom and producing some amazing food. The Harrington restaurant will have a star in no time.'

'That's great. No star here,' she said as they reached a busy bistro. Despite the cold there were people sitting outside, drinking coffee and smoking. Inside it was warm and, as they waited for someone to spot them and seat them, Chloe was enveloped in a hug.

'*Chérie!* It's so good to see you! Have you changed your mind?'

'Sorry, Augustin, I'm just here for lunch with my friend from England.'

'England?' Augustin gave him a long look. 'Your face is familiar, *monsieur.*'

'James is a chef, Augustin. His restaurant has a Michelin star. He's a bit of celebrity but he loves honest French cooking. So, do you have a quiet table for us?'

'That depends, darling girl, on whether or not he is the reason I found you in tears the last time you were here.'

The clink of cutlery on dishes, the lively hum of conversation, dimmed as Jay turned to look at Chloe.

'Tears?'

'I had just discovered that I'd lost my hairpin,' she said, taking his hand before turning to Augustin. 'The silver one that your wife admired so much? James found it, bent and broken. He's had it repaired and has travelled from London today for the sole reason of returning it to me. I wanted to buy him lunch to thank him and where else would I bring him?'

The man melted, made a slight bow in his direction and a few moments later they were seated in a quiet corner. Menus were produced but Jay shook his head.

'I am in your hands, Augustin.'

Wine arrived. White, and crisp as a winter morning. Water. Warm bread, fresh from the oven. Butter from Normandy. A wonderful vegetable broth…

'This is the way to live,' he said. 'Everyone relaxed, focussed on the good food Augustin has placed in front of them.'

'He would be flattered to hear you say that.'

'It's not flattery,' he said. 'It's the truth. In London lunch is something to be grabbed on the run. Traders come into the ground-floor bar and are never off their phones. I doubt they even taste the food.'

'That's terrible, but it must be different upstairs?' she said. 'I've seen the photographs on the website. Your dining room is so elegant, and the food looks just beautiful.'

'Fine food for people who are counting every calorie. Pictures for their social-media pages to show the world that they are living an aspirational lifestyle. Businessmen and women whose only interest is the deal they're making.'

He heard the words he was saying and didn't know where they'd come from.

'You sound a little disillusioned.'

'Am I being ungrateful?' he asked.

'Honest, maybe.'

'It's not all like that. In the evening there are family parties, celebrations, couples getting to know one another. The occasional proposal, choreographed with the help of my staff.'

'That must be fun.'

'Yes, it is. The best part, but an occasional proposal is not enough. I seem to have reached a peak, Chloe. Fulfilled all those early ambitions I bored you with when we were at school. I'm not yet thirty and suddenly I'm wondering where do I go from here?'

'Another star?' she suggested, and there had been a time when that had seemed important, but he shook his head. 'Is that what the tea-service idea is about? A new challenge?'

'I suppose so, but, put like that, it seems like a very small ambition.' He managed a smile. 'First-world problems, Chloe,' he said, shaking it off. He wasn't there to talk about him. He was in Paris to listen to Chloe. 'Tell me about your meeting with your father. How did you set it up?'

'After you left, Marie insisted I stay the night with her. While I was there Claud, her chef, phoned to tell her that his wife had broken her hip in the fall. She's not young, it's going to be a long job.'

'Poor woman.'

'It's not good. Marie is fairly certain that even if she recovers fully, she'll decide not to return to work. In the meantime, Claud is spending all his time at the hospital and when she comes home, he'll be needed to take care of her.'

'Will they manage?' he asked, concerned.

She nodded. 'They don't have to work. They both have good pensions, but they enjoyed working at the château because it was not full time. It was Marie who was in a fix. She had a full house that weekend for a Christmas craft workshop being run by a television celebrity.'

He grinned. 'And of course, you offered to help.'

'I was happy to stay for the weekend and pitch in.'

'Happy, full stop,' he said. 'I saw your face when we drove through the gates of the château and I know what love at first sight looks like. I take it she's offered you a job?'

'I'd already asked her if she'd take me on as an intern. I wanted to learn about the events business.' She nodded. 'I just came back to Paris to pack up.'

'And to meet with your father.'

'Yes, that.'

Chloe smiled up at Augustin, who had paused at a discreet distance to check whether they needed anything. Whether the food was to their liking.

He would have given it five stars no matter what it tasted like, but it was excellent and, curbing his impatience to hear Chloe's story, he said so and received a compliment on his French in return.

They ate while the soup was still hot but when the plates were cleared Chloe said, 'I told you that meeting you again was a moment I'd dreamed about, James. And it was a dream. But my first instinct was to run, disappear...'

She paused but he didn't leap in to reassure her, tell

her that he understood. A passing waitress topped up their water glasses.

'It was wonderful being together,' she said, once they were alone, 'but while you were offering me your life, I was still running away.'

'Because you want your own life,' he said. 'It took me a while. A verbal slap around the head from Sally, but you deserve to be so much more than an add-on to mine.'

The one he'd thought so perfect until he was faced with living the rest of it without Chloe.

'That is true,' she said, 'but being with you showed me that I had no life at all. When I left home, when I began running away, I didn't imagine I'd still be living like this years later.'

She paused and smiled up at Augustin as he placed a simple chicken casserole before them, listed the ingredients, then said a brief, *'Bon appetit!'* and left them to their meal.

'Not like this,' Chloe said, with a smile, as she turned her hand to indicate the table in front of them.

'I know.'

'You were right when you said that my father was controlling my life and I'm not denying that it was a shock, painful to hear, but that didn't make it any less true. If I was Sleeping Beauty, your kiss was a lot more than a wake-up call.'

'It was a lot more than a kiss,' he said.

'It was and I loved every minute of it.' And her smile was a lot more than going through the motions. It reached out, warming him as if she'd got up and put her arms around him.

'Marie's son is a lawyer and, once I'd decided that I had to face my father, I asked him if he'd be prepared to contact my father and set up a meeting in his office.' She took a sip of water. 'I did warn him that he'd be making an enemy.'

'But he agreed. Brave man.'

'Yes. He's been amazing.'

He heard the warmth in her voice and discovered that he possessed a hitherto undisturbed streak of jealousy.

'How did that go?' he asked. 'Did you get a grovelling apology? Did he go down on his knees begging for forgiveness?' he asked, hating that he sounded so cynical.

The man was Chloe's father and, no matter what he'd done, nothing could ever change that.

'What do you think?' she asked.

'You know what I think, Chloe. I'd have gone after him myself when you told me what he'd done but his lawyers would have shut me down in a heartbeat. All it would have done was expose you.'

'My hero.' She reached across the table. Briefly laid her hand over his. Her touch went through him like a charge of electricity and, as if she felt it too, she quickly removed it to push back a strand of hair that hadn't moved.

'No hero,' he said. 'And no begging, I'm guessing.'

'He said my name. I acknowledged him in return and then he asked me if I had anything to say to him. Clearly he thought I was the one who was going to be on my knees pleading to be allowed to return to the family fold.' She managed a shaky little laugh. 'I have to admit the knees were a bit wobbly.'

'But they did not bend.'

'No.' She pulled a face. 'Like it or not, James, I'm his daughter. The genes cannot be denied.'

'You have his strength, Chloe. Something I failed to understand and for that I'm sorry. But you don't have his weakness.'

She frowned. 'Weakness?'

'His pride, his arrogant belief that he is superior to the rest of us mere mortals. His vanity.'

'Oh.' She sat back in her chair. 'But that is what gives him his power.'

'It's not a power that I would want.'

'No.' His pride had denied him the joy of a granddaughter. She very much doubted the earl-in-waiting would have allowed the inconvenience of a love child to stand between him and a handsome dowry, should she have been prepared to knuckle under and marry him. Everyone had mix-and-match families these days.

'What happened, Chloe? What did he say? What did you say?'

'Um... Not much. But you can rest assured that there no longer exists any risk to you or any member of your family. Or to me.'

He stared at her for a moment. 'You threatened him?'

'Yes. Georges was right after all. He was like the Wizard of Oz, all smoke and mirrors. I hadn't realised it, but I always held the power.'

'Chloe? What did you do?'

'I looked him in the eyes, James, and offered him a choice. On the one hand public exposure, disgrace, his name dragged through the mud for conspiring in an illegal adoption to hide his own granddaughter. On the other, his assurance that everyone I know and love will live free from his malice.'

He let slip an expletive.

'What did he say?'

'Nothing. But he looked away first.'

'That was it?'

'There was a document for him to sign, family business, nothing to do with any of this. When he'd done that he left.'

'Without another word?'

'There was nothing left to say.'

'I guess not.' Then, 'Who's Georges?'

'Georges Bernier. Marie's son.'

'The brave lawyer.'

'Yes.' She smiled as if she knew what he was thinking. 'It was his very chic wife who helped me to put this outfit together.'

'I'm glad you had people to help you,' he said. 'And tomorrow you'll be moving to the château to start a new life?'

She nodded. They ate their lunch, declined a dessert. And Jay sat on his hands while Chloe paid.

Outside, a light flurry of snow caught them and he hailed a taxi, but when he opened the door for her she said, 'You take it, James. I can walk.'

'And get wet. I've plenty of time so why don't I take the cab and ask the driver to drive me to the Gard du Nord via your apartment?'

It was a short ride to the apartment but, when the car stopped outside her building, she made no move to leave.

'Thank you for today, James.'

'As I recall, you paid for lunch. I should be thanking you.'

'Lunch was really nice, but I meant thank you for having my pin repaired. For taking the trouble to bring it back to me.'

'Did you think I'd throw it in the bin?'

'Most men would have done, but then you are not most men.' She looked across at him. 'Take care of yourself, James.' He made a careless gesture and she caught his hand. 'No. I mean it. I'm concerned about you.'

'There's a switch,' he said, but Chloe not only looked fabulous, there was a real change in her.

His instinct to protect her had not been wrong. All the time that she'd been with him, she had been mentally looking over her shoulder.

Now she was looking forward and she credited him with

helping her to do that, which gave him hope that they could, maybe, find their way to a future together.

The taxi driver, who was paid less when he was moving slowly or at a standstill, held up his wrist and pointed at his watch.

He promised him extra to cover the time and then turned back to Chloe. 'Do you realise that we've never dated?'

'You have to go, James. You'll miss your train.'

'There'll always be another train,' he said, but there would never be another Chloe.

'We've spent a lot of time together, had a lot of sex, had a baby, but we've never done that thing where a guy calls for a girl, takes her out and then, at the end of the evening, walks her back to her front door and if he's lucky gets a kiss goodnight.'

'Do people do that any more?'

'I have no idea, but I think they should.' She was still holding his hand. 'If I come to Paris, can we do this again? Just have lunch while you tell me what you're doing?'

'But I won't be here, James. I'll be at the château.'

A caveat, but she hadn't said no.

'I can come and pick you up.'

'You'd do that?' she asked, but she was smiling. 'Okay. Let me know when you're coming and if it doesn't clash with an event at the château it would be lovely to see you. But you don't have to drive all the way out to Thoiry. I could meet you in Paris...'

'I'm afraid the dating rules state that I have to pick you up from your home and return you safely to your door.'

'The front door or the bedroom door?'

'The dating rules are clear on that, too. No sex before the third date. And only then if all parties think it would be fun.'

'Oh, I know it would be fun.'

'Maybe we need to concentrate on the things that we don't know, Chloe.'

'James…'

'I think we've tried this man's patience long enough,' he said, because leaving her while she still had something to say seemed like a smart idea.

Doubts, he didn't want to hear.

Questions, on the other hand, meant she would be all the more eager to meet him when he called.

Still holding her hand, he climbed from the back of the taxi and when she was standing on the pavement beside him, he lifted it briefly to his lips.

'I'll call you.'

Chloe remained on the footpath watching the taxi until it disappeared around the bend, stepping sideways to catch the last sight of James, hoping that he might look back. Not entirely sure what had just happened. Only that she was both happy and confused and a little bit afraid.

She was happy that James had taken so much trouble to bring back her hairpin. She was very happy that they were friends.

Was she happy that he wanted to see her again? That was confusing because it had to be pretty stupid on both counts. They both knew there was no future for her and James when their lives were in different countries.

And she was a little bit afraid because, although she knew how thorny this could get, how great the possibility of hurt for either or both of them, right at that moment she didn't care.

All she cared about was how soon it would be before he called her.

CHAPTER THIRTEEN

'HOW DID IT GO, JAY?'

He'd seen the missed call and picked up Sally's voice-mail as he walked from the underground to L'Étranger and she rang again while he still had the phone in his hand.

'Hi, Sal. I was on the Tube when you rang. I was going to call you as soon as I got home.'

'Well?' she demanded. 'What happened?'

'I gave her the hairpin. Kept my distance. Listened more than I spoke but Chloe had just seen off her father and she asked me to lunch so that she could tell me what happened.'

'Lunch? Were you not listening? The plan was for you to stay for no longer than ten minutes!'

'The first casualty of any battle is the plan, Sally.'

'Really? I despair!'

'Don't do that. Chloe was bubbling. She needed to talk to someone who didn't need explanations. Someone who knew how important that meeting was.'

'Okay. We can recover from this. What happened?'

'Chloe took me to the bistro where she used to work, defended me to her ex-boss, who was ready to do me serious harm because he thought I'd made her cry, and, when she insisted on paying for lunch, I managed to restrain the macho urge to snatch the bill from her hand.'

Sally laughed. 'I'd have paid good money to see that.'

'This is the new, listening James Harrington.'

'Just listening? How close did you get?'

'Opposite sides of the table, I swear. No footsy.'

'Did you kiss?'

'Only her hand.'

'Ooh…'

'Was that wrong?'

'How could that ever be wrong? I'm melting at the thought of it. How did you leave things?'

'That we should try dating for a while.'

'Dating?'

'Lunch, cinema, ice skating. "Holding hands in the old-fashioned way" dating.'

'Sweet.'

'Don't mock,' he said, dodging around a group of girls blocking the path.

'I'm not. I wish I'd thought of it. It's brilliant.'

'But complicated by the fact that Chloe is moving out of the vile flat to go and work for Marie Bernier at the château.'

'I don't blame her. I looked at it online and immediately wanted to spend a night or two there myself.'

'No reason why you shouldn't. You could mix business with pleasure and run an interior-design weekend course there.'

'You could cut down on the travelling and offer a cordon bleu cookery masterclass,' she suggested. 'Maybe one of your television contacts would like to film it?'

'Nice thought but I've just got to the restaurant, Sally. We'll talk soon.'

He disconnected, slipped the phone into his pocket and, instead of using the side entrance that led directly up to his apartment, he walked through the front door of L'Étranger.

The place was buzzing as the early evening traffic began to build up.

He'd only handed over the kitchen to Freya a couple of weeks earlier, but already he could feel a subtle change. Nothing anyone else would notice. Nothing he could put his finger on.

He spoke to members of staff as he walked through the ground-floor bar. Stopped to talk to customers who knew him, congratulating those who were there to celebrate some special occasion.

He thought about going into the kitchen, but it was Freya's domain now. The job of an executive chef was to advise, to plan for future growth, to approve and direct. Not to turn up and get in the way when service was in full swing.

Upstairs, in his flat, he sat down in his armchair, still in his overcoat and scarf, and wondered how long he had to leave it before he called Chloe.

Sally would almost certainly say a week.

There wasn't a chance in hell that he could wait that long, but when he checked his calendar on his phone, he discovered that there was something every day into the distance.

Hugo had some legal stuff he wanted to clear with him. He was booked to be a guest chef on a cookery show that was being filmed live on Saturday. His publisher's publicity people were desperate to tie up dates for interviews and a book tour. It had sounded like fun when he was signing the contract, but it would take a couple of weeks out of the spring when getting to France would be almost impossible. He went through it, trying to work out what was immovable and what he could shift...

Chloe's phone was ringing.

It had been five days. Five unbelievably busy days. The

many strands of delivering an events package were a huge learning curve. There were bookings up to two years ahead that already involved putting details in place. Prompts in the diary at the point when menus, flowers, a dozen details needed to be actioned, confirmed, chased.

It had kept her mind occupied throughout the day and sometimes into a sleepless night, but always, in the background, every time her phone rang, she felt that dangerous little heart leap.

James had texted a sweet thank you for lunch. Sent her an animated 'good luck' card for the new job. The kind of thing you'd send a friend. Which was lovely.

She wanted them to be friends, always.

She wanted more but was always conscious of walking a tightrope between two incompatible dreams.

Mostly, though, she just hoped that it was him, but when she finally saw his name come up on the caller ID her hand was shaking as she answered and, suddenly stupidly shy, said, 'Hello, James.'

'Hello, Chloe. How did the move go? Are you settled in at the château?'

Normal, everyday questions. But then he'd had time to work out what he was going to say before he called.

'The move went as they always do,' she said. 'There was a certain amount of stress and disaster, but I'm here, nothing of any great value was broken and I'm learning a lot.'

'That's wonderful. Obviously you're not in one of the guest suites, but do you have a room with a view?' he asked.

Talk about a conversation with your maiden aunt!

'I'm on the top floor in a big room that is twice the size of my Paris flat with a view over the lake.'

'Does it have a mantelpiece?'

Okay, now it was getting weird. 'Yes. Is it important?'

'It could be. I had a sudden wild impulse to buy a big old

gilt mirror at a *brocante*, recently. It's going to be picked up next week, but I don't actually have room for it. I was going to arrange storage but then I wondered if you had a handy mantelpiece where it might feel at home.'

'My mirror?' she asked. 'You bought my mirror?'

'And the armchair, but I have a home for that. So? Would you like it?'

'Yes, James…' She swallowed, took a breath. She would not cry… 'I would be very happy to save you the expense of storage.'

'That's very kind of you. I'll ask the driver to text you when he'll be arriving.'

Was that it? The reason for his call?

'Apart from an excess of furniture, how are you doing?' she asked.

'I'm good. Busy. Sally sends her love. She's fallen in love with the château, too. I suggested that she could run an interior design class there one weekend.'

'That's a wonderful idea. I'd love to see her. Tell her to give me a call and we can talk about it.' Then, because this conversation was setting up all kinds of tugs, both physical and emotional, and she was in danger of keeping him talking just to hear his voice, she said, 'I have to go, James.'

'Wait… Sorry, the mirror wasn't actually the reason for my call. I know it's ridiculously short notice, but someone just cancelled a meeting for tomorrow. Is there any chance that you'll be free? I'll completely understand if you have an event coming up this weekend and you're neck-deep in preparations. The job has to come first.'

'It does,' she agreed, 'but this weekend is clear, so we are not at panic stations. What did you have in mind?'

'A walk by the Seine if it's not raining. Lunch somewhere. Skating and hot chocolate, or maybe cocktails, at the Plaza Athénée?'

'I'll have enough trouble keeping on my feet with hot chocolate. And won't you be driving?'

'I thought I'd book a car with a driver,' he said. 'That way I'll be able to sit in the back and hold your hand. Maybe, after skating and cocktails, you'll fall asleep on my shoulder.'

'That is entirely possible,' she said, smiling at the thought.

'So? Is that a yes?'

Who was this James Harrington who took nothing for granted? Asked questions and listened to the answers?

'I would love to do all of that with you,' she said, 'but, James…'

'Chloe?'

'I want to be quite clear on one point.' He waited. 'Will this be our first or second date?'

He just laughed. 'Give my best to Marie,' he said, and then he was gone.

The two excitable French bulldogs, Beau and Felix, greeted him with unalloyed joy and a much more relaxed Marie with kisses on both cheeks.

'It makes me very happy to see you here, James.'

'Thank you, Marie. I hope Chloe feels the same way. How are things with you?'

'Perfect. Chloe…' She turned as she heard her on the stairs. 'Chloe is my angel.'

She was wearing a soft cream sweater, her gold curls fastened up in the silver pin.

'An angel?' He kissed her on both her cheeks with the same formality with which he'd greeted Marie, but drinking in the scent of her, holding it in his lungs. Desperately trying to block out what his life would be like if he could not see her.

She whirled around, laughing at his doubt. 'See my wings, baby. Watch me fly...'

It was true, he thought. She looked as if all it would take was a leap into the air and, like Peter Pan in a show his mother had taken them to see one Christmas when he and Sally were six years old, she would be flying around the room.

'Let's stick to the road for now,' he suggested as she tugged on her coat, wrapped a scarf around her neck. Unnerved by her joy.

What the hell did he think he was doing?

What would he do if Chloe had found her dream and there was no place in it for him?

'Sorry, guys,' he said, distracted by the dogs as they tried to follow Chloe into the car.

'Next time you must stay,' Marie said as she grabbed them by the collar, 'and take them for a walk.'

He was momentarily lost for an answer, his brain freewheeling, then catching as he realised that right now that was exactly what he wanted to do. But the driver had closed the door and, before he could think of a way to say that, the car was pulling away.

'The dogs like you,' Chloe said. 'Have you ever had one of your own?'

He shook his head. 'My mother was nervous around them and, although we didn't live in the hotel, the house was, is, in the grounds and my father was concerned about the guests.'

'The guests here don't mind them,' she said. 'I suspect your father was protecting your mother.'

'You may be right. I was only six when Dad died, but recent events have brought back so many memories. I can see now that while she was his light, had enormous charm, had enchanted the hotel guests, there was a fragility to her.'

Had he absorbed that as a small child? Subconsciously recognised the way his father had protected her? Tried to do the same with Chloe? He looked at her, so confident, so strong... 'You are nothing like her,' he said. 'Apart from the light. It shines from you, too.'

She reached out her hand and found his. 'There was a moment when I could have broken. It was only the anger that kept me from going under all those years. It was anger that drove me to see my father.' Her hand tightened on his. 'I've been given a new life, James, and I have you to thank for that.'

'You did it for yourself.'

'But you were the catalyst.'

'I was cruel.'

'You said what you saw, and I wasn't angry with you. I was angry with myself. If you hadn't been so determined to find me, nothing would have changed.' She looked at him. 'I was so deep in the rut I'd worn for myself that I wasn't able to see over the top. See that there was another life out there.'

'Then I'm glad. I don't think I've ever seen you look so happy,' he said. 'Not even when we were young.'

'I'm having such a good time,' she said. 'The château, of course, but I'm able to use everything I know. Use the management skills and the financial acuity that I learned at my father's knee. That stood me in good stead while I've had to earn my own living. And Marie is teaching me about planning events. The details...'

She filled the journey to Paris with all that she'd done, learned, since he'd last seen her. Bubbling with an enthusiasm that he had once felt in the early days in the restaurant.

Envied.

He didn't have to ask what he'd do if Chloe's dream

wasn't his. What he needed was a new dream that would live alongside hers.

They walked for a while, had a simple lunch, took to the ice in the beautiful courtyard of the Plaza Athénée, laughed a lot as they made idiots of themselves, drank hot chocolate and a final cocktail, before they climbed back into the car to be driven back to the château.

Chloe didn't fall asleep, but she leaned against him and he put his arm around her, holding her until they were home, and walked her up the steps to the door, where she turned to him.

'I don't want this to end, James.'

It was an invitation to stay, but he opened the door. 'Hold that thought.'

Marie appeared. 'Don't keep him on the doorstep, Chloe. Bring him in for coffee. I'm off to bed.'

It was a conspiracy, he thought, but, much as he wanted to stay, to wake up with Chloe beside him, he fought the temptation.

'Thanks, but it's going to be tight as it is to catch my train and I have a meeting first thing. But maybe next time I could talk to you about your wine, Marie?'

'Of course. It will be a pleasure.' She nodded, disappeared, leaving them to their goodbyes.

'Is there going to be a next time, Chloe?'

'You're afraid of being hurt.'

'Right now,' he said, 'I'm just afraid you'll decide that there's no future in this. No future for us.'

'Don't overthink it, James. Call me when you've got a spare day,' she said, 'and we'll enjoy what we have.' Then, almost as an afterthought, 'Just checking, here. Do the dating rules say that I'm allowed to call you?'

'Whenever you like,' he said. 'To talk, to arrange a date, or just so that I can listen while you breathe.'

'I'll do that,' she said, then leaned forward to kiss him lightly on the lips.

'Send me a text to let me know that you've got home safely.'

'James, is this a convenient time?'

He made an *I've got to take this* gesture and, as he walked in the corridor, said, 'It couldn't be more perfect.'

'You've just walked out of a meeting, haven't you?'

'I was in a meeting with my accountant so when I said it was the perfect moment, that was exactly what I meant.'

She laughed, but said, 'I'll keep it brief—'

'Don't! He's talking about some new accounting program.'

'Then listen to him. It's important.'

'I'd rather listen to you.'

'I've noticed, so listen. I called to let you know that the mirror has arrived, and I was wondering if you'd like to come and see how good it looks on my mantelpiece.'

Oh, the innocence in that voice. The temptation in that invitation.

He'd introduced the mirror into her bedroom so that she would think about him every time she looked in it, but his sneaky little ruse had just spectacularly backfired on him.

He knew she would be smiling at her cleverness, while he was leaning against the wall, catching his breath and trying desperately not to think about the silky skin of her breasts, the brief touch of her lips that had burned him up all the way back to London.

'We have date number two before we can even think about that,' he said, in an attempt at cool amusement, but there was no disguising the rasp of sexual desire in his voice. 'When were you thinking?'

'Tuesday or Wednesday?'

'Tuesday,' he said, without checking his calendar. Whatever was on it, he'd cancel. 'We can take the dogs for that walk. And I want to talk to Marie and her *vigneron* if that can be arranged,' he said, in an effort to restore the balance a little.

'I'll tell her.'

'It has been a most interesting day, Marie. Thank you.'

'I had no idea that you were so knowledgeable about viticulture, James.'

'I've been reading a lot about wine making in the last couple of weeks. Tasting with my own sommelier and the man my brother has taken on for the family hotel. They were both impressed with the character of your wine.'

'My husband hoped to achieve *grand cru*. He was close, but the first heart attack took the fire from his belly,' she said. 'But what is your new interest?'

'English winemakers are producing sparkling wines that, these days, are winning world-class medals.'

'You are considering planting a vineyard? In England?' she asked. 'It takes many years before you can harvest a vintage.' She lifted her hands. 'Don't waste your precious time talking to an old woman. Chloe wants to show you her part of the château.'

'*Madame...?*'

'Go, foolish boy. It's on the top floor. The third door on the left.'

He climbed the stairs, tapped on the door, opened it when Chloe called out for him to come in.

She was sitting at a little desk beneath the window, the dogs curled up at her feet. She had been working on her laptop and looked up as he entered.

'Did you enjoy your time with the *vigneron*?' she asked.

'Yes. I learned a lot.' He looked around the room, which

had been prettily furnished. 'This is rather lovely. And the mirror looks as if it's been there for ever,' he said as she got up and joined him.

'And the little blue vase looks perfect next to it. I'd very much like to give you a thank-you kiss for that. Kisses are allowed on a second date, aren't they?'

'Chloe…' He wanted to hold her, kiss her, but he shook his head. 'I'm not sure I can handle this.'

'No more dates?' The little crack in her voice gave him hope.

'Being apart. We're not kids any more, and this isn't a game. I wanted to build something solid, from the ground up. I love you. What we have is the reason I draw breath…'

'James…'

'I know. You don't want London, or a tea room, or my life. But without you, all of that is meaningless.'

'But it was your dream, James. I can't take that from you.'

'If it was still my dream,' he said, 'I'd be there now, but something has changed at L'Étranger. I thought at first it was because Freya is now in charge of the kitchen, but it wasn't that. The only thing that has changed is me.' He swallowed down the boulder that was building in his throat. 'I have become the outsider in my own life.'

'Sweetheart…' She put her arms around him. 'How can I help?'

He clung to her. 'Just tell me what you want, Chloe, what you dream about when you're awake and the moon is shining in your window, and if I have to rattle the stars to make it happen, I'll give it to you.'

'This is my dream, James. The weddings, the events. I can see such possibilities. Even vintage English tea parties…'

'Don't tease. Just tell me that there's a place for me in that dream?'

She leaned back so that she could look at his face, look into his eyes. 'You're serious? You'd move to France?'

'I'd move to the moon if you were there. But I have to admit that France is a lot more attractive.'

'But what about your restaurant? Your book tour? Your television appearances? Your family? You can't just walk away.'

'I have already begun to. As executive chef at L'Étranger I remain the hand on the tiller, but Freya runs the restaurant. If she needs me, she can pick up the phone, or we can video call, and I can spend a day in London once or twice a month. It's only a couple of hours on the train, and I'd always be home by nightfall.'

Her smile emboldened him.

'There's nothing I can do about the book tour. I signed a contract and it will be an intense couple of weeks when getting home might not be possible, but I'll never go to sleep without calling you.'

'And television?'

'Sally suggested I might run some masterclasses here.'

'And get a television company to film them?'

'She suggested it would be better to set up our own company, hire in the talent and sell the programmes we make to the networks. Cookery, craft, wedding planning...?'

She clapped a hand over her mouth. 'That is a genius idea! The possibilities are endless...'

She flung her arms around him and this time there was no holding back and her kiss had only one destination, but even as she was backing him towards the bed he broke away.

'Wait. Love...'

'Really? You're going to insist on waiting for a third date?'

'When we've talked to Marie, settled the deal, you can do whatever you want with me,' he promised.

'Oh,' she said, then added an uncharacteristic expletive.

'Oh?' He didn't like the sound of that 'oh' or what had followed. 'Oh, what?'

'You're too late. Marie has already found a buyer.'

'What?' He pulled away, dragged a hand through his hair. 'I'm so sorry. I'm such a fool. I've been playing at dating when I should have been—'

'No!' She put her arms around him. 'The dating has been lovely. Very frustrating, but right. We're different people from those desperate teenagers. We needed time...'

'We'll find somewhere else,' he promised. 'France is full of châteaux. When you fall in love with one, we'll make it our own dream.'

'No, James.'

'No...'

'This is awkward. I was going to wait until the third date to tell you that you were having breakfast in bed with the new chatelaine of Château St Fleury.'

It took him a moment.

'You? You've bought it? How?'

'The papers my father signed the day I met him were to release an inheritance from my great-grandmother. She died when I was seven and I didn't know about the bequest until Georges did some searches and turned it up. It wasn't a huge amount, but my father has been administering it and over nearly twenty years it had become quite substantial.'

'So that first day, when I came to give you your hairpin, you already knew you were going to buy it?'

'Are you annoyed with me for keeping it from you?'

He shook his head. 'On the contrary, I think you're

the most amazing woman I've ever met. I just have one question.'

'Yes?' she asked.

'Will you give me a job?'

'How about I give you half the château?'

'I've got a better idea. Sell me the vineyard.'

'The vineyard?'

'I told you I needed something new and planting a vineyard in Sussex was my fall-back plan. A project to bury myself in if you decided that you didn't want me in your future.'

'Doesn't it take years to establish a vineyard?'

'I'd have had years.'

'And one day you would have been winning gold medals.' She lifted her hands to cup his face. 'I'm in need of a little cultivation myself, James Harrington. If I agree to sell you the vineyard,' she said, 'can we forget the damn third date and go to bed?'

EPILOGUE

SEAN STOOD BENEATH a canopy of spring blossoms and waited for his bride.

He and Fiona had done all the legal bits in a simple register office ceremony back home in Edinburgh, but this was their big day. The celebration of their marriage, with the fabulous dress, the flowers, the special, for-ever vows made in the company of their family and friends.

The grass had been cut, huge pots were overflowing with plants in the bride's chosen colour scheme.

Every pane of glass in the orangery had been polished. The tables were laid with white damask cloths, heavy silver, crystal glasses. The pastel napkins had been embroidered in the French style, with the name of each guest—a keepsake for them to take home.

The champagne was on ice, the château's finest vintage wines at a cool room temperature, the wedding breakfast created by a famous chef and waiting to be served by the army of helpers from the village for whom the château provided a little extra income.

A harpist played and as Fiona, looking serene and lovely in a simple cream lace dress, was walked down the aisle between the chairs on the arm of her kilted father, a young French baritone began to sing Robert Burns' 'My Love Is Like a Red Red Rose...'

It was Chloe and James's first wedding at the Château St Fleury, but Marie had remained on hand with advice, and the families were now close friends.

Chloe saw James take a breath as Fiona joined her new husband, remember to smile before addressing the gathering and then invite Sean to make his vows.

They were simple, heartfelt, and Chloe had to blink back a tear as she remembered the moment that she and James had sworn their own vows in the *mairie*.

He had encouraged her to reach out to her mother and invite her to the ceremony. He had been too young to understand about emotional coercion, the abusive mind control that Nick had exerted over his mother, and she was long beyond his help.

But he knew Chloe hoped that one day her own mother might break free and he wanted her to know that she had a refuge with them if she needed it.

Friends and family had gathered to witness their marriage. Marie and all her family. People who worked for James. Even his publisher had travelled from London. It was only after they had made their vows and had turned around to acknowledge the clapping that she had seen her mother standing at the back of the room. Older but still elegant and beautiful, and with tears pouring down her cheeks.

She would not stay for the party, but she had come. And she sent them postcards from wherever she was. And last week they had met in Paris.

Baby steps…

She smiled as James invited Sean to kiss his bride and then it was non-stop with lunch in the orangery, dancing on the terrace, children playing games organised by a professional nanny. Tea… And then there was a quiet moment while everyone drew breath before more guests arrived for the evening buffet.

The stars were blazing by the time they left their guests to enjoy the rest of the evening and take a quiet walk around the lake, Beau and Felix, for whom Paris was a move too far, snuffling in the long grass alongside them.

'Your first wedding, James. How was it?'

'Awesome. I'm so glad it was Fiona and Sean. Did we do well?'

'It's not too late for one or more of the guests to get falling-down drunk, or the bride and groom to have a hooley of a row, but all last-minute calamities were averted, the food was amazing and I think we can count that a success.'

'So you'll do it again?' he asked.

'In three weeks, if I've got the date right in the diary.'

'We're booked pretty solid through until the autumn. Is it too early to be thinking about something special for Christmas?'

'James, about Christmas—'

'I've been thinking about how we're going to decorate the place. And I thought we might have a carol concert for the village, mulled wine, food…'

'That's great. All lovely…'

James stopped. 'Sorry. You had something to say and I'm listening. Tell me what's bothering you about Christmas.'

'Not a thing, my love, but, before you get carried away on some wassail extravaganza involving paying guests, I think you should know that we're going to be having company.'

'Well, that's okay. We've got plenty of room. Who have you invited?' He paused. 'Your mother?'

'Not my mother. And you were the one who did the inviting.' He looked so confused that she finally took pity on him, took his hand and placed it on her waist. 'We're going to have a Christmas baby, James.'

For a moment he just looked at her, too stunned to speak. Then the words began to tumble out. 'Oh. Oh, good grief. That's incredible…' He put his arms around her and hugged her very gently, as if she were made of porcelain. 'I don't know what to say…'

'I know, my love. I know,' she said, putting her arms around his neck, her cheek against his so that their tears mingled and ran together. 'I am so happy I could weep.'

'That makes two of us.' He pulled back to look up at her. 'You've been holding that in all day?'

'It was Fiona and Sean's day, James. And I wanted us to have a little time to ourselves when I told you.'

'Good call. I'd have been an emotional basket case if I'd known.'

Chloe lifted her head as she caught the strains of 'Unchained Melody' drifting over the lake.

'I love this song. Will you dance with me, James?'

'I'll dance with both of you.'

He drew her close and, as she laid her head against his shoulder, he began to hum the tune so that it vibrated through her body to the tiny being that was just beginning his or her life.

* * * * *

TEXAS PROUD

DIANA PALMER

In loving memory of Glenda Dalton Boling
(1945–2019) of Homer, Georgia.

You were my cousin, my friend,
my favorite bookseller, my hostess
for over twenty years of book signings with
my friend Jan Walker. You left a hole in the world
with your passing, Glenda. And all of us who loved
you will miss you, as long as we live.

Chapter One

Her name was Bernadette Epperson, but everybody she knew in Jacobsville, Texas, called her Bernie. She was Blake Kemp's new paralegal, and she shared the office with Olivia Richards, who was also a paralegal. They had replaced former employees, one who'd married and moved away, the other who'd gone to work in San Antonio for the DA there.

They were an interesting contrast: Olivia, the tall, willowy brunette, and Bernie, the slender blonde with long, thick platinum blond hair. They'd known each other since grammar school and they were friends. It made for a relaxed, happy office atmosphere.

Ordinarily, one paralegal would have been adequate for the Jacobs County district attorney's office. But the DA, Blake Kemp, had hired Olivia to also work as a

part-time paralegal. That was because Olivia covered for
her friend at the office when Bernie had flares of rheumatoid arthritis. It was one of the more painful forms
of arthritis, and when she had attacks it meant walking with a cane and taking more anti-inflammatories,
along with the dangerous drugs she took to help keep
the disease from worsening. It also meant no social life
to speak of. Bernie would have liked having a fellow
of her own, but single men knew about her and nobody
seemed willing to take on Bernie, along with a pro-
gressive disease that could one day make her disabled.

There were new treatments, of course. Some of them
involved weekly shots that halted the progression of the
disease. But those shots were incredibly expensive, and
even with a reduced price offered by kindly charitable
foundations, they were still out of her price range. So
it was methotrexate and prednisone and folic acid. And
trying not to brood about the whole thing.

She was on her way to her room at Mrs. Brown's
boardinghouse. It was raining, and the rain was cold.
It was October and cool. Not the best time to forget her
raincoat, but she'd been in a hurry and late for work, so
it was still hanging in her closet at home. Ah, well, she
thought philosophically, at least she had a nice thick
sweater over her thin blouse. She laughed hysterically
to herself. The sweater was a sponge. She felt water
rolling down over her flat stomach under her clothes.

She laughed so hard that she didn't see a raised por-
tion of the sidewalk. It caught her toe and she tripped.
She fell into the road just as a big black limousine came
along. Her cane went flying and she hit the pavement

on her belly. She was fortunate enough to catch herself on her forearms, but the impact winded her. Luckily for her, the driver saw her in time to stop from running over her. It was dark and only the streetlights showed, blurry light through the curtains of rain.

A man got out. She saw his shoes. Big feet. Expensive shoes, like some of the visiting district attorneys who showed up to talk to her boss. Slacks that were made of wool. She could tell, because she used wool to knit with.

"You okay?" a deep, velvety voice asked.

"Yes," she panted. "Just…winded."

She rolled over and sat up.

A tall man, built like a wrestler, with broad shoulders and a leonine head, squatted down, staring at her with deep-set brown eyes in an olive complexion. His jet-black hair was threaded with just a little silver, and it was thick and wavy around his head. A lock of it fell onto his forehead as he bent over her. He had high cheekbones and the sort of mouth that was seen in action movies with he-men. He was gorgeous. She couldn't help staring. She couldn't remember ever having a man send her speechless just by looking at her.

"Nice timing," he mused. "Saw the limo coming, did we? And jumped right out in front of it, too."

She was too shaken to think of a comeback, although she should have. She checked her palms. They were a little scraped but not bleeding.

"I tripped."

"Did you really?"

That damned sarcastic, mocking smile made her very angry. "Could you find my cane, please?" she asked.

"Cane?"

She heard his voice change. She hated that note in it. "It went flying when I hit the raised part of the sidewalk. It's over that way." She indicated the sidewalk. "On the other side, probably. It's red enamel. With dragons on it."

"With dragons. Mmm-hmm."

A car door opened. Another man came around the front of the car. He was older than Bernie but younger than the man squatting down next to her. He was wearing a suit.

"What's that about dragons?" the man asked, faintly amused.

"Her cane. That way, she says." He pointed.

The other man made a sound in his throat.

"Look anyway," the big man told him.

"All right, I'm going." There was a pause while Bernie sat in the road getting wetter by the minute.

"Well, I'll be...!"

The other man came back, holding the cane. He was scowling. "Where the devil did you get something like that?" he asked as he handed it down to her.

"Internet," she said. The pain was getting worse. Much worse. She needed a heavy dose of anti-inflammatories, and a bed and a heating pad.

She swallowed hard. "Please don't...stare when I get up. There's only one way I can do it, and it's embarrassing." She got on all fours and pushed herself up with difficulty, holding on to the cane for support. She lifted her head to the rain and got her breath back. "Thanks for not running over me," she said heavily.

The big man had stood up when she did. He was scowling. "What's the matter with you? Sprain?"

She looked up. It was a long way. "Rheumatoid arthritis."

"Arthritis? At your age?" the man asked, surprised.

She drew herself up angrily. "Rheumatoid," she emphasized. "It's systemic. An autoimmune disease. Only one percent of people in the world have it, although it's the most common autoimmune disease. Now if you don't mind, I have to get home before I drown."

"We'll drive you," the big man offered belatedly.

"Frankly, I'd rather drown, thanks." She turned, very slowly, and managed to get going without too much visible effort. But walking was laborious, and she was gritting her teeth before she'd gotten five steps.

"Oh, hell."

She heard the soft curse before she felt herself suddenly picked up like a sack of potatoes and carried back toward the limousine.

The other man was holding the door open.

"You put me down!" she grumbled, trying to struggle. She winced, because movement hurt.

"When I get you home," he said. "Where's home?"

He put her into the limousine and climbed in beside her. The other man closed the door and got in behind the wheel.

"I'll get the seat wet," she protested.

"It's leather. It will clean. Where's home?"

She drew in a breath. She was in so much pain that

she couldn't even protest anymore. "Mrs. Brown's boardinghouse. Two blocks down and to the right. It's a big Victorian house with a white fence around it and a room-to-rent sign," she added.

The driver nodded, started the engine and took off.

The big man was still watching her. She was clutching the cane with a little hand that had gone white from the pressure she was using.

He studied her, his eyes on the thick plait of platinum blond hair down her back. Her clothes were plastered to her. Nice body, a little small-breasted and long legs. She had green eyes. Very pale green. Pretty bow mouth. Wide-spaced eyes under thick black eyelashes. Not beautiful. But attractive.

"Who are you?" he asked belatedly.

"My name is Bernadette," she said.

"Sweet," he mused. "There was a song about Saint Bernadette," he recalled.

She flushed. "My mother loved it. That's why she gave me the name."

"I'm Michael. Michael Fiore, but most people call me Mikey." He watched her face, but there was no recognition. She didn't know the name. Surprising. He'd been a resident of Jacobsville a few years back, when his cousin, Paul Fiore of the San Antonio FBI office, was investigating a case that involved Sari Grayling, who later became Paul's wife. Sari and her sister, Meredith, had been targeted by a hit man, courtesy of a man whose mother was killed by the Graylings' late father. Mikey had made some friends here.

"Nice to meet you," she managed. She grimaced.

"Hurts pretty bad, huh?" he asked, his dark eyes narrowing. He looked up. Santelli was pulling into a parking spot just in front of a Victorian house with a room-to-rent sign. "Is this it?" he asked.

She looked up through the window. She nodded. "Thanks so much…"

"Stay put," he said.

He went out the other door that Santi was holding open for him, around the car and opened her door. He reached in and picked her up, cane and purse and all.

"Come knock on the door for me, Santi," he told his companion.

Bernie tried to protest, but the big man kept walking. He smelled of cigar smoke and expensive cologne, and the feel of his big arms around her made her feel odd. Trembly. Nervous. Very nervous. She had one arm around his broad shoulders to hold on, her hand spread beside his neck. He was warm and comforting. It had been a long time since she'd been held by anyone, and it had never felt like this.

Santi knocked on the door.

Bernie could have told him that he could just walk in, but he wasn't from here, so he didn't know.

Plump Mrs. Brown opened the door, still wearing her apron because she offered supper to her roomers. She stopped dead, with her mouth open, as she saw Bernie being carried by a stranger.

"I fell," Bernie explained. "He was kind enough to stop and bring me home…"

"Oh, dear, should you go see Dr. Coltrain?" she said worriedly.

"I'm fine, really, just a little bruised dignity to speak of," she assured the landlady. "You can put me down," she said to Mikey.

"Where's her room?" Mikey asked politely. He smiled at the older woman, and she flushed and laughed nervously.

"It's right down here. She can't climb the stairs, so she has a room near the front..."

She led the way. He put Bernie down in a chair beside her bed.

"You need a hot bath, dear, and some coffee," Mrs. Brown fussed.

There was a bathroom between Bernie's room and the empty room next door.

"Can you manage?" the big man asked gently.

She nodded. "I'm okay. Really. Thanks."

He shrugged broad shoulders. He frowned. "You shouldn't be walking so far."

"Tell her, tell her," Mrs. Brown fretted. "She walks four blocks to and from work every single day!"

"Dr. Coltrain says exercise is good for me," she retorted.

"Exercise. Not torture," Mrs. Brown muttered.

The big man was thinking. "We'll see you again," he said quietly.

She nodded. "Thanks."

He cocked his head. His eyes narrowed. "First impressions aren't always accurate."

Her eyebrows arched. "Gosh, was that an apology?"

He scowled. "I don't apologize. Ever."

"That didn't hurt, that didn't hurt, that didn't hurt,"

she mimicked a comedian who'd said that very thing in a movie. She grinned. Probably he didn't have a clue what she was talking about.

He threw back his head and roared. *"Police Academy,"* he said, naming the movie.

Her jaw fell.

"Yeah. That guy was me, at his age," he confessed. "Take a bath. And don't fall in."

She made a face at him.

His dark eyes twinkled. "See you, kid."

He walked out before she could correct the impression.

He stopped at the front door. "That room to let," he asked Mrs. Brown. "Is it still available?"

"Why, yes," she said, flushing again. She laughed. "You'd be very welcome. We have three ladies living here, but…"

"I'm easy to please," he said. "And I won't be any trouble. I hate hotels."

She smiled. "So do I. My husband was in rodeo. We spent years on the road. I got so sick of room keys…"

He laughed. "That's me. Okay. If you don't mind, I'll have my stuff here later today."

"I don't mind at all."

"How much in advance?" he asked, producing his wallet.

She told him. He handed her several bills.

"I don't rob banks, if that's what you're thinking," he said with a wry smile. "I'm a businessman. I live in

New Jersey, and I own a hotel in Vegas. Which is why I hate staying in them."

"Oh! You have business here, then?"

He nodded solemnly. "Business," he agreed. "I'll be around for a while."

"It will be nice to have the room rented," she confessed. "It's been vacant for a long time. My last tenant got married."

"I'll see you later, then." He hesitated, looking back toward the room where he'd left Bernadette. "She'll be okay, you think?"

"Yes. She might look fragile, but Bernie's tough. She's had to be."

"Bernie?" His eyes widened.

She laughed. "That's what we call her. We've known Bernadette all her life."

"Small towns." He smiled. "I grew up in one, myself. Far from here." He pulled out a business card and handed it to her. "The lower number is my cell phone. If she needs anything tonight, you call me, okay? I can come and drive her to the hospital if she needs to be seen."

Mrs. Brown was surprised at that concern from a stranger. "You have a kind heart."

He shrugged. "Not always. See you."

He went out, motioning for Santi to follow him. They got in the limo and drove off. Mrs. Brown watched it go with real interest. She wondered who the outsider was.

Mikey was all too aware of the driver's irritation. "They told me to keep an eye on you all the time," he told Mikey.

"Yeah, well, I'm not sharing a room with you, no matter what the hell they told you. Besides," he added, settling back into his seat, "Cash Grier's got one of his men shadowing me with a sniper kit."

"It's a small town," Santi began.

"A small town with half the retired mercs in America," Mikey cut in. "And my cousin lives right down the road. Remember him? Senior FBI agent Paul Fiore? Lives in Jacobsville, works out of San Antonio, worth millions?"

"Oh. Him. Right."

"Besides, I know the sniper Grier's got watching me." He chuckled. "He doesn't miss. Ever. And they snagged *The Avengers* to watch when the sniper's asleep."

"The Avengers?" Santi roared. "That's a comic book!"

"Rogers and Barton. They're called the Avengers because Captain America's name in the series is Rogers, and Hawkeye's is Barton. Get it?"

"Yeah."

"I know how bad Mario Cotillo wants me, Santi," Mikey said quietly. "I'm the only thing standing between Tony Garza and a murder-one conviction, because I know Tony didn't do it and I can prove it. Tony's in hiding, too, in an even safer place than me."

"Where?" Santi asked.

Mikey laughed coarsely. "Sure, like I'm going to tell you."

Santi stiffened. "I'm no snitch," he said, offended.

"Anybody can hack a cell phone or the elaborate two-way radio we got in this car, and listen to us when we talk," Mikey said with visible impatience. "Use your brain, okay?"

"I do!"

"Well, you must be keeping it in a safe place when you're not using it," Mikey muttered under his breath, but not so that Santi could hear him. The guy was good muscle and a capable driver. It wouldn't do to upset him too much. Not now, anyway.

Mikey leaned back with a long sigh and thought of the woman he'd met tonight. He was sorry he'd misjudged her, but plenty of women had thrown themselves into his path. He was extremely wealthy. He had money in Swiss banks that the feds couldn't touch. And while he'd been accused of a few crimes, including murder, he'd never even been indicted. His record was pretty clean. Well, for a guy in his profession. He was a crime boss back in Jersey, where Tony Garza was the big boss. Tony owned half the rackets around Newark. But Tony had some major new competition, an outsider who saw himself as the next Capone. He'd targeted Tony at once, planned to take him down on a fake murder charge with the help of a friend who worked in the federal attorney's office. It had backfired. Tony also had friends there. So did Mikey. But Mikey had been with Tony in a bar when the murder had taken place and by chance, Mikey had a photo of himself and Tony with a date stamp on his cell phone. He'd sent copies to Paulie and Cash Grier and a friend down in the Bahamas. Before the feds could jump Tony, who might have been dealt with handily and at once before it even came to trial, Mikey and Tony had both skipped town.

The next obvious play by Cotillo would be to put out contracts on Mikey and Tony. Mikey smiled. He knew most of the heavy hitters in the business. So did Tony. It wouldn't work, but Cotillo didn't know that. Yet. Meanwhile, Mikey and Tony were playing a waiting game. Both had feds on the job protecting them. Mikey wasn't telling Santi that, however. He didn't trust anybody really, except his cousin Paul. The fewer people who knew, the safer he was going to be.

Not that life held such attractions for him these days. He had all the money he'd ever need. He had a fearsome reputation, which gave him plenty of protection back home in New Jersey. But he was alone. He was a lonely man. He'd asked a woman to share his life only once, and she'd laughed. He was good in bed and he bought her pretty things, but she wasn't going to get married to a known gangster. She had her reputation to think of. After all, she was a debutante, from one of the most prominent families in Maryland. Marry a hood? Ha! Fat chance.

It had broken his heart. Even now, years and years after it happened, it was a sore spot. He was more than his reputation. He was fair and honest, and he never hurt anybody without a damned good reason. Mostly, he went after people who hurt people he cared about.

Well, there was also the odd job for Tony when he was younger. But those days were mostly behind him. He could still handle a sniper kit when he needed to. It was just that he didn't have the same need for notoriety that had once ruled his life.

Nobody needed him. Funny, the main reason he'd

enjoyed the debutante was that she'd pretended to be
helpless and clingy. He'd enjoyed that. Since his grandmother's death, there had been nobody who cared about
him except Paul, and nobody who needed him at all.
Briefly, he'd helped his cousin protect a young woman
from Jacobsville, Merrie Grayling, before she married
the Wyoming rancher. But that had been sort of an ac-
cessory thing. He'd liked her very much, yet as a sort of
adoptive baby sister, nothing romantic. It had been nice,
helping Paulie with that little chore, especially since he
knew the contract killer who'd been assigned to get Merrie. He had known how to get the hit called off—actually, by getting Merrie, an artist of great talent, to do a
portrait of Tony. The contract killer had ended badly,
but that happened sometimes. Most sane people didn't
go against Tony, who'd told the guy to call off the hit.

But all that had been three years ago. Life moved
on. Now here was Mikey, in hiding from a newcomer
in Jersey, trying to protect his friend Tony.

He thought again about the young woman who'd
fallen in front of the limo. He felt bad that he'd misjudged
her. She was pretty. What had she called herself—Bernadette? He smiled. He'd been to France, to the grotto
where Saint Bernadette had dug into a mudhole, found
a clear spring and seen the apparition she referred to as
the Immaculate Conception, and he'd seen Bernadette
in her coffin. She looked no older than when she'd died,
a century and more ago, a beautiful young woman. He
wondered if her namesake even knew who Saint Bernadette was. He wondered why she'd been given that name.

So many questions. Well, he was going to be staying in the same rooming house, so he'd probably get the chance to talk to her, to ask her about her family. She was nice. She didn't like pity, although she had a devastating medical condition, and she had a temper. He smiled, remembering that thick plait of blond hair down her back. He loved long hair. It must be hard to keep, for someone with her limitations.

His little Greek grandmother had been arthritic. He recalled her gnarled hands and the times when she hadn't been able to get out of bed. Mikey had carried her from room to room when she had special company, or outside when she wanted to sit in the sun. He couldn't remember what sort of arthritis she'd had, but it was in the family bible, along with plenty of other family information. He kept the bible in a safe-deposit box back in Jersey, along with precious photographs of people long dead. There had been one of the debutante. But he'd burned that one.

The car was eating up the miles to San Antonio, where Mikey had left his luggage in a hotel under an assumed name. He'd send Santi in to pick it up and pay the bill, just in case, while he waited outside in the parking lot. You couldn't be too careful. He needed to send a text to Paulie, as well, but that could wait until he was back in Jacobsville. He should ask Paulie about hackers and what they could find out, and how. He still wasn't up on modern methods of surveillance.

He leaned back against the seat with a long sigh. Bernadette. He smiled to himself.

Bernadette took a hot bath, and it did help ease some of the discomfort. Mrs. Brown had been kind enough

to add a handhold on the side of the tub so that Bernadette would find it easier to get in and out of the tub.
She took showers, however, not baths. It was so much
quicker to stand up. Besides, the bathroom was used by
all the boarders on the ground floor, although there had
been just Bernadette for several weeks, and poor Mrs.
Brown had enough to do without having to scrub the
tub all the time. She did have a daily woman who came
in to help with the heavy chores. But Bernadette was
fastidious and it bothered her, the idea of baths when
at least one of the former boarders had been male and
liked lots of musk-smelling bath oil. For women, especially, baths in a less than spotlessly clean tub could
lead to infections. Bernie had enough to worry about
without those. So, she took showers.

She dressed in her pajama bottoms and one of the
soft, thick T-shirts that she wore with it.

There was a tap at the door and Mrs. Brown came in
with a cup of tea in a beautiful ceramic cup on its delicate saucer. "Chamomile tea," she said with a smile. "It
will help you sleep, sweetheart."

"You're spoiling me," Bernadette complained softly.
"You have enough to do without adding me to your
burdens."

"You're no burden," Mrs. Brown said gently. "You
keep your room spotless, you never mess anything up,
and I have yet to have to pick up after you anywhere."
She sighed. "I wish we could say the same for the two
nice women on the second floor, and don't you dare tell
them I said that!"

Bernadette laughed. "I won't. You know I don't gossip."

"Of course you don't." She put the cup and saucer on the bedside table. "What a nice man who brought you home," she added with a speculative glance that Bernadette missed. "He's renting a room here, too!"

Bernadette caught her breath. "He is?" she stammered, and flushed a little.

Mrs. Brown chuckled. "He is. The one on the other side of the bathroom, but that won't be a problem. I'll make sure he knows to knock first when he needs to use it."

"Okay, then." She sipped tea and smiled with her eyes closed. "This is so good!"

"I put honey in it, instead of sugar, and just a hint of cinnamon."

Bernadette looked up at the older woman. "You know, he thought I'd fallen in front of his car on purpose."

"You fell? You didn't tell me!"

She sipped her tea. "The sidewalk was slippery and my toe hit a brick that was just a little out of place. I went flying into the street. Lucky for me that his driver had good brakes." She frowned. "It was a limousine."

"I noticed," Mrs. Brown said with a wry smile. "He was wearing a very expensive suit, as well. I think I recognized him. He looks like Paul Fiore's cousin."

"I heard about that," Bernadette said, "when I was working as a receptionist for a group of attorneys, before I got my paralegal certification from night school and Mr. Kemp hired me. I never saw him, but people talked about him. He was helping protect Merrie Grayling, wasn't he?"

"That was the gossip. Goodness, imagine having contract killers stalking two local girls in the same family!" She shook her head. "I had it from the Grayling girls' housekeeper, Mandy Swilling. She said the girls' father had killed a local woman for selling him out to the feds on racketeering charges, and the woman's son put out contracts on both Grayling's daughters, to get even. He thought their father loved them so much that it would really hurt him." She sighed. "Well, the man was dead by then, and the woman's son was charged with conspiracy to commit murder. They say he'll be in prison for a long time, even though he did try to help them find the killers."

"Good enough for him," Bernie said. "Murder is a nasty business."

"That's another thing. They say that Mr. Fiore's cousin Mikey is mixed up with organized crime."

"His cousin?"

"The man who carried you inside the house tonight," Mrs. Brown replied.

Bernie sat with the cup suspended in one hand. "Oh. Him." She laughed. She hadn't really been paying attention.

"Him." She laughed. "But I don't believe it. He's so nice. He was really concerned about you."

"Not when I first fell, he wasn't," Bernie said, wrinkling her nose. "He thought I did it on purpose to get his attention." She hesitated. "Well, you know, he is drop-dead gorgeous. When I first saw him, I could hardly even get my breath," she confessed. "It was like being hit in the stomach. I've never seen a real live man who looked like that. He could be in movies." She flushed. "Well, he's good-looking, I mean."

"I suppose some women do find excuses to attract men like that," Mrs. Brown said in his defense.

"I suppose. He changed his mind when he saw the cane, though." Her face grew sad. "When I was in high school, there was this really nice boy. I thought he was going to ask me to the senior prom. I was so excited. One of my girlfriends said he was talking about me to someone else, although she didn't hear what he said." She looked down into the now-empty cup. "Then another friend told me the truth. He said that I wasn't bad to look at, but he didn't want to take a disabled girl to a dance." She smiled sadly, aware of Mrs. Brown's angry expression. "After that, I sort of gave up on dating."

"There must have been nicer boys," she replied.

"Oh, there were. But there were prettier girls who didn't walk with canes." She put down the cup and saucer. "I didn't need the cane all the time, of course. But when I had flares, I'd just fall if I made a misstep." She shook her head. "No man is going to want a woman who may end up an invalid one day. So I go to work and save all I can, and hope that by the time I need to give up and apply for disability, I'll have enough to tide me over until I can get it." She made a face. "Gosh, wouldn't it be nice not to have health issues?"

"It would. And I'm sorry that you do. But, Bernie, a man who loves you won't care if you have them." She added, "Any more than you'd care if he had them."

Bernie smiled. "You're a nice woman. I'm so lucky to live here. And thank you for the tea."

"You're very welcome. You get some sleep. Tomorrow's Saturday, so you can sleep in for a change."

"A nice change." She grimaced. "But I don't want you to wait breakfast for me…!"

"I'll put it on a plate in the fridge and you can heat it up in the microwave," said Mrs. Brown. "So stop worrying about things."

Bernie laughed. "Okay. Thanks again."

"You're very welcome." She hesitated at the door. 'What a very good thing that we don't have many young women living here, except you."

"Why?"

"Well, that nice man who brought you in is really good-looking, and we don't want a line forming at his door, now do we?" she teased.

Bernie blushed, but Mrs. Brown had closed the door before she saw it.

Chapter Two

Mikey waited for Santi in a parking spot near the front door of the San Antonio hotel. He hoped it wouldn't take too long. The streets were busy, even at this time of night, and some of the people milling around were wearing gang colors and had multiple tats. He knew about the Los Serpientes gang. Although they were technically based in Houston, they had a presence here in San Antonio. Paulie had told him about them. They looked out for children and old people. Amazing. Kind of like the Yakuza in Japan.

Japan was a great place to visit. Mikey had gone there for several weeks after his tour of duty in the Middle East. He'd needed to wind down and get over some of the things he'd seen and done there. He'd been with a group of military overseas that included two men from here, Rogers and Barton, who'd been protecting the Grayling girls from contract killers. He hadn't served directly with them, but Cag Hart and the local DA, Blake Kemp, had been overseas at the same time. From Afghanistan to Iraq, he'd carried a rifle and served his country. The memories weren't good, but he had others he lived with. He just added the more recent ones to them.

He'd been surprised to find his company commander involved with Merrie Grayling. The Wyoming rancher, Ren Colter, had been the company commander of his sniper unit overseas. In fact, the Grayling girls' protectors, Rogers and Barton, had also been part of his group. What a homecoming that had been. Not a really great one, because Mikey had gotten in trouble scrounging materials for a brothel. But his commanding officer had gotten him out of trouble with Ren, because Mikey had the greatest luck in the world at poker. He never lost. It was one reason he was so rich. Of course, he couldn't get into casinos anymore. He didn't cheat. He didn't have to. But that luck had gotten him barred all over the world, even in Monte Carlo. He chuckled. It was sort of a mark of honor, being barred from those places. So he didn't mind that much. He had all the money he'd ever need until he died an old man, so who cared?

The car trunk opened suddenly. Mikey's hand had gone automatically under his jacket to the .45 he'd put there before Santi went into the hotel. He kept it in a secure compartment under the seat, custom-made. He hadn't needed it in Jacobsville, but this was unknown territory, and it was dangerous not to go heeled. He had a concealed carry permit, but for Jersey, not here. He supposed he'd have to go see the sheriff in Jacobs County and get one for Texas. That would be Hayes Carson. He knew the sheriff from three years ago. They got on.

Santi opened the door and got in behind the wheel. "All the bags are in the trunk, chief," he told his boss. "We need to stop anywhere else before we head south?"

"Not unless you're hungry."

"I could eat."

"Well, there's a nice restaurant in a better part of town. Let's go looking." He glanced out through the tinted windows at a young man who was giving the limo a real hard look. "I'm not overjoyed with the clientele hereabouts."

"Me, neither."

"So, let's go. We'll drive around and see if we can find someplace Italian. I think Paulie said a new place had just opened recently. Carlo's. Put it in the computer."

Santi fed it into the onboard GPS. "Got it, chief. Only three blocks away."

"Okay! Head out."

They were well into their plates of spaghetti when Mikey noticed a couple of customers in suits giving them a cursory inspection.

"Feds," Mikey said under his breath. "At the second table over. Don't look," he added.

"Know them?"

"Nope," Mikey said.

"FBI, you think?"

Mikey chuckled. "If they were, Paulie would have mentioned that I had a tail here in the city."

"Then who?"

"If I were guessing, US Marshals," he replied. "The big dark one looks vaguely familiar, but I can't quite place him. He was working with Paulie during the time I spent in Jacobsville three years ago."

"Marshals?" Santi asked, and he shifted restlessly.

"Relax. They aren't planning to toss our butts in jail. There's this thing called due process," Mikey said imperturbably. "We'll have fewer worries down in Jacobs County. Jacobsville is so small that any stranger sticks out. Besides, we've got shadows of our own."

"Good ones?"

"You bet," Mikey replied with a smug grin. "So eat your supper and I'll move into my new temporary home."

"I don't like being down the road in a motel," Santi muttered. "Even with all the other guys watching your back."

"Well, I'm not sharing the room," Mikey said flatly. "It's barely big enough for me and all my stuff, without trying to fit you into it. No room for another bed, anyway."

"I guess you got a point."

"Of course I do. Besides, it's not like I'm going to get hit until they track me down here."

"The limo is going to attract attention," Santi said worriedly.

"Yeah, well, no more attention than the gossip will,

but there's not a place in the world I'd be safer. Strangers stick out here. Remember, I told you about Cash Grier's wife being tracked here by a contract killer, and what happened to him?"

Santi chuckled. "Yeah. Grier's wife hit him so hard with an iron skillet that he ran to the cops for protection."

"Exactly. Nobody messes with Tippy Grier. What a knockout. A movie star, and she's married to the police chief and has two kids. I never thought Grier could settle down in a small town. He didn't seem the sort."

"That's what everybody says." Santi paused. "I feel bad about that poor girl we almost hit," he added, surprisingly, because he wasn't sentimental. "She was nice, and we thought she was trying to play us."

"We come by our suspicious natures honestly," Mikey reminded him. "But, yeah, she was nice. Needs looking after," he said quietly. "Not that she seems the kind of woman who'd let anybody look after her."

"I noticed that."

Mikey glanced at his watch. "We'd better go." He signaled to a waiter for the check.

Bernadette was reading in bed. The pain was pretty bad, a combination of the rain and the fall. She needed something to take her mind off it, so she pulled out her cell phone, on which she kept dozens of books. Many were romance novels. She realized that her condition would keep most men away, and it was nice to daydream about having a kind man sweep her off her feet.

She couldn't stop thinking about the big dark-haired

man who'd done that earlier in the evening. He was kin
to Paul Fiore, who was married to Sari Grayling. Bernie
worked with Sari in the local DA's office. She wondered
if she could get away with asking her anything about
the man, who'd been very kind to her after mistaking
her for some kind of con woman.

She shouldn't be thinking about him. A man that
handsome probably had women hanging on to his ankles everywhere he walked. He was apparently rich, as
well. There was another woman in her office, the receptionist, Jessie Tennison, a gorgeous brunette in her late
twenties, who was crazy about men and openly solic-
ited any rich one who came into the office. Mr. Kemp,
the DA, had already called her down about it once. A
second offense would cost her the job, he'd added. Her
position didn't include sexual harassment of clients.

What a new world it was, Bernie mused, when a
woman could be accused of what was often seen as a
man's offense. But, then, her coworker was very pretty.
She was just ambitious. She had a failed marriage behind her. Gossip was that her ex-husband had been
wealthy but had a gambling habit and lost it all on one
draw of a card. Nobody knew, because the woman didn't
talk about herself. Well, not to the women in the office.

A sudden commotion caught her attention. There was
movement in the hall. Some bumping and a familiar
deep male voice. Her heart jumped. That was the man
who'd brought her home earlier. She knew his voice already. It was hard to miss, with that definite New Jersey accent. She knew about that because of Paul Fiore.
He had one just like it.

There was more noise, then a door closing. More footsteps. Voices. The front door opening and closing, and then a car driving away.

Mrs. Brown knocked at Bernie's door and then slipped in, closing it behind her. "Sorry about the noise. Mr. Fiore's just moving in," she added with an affectionate smile.

Bernie tried not to show the delight she felt. "Is he going to stay long? Did he say?"

"Not really," she said. "His driver is staying at a motel down the road." She laughed. "Mr. Fiore said no way was he sharing that room with another man, especially not one as big as his driver."

Bernie laughed softly. "I guess not."

"So you'll need to knock before you go into the bathroom, like I mentioned earlier," Mrs. Brown continued. "Just in case. I told Mr. Fiore again that he'd need to do the same thing, since you're sharing." She looked worried. Bernie was flushed. "I'm so sorry. If I had a room with a bathroom free, I'd—"

"Those are upstairs," Bernie interrupted gently, "and we both know that I have a problem with stairs." She sighed and shook her head. "The rain and the walk and the fall pretty much did me in today. You were right. I should have gotten a cab. It isn't that expensive, and I don't spend much of what I make, except on books." That was true. Her rent included all utilities and even the cable that gave her television access—not that she watched much TV.

"I know that walking is supposed to be good for you," the older woman replied. "But not when you're having a flare." She drew in a breath. "Bernie, if you wrote the company that makes that injectable medicine, they might…"

"I already did," Bernie said softly. "They offered me a discount, but even so, it's almost a thousand dollars a month. There's no way I could afford that, discount or not. Besides," she said philosophically, "it might not work for me. Sometimes it doesn't. It's a gamble."

"I guess so." Mrs. Brown looked sad. "Maybe someday they'll find a cure."

"Maybe they will."

"Well, I'll let you get back to your book," she teased, because she knew about the late-night reading habit. "Need anything from the kitchen before I turn out the lights?"

"Not a thing. I have my water right here." She indicated two bottles of water that she kept by her bedside.

"You could have some ice in a glass to go with it."

Bernie shook her head. "It would just melt. But thank you, Mrs. Brown. You're so good to me."

The older woman beamed. "I'm happy to have you here. You're the only resident I've ever had who never complained about anything. You'll spoil me."

"That's *my* line," Bernie teased, and she laughed. It made her look pretty.

"Sleep well."

"You, too."

Mrs. Brown went out and closed the door.

Bernie thought about that injectable medicine. Her rheumatologist in San Antonio had told her about it, encouraged her to try to get it. At Bernie's age, it might retard the progress of the disease, a disease that could lead to all sorts of complications, the worst of which was deformity in the hands and feet. Not only that, but RA was systemic. It could cause a lot of issues in other parts of the body, as well.

Chance, Bernie thought, would be a fine thing. She'd have to be very well-to-do in order to afford something so expensive as those shots. Well, meanwhile she had her other meds, and they worked well enough most of the time. It wasn't every day that she fell in a cold rain almost in front of somebody's fancy limousine. She smiled to herself and went back to her book.

Breakfast the next morning would have been interesting, Bernie thought to herself as she ate hers from a tray her kindly landlady had provided. But she couldn't get up. A weather system had moved in, dropping even more rain, and Bernie's poor body was still trying to cope with yesterday's fall. What a good thing it was Saturday. She'd have had a time getting to work.

Just as she finished the last drop of her coffee, there was a perfunctory knock and the man who'd rescued her walked in.

She pulled the sheet up over her breasts. The gown covered her nicely, but she'd never had a man in her bedroom in her life, except for her late father and her doctor. She flushed.

Mikey grinned from ear to ear. He loved that reaction. The women in his life were brassy and easy and unshockable. Here was a violet under a staircase, undiscovered, who blushed because a man saw her in her nightgown.

"Mrs. Brown said you might like a second cup of coffee," he said gently, approaching the bed with a cup and saucer.

"Oh, I, yes, I...thank you." She couldn't even talk normally. She was furious with herself, especially when her hands shook a little as she took the cup and saucer from him. He lifted the empty one from the tray, so she'd have someplace to put the new one.

He cocked his head and looked at her, fascinated. Her long blond hair was in a braid, a little frizzled from being slept on. She was wearing a cotton gown, and he could see the straps with their eyelet trim. It reminded him of his grandmother, who'd never liked artificial fabric.

"You aren't feeling so good today, are you?" he asked. "Need me to run you over to the doctor?"

The flush grew. "Oh. Thank you. No, I'm...well, it's sort of normal. When it rains, it hurts more. And I fell." She bit her lip because he looked so guilty. "It wasn't your fault, or your driver's," she added quickly. "I'm clumsy. My toe hit a brick on the sidewalk that was just a little raised and it caused me to lose my balance. That's why I use the cane on bad days. I'm clumsy even on flat surfaces..."

"My grandmother had arthritis," he said softly. "Her little hands and feet were gnarled like tree roots." He wasn't watching, so he didn't notice the discomfort in Bernie's face—her poor feet weren't very pretty, either. "I used to carry her in and out of the house when she had bad spells. She loved to sit in the sun." His dark eyes were sad. "She weighed barely eighty pounds, but she was like a little pit bull. Even the big guys were afraid of her."

"The big guys?" she asked, lost in his soft eyes.

He shrugged. "In the family," he said.

She frowned. She didn't understand.

"You really are a little violet under a stair," he mused to himself. "The family is what insiders call the mob," he explained. "The big guys are the dons, the men who run things. I'm from New Jersey. Most of my family was involved in organized crime. Well, except Paulie," he added with a chuckle. "He was always the odd guy out."

She smiled. "He's married to Sari Grayling, who works in our office."

He nodded. "Sweet woman. Her sister is one hel— heck of an artist," he said, amending the word he'd meant to use.

"She truly is. They had her do a portrait of our local college president, who was retiring. It looked just like him."

He chuckled. "The one she painted three years ago saved her life. Her father whacked a woman whose son hired contract men to go after Grayling's daughters. Merrie painted the big don from back home, and he called off the hit." He didn't add how Tony Garza had called it off.

"We heard about all that. I wasn't working for the district attorney's office at the time. I was working for a local attorney who moved his practice to San Antonio.

But we all knew," she added. "Everybody talked about it. He actually gave her away at her wedding, didn't he?"

He nodded. "Tony's wife died young. He never had kids, never remarried." He grinned. "He tells everybody he's Merrie's dad. Gets a reaction, let me tell you, especially when he mentions that her brother-in-law is a fed."

She sipped coffee, fascinated by him.

It was mutual. He smiled very slowly, his heart doing odd things in his chest. It had been many years since he'd felt such tenderness for anything female, except his grandmother.

"Do you have family?" he asked suddenly.

Her face clouded. "Not anymore," she said softly, without elaborating.

"Me, neither," he replied. "Except for Paulie. We're first cousins."

"Mr. Fiore's nice," she said.

He nodded. He was thinking about Tony, in hiding and waiting for developments that would save him from life in prison. Mikey had the proof that could save him. But he had to stay alive long enough to present it. Here, in Jacobsville, was his best bet. He'd agreed, knowing how many ex-mercs and ex-military lived here.

But as he stared at this sweet, kind young woman, he thought about the danger he might be putting her in. Even in a foolproof situation, there could be snags. After all, the contract killer who'd been after Merrie actually got onto Ren Colter's property in Wyoming and had her bedroom staked out before she came back to her sister and brother-in-law.

Bernie cocked her head. "Something's worrying you."

He started. "How do you know?"

She drew in a slow breath and averted her eyes. "People think I'm strange."

He moved a step closer to the bed. "How so?"

She shifted restlessly. "I...well, I sort of know things about people." She flushed.

He nodded. "Like Merrie. She has that sort of perception. She painted a picture of me that nailed me to a T, and she'd never even met me."

She looked up. "Oh. Then you're not...intimidated by strange things."

He chuckled. "Nothing intimidates me, kid," he teased.

She smiled.

"So. You think something's worrying me." One brown eye narrowed. "What, exactly?"

She drew in a long breath and stared into his eyes. "Somebody wants to keep you from telling something you know," she said after a minute, and saw the shock hit his face.

"Damn."

"And it worries you that somebody might hurt anybody around you."

"Need to get a crystal ball and a kerchief and set up shop," he teased gently. "You're absolutely on the money. But that's between you and me, okay? The fewer people who know things, the fewer can talk about them."

She nodded. "I don't talk about things I know, as a

rule. I work for the DA's office. Gossip isn't encouraged."

He chuckled. "I guess not."

Her coffee was now stone-cold, but she sipped it, for something to do.

He stared at her with conflicting emotions. She was unique, he thought. He'd never met anybody in his life like her.

She stared back. Her heart was almost smothering her with its wild beat. She was grateful that she had the covers pulled up, so he couldn't see her gown fluttering with her heartbeat.

There was another quick knock and Mrs. Brown came in. "Finished, dear?" she asked as she went to pick up the tray. "You can just set that on here, Mr. Fiore," she told Mikey with a smile. "I'll…"

He put it on the tray and then took the tray from her. "You're too delicate to be lifting heavy weights," he said with a grin. "I'll carry it for you."

"Oh, Mr. Fiore," she laughed, and blushed like a girl. "If you need anything, you just call me, Bernie, ok?"

"I will. Thanks. Both of you," she added.

Mrs. Brown smiled. As Mikey went through the door, he turned and winked at her.

That wink kept her heart fluttering all day, and it kept her awake most of the night.

She was able to go to the table for breakfast the next morning, even if she moved with a little difficulty. Her medicines worked slowly, but at least they did work.

She had prednisone to take with the worst attacks, and it helped tremendously.

"You look better today," Mrs. Brown said. "Going to church?"

"Yes," she replied with a smile. "I'm hitching a ride with the Farwalkers."

Mikey frowned. "The Farwalkers? Wait a minute. Farwalker. Carson Farwalker. He's one of the doctors here. I remember."

Bernie laughed. "Yes. He's married to Carlie Blair. Her dad is pastor of the local Methodist church. I don't have a car, so they come by to get me most Sundays for services. Sometimes it's just Carlie and their little boy, Jacob, if Carson's on call."

He didn't mention that he knew that pastor, Jake Blair. He also knew things about the man's past that he wasn't sharing.

"My whole family was Catholic," he said. "Well, not Paulie. But then, he always went his own way."

"The Ruiz family here is Catholic," she said. "He's a Texas Ranger. His wife is a nurse. She works in San Antonio, too, so they commute. They're very nice people."

"I never met Ruiz, but I heard about him. Ranch the size of a small state, they say."

Bernie grinned. "Yes. It is rather large, but they aren't social people, if you get my meaning."

"Goodness, no," Miss Pirkle, one of the tenants said with a smile. "Your cousin and his family are like that, too, Mr. Fiore," she added, her thin face animated as she spoke. "Down-to-earth. Good people."

"Thanks," he said.

"We have a lot of moneyed families in Jacobsville and Comanche Wells," old Mrs. Bartwell interjected with a smile. "Most of them earned their wealth the hard way, especially the Ballengers. They started out with nothing. Now Calhoun is a United States senator and Justin runs their huge feed lot here."

"That's a real rags-to-riches story," Miss Pirkle agreed. "Their sons are nice, too. Imagine, two brothers, three children apiece, and not a girl in the bunch," she added on a laugh.

"I wouldn't mind a little girl," Mikey said, surprising himself. He didn't dare look at Bernie, who'd inspired the comment. He could almost picture her in a little frilly dress at the age of five or six. She would have been a pretty child. He hadn't thought about children in a long time, not since his ex-fiancée had noted that she wasn't marrying some famous criminal. It had broken Mikey's heart. Women were treacherous.

"Children are sweet," Bernie said softly as she finished her bacon and eggs. "The Griers come into our office a lot with their daughter, Tris, and their son, Marcus. I love seeing their children."

"The police chief," Mikey said, nodding. He chuckled. "Not your average small-town cop."

"Not at all," Bernie agreed, tongue-in-cheek.

"That's true," Miss Pirkle said. "He was a Texas Ranger!"

Bernie caught Mikey's eyes and held them. He got the message. Their elderly breakfast companion didn't know about the chief's past. Just as well to keep it quiet.

"Are you from here, too?" Mikey asked Miss Pirkle.

"No. I'm from Houston," she replied, her blue eyes smiling. "I came here with my mother about two years ago, just before I lost her." She took a breath and forced a smile. "I loved the town so much that I decided I'd just stay. I don't really have anybody back in Houston now."

"I'm not from here, either," Mrs. Bartwell said. "I'm a northern transplant. New York State."

"Thought I recognized that accent," Mikey teased.

Mrs. Bartwell chuckled. "I have a great-niece who lives in Chicago with her grandmother. Old money. Very old. They have ancestors who died in the French Revolution."

"My goodness!" Miss Pirkle exclaimed, all ears.

"My sister and I haven't spoken in twenty years," she added. "We had a minor disagreement that led to a terrible fight. My husband died of cancer and we had no children. My great-niece's mother was from Jacobsville. She was a Jacobs, in fact."

"Impressive," Bernie said with a grin. "Was she kin to Big John?"

"Yes, distantly."

"Big John?" Mikey asked curiously.

"Big John Jacobs," Bernie replied, because she knew the history by heart. "He was a sharecropper back in Georgia before the Union Army burned down his farm and killed most of his family, thinking they were slave owners. They weren't. They were poor, like the black family he saved from real slave owners. One of the Union officers was going to have him shot, but the black family got between him and the Army man and made him listen to the truth. They saved his life. He came here just after the Civil War with them. He didn't even have a proper house, so he and their families lived in one big shack together. He hired on some Comanche men and a good many cowboys from Mexico and started ranching with Texas longhorns. He made people uncomfortable because he wasn't a racist in a time when many people were. He married an heiress, convinced her father to build a railroad spur to the ranch, near present Jacobsville, so that he could ship his cattle north. Made a fortune at it."

"What a story," Mikey chuckled.

"And all true," Miss Pirkle said. "There's a statue of Big John on the town square. One of his direct descendants is married to Justin Ballenger, who owns one of the biggest feed lots in Texas."

"All this talk of great men makes me weak in the knees," Mikey teased.

"Do you have illustrious ancestors, Mr. Fiore?" Mrs. Brown asked with a mischievous grin.

"Nah," he said. "If I do, I don't know about it. My grandmother was the only illustrious person I ever knew."

"Was she famous?" Mrs. Bartwell asked.

"Well, she was famous back in Jersey," he mused. "Got mad at a don and chased him around the room with a salami."

There were confused looks.

"Mafia folks," he explained.

"Oh! Like in *The Sopranos*, that used to be on television!" Miss Pirkle said. "I never missed an episode!"

"Sort of like that," he said. "More like Marlon Brando in *The Godfather*," he said, chuckling. "Afterwards, he sent her a big present every Christmas and even came to her funeral. She was fierce."

"Was she Italian?" Mrs. Brown asked.

He laughed. "She was Greek. Everybody else in my whole family was Italian except for her. She was a tiny little thing, but ferocious. I was terrified of her when I was a kid. So was Paulie. Our folks didn't have much time for us," he added, not explaining why, "so she pretty much raised us."

"I never knew either of my grandmothers," Bernie said as she sipped coffee.

Mikey was studying her closely. "Where were your grandparents from?" he asked.

She closed up like a flower. She forced a smile. "I'm not really sure," she lied. "My father and mother were from Jacobsville, though, and we lived here from the time I was old enough to remember things. I have to get ready for church. It was delicious, Mrs. Brown," she added.

"Thank you, dear," Mrs. Brown said, and grimaced a little. She knew about Bernie's past. Not many other local people did. She could almost feel Bernie's anguish. Not Mr. Fiore's fault for bringing it up. He didn't know. "Want a second cup of coffee to take with you while you dress?"

"If I drink two, I can fly around the room and land on the curtain rods," Bernie teased. "I'm hyper enough as it is. But thanks."

She glanced at Mikey, puzzled by the look on his face. She smiled at the others and went back to her room.

Jake Blair was a conundrum, Bernie thought as she walked in line out the front door to shake hands with him after the very nice sermon. He seemed to be very conventional, just like a minister was expected to be. But he drove a red Shelby Cobra Mustang with a souped-up engine, and there were whispers about his past. The same sort of whispers that followed Jacobsville's police chief, Cash Grier, wherever he went.

Bernie gripped her dragon cane tightly and glanced at the toddler in Dr. Carson Farwalker's arms as he and Carlie walked beside her.

"Imagine you two with a child." Bernie sighed as she went from one face to the other.

Carlie grinned. "Imagine us married!" she corrected with a loving look at her husband, which was returned. "They were taking bets at the police station the day we got married about when he'd do a flit."

"They're having a long wait, don't you think?" Carson chuckled.

"Very long," she agreed. "Imagine, we used to fight each other in World of Warcraft on battlegrounds and we never knew it. Not until my life was in danger and Dad had you watching me."

"I watched you a lot more than he told me to," Carson teased.

She laughed.

They'd moved up to Jake by now and he was giving them an amused grin. "There's my boy!" he said softly, and held his arms out for Jacob, who was named after him."

"Gimpa." The little boy laughed and hugged the tall man.

Jake hugged him close. "If anybody had told me ten years ago that I'd go all mushy over a grandchild, I guess I'd have laughed."

"If anybody had told me ten years ago that I'd be practicing medicine in a small Texas town, I'd have fainted," Carson chuckled.

"I like having family," Jake said, and smiled at his daughter and son-in-law. "I never belonged anyplace in my life until now."

"Me, neither," Bernie said softly.

Jake looked at her kindly, and she knew that he'd heard the rumors. She just smiled. He was her minister, after all. Someday maybe she'd be able to talk about it. Mrs. Brown knew, but she was a clam. Not a lot of other people had any idea about Bernie's background because she'd lived for a few years, with her parents, in Floresville before coming back here with her father just before he died. She didn't like to think about those days. Not at all.

Jake looked behind his family at the few remaining, obviously impatient worshippers and handed his grandson back to Carson. "Ah, well, I'll see you all at the house later. I'm holding up progress," he added, and looked behind Carson at a man who actually flushed.

"Not a problem, Preacher," the man said. "It's just that the line's already forming for lunch at Barbara's Café…"

"Say no more," Jake chuckled. "Actually, I'm heading there myself. I can burn water."

"You can cook," Carlie chided.

"Only when I want to. And I don't want to," he confided with a grin. He kissed her cheek and shook hands with Carson. "I'll see you all for supper. You bringing it?"

"Of course," Carlie replied with a grin. "We know you can't boil water!"

He just laughed.

Bernie walked into the boardinghouse a little tired, but happy from the few hours of socializing with friends.

She wasn't looking where she was going, her mind still on the Farwalkers' little boy, whom she had sat beside in the back seat and cooed at all the way home. She ran right into Mikey and almost fell.

Chapter Three

Mikey just stared at her, smiling faintly as he caught her by both shoulders and spared her a fall. She did look pretty, with her long, platinum blond hair loose around her shoulders, wearing a pink dress in some soft material that displayed her nice figure without making it look indecent. He thought of all the women he'd known who paraded around in dresses cut up to the thigh and slashed to the waist in front. He compared them with Bernie, and found that he greatly preferred her to those glitzy women in his past.

"Thanks," she said, a husky note in her voice as she looked up at him with fascinated pale green eyes. It was a long way. He was husky for his height, and his head was leonine, broad, with a straight nose and chiseled lips and a square chin. He looked like a movie star. She'd never even seen a man so handsome.

"Deep thoughts?" he asked softly.

She caught her breath. "Sorry. I was just thinking how handsome you are." She flushed. "Oh, gosh," she groaned as that slipped out.

"It's okay," he teased. "I'm used to ladies swooning over me. No problem."

That broke the ice and she laughed.

He loved the way she looked when she laughed. Her whole face became radiant. Color bloomed on her cheeks. Her green eyes sparkled. Amazing, that a woman with her disability could laugh at all. But, then, his little grandmother had been the same. She never complained. She just accepted her lot in life and got on with living.

"You never complain, do you?" he asked suddenly.

"Well...not really," she stammered. "There's this saying that the boss has on the wall at work, a quote from Saint Francis of Assisi..."

"'God grant me the serenity to accept the things I cannot change; courage to change the things I can; and wisdom to know the difference,'" he quoted.

She smiled. "You know it."

He shrugged. "My grandmother dragged me to mass every single Sunday until I was old enough to refuse to go. She had a plaque with that quote on it. I learned it by heart."

"It's nice."

"I guess."

He let her go belatedly. "You okay?"

"I'm fine. I wasn't paying attention to where I was going. Sorry I ran into you."

"Feel free to do it whenever you like," he said, and his dark eyes twinkled. "You fall down, kid, I'll pick you up every time."

She flushed. "Thanks. I'd do the same for you, if I could." She eyed his height. Her head came up to just past his shoulder. He probably weighed twice what she did, and the expensive suit he was wearing didn't disguise the muscular body under it. "I don't imagine I could pick you up, though."

He laughed. "Don't sweat it. I'll see you later."

She nodded.

He went around her and out the door, just as she heard a car pull up at the curb. His driver, no doubt. She wondered where he was going on a Sunday. But, then, that was really not her business.

It was the next morning before Bernie saw Mikey again, at the breakfast table. He was quiet and he looked very somber. He felt somber. Somebody had tracked Tony to the Bahamas and Marcus Carrera had called in some markers to keep him safe. Tony had used one of his throwaway phones to call Mikey—on the number Mikey had sent through a confederate.

Carrera, he recalled, was not a man to mess with. Once a big boss up north, the man had done a complete flip and gone legit. He was worth millions. He'd married a small-town Texas girl some years ago and they had two sons. The wife was actually from Jacobsville, a girl who used to do clothing repairs at the local dry cleaner's. Her father was as rich as Tony. Her mother had pretended to be her sister, but the truth came out when Carrera was threatened and his future wife saved him. Mikey knew Carrera's in-laws, but distantly. At least Tony was safe. But if they'd tracked him down, they probably had a good idea where Mikey was. It wouldn't take much work to discover that Mikey had been down here in Jacobsville three years ago to help out his cousin Paulie. That being said, however, it was still the safest place he could be. He had as much protection as he needed, from both sides of the law.

He looked around at the women at the table. His eyes lingered on Bernadette. He didn't want to put her in the line of fire. This had been a bad idea, getting a room at a boardinghouse. Or had it?

"Deep thoughts, Mr. Fiore?" Mrs. Brown teased. "You're very quiet."

He laughed self-consciously when he felt eyes on him. "Yeah. I was thinking about a friend of mine who's been in some trouble recently."

"We've all been there," Miss Pirkle said warmly. "I guess friends become like family after a time, don't they? We worry about them just as we would about kinfolk."

"And that's a fact," he agreed.

"My best friend drowned in a neighbor's swimming pool, when my family lived briefly in Floresville," Bernie commented.

"Did you see it?" Mikey asked.

She looked down at her plate. Her whole face clenched. "Yes. I didn't get to her in time."

"Listen, kid, sometimes things just happen. Like they're meant to happen. I'm not a religious man, but I believe life has a plan. Every life."

Bernie looked up at him. Her face relaxed a little. She drew in a long breath. "Yes. I think that, too." She smiled.

He smiled back.

The smiles lasted just a second too long to be casual. Mrs. Brown broke the silence by putting her cup noisily in the saucer without glancing at her boarders. It amused her, the streetwise Northerner and the shy Texas girl, finding each other fascinating. Mrs. Brown's husband had died years ago, leaving her with a big house outside town and a fistful of bills she couldn't pay. Opening her home to lodgers had made the difference. With her increased income, she was able to buy this house in town and turn it into a new boardinghouse. The sale of the first house had financed the purchase and remodeling of this one. The new location had been perfect for her boarders who worked in Jacobsville. She found that she had a natural aptitude for dealing with people, and it kept her bills paid and left her comfortably situated financially. But romance had been missing from her life. Now she was watching it unfold, with delight.

Mikey glanced at his wrist, at the very expensive thin gold watch he wore. "I have to run. I'm meeting Paulie up in San Antonio, but I'll be home in time for dinner," he told Mrs. Brown. He got up and leaned toward her. "What are we having?"

"Lasagna," she said with a grin. "And yes, I do know how to make it. Mandy Swilling taught me."

"You angel!" he said, and chuckled. "I'll definitely be back on time. See you all later."

They all called goodbyes. Bernie flushed when he turned at the doorway and glanced back at her with dark, soft eyes and a smile.

She felt good enough to walk the four blocks to work and she hardly needed the cane. Her life had taken a turn. She was happy for the first time in recent memory. Just the thought of Mikey Fiore made her tingle all over and glow inside.

That was noticed by the people she worked with, especially the new girl, Jessie Tennison. Jessie was older than Bernadette's twenty-four years. She had to be at least twenty-seven. She'd been married and was now divorced, with no children. She had a roving eye for rich men. It had already gotten her in trouble with their boss, Mr. Kemp, the district attorney. That hadn't seemed to stop her. She wore very revealing clothing—she'd been called down about that, too—and she wasn't friendly to the women in the office.

Bernie put down her purse, folded her cane and took off her jacket before she sat down.

"I don't see why you work," Jessie said offhandedly, looking down her long nose at Bernie with a cold blue-eyed stare. "I'd just get on government relief and stay home."

"I don't need handouts. I work for my living," Bernie said. She smiled at the tall brunette, but not with any warmth.

Jessie shrugged. "Suit yourself. I'm going over to the

courthouse on my break to talk to my friend Billie," she added, slipping into a long coat.

Bernie almost bit her tongue off to keep from mentioning that their breaks were only ten minutes long and it would take Jessie that long just to walk to the courthouse. The district attorney's office had been in the courthouse, but this year they'd moved to a new county building where they had more room. The increased space had delighted the office staff, which had grown considerably. Their new office was closer to Mrs. Brown's boardinghouse and Barbara's Café, but farther from the courthouse.

She didn't say it, but her coworker Olivia did. "Who's in the courthouse today, Jessie?" she asked with a blank expression. "Some really rich upper-class man who might need a companion…?"

"You…!" Jessie began just as Mr. Kemp's office door opened. She smiled at him, all sweetness. "I'm going to the courthouse on my break to see my friend Billie for just a minute, Mr. Kemp. Is that all right with you?" she added with a cold glance at her coworker.

"If it's absolutely necessary," he replied tersely. He wasn't pleased with his new employee. In fact, he was beginning to think he'd made a big mistake. A glowing recommendation from a San Antonio attorney had gotten Jessie the job, mainly because there were no other applicants. Competent receptionists with several years' experience weren't thick on the ground around Jacobsville.

"It really is," she said, and looked as if it wasn't the

whole truth. "I have a friend in the hospital in San Antonio. Billie's been to see him," she added quickly.

"Okay. Try not to take too long." He paused and looked at her for a long time. "You get a ten-minute break. Not an hour."

"Oh, yes, sir." She was all sugary sweetness as she walked out the door in a cloud of cloying perfume.

Bernie's coworker fanned the air with a file folder, making a face.

Not five minutes later, assistant DA Glory Ramirez walked in the door and made a face. "Who's been filming a perfume commercial in here?" she asked.

"Somebody who's mad at me, probably," Sari Fiore, their second assistant DA, laughed as she came in behind Glory. "Perfume gives me a migraine."

"I'll turn the air conditioner on long enough to suck it out of the building," Mr. Kemp volunteered.

"Ask her to wash it all off. I dare you," Sari said to the boss.

He laughed and went back into his office. The phone rang. Sari picked it up, nodded, spoke into the receiver and pressed a button. It was for Mr. Kemp. She hung up.

"Where's Jessie?" Sari asked curtly. "The phone is her job, not ours."

"There's some rich guy at the courthouse," Olivia told her. "She had a call from her friend Billie, who works as a temporary assistant in the Clerk of Court's office. I guess that was what it was about, although she said she was going to ask about a sick friend."

"She can't do that on the phone?" Sari asked, aghast.

"Well, she can't see the rich guy over the phone," Olivia said demurely and with a wicked smile.

"Jessie's a pill," Glory added. "I wonder how she ever got past the boss to hire on here. She's definitely not like any legal receptionist I've ever known."

"She's big-city, not small-town," Sari said. "She's got an accent like that lawyer from Manhattan who was down here last month."

"I noticed," Glory replied. "How are you feeling, Bernie?"

Bernie flushed and grinned. "I'm doing fine."

"Oh?" Sari teased. "We heard about your new boarder at Mrs. Brown's."

Bernie went scarlet.

"That was mean," Glory told Sari.

"Sorry," Sari said, but she was still grinning. "Isn't Mikey a doll?" she added. "He could pose for commercials."

"I noticed," Bernie said. "He's very good-looking."

"We heard about the fall. You okay?"

Bernie gasped. "Does he tell you guys everything?"

"Well, not everything. Just when he feels guilty about something." She smiled gently. "He felt really bad that he'd misjudged you. But it's not surprising. He's had women jump in front of his car before."

"My goodness!" Bernie exclaimed, fascinated.

"He is very rich," Glory pointed out. "And some women are less than scrupulous."

"Very true," Bernie said. "But I'm not."

"He noticed," Sari replied, tongue in cheek. "He said you remind him of his grandmother."

Bernie's eyes widened to saucers, and she looked absolutely horrified.

"No!" Sari said quickly. "He didn't mean he thought you were old. He said you had the same kind heart and the same sharp tongue she did. He was tickled when you compared him to that guy in the *Police Academy* movie." Her blue eyes sparkled as she looked at Bernie. "Paul said he really was like that guy, too."

Bernie laughed. "He's a lot of fun around the boardinghouse. He makes our two older ladies very flustered. Mrs. Brown, too."

"He's a dish. But he's not really a ladies' man, despite the appearance," Sari added. "In fact, he doesn't like most women. He had a hard experience some years back. I guess it affected him."

"We've all had hard experiences," Glory remarked. She shook her head. "If anybody had ever told me I'd marry Rodrigo…!"

"If anybody had ever told me that I'd finally marry Paul…" Sari countered, and they both laughed.

Both women had had a hard path to the altar, with some painful experiences along the way. Now they were happy. Glory and Rodrigo had a son, but Paul and Sari hadn't started a family. Despite being filthy rich, they were both career oriented. Paul was FBI at the San Antonio office and Sari was an assistant DA here in Jacobs County. Children were definitely in their future, Sari often said, but not just at the moment.

Bernie would have loved a child. It would have been difficult for her with her physical issues, but that wouldn't deter her if she ever found a man who loved her enough to marry her. She thought briefly of Mikey and her heart fluttered, but she knew she wasn't beautiful or cultured enough to appeal to a man so sophisticated. And if he'd reached his present age, which had to be somewhere in his thirties, unmarried, he was unlikely to be thinking of marrying anybody in the future. What a depressing thought, she realized, and how silly of her to be thinking of it in the first place. He was only here temporarily. He belonged up north.

She sat very still, aware of conversation around her and not hearing it. Mikey belonged up north. But he was in Jacobsville for no apparent reason, and he'd taken a room at a boardinghouse, which meant he was staying for a while. Why?

She knew he was worried about the people around him in the boardinghouse. Had he made somebody really mad, and they were after him? Was he in Jacobsville because he was safe here? She'd heard just a snippet of gossip from Mrs. Brown, that Mr. Fiore was being watched by one of Eb Scott's men. Nobody knew why. But Eb's men were mercenaries, experienced in combat. Bernie hoped that Mikey wasn't being hunted.

What an odd word to think of, she mused as she pulled up the computer program she used in her work. Hunted. She'd guessed that Mikey was worried about somebody else. Her heart jumped. Was it a woman, perhaps? No. Sari said he was sour on women. A man? Somebody from his past with a grudge? He knew a lot about organized crime. Maybe it was somebody he'd come across in his job, because Mrs. Brown said he told her he owned a hotel in Las Vegas. He must, she thought, be very rich indeed if he owned property in that expensive place.

She was well into research on a new case precedent for the boss when Jessie breezed back in, wafting her expense perfume everywhere.

Sari glared at her. "Jessie, I've told you that heavy perfume brings on migraines. I'd hate to have to speak to Mr. Kemp about it."

"Oh, I'm sorry!" Jessie said at once, feigning surprise. "I won't wear so much from now on."

"Thanks." Sari gave her a look she didn't see and went back to work.

"Well, was he there, your rich mark?" Olivia drawled.

Jessie glared at her. "I don't have a rich mark."

"Some wealthy gentleman?" Olivia probed further.

Jessie took off her coat and sat down at her desk. "I don't know. He was riding in a black limousine. He's from New Jersey."

Bernie's heart dropped to her feet. She only knew one rich man in Jacobsville who rode around in a black limousine. It had to be Mikey. Jessie was beautiful and sophisticated, probably the sort of woman Mikey would really go for. Jessie was an oddity in Jacobsville, where most women weren't streetwise. The older woman probably charmed him.

While she was thinking, Jessie's cold eyes stabbed into her face. "He said he's living at Mrs. Brown's boardinghouse. That's where you live, isn't it, Bernadette?"

"Yes," Bernie said shortly.

Jessie laughed, her scrutiny almost insulting. "Well, you won't be any sort of competition, will you? I mean, no sane man is going to want to take on a woman who can't stand up without a cane—"

"That's enough," Mr. Kemp said shortly from his open office door, and he looked even more formidable than usual. "You get one more warning, Jessie, then you're on your way back to San Antonio. You do not disparage coworkers. Ever."

Jessie actually flushed. She hadn't realized the boss could hear her. She'd have to be a lot more careful. There weren't any other jobs available in Jacobsville right now, and she couldn't afford to lose this one.

"I'm very sorry, Mr. Kemp," she began.

"Bernie's the one who's owed an apology."

"Yes, sir." Jessie turned to Bernie. "I'm sorry. That was wrong of me."

"Okay," Bernie said, but she didn't really look at the other woman.

Mr. Kemp hesitated for just a minute before he went back into his office.

"Careless, Jessie," Olivia said in a biting undertone. "Better make sure the boss isn't listening when you start making rude comments about one of us."

Jessie looked as if she might explode. The phone rang and saved her from making her situation any worse.

At lunchtime, Olivia and Bernie went to Barbara's Café to eat. Glory and Sari went home, where Glory had a babysitter and she could visit with her son while she ate. Sari had lunch with Mandy Swilling, the Grayling housekeeper. Jessie was stuck in the office until the others returned, thanks to Mr. Kemp who insisted that somebody had to answer the phone while he was out of the office. Jessie was almost smoking when the other women went out the door.

* * *

"Jessie's a pain," Olivia said curtly.

Bernie's pale green eyes sparkled as she dug into her chef's salad. "You really made her mad."

"Well, nobody else says anything," the other woman defended herself. Her voice softened. "Least of all you, Bernie. You're the sweetest woman I've ever known, except for my late grandmother. You could find one kind thing to say about the devil," she teased.

Bernie laughed softly. "I guess so."

"At least Sari finally said something about the heavy perfume. I know it gives her fits. She's prone to migraines from just the stress of her job. Jessie doesn't care what she does or says unless the boss loses his temper." She frowned. "What's she doing down here?" she added with a frown. "I mean, she worked in San Antonio, where salaries are a lot higher. She doesn't know anybody in Jacobsville."

"The boss said she wanted a slower pace," Bernie replied.

"Sure. Like she has any stress. Unless answering the phone gives you ulcers," Olivia said drily. "Or bending over the desk to show as much cleavage as possible when a wealthy client comes in."

"Oh, shame on you!" Bernie said, laughing.

"I know. I'm bad. But Jessie's worse. She met your fellow boardinghouse occupant, too," Olivia added with a pointed glance at Bernie's flushed face. "She'll be after him soon. Nobody here rides around in a limo except Paul's cousin Mikey. Sari used to, but she mostly just drives now that all the threats to her and her sister are gone."

"He's here for a reason, too," Bernie said.

"A guess, or that intuition that makes most people nervous?" Olivia teased.

Bernie laughed. "Maybe a bit of both."

"Or maybe not." Olivia glanced up and then down again. "Any idea about what he might be doing today?"

Bernie's heart jumped and she felt it flutter. Incredible, that she knew absolutely where he was, without even looking. "He's coming in the door."

She hadn't looked up. She did now, and there he was, in a dark suit with a patterned blue tie, looking around until he spotted Bernie. He grinned as he went to the counter and placed his order, paying for it before he joined Olivia and Bernie at their table.

"Room for one more?" he asked with a grin at both women. "I don't really know anybody else in here, and I'm shy."

"Oh, sure you are," Olivia said with a wry smile. She wiped her mouth. "I have to get back before Jessie turns purple and says we're starving her. You stay and finish your salad, Bernie," she added as she stood up. "You have a half hour before you have to come back."

"Jessie. That the underdressed brunette who works in your office?" he asked.

They nodded.

"Don't tell her I'm here, okay?" he asked Olivia. He shook his head. "I know how deer feel in hunting season."

They both laughed.

"I won't. I promise," Olivia said. She winked at Bernie and went to carry her tray back.

Mikey looked at Bernie slowly, taking in the blond

braid and the nice gray suit she was wearing with a pink camisole. "You look pretty," he said softly.

She flushed and laughed self-consciously. "Thanks."

"You're a breath of spring compared to the women I know," he added quietly, watching her. "Brassy, overbearing women don't do a thing for me these days. I guess I'm jaded."

She smiled shyly. "You're very handsome and you're wealthy. I guess women do chase you. Even movie stars and rich women."

He pursed his lips. "They used to. It's the other stuff that puts them off."

Her thin eyebrows lifted. "The other stuff?" she asked.

He shrugged. "My connections."

She still wasn't getting it. While she tried to, Barbara brought his steak and salad and black coffee, and put it down in front of him.

"I hope it's done right," she told Mikey. "My cook tends to get meat a little overdone. One of our customers actually carried his back into the kitchen and proceeded to show him how to cook it properly."

"Jon Blackhawk," Bernie guessed.

"How did you know?" Barbara asked.

"He's the only gourmet chef I know, and he's Paul's boss at the FBI office in San Antonio. They were both down here recently on a case. And nobody eats anywhere else in Jacobsville except here," she teased.

Barbara chuckled. "Exactly. It didn't come to blows, but it was close. My temporary cook's from New Jersey," she added.

Mikey's ears perked up. He glanced at Barbara.

She made a face. "His people are heavily federal, if you get my meaning. His brother works for the US Marshals Service in San Antonio, and he's a former policeman where he came from. He's retired."

"Oh." Mikey relaxed, just a little.

"I was going to add... Goodness, excuse me," she said, suddenly flustered as she went back to the counter.

Bernie's eyes followed her, and she grinned to herself as she watched a husky man in a police uniform smile at Barbara as she went to wait on him.

"Okay, what's that little smirk all about?" Mikey teased.

"That guy at the counter. That's Fred Baldwin. He worked as a policeman here for a while, then at a local ranch. Now he's back on the police force. He's sweet on Barbara and vice versa."

Mikey glanced in that direction and laughed softly. "I can see what you mean."

"Her son's a lieutenant of detectives with San Antonio PD," Bernie added.

He nodded. "I met him, last time I was here. Nice guy."

"Her daughter-in-law's father is the head of the CIA," she added.

"I heard that, too. Her son's dad is a head of state, down in South America."

"He does have some interesting connections," Bernie agreed.

Mikey finished his steak. "What's there to do around here at night?" he asked.

She pursed her lips. "Well, people go to concerts at

the local high school on the weekends sometimes. Other people drive in the Line."

"What the hell...heck's the Line?" he amended.

"A bunch of people drive around in a line. Teenagers, married people, even old people sometimes. They have a leader, and they go all around the county, one after the other, sometimes even up to San Antonio and back."

He shook his head. "The things I miss, living in a city." His dark eyes met hers. "How about movies?"

"Jack Morris and his son just opened a drive-in theater outside town," she said. "He even built a snack bar with restrooms. He says he's bringing back the 1950s all by himself. It's pretty successful, too."

"What's playing right now?"

She named the movie, an action one about commandoes.

He smiled. "You like movies like that?" he asked.

"Well, yes," she confessed.

He chuckled. "I thought you had an adventurous nature. Mrs. Brown told me about those books you read in bed. She said you have some on outfits like the British SAS and the French Foreign Legion."

She blushed. "My goodness!"

"So, how about a movie Friday night?" he asked. "I'll have Santi rent a smaller car, one that won't get so much attention from the populace."

Her heart skipped a beat and ran wild. "You want to take me out, on a date?"

"Of course I do," he said softly.

She thought she might faint. "But I... I have all sorts of health issues..."

"Bernadette, you have a kind heart," he said quietly, his dark eyes soft on her face. "None of the other stuff matters. Least of all an illness you can't help." He grinned. "I won't ask you to go mountain climbing with me. I promise."

She laughed. "That's a deal, then."

He shook his head. "Why would you think you're untouchable?"

"A local boy told me that when I was in high school. He said he didn't want to get mixed up with a handicapped girl."

"Idiot," he muttered.

She smiled at him. "Thanks."

"How long ago?"

She blinked. "How long ago was it?"

He shifted. "Clumsy way to put it. How old are you?" he added. His dark eyes twinkled. "Past the age of consent?" he probed.

She closed up and looked uncomfortable.

He put a big, warm hand over hers on the table. "I don't proposition women I haven't even dated yet," he said softly. "And you aren't the sort of girl who'd ever get such a proposition from me. Honest."

She caught her breath. He was so unexpected. "I'm twenty-four. Almost twenty-five."

He was shocked and looked it. "You don't look your age, kid."

She beamed. "Thanks."

He laughed and curled his fingers around hers, enjoying the sensations that ran through him. Judging by the flush, she was feeling something similar.

"Careful," she said under her breath as more people came in the front door.

"Careful, why? Somebody with a gun looking our way?" he asked, and not entirely facetiously.

"Gossip."

He scowled. "What?"

"Gossip," she repeated. "If people see you standing close together or holding hands, they start talking about you, especially if you're local and unmarried. You'll get talked about."

"Like I care," he teased.

She felt as if she could float. "Really?"

His teeth were perfect and very white. She noticed, because he didn't seem to smile much. "I don't mind gossip. Do you?"

She hesitated. But, really, nobody here was likely to gossip about her to him, at least. Not many people knew about her parents or, especially, her grandparents. "No," she said after a minute. "I don't mind, either."

"Just as well. I have no plans to stop holding hands with you," he said. "It feels nice."

"It feels very nice," she said.

He had Santi drive her back to her office. He even got out, helped her from the car and walked her to the door.

"That woman in the courthouse said she works here. That right?" he asked.

She made a face and nodded.

"Then I won't come in. Phew," he added. "She could start a perfume shop on what she was wearing."

"She could in there, too," she said.

He laughed. "Well, I'll see you back at Mrs. Brown's later. If it starts raining, you call me and I'll come pick you up."

She looked hesitant.

"Oh. Right." He pulled out his wallet, extracted a business card and handed it to her. "Cell phone. At the bottom. You can call me or you can text me. Texting is better. I hate talking on the damned phone."

She laughed. "So do I."

"Okay, then. See you later, kid."

"See you."

He got back in the car. She went into her office and closed the door behind her.

Jessie was watching. Her face was livid. She'd tried to cadge a ride back to the office in that nice limo and been refused. It made her furious that little miss sunshine there had managed it. And she was late back to work, to boot!

Chapter Four

Bernie didn't have to look to feel Jessie's fury, but she sat down at her desk without even glancing toward the front desk. Apparently Jessie wasn't going to push her luck by attacking Bernie, though. She settled down at her desk and busied herself typing up letters for the boss while she answered the phone.

It wasn't hard to avoid her at quitting time. Jessie was always the first one out the door, just in case the phone rang and somebody had to answer it. She was never on time in the mornings, either, something resented by all her coworkers.

"Phew," Bernie said with heartfelt thanks when Jessie was out of sight. "I thought my number was up when we got back from lunch."

"Jessie won't quit," Olivia said quietly. "She's got that

nice rich visitor in her sights and she'll do anything to get his attention. You watch out," she added.

Bernie sighed. "I guess she'll really hit the ceiling when she finds out I'm going to a movie with him."

"Movie?" Sari asked, all ears.

"When?" Glory asked.

She laughed. "Friday night. He's taking me to the drive-in."

"Ooh," Sari mused. "Heavy stuff."

Bernie blushed. "He's so good-looking. Honestly, I feel dowdy compared to Jessie."

"He didn't like Jessie, though, did he?" Olivia reminded her. "He told me not to mention he was having lunch with us when I went back to the office. He wasn't impressed by her. In fact," she added with a chuckle, "he said he knew how deer felt during hunting season."

"Wouldn't that get her goat?" Sari teased. "I wasn't kidding about Mikey," she added to Bernie. "He really isn't a ladies' man."

"He could be in movies," Bernie said.

"Yes, he could," Glory agreed. "I wonder." She glanced at Sari. "Didn't anybody ever try to get him to audition for a movie?"

"In fact, Paul says he was pursued by a Hollywood agent who saw him in Newark. He just smiled and walked away. He's shy, although that never comes across. He puts on a good act," Sari added.

"He's good with people," Bernie told them as they went out and locked the door, Mr. Kemp having gone home from a day in court already. "The ladies at the boardinghouse think he's just awesome."

"And what a lucky thing that Mrs. Brown only had one vacancy," Sari said. "Or Jessie would be over there like a flash."

"I still can't figure what she's doing down here," Glory said. "She's a bad fit for our office, and she doesn't mix with anybody in town except her friend Billie at the county clerk's office." She frowned. "In fact, Billie hasn't been here long, either, and she's a city girl from back east somewhere. They're both of them out of step with local people."

"Do they room together?" Bernie asked.

"Yes, at some motel out of town. That's got to be expensive, too, since none of our local hotels serve meals."

"Which one do they stay at?" Glory asked.

"The one where all the movie stars live when they're in town filming," Sari told her. "The one with whirlpool baths and feather pillows and mini bars."

"Ouch," Glory laughed. "That's the most expensive place in town. Jessie doesn't make enough here to afford such luxury."

"Well, she and Billie share," Sari said. "I guess they share meal expenses, too. Jessie would never manage it alone."

"Don't mention your upcoming date in the office," Glory cautioned Bernie.

"I might not need to," Bernie said, waving Olivia goodbye as she drove off in her car. "We were sort of holding hands in Barbara's Café," she confessed.

Sari whistled.

Bernie looked at her curiously.

"And Mikey knows about small towns, too," she

mused. "Apparently he doesn't mind people knowing that he likes you."

Bernie flushed. "Really? You think he does?"

"Paul does," Sari said. "And he knows Mikey a lot better than the rest of us do."

"Wow," Bernie said softly.

"There's my ride. My boys," Glory gushed, waving to Rodrigo at the wheel of their car and their little boy in the back seat. "See you tomorrow!"

"Have a good night," Bernie called. Glory waved as she got into the car and fastened her seat belt. Rodrigo waved at the women on his way past.

"There's just one thing," Sari said gently, turning to Bernie when they were alone. "Mikey's down here for a reason, and it's a dangerous one. I can't talk about it. But you should know that there's a risk in going around with him."

"I do know," Bernie replied. "I don't care."

"So it's like that already." Sari smiled. "I'd feel the same way if Paul was like Mikey. You know that Mikey's past isn't spotless?" she added a little worriedly.

"You mean, about his hotel business?"

Sari didn't know what to say. She felt uncomfortable telling tales. Well, better to let sleeping dogs lie. "It was a long time ago," she lied, smiling. "He'll tell you himself when he's ready."

"I don't care about his past," Bernie said softly, and she smiled. "I've never been so happy in my whole life."

"Judging by how much he smiles lately, neither has Mikey," Sari laughed. "Paul said he was the most somber man you've ever seen until lately. They grew up together."

Bernie nodded. "Their grandmother raised them. Mikey loved her."

"Yes, he did. Paul and Mikey had a rough childhood. Their grandmother was all they had. Well, and each other, although neither of them would admit it."

"They seem to get along well, from what Mikey says."

"They do now. It wasn't always that way." She glanced toward the curb. Paul was sitting at the wheel of their Jaguar. He waved. "Well, I'll go home. Can we drop you off?" she added.

Bernie laughed. "I'm doing really good today, and Dr. Coltrain says I need the exercise when I can get it. But thanks."

"No problem. Anytime. See you tomorrow."

Bernie waved them off and walked the four blocks to Mrs. Brown's boardinghouse. She felt as if her feet didn't even touch the sidewalk. Life was sweet.

She got through the rest of the week relatively unscathed by Jessie, although she received a lot of irritated looks when a couple of local people coming into the office mentioned that Bernie had been seen holding hands with Mikey at Barbara's Café. But apparently Jessie still thought Bernie was no competition for her. She did mention, loudly, that she was going to spend more time at Barbara's herself.

"And good luck to her," Sari laughed when Jessie

left ahead of them all, as usual, at the end of the day. "Mikey's been in San Antonio for the past two days."

Bernie smiled with obvious relief. She hadn't seen him since their lunch at the café. He'd been out of town apparently. She'd wondered if he was leaving town. She'd hoped he'd say goodbye first, but his absence at the boardinghouse had worried her. Mrs. Brown only said that he had business to take care of, but she hadn't said how long it might take him to conduct it. Bernie figured it was something to do with the hotel he owned. It must take a lot of work to coordinate something so big, and he must have a lot of employees who had to be looked after as well.

"You didn't know," Sari guessed when she noted Bernie's expression.

"Well, no. He just told Mrs. Brown that he had business to take care of. We didn't know where he was."

"He and Paul have something going on together," Sari said, without mentioning what, although she knew. It was top-secret stuff, nothing she could tell even her worried coworker about.

"I hoped he wouldn't leave town without saying goodbye," Bernie replied.

"Are you kidding? He's taking you to a movie, remember?" Sari teased. "How could he leave town?"

Bernie laughed. "I guess he wouldn't, at that." She was beaming. "You know, I've only ever been on a few dates in my life." She hesitated and looked at Sari worriedly. "Mikey's sophisticated, you know? And I'm just a small-town girl with old-fashioned ideas about stuff."

"So was Della Carrera before she married Marcus

here in town," she reminded the other woman. "No-body's more sophisticated than Marcus Carrera."

Bernie smiled. "I guess not." She frowned. "Mr. Carrera was big in the mob, wasn't he?" she added absently.

"He was. He went legitimate, though. He was actually working with the FBI to shut down a crooked crime figure who planned to open a casino near Marcus's."

"I heard something about that." Bernie shook her head. "I don't understand how people ever get involved with organized crime. It seems a shameful way to earn a living."

"That it is," Sari said, but became reserved. Bernie didn't know about Mikey and she didn't feel comfortable blowing his cover. "Well, I'm off. See you tomorrow!"

"Have a good night."

"You, too."

Bernie watched them drive away and started back to Mrs. Brown's. She could hardly contain her excitement about the coming date with Mikey.

Mikey, meanwhile, had been in conference with Paul, Jon Blackhawk and a US Marshal in San Antonio, while the three of them hashed out what they knew and what they didn't know about Cotillo. Mikey had stayed at a safe house with the marshal while they discussed the case and what they were going to do about the threat.

"I don't want the women in my boardinghouse hurt," Mikey said during one long session. "Just being around me could put them in danger."

"They won't be," Paul replied. "You've got more protection than you realize."

"Yeah, well, Merrie Colter had plenty of protection, too, and she ended up in the hospital when that contract man was after her," Mikey pointed out.

"No plan is foolproof," Jon Blackhawk, assistant SAC at the San Antonio FBI office agreed. "But we've got most of our bases covered. And, frankly, no place is going to be perfectly safe. If you leave your boardinghouse, the women who live there could still be in danger if the contract man decides they might know where you were."

Mikey felt sick to his stomach, although nothing showed in that poker face. "I suppose that's true," he said heavily.

"I've never lost a person I was protecting yet," US Marshal McLeod interjected. He was tall and husky like Mikey, but he had pale gray eyes in a face like stone and a .357 Magnum in a leather holster at his waist.

"You and that damned cannon," Paul muttered. "Why don't you move into the twenty-first century, McLeod, and sport a piece that didn't come out of the eighties?"

"It's a fine gun," McLeod said quietly. "It belonged to my father. He was killed in the line of duty, working for our local sheriff's office back home."

"Sorry," Paul said sheepishly.

McLeod shrugged. "No problem."

"I hope you got earplugs when you have to shoot that thing," Mikey mused.

"I got some, but if I take time to put them in, I'll be wearing them on the other side of the dirt."

Mikey chuckled. "Good point."

"Where's your piece?" Paul asked suspiciously.

"My piece?" Mikey opened his suit coat. "I don't carry a gun, Paulie. You know that."

"I know that you'd better get a Texas permit for that big .45 you keep in your car, before Cash Grier knows you don't have one," Paul said with a smirk.

Mikey sighed. "I was just thinking about that the other day. So. Where's Cotillo?"

There was a round of sighs. "Well, he was in Newark," McLeod said. "I checked with our office there, but he's out of sight now. Nobody knows where he went. We have people checking," he added. "One of our guys has a Confidential Informant who's close to him. We'll find him."

"It's his contract killer we need to find," Paul interrupted. "If he offs Mikey, we have no case, and Tony Garza will go down like a sack of beans for murder one."

"Speaking just for myself, I'd prefer to live a few more years," Mikey mused.

"Especially since you have a hot date tomorrow night, I hear?" Paul said with an unholy grin.

Mikey embarrassed himself by flushing. The tint was noticeable even with his olive complexion.

"Hot date?" Jon asked.

Mikey cleared his throat. "She's a nice girl. Works as a paralegal for the district attorney's office in Jacobsville."

"Bernie," Paul said.

There were curious looks.

"Bernadette," Mikey muttered. "It's short for Bernadette."

"Pretty name," Jon said.

"She's a sweetheart," Paul told them. "Takes a real load off the district attorney, and the other women who work in the office love her, especially my wife." He glanced at Mikey. "Which begs the question, why don't you ever bring her over to the house to eat? You know Mandy wouldn't mind cooking extra."

Mikey shifted his feet. "It's early days yet. I just asked her to a movie."

"A drive-in, at that," Paul mentioned with a grin.

"You've got a drive-in theater in Jacobsville?" Jon exclaimed. "They went out in the fifties, didn't they?"

"In the sixties, mostly, but we've got a local guy who's trying to bring them back. He even built a small café on the premises with restrooms and pizza. So far, he's a raging success."

"My dad talked about going to drive-ins," McLeod mused. "He said it was the only place he could kiss my mother without half-a-dozen people watching. Big family," he added.

"I can't place that accent, McLeod," Paul said. "You sound Southern, but it's not really a Texas accent."

"North Carolina," McLeod said. "My people go back five generations there in the mountains. The first were Highlanders from Argyll in Scotland."

"Mine came from Greece and Italy," Paul said.

"Well, mine and Mikey's," he added with a glance at his cousin.

"Mine met the boat yours came over on," Jon said with a straight face. He was part Lakota Sioux.

There was a round of laughter.

"I have some Cherokee blood in my family," McLeod volunteered. "My great-grandmother was Bird Clan. But we're mostly Scots."

"Can you play the pipes?" Jon asked curiously.

McLeod shrugged. "Enough to make the neighbors uncomfortable, anyway."

"I had a set of trap drums," Paul recalled wistfully. "We had some really loud, obnoxious neighbors upstairs when I lived in Newark, long before I moved here." He didn't add that at the time he'd had a wife and child who were killed by operatives of a man he put in prison. "I was terrible at playing, but it sure shut the upstairs neighbor up."

"You bad boy," Mikey teased.

"A man has to have a few weapons," he said drolly.

"Back to Cotillo," McLeod said. "We have someone watching you from our service down in Jacobsville. You don't need to know who, but we're on the job. I offered, but they shut me up immediately."

"They did? Why?" Mikey asked.

"They say my restaurant allowance is abused."

They all looked at him. He was substantial, but streamlined just the same.

A corner of his mouth pulled down. "They say I eat too much. Hey, I'm a big guy. It takes a lot of food. Besides, I hear some of the best food in Texas is at that café in Jacobsville."

"It is," Paul agreed. "Everybody eats there."

"So would I, if they'd let me. The boss said we needed somebody who liked salads and tofu."

Now they all really stared at him.

He glowered back. "She's a vegan," he said with spirit. "She gets upset if anybody mentions a steak."

"Tyranny," Paul teased.

"Anarchy," Mikey seconded.

"She should move back east, where she'll have plenty of company," Jon agreed. "I'm not giving up steaks, and I don't care if the SAC is a vegan or not."

"That's what I told her," McLeod replied. His black eyes sparkled. "Shut her up for ten minutes at least. But that's when she assigned me to him," he indicated Mikey. "She thinks it's a mean assignment." He chuckled. "I didn't try to change her mind."

"Good thing," Jon said. "I know your boss. She has a mean streak."

"She mustered out of the Army as a major," McLeod replied. "Honestly, I think she believes she's still in it."

"They make good agency heads," Jon said.

McLeod nodded. "But I'm still not eating tofu."

They all laughed.

"What about Cotillo?" Mikey asked after a minute.

"Why does that name sound so familiar?" Paul wondered. Then his face cleared. "Of course. It's that town across the border, you know, the one where an unnamed person that we all know offed the drug lord El Ladron and his buddies in a convoy." The unnamed person was

Carson Farwalker, now a doctor in Jacobsville, who'd thrown several hand grenades under El Ladron's limo and was never charged.

"There's a cactus called ocotillo," Jon Blackhawk mused, "but that little town over the border was actually settled by an Italian family back in the late 1800s."

"Interesting," Mikey remarked. He sighed. "But the man is more worrisome than the town right now."

Faces became somber.

"When our CI finds out anything, I'll pass it on," McLeod said. "Meanwhile, he's got somebody watching Carrera down in the Bahamas." He indicated Jon.

Jon nodded. "Our field office has him under surveillance. And Carrera has some protection of his own, for himself and Tony Garza. You know, just because Carrera went straight doesn't mean he doesn't still have some pretty formidable ties to his old comrades. We understand he has two of them staying in the house with Della, his wife, and his two little boys."

"Two of the best," Mikey agreed. "I know them from the old days."

"Mikey," Paul said with real affection, "you never left the 'old days.'"

"Well," Mikey said with a sigh, "we are what we are, right, Paulie?"

"Right."

Bernie didn't really know how to dress for a drive-in movie, so she settled for pull-on navy blue slacks topped with a blue-checked button-up shirt and a long blue vest that came midthigh. She thought about putting her hair up in some complicated hairdo, but she left it long and soft around her shoulders. She'd toyed with having it cut. It was hard for a woman with disabilities to keep it clean and brushed, but she couldn't bear the thought of giving up the length. She had all sorts of pretty ribbons and ties to put her hair up with when she went to work. Even jeweled hairpins for special occasions. Not that there had been many of those, ever.

She glanced in the mirror and smiled at the excited, almost pretty girl in the mirror. She was going on a real date, with a man who made movie stars look ugly, and he liked her. She almost glowed.

There was a hard tap on the door. She got her coat and purse and opened the door. Mikey was wearing slacks and a designer shirt under a nice jacket. His shirt was blue, like hers.

He grinned at her. "Well, we seem to match."

"I noticed," she teased.

He gave her a thorough appraisal and felt his heart jump as he locked eyes with her. She was unique in his experience of women, which was extensive. She was so different from the aggressive, sensual women he'd liked in his youth. His tastes had changed over the years. Right now, Bernie was the sweetest thing in his life. He hoped he wasn't putting her in danger by being close to her.

"You ready to go?" he asked. "We must both be insane. A drive-in movie and it's just a week until Halloween! It's cold, even for south Texas!"

"I love drive-ins," she said softly. "And I don't care if it snows."

He chuckled. "Me, neither, kid." He took her hand in his and felt her catch her breath. He felt just the same. "Come on. I've got something a little less noticeable than the limo to go in."

A little less noticeable, she thought with surprise when she saw what he was driving. It was a luxury convertible, very pretty and probably very fast.

"Oh, my," she said.

"It goes like a bomb," he said, as he helped her inside the late-model Mercedes convertible. It was a deep blue color. The interior was leather, with wood trim on the steering wheel and the dash. She sank into luxury as she fastened her seat belt.

"Oh, my," she said again as he touched a control and her seat heated up and began to massage her back. "This is heavenly!" She closed her eyes and smiled. "Just heavenly!"

He chuckled. "I'm glad you like it. I go first-class, kid. Always have, even when I was young and full of pepper." He didn't like remembering exactly how he'd gone first-class. She made him feel guilty about the things he'd done in his pursuit of wealth. She didn't seem to covet wealth at all.

"I've never ridden in a car that had heated seats," she said excitedly. "And even a massage! It's just amazing!"

He smiled. He hadn't considered how uptown the car was to someone who probably rode around mostly in cabs that barely had heaters and air-conditioning. "Don't you drive?" he asked.

She felt the words all the way to her feet and averted her eyes so that he couldn't see the sadness in them.

She couldn't have afforded a car. "I used to," she said softly. "Not anymore."

"You should go back to it," he replied as he pulled the car out into the street and accelerated. "I love to drive."

"This car must go very fast."

"It does. I'd demonstrate," he teased, "but you'd have to come bail me out of jail."

She laughed, the old fear and guilt subsiding. "I would, you know," she said softly. "Even if I had to sell everything I own."

He flushed.

"I mean, I'd find someone who could…" she began, all flustered because of what she'd blurted out. She was horribly embarrassed.

His big hand reached out for her small one and tangled with it. "Stop that," he chided gently. "You shouldn't feel guilty for enjoying somebody's company. Especially not mine." His hand contracted around hers. "I'm used to women who want what I've got," he added coldly.

"What you've got?" His fingers tangling gently with hers had her confused and shaky inside.

"Money, kid," he replied. "I've got enough in foreign banks to see me well into old age, even if I spend myself blind."

"Oh." Her hand stiffened in his.

He glanced at her and chuckled. "Now you think I suspect that you're only going out with me because I'm rich. Not you," he added in a deep, husky tone. "You're not the sort of woman who prefers things to people. I knew that right off. Proud as Lucifer, when you fell in front of the car and I made sarcastic remarks about how you'd fallen." He sighed sadly. "Worst mistake of my life, thinking you were like that. Believe me, I felt about two inches high when Santi found that cane you used."

She bit her lower lip. "I'm clumsy, sometimes," she said. "I fall over nothing when I'm having flares. I wish I was healthy," she added miserably.

"My little grandmother would sit and cry sometimes when the pain got really bad," he recalled quietly. "I'd fill a hot water bottle for her and read her stories in Greek to take her mind off it."

"You can speak Greek?" she asked.

"Greek, Italian, a little Spanish," he replied.

"I learned to read Greek characters," she said. "They're the Coptic alphabet, like Russian."

"Nice," he said, glancing at her with a smile. "Yes, they are. Hard for some people to learn, too."

"I love languages. I really only speak English and Spanish."

"Spanish?"

"Well, we deal with a lot of bilingual people, but some of the older people who come from countries south of ours don't understand English as well as their children. I can translate for them."

"Brainy," he teased.

"Not really. I had to study hard to learn the language, just like I had to study hard to learn to be a paralegal. I went to night school at our local community college," she added.

"I imagine that was hard," he said. "Working and going to school at the same time."

"It was," she confessed. "I wanted to learn the job, but I missed class sometimes. There was a nice woman who was studying it at the same time—Olivia, who works in our office—and she took notes so that I could catch up on what I missed. The professor was very understanding."

"You're a sweet kid," Mikey said softly. "I can imagine that most people bend rules for you."

She laughed. "Thanks." She glanced at him as they drove a little out of town to the wooded area that housed the new drive-in. "Did you go to school? I mean, after high school?"

"I got a couple of years of college when I was in the Army," he said. "Never graduated. I was too flighty to buckle down and do the work."

"What did you study?"

He chuckled. "Criminal justice. It seemed like a good idea at the time. I mean, considering what I did for a living."

She just stared at him, curious.

He felt his cheeks heat. He glanced at her. She didn't understand. "Didn't Sari talk about me at work?" he said.

"Just that you and her husband are first cousins and that you're close," she replied, and her eyes were innocent.

She wasn't putting on an act. She really didn't know what he'd been, what he still was. He hesitated to tell her. He loved the way she looked at him as if he had some quality that she'd never found in anyone else. She looked at him with affection, with respect. He couldn't remember another woman who'd cared about the man instead of the bank account. It made him humble.

He drew in a breath. "Well, Paulie and I are close," he agreed. His hand tightened around hers. "I meant, didn't you know about the trouble Isabel and Merrie had three years ago, when they were being stalked by a cleaner?"

"Oh, that," she said, nodding. "There was a lot of gossip about it," she added. "I don't remember much of what I heard, just that a man who was big in organized crime back east called off the hit man. She painted him." She laughed. "They said he walked her down the aisle when she married Paul. I didn't know her then, except I knew the family and that they were well-to-do. I never moved in those circles. I'm just ordinary."

"Honey, ordinary is the last thing you are," he said huskily as he pulled onto the dirt road that led to a drive-in with a huge white screen and a graveled lot with speakers on poles every few feet. "And we're here!"

He paid for their tickets and drove them through to a nice parking spot right in front of the screen. He looked at the ticket. "We've got a ten-minute wait," he said.

"What are we going to see?" she asked. "I didn't pay attention to the marquee."

He chuckled as he cut off the engine and turned to her. "You didn't notice?" he teased, black eyes sparkling as they met her pale ones.

"Not really," she confessed. "I was excited just to be going out with you." She flushed. "There are some very pretty single girls around Jacobsville, including Jessie, who works with us."

His fingers tangled softly with hers, caressing, arousing. "Jessie doesn't do a thing for me," he told her. "She's like the women I used to date back east. Brassy and out for everything they can get from a man."

"I guess so. We're not really like that here," she added. "Money is nice, but I have all I need. I'm not frivolous. My biggest expense is the drugstore. And the doctor," she said sadly.

"It doesn't matter," he said solemnly. "You're not of less value as a woman because you have a disability."

"Most local men thought I was," she replied. "I won't get better unless they come out with a miracle drug," she said. "There are shots I could take, but they're really expensive and there's no guarantee that they'd work. There's also infusion, where they shoot drugs into you with an IV and they last several weeks." She lowered her eyes to the big hand holding hers. It was strong and beautiful, as men's hands went. Long fingered, with perfectly manicured nails.

"I read about those shots," he replied. "Just before my grandmother died, I was researching new drugs that might help her. The pain got so damned bad that they had to give her opiates to cope with it." He made a face. "Then the government steps in and says that everybody's going to get addicted, so now you get an over-the-counter drug for pain even if you've got cancer," he added angrily. "Like that's going to help get illegal narcotics off the street! Hell, you can buy drugs, guns, anything you want in the back alley of any town in America, even small towns."

"You can?" she asked curiously.

"Of course you can. Even in prison."

"Wow."

He chuckled. "Kid, you really aren't worldly."

"I guess not," she said with a good-natured smile. "I don't have much of a social life. Well, I do have Twitter and Facebook, but I don't post very often. Mostly, I read what other people write. My goodness, I must be sheltered, because some of the things people post I wouldn't even tell to my best friend!"

"What sort of things?" he teased.

"I'm not saying," she replied.

He made a face. "That didn't hurt, that didn't hurt, that didn't hurt…" And he laughed, softly and with so much mischief that she burst out laughing, too.

He looked around. "Not so many people just yet. So." He caught a handful of her long, beautiful platinum hair and tugged her face under his. "Don't panic," he whispered as he bent his head. "This is just a test. I'm practicing mouth-to-mouth resuscitation, in case I ever have to save you…!"

Chapter Five

Bernie held her breath as she watched his firm, chiseled lips hover over hers. She could taste the coffee on his mouth, feel his breath as his face came closer, so that his dark eyes filled the world.

She clutched at his jacket, more overcome with emotion than she could have dreamed even a few weeks ago.

"I love your hair, Bernadette," he whispered as his hand contracted in it and his mouth slowly covered hers for the first time.

She gasped under the soft pressure, but she wasn't trying to get away. He gazed down at her. Her eyes were closed, her eyebrows drawn together. She looked as if she'd die if he didn't kiss her.

Which was exactly how he felt, himself. He settled his mouth over hers, gently because he could sense her attraction and her fear. It was hard to give control to another person. But it was a lesson she would have to learn. He was glad that she was learning it with him.

He guided her arms up around his neck as his lips became slowly more insistent, giving her time to absorb the newness of it, giving her time to let go of her restraint. It melted out of her as he drew her closer across the console, his lips opening now, pressing hers gently apart.

She heard his breath sigh out against her cheek, felt his arms enfolding her, protecting her. She moaned as the feeling became almost overpowering and her arms tightened around his neck.

"That's it, baby," he whispered. "Just like that. Don't hold back. I'll go slow, I promise."

And he did. He didn't force her or do anything to make her uncomfortable. His mouth slid finally against her cheek to rest at her ear. His heart was doing the hula in his chest. He could feel hers doing the same thing.

It was odd, to be chaste with her. Most women in his past would have been tearing his clothes off at this point, but Bernie was gentle and inexperienced. He could feel the need in her because he felt it, as well. It was new to want to protect and cherish someone. He felt as if he could fly.

"You taste like sugar candy," he whispered at her ear.

Her arms tightened and she laughed softly. She didn't know what to say.

His big hand smoothed the length of her hair. "I'm glad you left it down tonight," he murmured. "Just for me?"

"Just for you." Her voice sounded husky. She felt

swollen all over. It was a delicious sensation, like going down on a roller coaster.

His face nuzzled hers. "I never expected something like this," he said in a deep, lazy tone. "I was going to stay in this little town for a while and bide my time, maybe find a poker game to get into or something. And here's this beautiful little violet, right in my boarding-house."

"Me?" she stammered.

His hand slid under her hair. "You, Bernadette." His cheek slid against hers and his mouth covered hers again, but harder this time, hungrier.

She couldn't resist him. She didn't have the sophistication to even pretend that she didn't like what he was doing. Her fingers tangled in his thick, cool, wavy hair. She loved what he was doing to her. She couldn't hide it.

And he loved that about her. He loved that she felt the same attraction he did, and that she was innocent, untouched, vulnerable. She needed someone to take care of her. He needed someone to take care of. Since his grandmother's death, there had been nobody in his life to fill that need. Bernie's disability didn't put him off in the slightest. It made him feel protective.

Which made him slow down. He was taking things too far, too fast. He drew back very slowly, his dark eyes intent on her face, her eyes half-closed, her pretty mouth swollen, her body warm and soft in his arms. She radiated tenderness.

"It's been a long time since I felt like this," he whispered at her lips, brushing them with his own. "And even then, it wasn't so sweet."

She smiled against his mouth. "I've never felt anything like this," she confessed softly. "Not with anybody." She grimaced. "Not that there's ever been anybody, except a boy who kissed me at a party when I was sixteen." She sighed. "That was just before he said he liked me a lot but he didn't want to get involved with a crippled girl."

"You aren't crippled," he said shortly. "You have as brave a spirit as anybody I ever knew. You're strong and capable. You're a woman with a disability, not a disability that's female. If that makes sense."

"You mean, I have a disability but it doesn't define who I am," she translated.

He smiled. "Yeah. It's like that." He searched her pale green eyes. "I don't mind it. I told you about my grandmother, that she had it, too. Somebody who minds it isn't interested in you the right way. He's looking for somebody more…casual."

She knew what he meant. Her fingers went up to his face and traced it while she studied him with fascination. "I never knew anybody like you," she whispered.

"I never knew anybody like you," he replied, and he was serious. "I can't imagine how I missed seeing you when I was here before, three years ago."

"I heard about you back then. I was working for a firm of attorneys. But people just said you were helping your brother-in-law with some case," she added.

That might be a good thing. He wasn't sure how she'd feel if she knew the truth about him, about exactly why and how he'd helped the Grayling girls.

"You don't know much about me," he said after a minute.

"That's okay. You don't know much about me, either," she replied.

He grinned. "Don't tell me. You're a spy and you have a trench coat in your closet back in the boardinghouse."

"Don't you dare tell a soul," she chided. "They'd send people to sack me up and take me away."

"I'd never do that," he said softly, and he smiled. "Not in a million years."

In the back of his mind, he was hearing a song recorded by Meatloaf about doing anything for love. He sang softly, a little off-key.

She caught her breath. "It's one of my favorite songs," she confessed. "Did you see the video?"

"I did. I watch it on YouTube sometimes." He laughed. "It's one of my favorites, too. What other sort of music do you like?"

Just as she started to answer, there was a gentle rap on the window.

Startled, Mikey let go of Bernie and put her gently back into her own seat before he powered down the window.

Cash Grier was standing there with a very knowing smile on his face, in his uniform.

"I have not been speeding in your town, and I never even jaywalked," Mikey began. "Besides that, we are outside the city limits."

Cash chuckled. "That's not why I'm here."

Mikey just waited.

Cash grimaced. "We've had a development," he said. "Nothing major. But Paul wants to talk to you, at the house."

"We just got here," Mikey said, visibly disturbed. "Can't it wait?"

"Sorry. No, it can't. Paul said to bring Bernie with you," he added with a smile in her direction.

"Oh." Mikey brightened. He turned to her. "Okay with you?"

She grinned. "Okay with me."

"We'll catch the movie another time," Mikey promised. He turned back to Cash. "You headed that way, too?"

Cash nodded. "You'll have two other cars following behind you, as well."

"Following us?" Bernie asked, concerned.

Cash and Mikey exchanged a long look. Mikey shook his head, just a jerk, but Cash understood at once that he wasn't to tell Bernie anything. "It's something to do with a case Paul's working on," Cash told Bernie with an easy smile. "No worries."

"Okay," she said, and smiled shyly.

"We'll be right along." Mikey took the speaker off the window and put it on its stand, powering the window up afterward. "Sorry about this," he told Bernie.

"You're related to an FBI agent," she said. "And I don't mind. Really."

He caught her hand in his as he turned onto the road. "You're easy to be with," he said softly. "You don't complain, you don't fuss. Even when you probably should."

She laughed. "I love being with you. Anywhere at all."

"That's how I feel." He curled her fingers into his and drove the rest of the way to Paul's house in silence. He was worried, and couldn't let it show. It must be something big if Paulie wanted to interrupt a date. His cousin wasn't the sort to interfere unless it was warranted. Which led Mikey to worry about exactly what the new development was.

His first thought was that they'd found Tony in some sort of horrible condition. They knew that Cotillo had a contract out on him, and that he could probably figure out that Tony was in the Bahamas since he and Marcus Carrera were close. He hoped Tony was still alive, even though it put Mikey in more danger.

He glanced at Bernadette and felt his heart clench. He was already attached to her. He couldn't bear the thought of letting her get hurt because of him. And she still didn't know anything about him, really, or the danger he was in. He was putting her in danger. If someone came looking for him, they'd go after the weakest link. An hour in any restaurant or bar around, and they'd know that Mikey was dating this cute little paralegal who worked for the DA. Bernadette could be used against him. In fact, so could Mrs. Brown and her other residents. Mikey had a weakness for motherly women, and people knew about it.

"You're worried," she said softly from beside him.

His head turned. His shocked expression said it all.

"You hide things very well," she continued. "You really do have a poker face. But it's inside you. I can feel it."

He let out a long breath and his fingers contracted. "You see deep, just like Paulie's sister-in-law."

"Merrie was always like that, even in school."

"You've lived here a long time, haven't you?"

"Well, off and on, yes. I was born here, but when I was little, my parents moved to Floresville. My dad worked on a cattle ranch there as a foreman." Her face closed up. "Dad and I moved back here when I was about ten years old."

He was reading between the lines. Something had happened in Floresville that still caused her pain after all that time. He wondered what it was. But he wasn't going to ask. Not yet. They had time.

"I lived all my life in Newark," he said.

"Yes, you told me. You said you own a hotel in Las Vegas," she added, fascinated. "It must be a lot of responsibility, taking care of something so big," she added.

He chuckled. "You have no idea. I didn't know what I was getting into. I had some spare cash and I thought it would be fun to own something big and elegant. It's not what it's cracked up to be. The labor problems alone are enough to send me to the nearest bar."

"I guess a lot of people work for you."

They did, but not in the hotel business. He employed a number of men who worked just a little outside the law on various projects for him. He wasn't about to go into that with her. He thought about the life he'd lived, the things he'd done to get rich. It had seemed so important at the time, as if nothing was more important than having things, having expensive things, having money. He'd come out of the armed forces with a lot of contacts and even more ideas, and he'd put them into practice in the years since then. Now, when he thought of Bernadette and what a straight arrow she was, he felt uncomfortable. What would she think of him when she knew what he was, what he'd been, what he'd done? Already, the thought of losing her trust was painful.

"You have to stop worrying about things you can't change," she said, reminding him of a conversation they'd had some time ago about that.

He chuckled. "That's the thing, kid. There's a lot of stuff I *can* change. I just don't know how to go about it without getting thrown in the slammer."

She laughed because she thought it was a joke.

He smiled. It wasn't a joke at all. He had men who could take on a contract killer with great success, but it would put him in bad stead with the FBI and the US Marshals Service, which was helping protect him. His hands were tied. He couldn't put Paulie on the firing line by acting on his own. Besides, if he helped put Cotillo away, it put him in a great bargaining position with Uncle Sam. He might need a favor one day. It was to his advantage not to use his usual methods of dealing with threats.

"If you get arrested, I can bake a nail file in a cake and come to see you," she said with a wicked little grin.

He sighed. "Honey, they don't have iron bars on the outside of cells anymore. They're all inside and all the doors lock along the way. You'd never get out that way."

She frowned. She'd never been in a real jail, but he seemed to know a lot about them. She reasoned that he'd probably been with his cousin to see somebody in jail on a case or something. It didn't worry her.

He glanced at her and smiled. She really didn't see the bad part of him. It was amazing—that she had such insight but didn't see wickedness in his actions. Probably she didn't look for it. Apparently, her own life had been a sheltered one.

The big house at Graylings was ablaze with lights when Mikey pulled up into the driveway. There were two black sedans and a black SUV. The sedans had government license plates.

"Feds," Mikey said with a sigh as he helped Bernie out of the car.

She glanced at the backs of the cars parked side by side. She smiled. "Government plates. I guess they think people won't know as long as they don't have flashing lights on top," she teased.

He chuckled. "Good one." He caught her hand in his as they walked up to the front door. He drew in a breath. "Listen, kid," he said as they reached it, "there are things going on that I can't tell you about."

"I don't mind," she said, and looked up at him with perfect trust. In fact, she was in so far over her head that she wouldn't have minded if he robbed banks for a living.

He smiled slowly. "You're almost too good to be true," he chuckled. "Don't you have any wicked, terrible things in your past?"

The door opened, but not before he saw the expression that washed across her face, quickly hidden when

Sari Fiore opened the door and grinned at them, holding hands.

"Sorry to have to break up your date," she told Bernie, "but we didn't have a choice. You can keep me company while the men talk. Mandy's gone to bed with a headache, so I'm alone. Well, almost alone," she amended when three men walked into the hall.

"Hey, Mikey," Paul Fiore greeted his cousin.

"Hey, Paulie."

"You know McLeod already," he said to Mikey, indicating a big, dark man, "and this is Senior FBI Agent Jarrod Murdock from our San Antonio office."

"I heard about you," Mikey mused as he looked at tall, blond Murdock, an imposing man who never seemed to smile. "Didn't they threaten to dress up like a ninja and throw you in the back of a pickup if you made coffee again…?" he teased.

Murdock made a face. "Not my fault I can't make good coffee," he scoffed. "I wasn't raised to be a woman."

The two women present gave him a wide-eyed, shocked look.

He cleared his throat. "Well, men aren't built right to make coffee," he amended. "Our hands are too big." He added that last bit tongue in cheek. And he wasn't smiling, but his pale blue eyes were twinkling just the same.

"That's the only comment that saved you from a picket line outside your office," Sari said in a mock threatening tone.

"God forbid!" Murdock said. "They'd fire me for sure."

"Not really," Paul commented. "You're too good a

shot. You and Rick Marquez's wife hold the record for the most perfect scores in the city in a single year."

"She missed one shot last month," Murdock replied. He grinned. "Morning sickness. So I hold the record right now."

"She's pregnant?" Sari asked. "Oh, that's so nice! I hope it's a boy this time."

"They already have two girls," Bernie told Mikey with a smile.

"I like little girls," Mikey said. "Little boys, too. Kids are sweet."

"Not all of them," Agent McLeod said coldly with glittering silver eyes.

"Oh, that's right," Paul commented. "That family you were looking after had a kid who stayed in juvie hall most of his life. What was that he painted your car with?"

McLeod eyes narrowed. "Skull and crossbones."

"And you couldn't touch him, because he was in protective custody."

"Oh, I wouldn't say that," McLeod replied. "I had a long talk with his probation officer. He's getting visits at school, at home, at his part-time job…"

"You vicious man," Sari chuckled.

"Maybe the skull and crossbones was more accurate than we know," Murdock commented.

"Watch it," McLeod said, "or I'll buy myself a ninja suit and a pickup truck."

They all burst out laughing.

"Well, come on into the study," Paul said to the men. He glanced at Sari.

"Bernie and I will be in the kitchen, discussing world politics," Sari replied.

Bernie looked up at Mikey with soft, pretty green eyes. "See you later."

He smiled slowly. "You will." He brought her fingers to his mouth and brushed them with it before he followed the men into the study.

Bernie had to be prompted to follow Sari into the kitchen. She was spellbound.

"If anybody had told me that Mikey would fall all over himself for a small-town Texas girl, I'd have fainted," Sari teased. "Honestly, you're all he talks about when he and Paul get together!"

Bernie flushed. "He's all I talk about at the boardinghouse. I've never met anybody like him. He's so... sophisticated and charming and sweet."

"Sweet?" Sari's eyes were popping.

Bernie laughed. "Well, he is."

"I suppose people bring out different qualities in other people," Sari said philosophically as she made coffee. "I owe Mikey a lot. So does my sister. He helped keep us alive."

"I heard that you were threatened, because of your father," Bernie said quietly. "Not the particulars, of course, just that Mikey helped your husband with the investigation."

"Mikey put us in touch with a gentleman who saved Merrie's life," Sari said, without going into any detail. "She was almost killed."

"I did hear about that. Some crazy man ran into her with a pickup truck, and then died in jail."

Sari nodded. She waited until the coffee perked and poured two cups of it. She put them on the table. She knew from the office that Bernie took hers black, just as Sari did.

Sari sat down across from her. "We lived through hard times," she recalled. "Our father was a madman. There were times when I thought he was going to kill us himself."

Bernie stared into her own coffee. "My grandfather had an unpredictable temper," she said. "You never knew which way he was going to jump. One time he'd laugh at something you said, and the next... Well, Mama and I had to be very careful what we said to him. So did my father."

"Your grandparents lived in Floresville, didn't they?" Sari asked gently.

Bernie's face clenched. She met the other woman's concerned blue eyes. "You know, don't you?" she asked.

Sari nodded. "From a former sheriff who moved here and had dealings with our office. But you know I don't gossip."

Bernie smiled. "Yes, I do." She put both hands around the coffee cup, feeling its warmth. "My grandfather wasn't a bad man. He just had an uncontrollable temper. But he could be dangerous. And he was, one time too many." She grimaced. "We lived out of town on a ranch, but gossip travels among country folk. After it happened, Dad lost his job and wasn't given references, so we came back to Jacobsville. I was only ten. Dad and I were targeted once by one of the victim's relatives."

"I've been through the wars myself, you know. But I don't blame people for what their relatives do," she added firmly.

"Neither do I. But there was some gossip even here. Fortunately, there wasn't so much that Dad couldn't find work. He went to Duke Wright and got a job. He never got like Granddaddy. I used to think if only somebody had forced my grandfather to see a doctor and get on medication. If only we'd realized that he had mental health issues," she said huskily.

"*If.* There's a horrible word. *If only.*"

"Yes." Bernie nodded. She looked up. "You won't tell Mikey? I mean, I'll tell him eventually, but it's early days yet and—"

"Mikey has secrets, too," Sari interrupted. "He won't hold anything against you. He's more worried about what you'll think of him. He's…had some problems in his past."

Bernie cocked her head. "Can you tell me about them?"

"I think he should tell you," Sari replied. "I don't like to carry tales. He's not a bad man," she added firmly. "Everybody has shameful secrets. Some get told, some never do, some we carry inside us forever like festering wounds."

Bernie nodded. "That's like mine. Festering wounds. They blamed all of us, you see, not just my dad. They blamed Mama and me, as well."

"Bernie, you were just a kid. How could anyone have blamed you?"

"They said Mama made him mad in the first place,"

she explained. She closed her eyes. "I was just ten years old, I didn't have anything to do with it. Neither did Dad. But people died, and I live with the guilt."

"You shouldn't have to," Sari said curtly. "There was no possible way you could have stopped it."

"Losing my grandmother and my mother was the worst of it, especially for Dad," Bernie confessed softly.

She put a hand over Bernie's. "You can't live in the past. I'm having a hard time with that myself. My father killed a woman. He more than likely killed my own mother. I have to live with that, and so does Merrie. We have our own guilt, although I don't know what we could have done to stop it. We were terrified of our father, and he was so rich that nobody around here would go against him. He made threats and people did what he wanted them to." She sighed. "It was like a nightmare, especially when he was arrested. He tried to make me marry a foreign prince so that he'd have money for his defense attorney," she recalled bitterly. "He came at me with the belt and I screamed for help. He died with the belt in his hand. I thought I'd killed him."

"You'd never hurt a fly," Bernie returned gently. "Neither would Merrie. Your father was an evil man. That doesn't mean you'd ever be like him. You couldn't be."

Sari smiled. "Thanks. I mean it. Thanks very much."

"I guess we're all products of our childhoods," she commented. She searched Sari's blue eyes in their frame of red-gold hair. "What was Mikey's like, do you know? He said he grew up in Newark, and his grandmother raised him and your husband."

Sari smiled. "She did. She was Greek, very small and very loving, even though she was strict with them."

"What about their parents?"

"The less said the better," Sari said coolly. "I'm frankly amazed that they both turned out as well as they did."

Bernie sighed. "I know how that feels, except it was my grandfather, not my parents."

Sari nodded. She smiled. "I hope you're prepared for Monday. When Jessie finds out about the hot date, she's going to be a handful. Glory and I will run interference for you. And it isn't as if Mikey even likes her."

Bernie sighed. "That's a good thing. She's really beautiful."

"She is. But as our police chief likes to say, so are some snakes."

They both laughed.

In the office, things were less amusing. One of Cotillo's henchmen had actually managed to get inside Marcus Carrera's Bow Tie Casino in the Bahamas while Tony Garza was in his private study there. Only quick thinking by Carrera's bodyguard, Mr. Smith, who sensed something out of the ordinary, had saved the day. The henchman was arrested and held for trial.

"They found the henchman dead in his cell the next day, of course," Paul told his cousin.

"Of course." Mikey stuck his hands in his pockets. "It's a good bet that Cotillo knows where I am, as well. I've got no place else to go in the world where I'd have protection like this," he added.

"True enough," McLeod said. His gray eyes narrowed. "Once you testify, we have plans for you."

"They'd better be plans for two people, because I'm not leaving here without Bernadette."

The words came as a pleasant shock to his cousin, who'd only known Mikey to get serious about a woman once in his life, and that had ended badly.

McLeod chuckled. "We can arrange that."

"Okay, then."

"But we're going to have to up the protection," Paul said. "Eb Scott wanted to lend us the Avengers," he added, referring to Rogers and Barton, two of Scott's top men, "but they're on a top-secret mission overseas. He sent us Chet Billings instead. And we've got Agent Murdock here assigned to you as well."

"So long as he doesn't try to make coffee for me, we're square," Mikey said with a glance at the tall FBI agent.

Murdock just laughed.

"What about Carrera?" Mikey asked. "Is his family going to be under threat, as well?"

"He hired on some old friends," Paul said. "Several old friends, from back home."

Mikey knew what he meant, without explanation. "If I were Cotillo, I'd fold my tent and go back to Jersey."

"Not a chance," Paul said quietly. "He thinks he has what it takes to put Tony Garza down and take over his whole operation."

"Sounds to me like a man with a huge narcissistic complex," Murdock murmured.

"Or a man on a raging drug high," McLeod inserted.

"Maybe both," Paul replied. "People are getting involved in this who don't even have ties to Tony's business. They just don't like the idea of an untried, arrogant newcomer trucking into their territory and trying to set everybody aside who's been in the business for generations."

"I know several low-level bosses who hate Cotillo's guts and would love to move on him, There's even a rumor that one of the bigger New York families wants him out," Mikey said. "But Tony's the only one with the power to put him away. If Cotillo hadn't tried to frame him on that murder one charge, Cotillo would be running south as fast as his fat little legs would carry him."

"We've got the video you made," Paul told Mikey. "It's even got the time stamp."

"Sure," Mikey replied with a wry smile. "But the defense could swear that it was photoshopped, that I lied to save my friend."

"Not if you testify," McLeod replied. "You're the best insurance we've got that Cotillo can't bring his murderous operation into Jersey. Listen, nobody thinks you and Tony sing with the angels, okay?" he added. "But there are levels of criminals. Cotillo is a cutthroat with no conscience, who's only in it for the money. He'll kill anybody who gets in his way. Tony has more class than that. And you," he said to Mikey, "never hurt a person unless they hurt somebody you cared about."

Mikey flushed. "Cut it out," he muttered. "You'll ruin my image."

Paul chuckled. "He's right, though," he told his cousin. "Merrie said that after she'd painted you."

"Hell of a painting," Mikey replied. "And she didn't even know me."

"What painting?" McLeod asked.

"Wait a sec." Paul pulled out his cell phone and turned to the photo app. He thumbed through it and showed it to McLeod. It was the painting Merrie had done of Mikey, which Paul had photographed before he sent it to his cousin.

"Damn," McLeod said, looking from the portrait to Mikey. "And she didn't know what you did for a living?"

Mikey shook his head. "She painted that from some snapshots Paul had. Well, from a couple of digital images, from his cell phone, like that one. I was amazed. She did Tony, too. Some artist!"

"Some artist, indeed." McLeod agreed.

"Back to the problem at hand," Paul said when he put down the phone. "We need to double security. And you need to find another way to hang out with Bernie. A safer way than a drive-in theater in the country."

Mikey muttered under his breath. "What, like having tea in her bedroom in the boardinghouse? That'll help her rep."

"You can bring her here," Paul said. "We have the best security in town."

"You mean it?" Mikey asked.

"You bet," Paul told him. "You can watch movies together in the sunroom." He pursed his lips. "Where Cash Grier isn't likely to tap on the window."

"Which brings to mind a question," Mikey said. "Why was Grier looking for me at a movie theater out of town? Not his jurisdiction, is it?"

Chapter Six

"Cash was home and Sheriff Carson wasn't answering his phone," Paul said, "to make a long story short. Our police chief volunteered. His kids were protesting bedtime, so he pretty much walked off and left Tippy and Rory with it," he added, naming Cash's wife and young brother-in-law.

"In which case, he might want to spend the night at a friend's house," Mikey chuckled, "if what I've heard about his missus is true. Did she really use an iron skillet on that guy who came in her back door with a .45?"

"Absolutely she did," Paul confirmed. "She's still a celebrity for that, not to mention being a former model and movie star."

"And gorgeous," Agent Murdock said with a sigh. "Even two kids haven't changed that."

Paul chuckled. "Tell me about it. Not that I did bad myself in the wife department. My Sari would give all the movie stars a run for their money."

"She's a doll," Mikey agreed. He sighed. "Well, what are you guys doing about Cotillo while he's plotting to have me and Tony killed?"

"We think he has somebody locally," Paul said, suddenly somber. "We don't know who. There are several people who just started working in Jacobsville recently, some of them with pronounced northern accents, like mine and yours."

Mikey grimaced. "I think I met one of them. She works with Isabel in the DA's office. A woman named Jessie." He shook his head. "Apparently she likes rich men and she's predatory. She actually got my cell phone number and called to ask me out."

"I'll bet that went over well," Paul replied tongue in cheek, because he knew his cousin inside out. Mikey didn't like aggressive women.

"It didn't go over at all," Mikey replied. "I told her the number was private and I wasn't interested. Then I hung up and blocked her number."

"I never attract women who want to date me." Murdock sighed. "I guess you have to be handsome."

"There's nothing wrong with you, Murdock, except the way you make coffee," Paul said. "And I did save you from that visiting attorney who mentioned how the ficus plant needed fertilizer."

"Yes, he was looking right at me when he said it," Murdock said and sighed. "Not my fault. Nobody else in the office will even try it."

"I would, but I'm never at my desk long enough."

"I live on the damned telephone," Murdock said heavily. "I get picked every time the boss needs information that he has to get from people out of town. I spend most of the day tracking down contacts."

"You should apply for the SWAT team," Paul suggested. "You'd do well."

"I'd get somebody killed is what I'd do," Murdock returned. "I don't think fast enough for a job like that. I guess, all in all, information gathering is important work and I'm pretty good at finding people."

"He used to be a skip tracer for a detective in Houston," Paul told Mikey. "He was good."

"I still am," Murdock said with a grin. "I tracked down an escaped murderer just a few days ago by calling his mother and telling her I was an old Army buddy. She told me exactly where he was. Sweet lady. I felt really guilty."

"People break the law, they do time," Paul said. "That's the rules."

"Rules are for lesser mortals," Mikey said with a hollow laugh. "I never followed any in my life."

"Until now," Paul said, with twinkling black eyes. "Rules are what's keeping you alive."

"Well, that and Bernie, I guess," Mikey said, and a faint ruddy color ran along his high cheekbones. "We went to the drive-in earlier. We were having a great time until Grier tapped on the window."

"What movie did you see?" Agent Murdock asked.

Mikey cleared his throat. "It was some sort of action movie, I think. The title escapes me."

"I'll bet it does," Paul said under his breath. "Isabel told me that Bernie poured coffee over ice when she went to get a cup, and then she toppled a bookcase, all in the same day. And she's not clumsy."

Mikey's eyes twinkled. "Well, well."

"She's a sweet woman," Paul said. "Sari's protective of her. That woman, Jessie, who works in the office, gives her a hard time."

"DA needs to take care of business and fire her," Mikey muttered.

"He's given her fair warning that she'll lose her job if she causes any more trouble," Paul replied. He put his hands in his pockets. "Back to the matter at hand, though. I phoned Marcus Carrera and asked him how things were going. He says Tony's getting restless. He doesn't like hiding from some cheap hood who wants to take over his territory. He's fuming that he didn't anticipate trouble from that quarter when the guy first moved in with his goons."

"If he comes back, he could die over here," Mikey said. "He knows that Cotillo will have people watching and waiting."

Paul nodded. "That's what I told Carrera. He said he'll talk some sense into Tony and make sure he stays put, no matter what it takes. He's got some old friends from his gangster days helping out. And he hired a group of mercs, one of whom used to live here—that Drake guy whose sister married the veterinarian, Bentley Rydel. Kell Drake, that was his name."

"That's some formidable backup," Mikey conceded.

"I hope he won't have to stay there too long. But what about Cotillo?"

"We've got plans for him," Paul said. "I have friends in Jersey, too. They're doing some scouting for me. The agency turned one of our best field agents onto the case, and he's digging into Cotillo's background. With any luck, he'll find something we can use for leverage while we wait for Tony's trial to come up."

"Tony fled the country," Mikey said sadly. "That's going to go against him. Flight from prosecution."

"He didn't fly, he was flown—by us," Paul said with a grin. "So that's not a charge he'll be facing."

Mikey sighed. "His past isn't lily-white. Neither is mine. So far, Cotillo hasn't ever been charged with a crime, for all we know."

"That's right," Paul returned. "For all we know. That's why we're digging. There's a federal prosecutor also on the case, and using his own investigators to look at Cotillo and his associates. Eventually, somebody's going to talk."

"So long as they don't talk about me and Tony and what's in our pasts," Mikey said with a resigned breath. "I've been a bad man, Paulie. I hope it doesn't come back to bite me."

"Not that bad, and you don't have a single conviction," Paul told him.

"No," Mikey conceded with a sad smile. "But that doesn't mean I haven't deserved one."

Paul put a lean hand on Mikey's broad shoulder. "We go one day at a time and leave tomorrow to itself. Right?"

Mikey smiled. "Okay. Right. Well," he added, "I'd better take Bernie home. So much for the movies."

"We have movies on DVD and pay-per-view," Paul reminded him with a grin. "You can watch them together right here, where it's safe. And the door has a lock," he added with amused eyes when Mikey blushed.

Mikey told Bernie about it when he took her back to the boardinghouse, reluctantly. "I'm sorry we had to break it up tonight," he said gently. "But Paulie says we can watch pay-per-view at his place, whenever we want."

"I'd like that," she whispered as he drew her close.

"Me, too, baby." He kissed her hungrily and then put her gently away. "I'm going back over to the house for a while. But we'll make a new movie date later, okay?"

She beamed. "Okay!"

Later, over supper at the house, Mikey drank a second cup of black coffee. He was unusually quiet.

"What's biting you?" Paul asked.

He shrugged. "I was thinking about Cotillo and his stooges. You know, I never stopped having Santi drive me in the limo. I've been pretty visible here…"

"Disguises don't work with people like Cotillo," Paul replied. "Besides, this is one of the safest places in the world when somebody's hunting you. It saved Sari and Merrie."

"It did," Sari added to the conversation. "It will save you, too, and Tony, I hope. Merrie's very fond of him, you know."

Mikey smiled. "Baby Doll's fond of everybody. It's just the way she is."

"That's true."

"Why are you so morose?" Paul asked his cousin.

"I worry about taking Bernie out now that I know I'm being watched by Cotillo's hoods," he said, pushing his coffee cup around.

"We told you that you could bring her over here any time you like," Sari reminded him with a smile. "She's so sweet. I love working with her."

Mikey seemed to perk up a little. "You really meant that? You wouldn't mind?"

"Not at all," Sari replied. "There are plenty of places to walk within sight of the house. We have calves she can pet and cats in the barn, and there's also the sunroom." She cleared her throat and didn't dare look at Paul, because some momentous things had happened there before the two of them married.

Mikey chuckled. "Okay, then," he said. "Thanks."

"No problem," Paul told him, his dark eyes twinkling. "So. How about Saturday?"

"Saturday sounds fine," Mikey replied. "You guys are terrific."

"Thanks," Sari said.

"You're terrific, too, Mandy," Mikey added when the housekeeper came from the kitchen with a cake pan.

Mandy grinned. "Nice of you to say that, and I baked you a chocolate cake, too!"

Mikey hesitated, looked guilty. His face drew up. He didn't want to tell her.

"Mandy, he won't say, but he gets terrible migraine

headaches," Paul told her gently. "Chocolate is one of his triggers."

"Oh, my goodness, I'm so sorry!" Mandy began.

"You're a sweetheart, and it's the thought that counts," Mikey told her with a smile. "I love chocolate. I just can't eat it."

"Well, I'll make you a nice vanilla pound cake tomorrow. How's that?" she teased.

"That, I'll eat, and thank you."

"It's no trouble at all. You helped keep my girls safe. I'll never forget you for it, not as long as I live."

Mikey flushed a little. "They're sweet girls, both of them." He glanced at Sari. "Sweet women," he amended.

Sari waved away the apology. "I don't get offended at every single word people come up with. Besides," she added with twinkling blue eyes, "I got called a whole new word in court by a man I was prosecuting for assault. The judge turned him every which way but loose."

Mikey chuckled. "Good for the judge."

"She's a great judge," Paul agreed. "I had to get a search warrant from her several years ago. We had a long talk about Sari's mother. The judge was friends with her."

"My mother was sweet, kind of like Bernie," Sari said. "She loved to plant flowers and grow things."

"My grandmother did, too," Paul said.

"Yeah, she always had an herb garden, and she grew tomatoes out in the backyard," Mikey added. "It was hard, losing her. She was the only real family Paulie and I ever had. Our parents weren't around much."

"Which was just as well," Paul said grimly.

Mikey nodded.

"Well, I've got some research to do," Sari said, rising. She bent to kiss Paul. "Don't eat my part of that cake," she warned. "I'll be back for it later."

"Would I do that?" Paul said with mock defensiveness.

"Of course you would," she replied. She chuckled as she left the room.

"Damn, you got lucky," Mikey said after she'd gone.

"I did. Maybe you got lucky, too," Paul said. "Everybody who knows Bernie loves her." He grimaced. "Shame what happened to her," he added.

"Yeah, the arthritis is pretty bad," Mikey agreed.

Paul frowned and had started to speak when his phone went off. He looked at the number and groaned, but he answered it. "Fiore," he said.

He listened, glanced at Mikey, grimaced again. "I see. Yeah, I'll make sure he knows. We'll double up down here. No worries. I wouldn't want to risk Carrera getting mad at me, either, but these guys aren't playing with a full deck, if you know what I mean. Sure. Okay. Thanks."

"Trouble?" Mikey asked.

Paul nodded. "Somebody made an attempt on Tony, a new one. He's in custody and they're hoping he'll sing like a bird when they extradite him back here."

"A break, maybe."

"Maybe. If they don't suicide him, like they did the other one."

"Yeah." Mikey drew in a breath. "You know, my life was going along so well up until now. I've got the hotel. I've got all the money I'll ever need. I was really thinking about a home and a family. I guess I lost sight of what I've been, what I've done." He looked up at Paul. "Maybe the universe is set up so that you get back what you give out, every time, in double measure. I don't mind for me. I just don't want to put her in the crosshairs. She's the sweetest woman I've ever met."

Paul didn't need prompting to know that his cousin was talking about Bernadette. There was a look on Mikey's face that his cousin hadn't seen in many years. "We've got all our bases covered," he told Mikey. "You have to remember, outsiders stand out here. There's already gossip about that woman Jessie in Isabel's office, and even Barbara's new cook at the café. Outsiders draw attention."

"Did you check out Jessie and the cook?" Mikey asked.

Paul gave him a sardonic glance. "What do you think?"

"Sorry."

"No worries. But we dug pretty deep. I think we'd have found anything obvious, like an arrest record. Well, unless the guy's working for one of the letter agencies," he added, referring to the federal intelligence and justice community.

"True."

"You going to bring Bernie over Saturday?" Paul asked.

Mikey chuckled. "What do you think?" he said, throwing his cousin's own words back at him, and they both laughed.

Bernie couldn't sleep. It had been raining all day and the pain was pretty bad. She had pain relievers, massive doses of ibuprofen for when all else failed, but she didn't like it. The medicine messed her stomach up, even when she took it with food. Besides that, there was a limited amount of time that she could take it. It was so powerful that it could cause major problems with the liver and kidneys if people used it for a long period of time without a break. She was afraid of that.

But this was one time when she had to have some relief. She could barely hold back the tears.

She got out of bed painfully and pulled on her white chenille robe. She was going to have to go and get a bottle of water out of the fridge. Mrs. Brown, bless her heart, kept it for her tenants, who were always welcome to anything to drink or any bedtime snacks they could find in her spotless kitchen.

Bernie walked very slowly into the kitchen and almost collided with Mikey, in burgundy silk pajama bottoms with a matching robe. His broad, hair-roughened chest was bare, with the robe open. He looked handsome and sensuous. Bernie's heart jumped wildly at just the sight of him.

Mikey smiled. He could see all that in her face. She was totally without artifice, he thought. An honest woman, who never hid what she felt.

"You look pretty with your hair down, honey," he said gently.

She did. Her long platinum hair waved around her shoulders and down almost to her waist in back. With her cheeks faintly flushed and her pale green eyes twinkling despite the pain, she was a dish.

She laughed self-consciously. "I was just thinking

how gorgeous *you* look," she confided with a bigger flush.

"What do you need?" he asked. He was holding a paper plate with crackers and sliced cheese on it, along with some slices of fresh pear.

"Just a bottle of water from the fridge and something to eat. I have to take one of the big pills. Pain's pretty bad," she said reluctantly.

"Here. Sit down. I'll get you some cheese and crackers."

"I can do that…"

"Don't fuss, honey," he said gently. He pulled out a chair and waited until she sat down. Then he fetched the water and sliced a little more cheese and put some more crackers on his paper plate. He sat down, too.

"The pears are nice," he said.

"I like fresh fruit," she said shyly.

They munched cheese in a pleasant silence. She washed it all down with her bottle of water, wincing every time she shifted in the chair.

"I'm sorry you had to have a disease that makes you hurt all the time," he told her quietly.

"Life happens," she said. "I learned to live with it a long time ago."

He frowned. "You aren't that old."

"I'm twenty-four," she reminded him. "But I've had it since I was about nine."

"Nine years old!" he exclaimed.

"Some children are born with it," she replied. "Arthritis isn't just a disease of old people. There's a little boy, five, who goes to the same rheumatologist I do.

He's got osteoarthritis and he has to take doses of ibuprofen just like I do."

Mikey winced. "What a hell of a life."

She nodded. "At least I've had it long enough to know how to cope with bad days and flares. It's much harder for a child."

"I can only imagine."

"Why are you up so late?" she wondered.

He moved crackers around on the plate, next to his opened soft drink. "You mentioned that I was worried about putting people in danger by living here," he said, recalling her uncanny perception.

She nodded. "You're in some kind of trouble, aren't you, and your cousin's trying to help."

"That's about the size of it." He leaned back with his soft drink in his hand. He looked gorgeous with his black, wavy hair tousled and his robe open.

He chuckled at her expression. "Your eyes tell me everything you're thinking, Bernie," he said softly. "You can't imagine how flattered I am by it."

"Really?" she asked, surprised.

He stared at her quietly. "I'm a bad man," he said after a minute, and he scowled. "Getting mixed up with me is unwise."

She just looked at him and sighed. "I never had much sense."

It took a minute for that to register. He burst out laughing. "Oh. Is that it?"

She grinned. "That's it."

"Then, what the hell. I've got all sorts of people looking out for me. That means they'll be looking out for you and everybody in the boardinghouse, too."

"Okay," she said, smiling.

He cocked his head. "Do you like chocolate cake?" he asked suddenly.

Her eyebrows arched. "Well, yes. It's my favorite."

"Mandy made me one and I couldn't eat it," he said with a grimace. "I get migraine headaches, real bad ones. Chocolate's a trigger."

"My dad used to get them," she replied. She frowned. "Isn't anything aged a trigger? I mean, like cheese?"

He looked at her and then at the plate of cheese and let out a breath. "Well, damn. I never thought about it. Every time I eat cheese I get a headache, and I never connected it!"

"Dad's neurologist said everybody's got more than one trigger, but sometimes they don't recognize them. He couldn't drink red wine or eat any dark fruit or cheese. And he loved cheese."

"How about chocolate?"

She laughed. "He never liked sweets, so it wasn't a problem."

"Do you get headaches?"

She shook her head. "I had one bad one when I was about thirteen. Never since."

"Lucky you," he told her.

"I guess so."

"Paulie says I can bring you over to the house to visit on Saturday, if you want."

Her heart skipped and ran away. "He did? Really?"

"So did Sari. There are kittens in the barn and horses to pet. I think there's a dog somewhere, too."

"Ooh, temptation," she cooed, and grinned at him.

He laughed. "I thought the kittens might do it."

She cocked her head and her eyes adored him. "The kittens would be a bonus. Spending time with you is the real draw."

He caught his breath. Amazing, the effect she had on him. He felt as if he could walk on air.

"It's like that with me, too, kid," he said softly. "I like being with you."

She felt exhilaration flow through her. "The cane doesn't put you off?"

He shrugged. "I'll get one, too. We'll look like a matched set."

Tears stung her eyes. She'd never dreamed that a man, especially a gorgeous, worldly man like this, would ever find her attractive and not be put off by her condition.

"Aw, now, don't do that," he said softly. He got up, lifted her into his arms and sat back down with her across his lap. "Don't cry. Everything's going to be all right. Honest."

She put her arms around his neck and snuggled close. "You think so?" she asked tearfully.

"Yes, I do." He rubbed her back, feeling protective.

The sound of a door opening broke the spell. But he wouldn't let Bernie up even when Mrs. Brown came into the kitchen.

"Oh, dear," she said, taking in Bernie's tears and Mikey comforting her. "Pain got you up, didn't it?"

"Yes. I came to get a bottle of water so I could take one of those horrible pills, but I have to eat something first. I hope you don't mind…"

"Bosh," Mrs. Brown said. "That's why I keep snacky foods and soft drinks in the fridge."

"The cheese is really good," Mikey said.

"It's hoop cheese," Mrs. Brown told him with a grin. "I get them to order me a wheel of it at the grocery store and I slice it and bag it up. I like it, too. I got peckish so I thought I'd get myself a snack. Is it bad, Bernie?" she added.

Bernie nodded. "I'm sorry if I woke you."

"I don't sleep much," Mrs. Brown said quietly. "You didn't bother me at all."

Bernie got off Mikey's lap reluctantly. "Thanks for the comfort," she said, wiping her eyes. "I don't feel sorry for myself, but the pain is pretty bad."

"Go to bed, honey. Don't forget your water," he told her. "Saturday, if you're better, we'll go see the kittens in Paulie's barn. Okay?"

Bernie's eyes lit up. "Okay."

"Want me to carry you down the hall?" he offered.

"Thanks," she said, a little self-conscious at Mrs. Brown's amused expression. "But I'm good. I hold on to the wall when I get wobbly. Good night," she added to both of them.

"Try to sleep, sweetheart," Mrs. Brown said. "If you need me, you call, okay?"

"I will. Thanks." She glanced at Mikey, flushed, smiled and went out the door.

"She's got grit," Mikey told the landlady.

"Yes, she really has," Mrs. Brown replied. "We all

try to look out for her, as much as she'll let us. She's very independent."

"I noticed," he chuckled.

"You're eating cheese," she said worriedly. "Didn't you tell us that you got migraine headaches?"

"Well, yes…"

"Cheese is a trigger," she said. "Like red wine and chocolate."

He made a face. "I can't eat chocolate at all, but I never thought of cheese bringing on a headache." He laughed. "You know, I used to get headaches all the time and never knew why. It was always after I'd been out with a colleague of mine. He loved cheese, so he always had a platter of it with his dinner, wherever we ate. I nibbled on it and then almost died in the night when the pain came."

"Do you get the aura?" Mrs. Brown asked.

He grimaced. "Yeah. Flashy lights or blind in one eye until the pain hits."

"Do you have something to take for it?" she persisted.

"Just over-the-counter stuff."

"You should see a doctor and get something stronger," she told him. "They even have a drug that can prevent them, if you don't have drug allergies."

"They do?" he asked, and was really interested.

"They do." She laughed. "It's why I don't have them much anymore," she confessed. "Cheese is one of my biggest triggers. But I haven't had a migraine since back in the winter," she added.

"Maybe I should do that," he said. "They get worse as I get older."

"You're not old, Mr. Fiore," she teased.

He shrugged. "Thirty-seven," he confessed. "Really too old for Bernie..."

"Nonsense. I was fifteen years younger than my late husband, and we had a wonderful life together."

His eyebrows arched. "Did people talk about you?"

She nodded. She smiled. "We didn't care. It was nobody's business but ours." She sighed. "I'm so glad you and Bernie are friends. She's never had much in the way of companionship. She's so alone."

"Yeah, me, too," he confided. "After my grandmother died, all I had left was Paulie. He's a great guy."

"So I hear."

He got up. "Well, I'll go off to bed and hope the cheese doesn't do me in. But it was worth it," he added with a chuckle as he put his empty plate in the trash can. "Best cheese I've had in a long time."

"I'm glad you like it. And if you get the preventative, you can eat all you like of it," she laughed.

"I guess so. Sleep well."

"You, too."

But he didn't sleep well. He woke two hours later with a headache that almost brought him to tears. He walked into the bathroom, half-blind, and almost collided with Bernie, who was wetting a washcloth in the sink.

"My goodness, what's wrong?" she asked, because he was deathly pale.

"Migraine," he said roughly. "Any Excedrin in there?" he asked, indicating the medicine cabinet. "I can't find mine. I think I put it in here…"

She opened the cabinet and looked. "Yes, there is."

"Shake me out a tablet, will you, honey?"

"Oh, yes." She did and handed it to him. "You need this more than I do," she said, indicating the wet washcloth. "Come on. I'll help you back to bed."

"You should go," he said, swallowing hard.

"Why?"

"I get sick…" Before he could say anything else, he managed to make it to the commode and lost his supper, the cheese, the crackers, the soft drink and just about everything else.

When the nausea passed, he found Bernie on her knees beside him with the wet cloth, wiping his face. She flushed the toilet.

"Better now?" she asked.

He swallowed and drew in a breath. "Yeah. I think so. Honey, you shouldn't…" he began.

"You looked after me when I was having a flare," she reminded him. "Tit for tat."

He managed a smile. "Okay."

"Come on. I'll help you back to bed."

He let her lead him back into his bedroom and help him under the covers. She put the washcloth over his eyes.

"I'll go get you something to take the tablet with. Want water or a soft drink?"

"Ginger ale, if there's any in the fridge," he said weakly, loving the comfort of her touch, the compassion in her voice. All his life, women had wanted him for his wealth, his power. This woman only wanted him. It was a revelation.

"I'll be right back."

"You shouldn't be walking," he said.

"It's just to the kitchen, and I took the big pill. It's helping. I'll be right back."

Mrs. Brown was just getting ready for breakfast in the kitchen. She turned as Bernie came in.

"Do you want some coffee, sweetheart?" the landlady asked.

"I'd love some, but Mikey has a migraine. I found his migraine medicine, but he wants ginger ale to take it with."

"There's one bottle left that's cold," the older woman said. "I'll get some more and put them in there. Is he all right?"

"He lost his supper," Bernie said. "He's really sick. I'm going to sit with him for a few minutes."

"If you need me, just call. We can get one of the Coltrain doctors to come over here and give him a shot if he needs them to. Those headaches are horrible. I used to have them before I got on the preventative."

"He should see a doctor," she said as she got the ginger ale out of the fridge.

"You make him do that," Mrs. Brown said.

Bernie flushed and laugh. "As if I could."

"Bernie," Mrs. Brown said gently, "can't you see that the man is absolutely crazy about you?"

Chapter Seven

Bernie stared at Mrs. Brown as if she'd sprouted grass in her hair. "He what?"

"He absolutely adores you," the older woman replied, smiling. "Everybody noticed, not just me."

Bernie flushed. "Well," she said, stumped for a response.

"You just go take care of your fellow," Mrs. Brown said. "I'll get breakfast ready. If he can eat anything, I'll make him whatever he likes."

"I'll tell him," Bernie replied. "Thanks."

"You come and eat whenever you like. I'll make you up a plate that you can reheat, okay?"

"Okay!"

Bernie went back to Mikey's room and closed the door. She sat down on the edge of the bed. "Still got the tablet?" she asked, because she'd handed it to him earlier.

"I got it."

"Here. It's open." She'd already taken the top off the bottle before she handed it to him. He swallowed down the tablet and handed her back the bottle. "Thanks, honey."

"No problem." She put his drink on the side table. "Will it stay down?" she worried. "Mrs. Brown said we can call one of our local doctors and they'll come give you a shot if you need it."

He swallowed. "Maybe the pill will work."

"Does it usually?"

He smiled. "No. It helps just a little. Nothing stops it."

She smoothed back his cool, wavy black hair. "You just let me know what you need. I'll get it."

His eyes adored her. "There was never a woman in my whole life who'd have taken care of me the way you just did. Well, except for my grandmother."

"I'm sure there were plenty who wanted to," she teased.

"Maybe a couple. But I'm funny about women. Most of them are jaded and glitzy," he added, his eyes cold with memory.

"Maybe you've been looking in the wrong places for them," she said, tongue in cheek.

His black eyes twinkled at her. "Think so?"

"It's a possibility."

He lay back and closed his eyes, wincing. "Of all the things to get from cheese," he groaned. "It's my favorite food."

"You can find a new favorite one. Maybe squash," she teased. "Or okra."

"Stop! You're killing me!"

She laughed. Most of the men she worked around hated both vegetables with a passion.

"Frozen yogurt, then."

"That sounds nice."

They were quiet for a few minutes, but it was obvious that even when the tablet had time to work, it wasn't doing much.

"Pill helping at all?"

He put his hand over his eyes. "Not so much." He closed his eyes and winced. "It's just over-the-counter stuff."

"Let me call a doctor. Please."

He drew in a breath. "Okay," he said finally.

"Be right back."

She phoned Lou and Copper Coltrain's office. The nurse said she'd ask Lou to come right out. Lou was short for Louise, she was blond and sweet and she knew exactly what to do for Mikey.

"You should see a neurologist," she told him after she'd given him an injection for the pain. First, of course, she'd examined him, asked what he'd already taken for the headache and inquired about any drug allergies. He had none. "But in the meantime, I'll write you a prescription for the preventative and something for the headaches that works when you get one." She turned to Bernie. "I'll give these to you, Bernie. You get them filled today."

"I will," Bernie said, smiling at the physician. "Thanks for coming."

"You're most welcome. If you have any more issues, Mr. Fiore, you call the office, okay?"

"Yes, ma'am," he said complacently. He smiled up at her through dark-rimmed eyes. "Thanks, Doc."

"You're welcome."

"I didn't think doctors made house calls anymore," he said.

"Jacobsville's not like most small towns," she laughed. "We do what's needed." She glanced at Bernie. "I thought you might be dying, from Bernie's description. She was very upset."

He opened both eyes and stared at Bernie. "She was?" he asked softly, and smiled at her.

She flushed even more. He laughed. Lou hid a smile, said her goodbyes and left.

"Can I get you anything else?" Bernie asked.

"No, but you can give the prescriptions to Santi. I'll text him." He pulled out his cell phone and made a face. "Damn, I can't see it," he murmured.

"Just a sec." She took the phone from him, pulled up messaging and looked at Mikey. "What do you want to tell him?"

"Ask him to come over right away."

She typed it in. The response was immediate. "On my way," it read.

"He'll think I'm dying or that Cotillo got me," he chuckled.

She frowned. "Who's Cotillo?"

"A bad man. Even worse than me," he said in a husky tone. His eyes tried to focus on her face. "There's a lot you don't know about me, kid."

"Well, there's a lot you don't know about me, too," she said.

His big hand searched for hers and held it tight. "We'll learn about each other. It takes time. Right?"

She smiled. It sounded like a future. She felt herself glowing inside. "It takes time," she agreed.

He took a deep breath and closed his eyes. "I'm going to try to sleep. Santi has plenty of cash for the prescriptions."

"Okay." She got up. "If you need anything, you just call, okay?"

He smiled without opening his eyes. "Okay. Thanks, honey."

"You're very welcome."

She went out of the room, the soft words lingering, touching, making her feel valued.

There was a knock at the front door. She went to answer it. Santi was standing there.

"What's wrong with the boss?" he asked at once.

"Migraine," she said. "We had to call the doctor."

"It's a doctor you know, right?" he asked, and his broad face looked troubled.

"Oh, yes, Dr. Louise Coltrain. She came out and gave him these prescriptions. He asked you to get them filled for him at the drugstore."

He took them from her and nodded. "I'll get right on it." He grimaced. "I don't like being away from him at night, even with all those other guys watching out for him. Listen, you hear any strange noises or if anybody tries to get in the house, you text me. Got your cell phone with you?"

"Yes." She pulled it out and handed it to him.

He pulled up the contact screen and put information into it. He handed it back. "That's my cell phone number. The boss isn't twitchy, so he might pass over something that could be dangerous."

"I'll call you if anything happens here," she promised. "Thanks," she added softly.

He smiled. "You're a nice kid. I'm sorry we were rough on you when you fell in front of the car. It's just that women have tried that before in the boss's old neighborhood."

"Really?" she asked, and she was honestly surprised.

He nodded. "He's loaded, you know? Plenty of women would do anything for money."

She smiled. "I've known one or two of those myself. I like having enough to pay the bills and eat out once in a while. That's about all. Money doesn't make people happy. Very often, it does just the opposite."

"Yes, it does." He held up the prescriptions. "I'll get these filled and bring them back to you. The boss, you're sure he's okay?"

"Why don't you look in and see, before you go?" she asked, leading him down the hall. "He's had a rough night."

"I used to nurse him through these headaches," Santi said. "They're a nightmare."

"I can see that."

She knocked briefly and opened the door. Mikey turned his head, wincing at the pain. He managed a smile.

"Hey, Santi. Had to make sure I hadn't croaked, right?" he teased.

Santi chuckled. "Something like that. You okay?"

"Getting better by the minute."

"Okay. I'll go get your meds and be right back."

"Bernie," Mikey called, when she started to go out, too. She went back in and paused by the bed. "You haven't even had breakfast, have you?" he asked.

"Well, not just yet…"

"Go eat something."

"Okay. Mrs. Brown said you can have anything you want to eat when you feel like food."

He smiled drowsily. "She's a doll. So are you. I'm not hungry yet. I think I'll just sleep for a while. Eat something."

"I will."

"Hey," he called softly when she was at the door.

She turned, her eyebrows arching.

"When I get better, suppose we take in another movie? Paulie says they've got all the latest movies on pay-per-view and DVD. And a door that locks," he added with a wicked smile.

She laughed, flushing as she remembered the last movie they'd gone to but not seen. The memory of his mouth on hers was poignant. "I'd like that," she said.

"Me, too."

"Get some rest. I'll check on you in a few minutes."

He sighed. "Sweet girl. Don't ever change."

"I'll do my best."

She went out and closed the door.

Paul came over to see about his cousin, alerted by Santi after the bodyguard had dropped off Mikey's prescriptions.

"You look rough," Paul said, sitting by his cousin's bedside. "I remember what a misery those headaches are."

"Misery is right. I lost everything I'd eaten. Bernie was right in the bathroom with me, mopping me up," he added. "What a hell of a woman. I never knew anybody like her."

"She's unique," Paul agreed. "Amazing how she keeps going. Her disability never seems to get her down."

"She has good days and bad ones."

"Don't they have shots for that condition now?"

"Yeah, they do," Mikey said. "I overheard her landlady saying what a shame it was that they were so expensive. Bernie can't afford them." His face tautened. "I can, but she'd never let me do it for her. She's proud."

"She is."

"Mikey, how well do you know Santi?" Paul asked.

Mikey's eyebrows rose. "As well as I know you," he said. "Honor's his big thing. He'd never sell me out because it would seem dishonorable to him. He takes his job seriously. Why do you ask?" he added.

"Just some gossip. They say Cotillo's got somebody close to you."

"It's got to be Mrs. Brown, then," Mikey said with

twinkling dark eyes. "Right? I mean, she's the obvious choice. Friendly, sweet, just the sort to set you up for a hit."

Paul chuckled. "Okay. I see what you mean. Just the same, we're checking out everybody who lives here. Just in case."

"That's not a bad idea. You still got Billings somewhere with a sniper kit?"

Paul nodded. "I don't think he ever sleeps. He seems to get by on catnaps, but we have an alternate in place anyway."

Mikey drew in a breath and laughed huskily. "These damned headaches. I didn't know there was a way to prevent them. Doc prescribed something, along with a prescription to take when the pain gets bad." He grimaced. "I hate drugs, you know? But this is a sort of pain that makes you want to hit your head with a hammer just to make it stop throbbing."

"Grandmama used to get them," Paul recalled. "They were bad."

"So are mine. Imagine a woman who doesn't run for the hills when a man's losing the contents of his stomach," he said. "Bernie didn't leave me for a minute, not until after the doctor came."

"I hear you did pretty much the same for her the day you met, when she fell in front of the car."

"Yeah," Mikey's mouth pulled down. "I thought it was a trick. You know how women used to come on to me. One even pretended to fall down a flight of stairs. I didn't know Bernie from an apple. I assumed she liked the looks of the limo and wanted a ride. Bad call." He drew in a breath. "She asked us to look for her cane, and we didn't believe her. Santi found it. I felt like a dog."

"Your past isn't full of guileless women," Paul said with a grin. "Understandable mistake."

"I guess." He put a hand to his head. "At least the throbbing has stopped. That doctor's pretty good. Nice looking woman. She married to the redheaded doctor?"

"Copper Coltrain," Paul agreed. "There was a mismatch. She worked with him for almost a year, and he hated her guts for something her father did years ago. It wasn't until she started to leave the practice that he got his ducks in a row. It was a rocky romance."

Mikey just sighed. "Mine's not rocky at all," he said. "You know, I never thought about having a family before. Little girls are sweet."

"Yeah." Paul didn't say any more. He and his former wife had a little girl. His wife and the child were gunned down by one of Paul's enemies, in revenge for his arrest and conviction. It was a sad memory.

"Sorry," Mikey said, wincing. "I forgot."

"I try to," Paul said. "I mean, I'm happier than I ever dreamed I could be, with Sari. But there are times when I think of my little girl…" He broke off.

"We all have bad memories, Paulie," Mikey said. "Mine aren't as bad as yours. I'm sorry for what happened to you. But the guy paid for it," he added coldly.

Paul glanced at him. "Yeah, one of the marshals in Jersey said he thought you might have had something to do with that."

Mikey just pursed his lips. "Who, me? I go out of my way to be nice to people."

"Yeah, but you know people who don't."

Mikey chuckled. "Lots of them."

"Have you told her?" he asked, his head jerking toward the door.

Mikey knew who he meant. He leaned back against the pillows. "I don't know how. At first, I didn't think there was a reason I needed to tell her. Now, I'm scared of what she'll think of me."

"She's a sweet woman."

"Sweet, and innocent. She doesn't see wickedness. She always looks for the best in people. Even in me. I'm not what she thinks I am. But how do I tell her what my life has been like? How do I do that, and keep her?"

"You underestimate how she feels about you, Mikey," Paul said. "You don't love or hate people for their actions mostly. You care about them because of what they are, deep inside. Bernie knows you aren't as bad as you think you are."

"I hope you're right. It hasn't been a long time, but if I lose her, it will be like having an arm torn off, you know?"

"I do know. That's how I feel about Sari."

"She's a winner."

He smiled. "I agree. Hey, if you're not better Saturday, you can bring Bernie over for lunch Sunday, you'll be welcome. You can take her walking around the property, maybe even catch that movie you went to see at the drive-in. It wasn't a new one, because it's on pay-per-view now."

"That sounds nice," Mikey replied. "I hope this stupid headache goes away before then," he added. "They usually last two or three days."

"I remember. You take your meds. Maybe they'll cut this one short."

"I hope so. Thanks for the cousinly visit," he added. "Anything more from Carrera?"

Paul shook his head. "He's got Tony in a safe place, he says, and not to worry."

"I'm in a safer place," Mikey chuckled. "Little bitty town in the middle of nowhere, with half the retired mercs in the country. Lucky me."

Paul grinned. "I'll second that. Ask Bernie over Sunday."

"I will. Thanks."

"No problem. See you later."

"Yeah."

Bernie was delighted with the invitation. It did take Mikey a few days to get over the headache, but he was fine Sunday afternoon. "Are you sure they don't mind?" she asked.

"They wouldn't invite you if they minded, honey," he told her as they sped toward Paul and Sari's house. "You warm enough?"

"I'm fine," she said, huddling down in her warm berber coat. "It's chilly tonight."

"Imagine that, chilly in south Texas," he teased. "Now if you want to see chilly, you have to come to Jersey. We know about cold weather."

"I guess you get a lot of snow."

"We used to get more, when Paulie and I were kids.

We had some great snowball battles in the neighborhood. These older boys would lie in wait for us and pelt us with frozen snowballs every chance they got. So Paulie and I got some ice cubes and put them inside our snowballs. Ouch! The bullies ran for their lives."

She laughed. "I'll bet they did."

"Our grandmother was so fierce that they were more afraid of her than even the big boss in the neighborhood," he recalled with a smile. "I told you about her hitting him with a salami. Chased him all the way out the front door with it, and his people didn't dare laugh. It taught him a whole new respect for women."

She laughed softly. "I wish I could have met your grandmother."

"Me, too, honey. She'd have loved you." His hand reached for hers and held it tight. "She had no time for modern women with modern ideas."

She sighed. "Me, neither. I'm a throwback to another generation, I guess. My dad pretty much raised me after we came back here." Her heart felt like lead in her chest. She hated remembering why they'd come to Jacobsville.

"What's wrong?" he asked, sensitive to her mood.

She grimaced. "Things I can't talk about. Bad things."

"Honey, I could write you a book on bad things," he commented. He drew in a breath. "One of these days we have to have a long talk about my past, and it isn't going to be nice."

"It won't matter," she said quietly. "The person you were isn't the man you are today."

"That's not as true as I wish it was," he replied.

"I can't believe you'd do anything terrible."

But he had. Really terrible things. They hadn't both-ered him much until now. This sweet, kind woman be-side him didn't have any idea about what sort of evil lived in his real world, the world she'd never seen.

"Listen, you read books?" he asked.

"Oh, yes. It's how I get through bad nights, when the pain overpowers the medicines I take for it."

"There's this book—I'll give you the title. It's about a man who paints houses."

"A painter?" she asked.

His fingers contracted. "It's a different sort of paint-ing. If you read the book, you'll begin to get some idea of the sort of world I live in." His face tautened. "It's a hard life. Dog eat dog, and I mean that literally. The man I work for is hiding out from a man even worse than he is. What I know, what I've seen, can clear him. The feds just have to keep me alive long enough until the trial comes up." He turned and glanced at her. "It's a business. Like regular business, in a way. It's just that somebody wants what you have and thinks up ways to get it, most of them illegal and deadly."

She frowned. "I don't understand."

"How could you? Raised in a tiny little town, sur-rounded by law-abiding citizens, most of whom love you." His face hardened. "In my whole damned life, my grandmother was the only person who really loved me."

Her heart almost stopped. She loved him. And she'd only just realized it. She was faintly disconcerted by a revelation that should have occurred to her much sooner. "There's your cousin Paul," she said after a minute.

"Yeah, Paulie. We're fond of each other. He'd do anything he could to help me. In fact, he already is. But that's not the same way I felt about my grandmother."

"I don't remember mine very well," she said tightly.

He glanced at her. "Bad memories?"

She swallowed. "They don't get much worse."

His fingers linked into hers. "Can you tell me about it?"

She hesitated. He was insinuating that his life had been a little outside the law. Perhaps he might understand better than most men what it had been like for her, for her family.

"I want to," she said. "Can it wait until later?"

He laughed. "It can wait." He was flattered that she wanted to trust him with something that was obviously a secret, something she kept hidden. It was an indication of feelings she was beginning to have for him. He was beginning to have the same sort for her. If she had something traumatic in her past, it might help her relate to his own life.

Then he stopped and considered what he'd be letting her in for, after the trial, when he went back to Jersey, back to the old life. He'd pledged his loyalty, his life, to the crime family he belonged to. Betraying that code, that omertà, would get him killed. Not that he had any plans to turn his people in to the feds. In fact, even Tony was working with the feds right now, to ward off the takeover by Cotillo. But that was a temporary truce. Nobody in Tony's employ was going to rat out anybody to the feds, least of all Mikey. That would get you killed quick.

On the other hand, if he wanted a life with the sweet woman at his side, and he was beginning to, how could he drag her into the shadows with him?

It would be her choice in the end. But she was sheltered and disabled. Not that his people would be bad to her, oh, no. Even the women would welcome her like a relative. His underlings would treat her like royalty. So it wouldn't be bad from that standpoint. But the rackets Tony and Mikey were mixed up in were illegal. They specialized in online gambling, in numbers running, in casinos in Vegas. One of Mikey's properties was a casino, in fact. He'd told Bernie that it was a hotel. It was a hotel, but it wasn't in Jersey. It was in Las Vegas, and big-name entertainers came regularly to appear there. He ran it like a legal business, but he did do things off the books that could land him in jail. Bernie was such a gentle, trusting soul. She liked the country, the outdoors, little animals. Mikey liked bright lights and casinos. It was going to be a difficult adjustment, if she was even willing to make it.

"You're brooding," she accused, watching the expressions cross his handsome face.

He laughed self-consciously. "I'm brooding." He turned his head for a minute and caught her eyes. "Sorry. I have things on my mind." He made a face. "Paulie said they've got somebody close to me."

"They?"

"The guy who's after Tony and me," he explained. He chuckled. "I told him it was probably Mrs. Brown.

You can tell she's just the kind of person who would set a man up," he added with a grin.

She burst out laughing. "Oh, that's wicked."

"I'm a wicked man, honey," he said, and he wasn't kidding.

She frowned. "He doesn't have any idea who it is?" she added.

"Not yet. He's checking people out."

"I'd check out that Jessie person in my office," she muttered. "She's one of the most horrible people I've ever known. She's always cutting at the other women in the office. Poor Glory has high blood pressure. It can be dangerous, you know, and she has a small child. Jessie makes all sorts of unpleasant remarks to her about the medicines she takes, even about the way she dresses."

"Your boss should get that woman out of the office," he commented.

"He'd like to, but he's the DA. He has to have a legitimate reason to let her go or she could take him to court. He'd like her to leave, too. She messes up appointments all the time, another reason Glory's so stressed."

His fingers stroked hers. "We all have our crosses, don't we, kid?"

She nodded. "Nobody gets through life without a few traumas." She sighed. "It's really sad, you know. She's so beautiful. How can a person who looks like that be such a pain to be around?"

"You never know what sort of background people come from," he said simply. "A lot of times, kids turn out bad because of the way they were raised. You know, I only saw my dad a few times in my whole life. My mother died of a heart attack when she was just in her twenties, not too long after she had me. Her mother, my grandmother, took me in. Paulie's mom bit the dust about the same time, so he ended up with our grandmother, too." He grimaced. "Paulie's dad was even worse than mine. He took some licks when the old man was home. Fortunately, it wasn't often."

"Did your fathers work in some sort of away job, like construction?" she asked innocently.

"They worked for the big bosses. They went where they were told, and did what they were told." He smiled sadly. "That's the life, kid. You pledge to obey and you do it. There's a code of honor. We call it omertà. It means you pledge your loyalty to a don and you never forget it. You sell out your colleagues, you meet with a quick and sad end."

Her heart jumped. "But you're going to testify against a man who's a, what did you call him, a don?"

His fingers contracted comfortingly around hers. "That's a different thing," he said. "This guy Cotillo is trying to muscle in on territory that doesn't belong to him. The other families are as much against him as Tony's is."

She frowned. "Tony's your family? Is he a relation?"

He chuckled. "Tony's a character," he said. "No, we're not related, but we'd die for each other. So in that sense, yeah, I guess you could say he's family. The feds are protecting him. Me, too. What we know can put Cotillo away for a very long time. The families are working toward that end, even making a temporary truce with the feds to keep them from prying too closely into our business."

She blinked. "You talk about federal people as if they're the enemy," she said. "But your cousin works for a federal agency."

"It's just a figure of speech, honey," he said, backtracking. "We're all grateful for their help. Nobody wants a guy like Cotillo in charge in Jersey. He's a weasel. First chance he got, he'd start lining up other families for elimination. They know that. So the feds are sort of the lesser of the two evils."

"I see."

"You don't, but you will," he promised. He sighed. "I just hope it isn't all going to be too much for you, Bernie. You've lived a sheltered life."

"Actually, I haven't. Not so much."

"Oh?"

"Well, I haven't lived in a commune or had lovers, or anything like that. But I'm anything but sheltered. I'll tell you," she added. "I promise."

He smiled. "I'll tell you, too."

"That's a deal."

Chapter Eight

They were heading down the long driveway to Gray-lings when his fingers contracted around hers. "No se-crets from now on," he said. "I'll tell you about my life today and you can tell me about yours."

"It might matter…" she said worriedly.

"It won't." He sounded very positive. "Nothing you tell me will change anything." One side of his sensu-ous mouth pulled down. "On the other hand, what I have to tell you, well, that may change a lot of things," he added heavily, and he was regretting things in his past that might drive her out of his life. It was a terrible thought. She was already part of him.

"Whatever sort of trouble you're in, I'll stand by you," she said.

He wanted to pull her over into his lap and kiss the

breath out of her for saying that, but he had to restrain himself. His fingers worked sensuously into hers, caressing them. "I never thought I'd get mixed up with a girl from a little town in Texas," he said, chuckling. "I feel just like Carrera must have."

"Carrera?" she asked. "Oh, yes, Delia's husband." She smiled. "Delia had a bad time of it. Her mother turned out to be a woman she'd always thought of as her sister, and her father turned out to be her mother's husband. She saved Mr. Carrera's life in the Bahamas, but she lost her baby. She came home and she was so miserable. It hurt me to see her when I had to go to the dry cleaner's." She sighed. "But then Mr. Carrera showed up with some sort of quilt he'd made for her, and the next thing we knew, they were getting married."

"Yeah, he quilts," he said with a soft laugh. "The guy looks like a wise guy. He's big and rough and he intimidates most people. The quilting habit gave him a lot of heat until he started throwing punches. Now nobody laughs at it. He wins international competitions with his designs, too."

She nodded. "They have one of his quilts in our library, on permanent display. It's a Bow Tie quilt. They say he has one just like it in a casino he owns. Gosh, imagine owning a casino! Those are the richest, flashiest places on earth!"

He hadn't told her that his hotel in Vegas was also a casino. "You ever been in one?" he asked.

"When I was small, my parents took me to the Bahamas on a cruise one year, on summer vacation. I wasn't allowed inside, but they drove me by one over on Paradise Island. It was fascinating to me, even as a child."

His fingers contracted. "Suppose I told you that the hotel I own is actually a casino," he said slowly, "and it's in Las Vegas?"

Her eyes widened. "You own a casino in Las Vegas?" she exclaimed. "Wow!"

He laughed, surprised at her easy acceptance. "I run it legit, too," he added. "No fixes, no hidden switches, no cheating. Drives the feds nuts, because they can't find anything to pin on me there."

"The feds?" she asked.

He drew in a breath. "I told you, I'm a bad man." He felt guilty about it, dirty. His fingers caressed hers as they neared Graylings, the huge mansion where his cousin lived with the heir to the Grayling racehorse stables.

Her fingers curled trustingly around his. "And I told you that the past doesn't matter," she said stubbornly. Her heart was running wild. "Not at all. I don't care how bad you've been."

His own heart stopped and then ran away. His teeth clenched. "I don't even think you're real, Bernie," he whispered. "I think I dreamed you."

She flushed and smiled. "Thanks."

He glanced in the rearview mirror. "What I'd give for just five minutes alone with you right now," he said tautly. "Fat chance," he added as he noticed the sedan tailing casually behind them.

She felt all aglow inside. She wanted that, too. Maybe

they could find a quiet place to be alone, even for just a few minutes. She wanted to kiss him until her mouth hurt.

He pulled into the long driveway and up to the house, which was all aglow with light. It was a huge two-story mansion with exquisite woodwork and a long, wide porch. The front door opened as Mikey helped her out of the car, retaining her hand in his as they approached the house.

"Paisano," Paul greeted him in Italian.

"Salve! Come stai?" Mikey replied, and let go of Bernie's hand long enough to hug his cousin.

"Sto bene, grazie, e tu?" Paul replied.

"Va bene," Mikey responded with a grin. *"Cosi, cosi. Non mi posso lamentare."*

"Benissimo!"

"English, English," Sari Fiore chided. "Bernie doesn't understand Italian," she laughed.

"Just greetings, honey," Mikey told her, and brought her hand to his lips. "I'll teach you some nice Italian words the minute we get some time together."

She grinned. "Okay."

"Come on in," Paul added as two feds got out of the sedan that had trailed Mikey's car. "McLeod, do you and Agent Murdock want coffee?"

"I'd love some," McLeod said, and glanced at Murdock. "As long as that guy doesn't offer to make it," he added firmly.

Murdock, a good-natured man, just chuckled. "I get stuck with making it at our office. People pour it in the ficus tree."

"Yeah, the poor damned thing shivers all the time,"

Paul commented on the way to the kitchen. "I think it's on the verge of a nervous breakdown. Hey, Mandy, can you make us a pot of coffee?" he called to the woman working to clean up the kitchen counters.

"Of course I can!" she exclaimed, and grinned. "Hey, Mikey! Hello, Bernie. Nice to see you both."

"Nice to see you, too, Mandy," Mikey replied, and kissed her cheek. "I miss your cooking. Not that Mrs. Johnson isn't good."

"I know she is," Mandy replied. She gave Mikey and Bernie a secret smile when she saw them holding hands.

Mikey noticed, but he didn't let go, even when they sat down together at the long kitchen table with Paul and the two feds.

"Okay," Mikey said. "What's up? You guys tailed us the whole way here," he added to McLeod.

"Cotillo sent one of his boys down here after you," McLeod replied quietly, watching Mikey's face harden. "We caught him at the courthouse yesterday."

Mikey blinked. "How?"

"We have facial identification software," McLeod said simply. "I used it. He's got wants and warrants outstanding in Jersey. Our guys took him into custody and they're delivering him right back to the authorities there."

US Marshals, that was, Mikey knew without being told. He let out a breath. "I guess I'd better be more careful about taking Bernie out to public places."

Her fingers, unseen, contracted around his.

"Not at all," Agent Murdock said. "As long as they're

pretty public. Drive-ins aren't a good idea. Too much opportunity for covert work."

Mikey sighed. "I guess so. Damn."

"It's okay," Bernie said. "We can sit in Mrs. Johnson's parlor anytime we like, and talk or watch television," she reminded him.

He smiled at her. "You're a rare girl, Bernie."

She flushed and laughed. "Not so much."

Mikey glanced at the government agents. "So why was he at the courthouse?" he asked.

"We think he was looking for a contact there. But he came after quitting time, so we didn't have the opportunity to find out. When we questioned him," McLeod added, "he said he was looking for San Antonio and got lost. He was just looking for directions."

"Oh, that sounds very sincere," Mikey said sardonically.

"Yeah, considering that he flew into the San Antonio airport," Paul added drily.

"Here's coffee," Mandy said. "And how about some nice pound cake? I made a chocolate one!"

Mikey made a face. "Gosh, I'd love that, but I'm just getting over a really bad migraine. Chocolate's one of my triggers," he reminded her.

"I'm sorry," Mandy said. She patted him on the shoulder. "But I've got a nice cherry pie?" she teased.

He chuckled. "I'll take that. Thanks. You know, she nursed me through the headache, sickness and all," he added, looking at Bernie with evident affection. "She never left me, and even called a doctor out to the boardinghouse to treat me. She's quite a girl."

Bernie's face flamed because everybody was looking at her.

"Yes, she is," Sari said, smiling. "At work, she's always the first one there and the last one to leave, and she never minds staying over if we need her." She made a face. "It's not the same with that new woman the boss hired. Jessie. She's constantly late and she makes clients uncomfortable. She made a real play for one of the wealthy married local ranchers, and the boss gave her warning." She sighed. "I wish she'd do something he could fire her for. Nobody likes her."

"She's an odd fit for a small town," Bernie said. "She's overly sophisticated."

"We have a few overly sophisticated people, like the police chief's wife, but she's nice," Mandy broke in, putting a platter of sliced pound cake, saucers and utensils on the table, along with a saucer containing a slice of cherry pie for Mikey.

"This looks delicious. Thanks, honey," he told the housekeeper and grinned at her.

"You're welcome. Go ahead, people, dig in. We don't stand on ceremony here."

"No, we don't," Sari said, smiling warmly at her husband.

"Oh, that's good coffee," Paul said with a long sigh. "I just hate trying to drink it at work," he added with a pointed glare at Murdock.

Murdock made a face. "Not my fault. My mother always drank tea. She never taught me how to make coffee and I never drink it."

"No wonder it tastes so bad," Paul teased.

Murdock sighed. "There have been threats, you know," he said complacently. "In fact, ASAC Jon Blackhawk's brother, McKuen Kilraven, was openly talking about men in ninja suits and a pickup truck and a big sack."

"You'd never fit in a sack, Murdock," Paul chuckled. "Besides, Kilraven's too occupied with their new daughter to do any such thing. That's two kids now. He and Winnie are over the moon."

"She still working 911 dispatch down here?" Murdock asked.

Paul shook his head. "She's got her hands full with two preschoolers. Kilraven's still with the company, but he's mostly administrative these days. No more hanging out of helicopters by one leg wrapped in camo netting while he fires at enemy agents."

"You're kidding!" Bernie gasped.

"Oh, no, I'm not," Paul chuckled. "The man was a maniac when he was after a perp. He's calmed down somewhat since he married, but he's still good at what he does."

"He was a patrolman here, working for Chief Grier as cover on a covert federal assignment, for a while," Bernie said as she nibbled cake and sipped coffee. She laughed. "There was gossip that Chief Grier wanted to put him in a barrel, drive him to the border and send him down the Rio Grande. They did butt heads a few times over procedure."

"The chief butts heads pretty good," Paul assured her. "He's lowered the crime rate with a vengeance since he's been in charge of our local police."

"Nobody thought he'd stay here when he first came," Bernie said. "He was really tough. Then they made a movie here with the Georgia Firefly, Tippy Moore, and before any of us realized it, he was married to her."

"She's a knockout," Paul said. He slid his hand over his wife's. "I'm partial to redheads, you know," he added, grinning as he studied Sari's red, red hair pinned up over big blue eyes.

She grinned back. "Thanks, sweetheart."

"So what do we do about Cotillo and the trial and Tony Garza?" Paul asked as he finished his pie and his coffee.

"First things first," Paul said. "We've got tails on Cotillo and his men, with interagency cooperation. Cotillo's killed a lot of people trying to forge new alliances and take over territory. He's made enemies."

"The killings are going to get him in trouble," Mikey said. "The big guys don't like that. It invites the feds in. They want problems solved with dialog, not automatic weapons."

"Well, they do kill people who rat them out," Paul replied solemnly.

Mikey nodded. "Omertà," he agreed. "Loyalty is life itself in the outfit. The number-one sin is selling out your people to the feds. Nobody likes a rat. They get put down and sometimes their whole families do as well, as a warning." He ground his teeth together when he saw his cousin's face. That had happened to Paul. His first family had been gunned down when Paul locked up one of the minor bosses and shut down a lucrative illegal operation. The man had gotten even in the worst possible way.

"I'm sorry," Mikey told his cousin. "Truly sorry. I should never have brought that up."

Paul's face relaxed. "It was a long time ago. Still stings," he said, and his eyes were filled with horrible memories.

"Just the same, I'm sorry."

Paul smiled. "We're family. Don't sweat it."

Mikey sighed. "You're the only family I've got. Well, except for Tony's family." He glanced at the feds. "I hope you guys understand that I'm only cooperating because Tony's being falsely accused. I'm not selling out my people. Not for anything."

"We know that, Mikey," Paul said quietly. "Nobody's asking you to rat out your colleagues."

Mikey sipped coffee, not looking at them. "I took a blood oath," he said very quietly. "I made a solemn promise. I swore to it, like you'd make a vow in church. I won't break it. Not if they lock me up forever."

"We only lock up people when we can prove they've broken the law," Paul assured him. He leaned closer. "So make sure we can't prove anything on you," he chuckled.

Mikey laughed. "I don't do that stuff anymore. I have a legit casino and I run it like a legit business."

"I know that," Paul replied. "You're not as bad as you make out, Mikey. You saved Merrie's life," he added, referring to Sari's younger sister. Both women had been targeted by an enemy of their late father, victims of professional hit men. Mikey's input had helped save both of them. "In fact, you helped save Sari's, as well."

"I just made a few calls," Mikey replied.

"Well, those few calls helped us catch all the perps," Paul replied.

Mikey grinned. "I like Baby Doll," he said, referring to Merrie. "How's she doing?"

"She and Ren are expecting again," Sari said with a wide grin. "She's over the moon."

"She still painting?" Mikey asked.

"Oh, yes. She never gives that hobby up," Sari told him.

He glanced at Bernie with real hunger. "I'd love her to do a portrait of Bernie for me," he said.

"You know she'd be happy to!" Sari said. She glanced at Bernie, who was flushed and beaming. "Bernie, do you have a few photos of yourself that we could send her?"

Bernie grimaced. "Well, no, not a lot. I don't have anybody to take pictures of me…"

While she was speaking, Mikey took out his expensive cell phone and snapped photos of her from all angles. He showed them to her in his photo app.

"You're really good at this," she said, surprised as she looked at herself in the pictures. She looked happy, mysterious, almost pretty. She laughed. "These don't even really look like me!"

"They do. You don't laugh a lot," he replied. His face tightened. "I love it when you laugh, Bernie," he added. "You're beautiful when you're happy."

She felt her heart almost bursting. He thought she

was beautiful. He wanted a painting of her. She could have floated up to the ceiling, she was so lighthearted.

"Thanks," she whispered.

He wrinkled his nose at her and grinned. "We'll have to wait until that movie we were watching comes out on pay-per-view and we can watch it together."

"I don't have pay-per-view," she said morosely.

"We do," Sari said, and grinned. "You can watch it in the library. In fact, we already have it. The drive-in is showing it, but it's not a first-run movie. Wouldn't you like to see the rest of it?"

Mikey pursed his lips. "Would I! It's a great movie."

"It is, but I'd need tissues," Bernie confessed. "One reviewer said it would twist your heart open."

"You can have tissues and more coffee," Sari said. "Mandy, can you do refills and find a box of tissues for Bernie?"

"You bet!" Mandy said, and went to get both.

The government agents left shortly after. Mikey took Bernie into the luxurious study with its plush couch and chairs and the expensive media center, with a fifty-five-inch television screen.

"Wow," Bernie said as Mikey closed the door behind them. "This is awesome."

"They've refurnished it since old man Grayling died," he told her as he went to turn on the television and set up the movie. "In fact, they've redone the whole house. It has some bad memories for Sari and her sister."

"I remember hearing about how badly their father

treated them," Bernie said. "He must have been a horrible father."

"From what I hear, he was." He grimaced. "Mine was pretty bad, too."

"My dad was a sweet, kind man," Bernie said sadly. "He died much too young. He lived through a lot of trauma. I think it affects people, you know? Affects their health."

"Maybe so."

He turned on the movie and brought the controller back as he dropped down onto the plush couch beside Bernie. He put the controller on the coffee table and turned to Bernie.

"Gee, look, we're all alone," he said with a grin, "and there are no cars around us."

"Isn't that fascinating?" she laughed.

"Oh, you bet." He pulled her onto his lap, letting her head fall back on his shoulder. "And I have some really interesting ideas about what we could do while the movie runs."

Her arms looped around his neck and her eyes riveted to his wide, sensuous, chiseled mouth. "You do?" she whispered.

He drew her close and bent his head, smiling. "Oh, yes. Very, very interesting."

As he spoke, his mouth slowly covered hers. She sighed and sank against his big, muscular body, letting him take her weight while he kissed her.

"I could get used to this," he whispered.

She smiled under his lips. "Me, too."

He nibbled her upper lip and traced under it with

just the tip of his tongue, loving the way she reacted to him. She wasn't coy or reticent. She met him halfway. If those long, soulful sighs were any indication, she loved what he was doing to her.

He shifted her and his fingers ran gently up and down her rib cage, setting fires, making her hungry. His mouth grew slowly insistent. She twisted against him, hungry and burning with new needs.

His big hand slid under the sweater she was wearing and teased around her breast while he kissed her slowly. She moaned and twisted up toward that maddening hand whose touch was making her wild for more.

He smiled against her soft lips because he knew that. His thumb slowly trespassed under the lacy cotton cup and against her firm breast. She gasped under his mouth, but she didn't try to stop him. He loved that. His mouth opened on hers, deepening the kiss, diverting her while his hand went to the hooks that held the bra in place and snapped them open. His hand, warm and strong, moved slowly back around, teasing just under her breast. He could hear her breathing change, feel the need in her grow, as it grew in him.

"Oh, baby," he murmured as his mouth grew hard on hers and his big hand tenderly swallowed her breast up whole, his palm rubbing gently at the hard little nub he found.

She caught her breath and moaned.

"This is sweet," he ground out. "Oh, God, it's sweet like sugar candy…"

He moved, turning her so that she was lying under him, full length, on the plush couch. He was on his side, his elbow taking his weight as his hand moved the bra out of his way so that he could touch her more easily.

Her body arched, helpless, as she reacted to the intimate tracing of his hand. She couldn't even pretend not to want it. She was aching, throbbing with hungers she'd never felt in her life. A faint whimper escaped the mouth that his was devouring.

"Yes," he whispered huskily. "It's not enough, is it? Try not to cry out," he added as he slid the sweater and bra up under her chin. "They might hear us…"

What he was saying didn't make sense until his mouth lowered, and she felt it cover and consume her whole breast, taking it slowly into the moist, warm darkness, his tongue sliding over the nipple and making her throb from head to toe.

She had to stifle a cry. She sobbed under the expert touch of his mouth, shivering, arching as she pleaded for something more, something to ease the ache that was slowly consuming her.

He began to suckle her, hungrier than he could ever remember being with a woman. She sobbed as if he was hurting her, but he knew he wasn't. His long, powerful leg inserted itself between both of hers in the slacks she was wearing and began to move sensuously, making the hunger even worse.

He rolled over onto her completely, hesitating just long enough to open the buttons of his shirt and pull it apart over the thick hair that covered his muscular chest. When he went down against her, it was bare skin against bare skin, something she'd never felt.

Her arms went under the shirt, around him, her

hands digging into his bare back. Odd how it felt there, she thought dimly, because there was a definite depression, a coin-shaped one. But he was moving on her and she felt the power and heat of him, the sudden surge of his body that told her graphically how capable he was.

His mouth ground into hers. He groaned as he pushed between her long legs and right against the heart of her in that soft fork of her body. She lifted up, shivering, and he moved roughly on her, feeling the passion burn him alive.

But his mind froze the passion as he realized how innocent she was. This was wrong. He could live with it, he could love it, but it would shame her, make her feel soiled. He couldn't do that to her. He couldn't, even if it was agony to stop.

He rolled over, shivering, and pulled her hard against his side. "Don't move," he whispered unsteadily. "Just lie still. Please, honey. Help me. I hurt like hell!"

She managed that, just. She was on fire and he'd stopped. Why had he stopped? She wanted him so desperately, just as desperately as he wanted her.

But sanity slowly returned. Was this what she really wanted, to have sex with a man on a sofa in a room with an unlocked door, a man to whom she had no real ties except physical ones? She was religious. She didn't believe in sex before marriage. But she wanted Mikey. She wanted him so badly that she'd have given in right here, without a single protest. In fact, she'd done that. But he'd stopped. She could feel how difficult it had been for him to do that. His body was shaking with unfulfilled needs. Now she felt guilty that she'd let it go so far. How would she have felt afterward? She didn't even know how to protect herself. What if she'd become pregnant? How would she live with that in a small town where everybody knew her, and knew that the only man she'd kept company with in recent years was the one lying so stiffly beside her right now? It would be no secret who the father was. Mikey had a casino in Las Vegas. He was a big-city man. It was highly unlikely that he'd throw all that up to live in a little town like Jacobsville with a woman who might end up an invalid in a very few years.

Besides that, he had a past, and bad men were after him because of a man he worked with, who was hiding from assassins. This was a terrible time to start an affair. In fact, she had to admit she wasn't the sort of woman who could even have an affair. It just wasn't like her, despite her aching hunger for Mikey and the violent attachment that she felt to him.

He was breathing easier now. He stretched and laughed softly when he felt her breasts against his bare rib cage.

"Well, that was a damned near thing," he whispered as he turned over, rolled her onto her back, and looked at her pretty firm pink breasts with their hard, dusky crowns. He touched them very gently. "I didn't want to stop."

"We're on a sofa," she began, flushing.

"Honey, all I had to do was push your pants down and go into you," he whispered blatantly, smiling at her expression. "It wouldn't have taken three minutes, as hot as I was. That's how easy it would have been. You didn't realize, did you?"

She caught her breath. "Not really," she confessed. "I haven't ever…"

"I noticed." He bent and brushed his mouth over her bare breasts. "God, woman, you're so beautiful," he whispered. "I'll dream of you every night of my life after this!"

"You will?" She thought how comfortable she was with him, how easily they'd slipped into intimacy. It felt so right. She wasn't even embarrassed.

He chuckled. "Yes, I will." He lifted his head and drew in a breath. "When all this is over, you and I are going to sit down and have a very serious talk." He brushed back her damp, disheveled hair. "Very serious."

She smiled slowly, her heart lifting. "Okay."

He laughed. "Everything's so easy with you, Bernie," he said, touching her cheek gently. "You never make waves, do you?"

"Not much, no."

"I love that about you," he said. "I feel at ease with you. Safe."

"I feel that way with you, too."

His big hand brushed tenderly over her breasts. "I guess we should put our clothes back on and watch the movie," he said with a sigh.

She nodded.

He pulled her up beside him, but before she could pull her sweater and bra back down, he turned her into his lap and pulled her inside his shirt, shivering as he felt her bare skin rub gently over his. His arms contracted hungrily and he held her, rocking her, in a blistering silence of passion.

"You'd do it with me, wouldn't you?" he whispered at her ear.

"Yes," she replied in a husky, shaky little voice.

"I don't even have anything to use," he confessed gruffly. He held her even closer. "You know what? I don't think I'd mind."

"You wouldn't?"

His hand went to the base of her spine, and he rubbed her against the hardness of him, holding her there firmly. "I like babies," he whispered.

She shivered. "Oh, Mikey," she sobbed, and her arms tightened.

He shivered, too. "Oh, God, I've got to get up and lock the door," he groaned. "On the sofa, on the damned carpet, against a wall—I have to have you, right now!"

"Yes," she whimpered, pushing closer. "Yes!"

He eased her away from him, his eyes blazing as he looked at her breasts. "I'll lock the door..." he said.

Just then, footsteps sounded down the wood floor of the hall and there was a sudden knock at the door.

"How's the movie going?" Sari called.

Mikey and Bernie looked at each other in a moment of shocked embarrassment while they waited for that doorknob to turn...

Chapter Nine

"Just a sec!" Mikey called in a strained, deep voice.

There was a muffled laugh from the door. "Mandy's got more coffee. Come on out when your movie finishes."

"We will. Thanks!" he called back.

The footsteps withdrew.

He let out the breath he'd been holding. Bernie sat beside him as if in a daze, her top still up around her neck, her breasts pressed hard into the thick hair on Mikey's broad chest. He looked down at her with wonder.

"I guess the jig would have been up if Sari had opened that door," he laughed.

She smiled dreamily up at him. "I guess."

He drew in a hard breath. "I suppose we'd better stop while we're ahead." He drew back and looked down at her bare breasts with fascination. "Over the years, I've seen a lot of women undressed," he murmured. "But none of them were half as beautiful as you are, honey." He stroked her soft, firm breast and leaned down, putting his lips reverently to it. "I'll live on this my whole life."

Her heart skipped. She just looked at him with everything she felt for him in her green eyes. His jaw clenched. He still wanted her, now more than ever. But he managed some control as he pulled down the bra and fastened it, then drew the sweater down over her waist.

She smiled and fastened the buttons of his shirt. He looked rumpled and his hair was mussed from her hands in it. She loved the way he looked. He was a little flushed, too, and his dark eyes danced as they met hers.

"You'd like Vegas," he said. "For visits, anyway, it's an exciting place. Plenty of music and neon lights. An oasis in the desert."

She put her hands on his chest, over the buttoned shirt. "I don't guess you'd like a little Texas town that draws the sidewalks in at dusk," she said without meeting his eyes.

"I'd like wherever you called home, Bernie," he said solemnly. "We come from different places. But that doesn't mean both of us can't adapt to something else, even if it's just for a little while." He bent and kissed her very softly. "I didn't want to stop. You go to my head like whiskey. It was like sailing on the clouds."

She laughed and pressed close. "For me, too."

His arms contracted, holding her close and rocking

her. "We'd better finish watching the movie. There may be a quiz after."

She laughed with pure delight. "Okay."

He drew her gently down beside him and clasped her hand tight in his. They watched the screen until the credits came on. Mikey turned off the entertainment center and drew Bernie along with him out the door and into the kitchen.

Paul and Sari looked up as they came into the room. Both were grinning.

"Yeah, we got a little friendly," Mikey said defensively. "It was me, mostly."

"It was me, too," she said, and smiled up at him.

"You don't need to excuse anything to us," Paul chuckled. "We've only been married three years."

"He means, we're still on our honeymoon," Sari teased. "So how about that coffee?"

"Sounds lovely," Bernie said, and stars were in the eyes she turned toward Mikey, who looked like a cat who'd just eaten a canary.

That expression went along with Bernie to work the following Monday, where Jessie saw it and grew sarcastic and insulting.

"We all heard about you and Mikey going over to his cousin's place. Some mansion," Jessie drawled sarcastically, glancing at Sari as she paused by Bernie's desk. "Got your eyes on that nice rich fish, don't you? But do you think a little hick like you could land a man that sophisticated?"

Bernie's face flamed, but she didn't back down.

"Backgrounds don't make much difference when people have feelings for one another," she said.

"As if he'd have feelings for you," Jessie said with a laugh. "I don't know him personally, but I know about him. He's had women who were movie stars, and debutantes and millionaires' daughters. He's not likely to take up with a woman who's looking at a wheelchair a few years down the road."

"That's enough," Sari said icily, standing up. "One more word and Mr. Kemp is going to get an earful."

Jessie knew when to quit. She shrugged. "Just stating facts, that's all."

"Ooh, somebody's so jealous she can't stand it," Olivia drawled with an amused look at Jessie. "What's the matter, sweetie, did he slap you down over at the courthouse and you're getting even?"

Jessie actually flushed. 'He did not," she spit. "I could have him if I wanted him."

"Do be my guest and try," Olivia taunted. "We heard that you made him sick."

Jessie was almost vibrating by now. She started to speak just as Mr. Kemp's door opened and he came out. She went quickly to her desk with a forced smile at the boss and pretended to work.

Kemp, no fool, looked from Bernie's flushed face to Sari's angry one and drew a conclusion. He didn't say a word, but the look he gave an oblivious Jessie wasn't one that would have encouraged her about her longevity in this office.

Glory Ramirez came in the door, a little fatigued.

"Court is bound over until tomorrow," she told Mr. Kemp. Glory was an assistant DA, like Sari.

"Does it look like the jury will convict?" Sari asked.

Glory made a face. "Who knows what a jury will do?" she asked with a sigh. "I hope I'm good enough to put this guy away. He lured a fourteen-year-old girl in with promises of true love and she fell for it. He's thirty-five," she added coldly.

"What a mess," Sari said.

"It's worse than that. She's pregnant," Glory said.

"Oh, that's no problem," Jessie laughed. "She can just go to a clinic and have them take it out."

"She and her people are deeply religious," Glory replied. "Not everybody thinks of termination as birth control, Jessie."

There was a whip in her voice. The other women knew why. Glory had lost her first baby after a horrible fight with her husband when they were first married, before they really knew much about each other. It had taken her two years to get pregnant again. She and Rodrigo had one child, a boy, and Glory's precarious health made another unlikely. Her blood pressure was extremely high and she'd already had angioplasty for a blocked artery that had caused a mild heart attack.

"You people take everything so seriously," Jessie muttered.

"Babies are serious business," Mr. Kemp broke in. Everybody except Jessie knew that he'd been in love and engaged, and his fiancée had died after a local woman spiked her drink with a drug. The fiancée had been pregnant at the time, and the child died with her.

"Babies are a nuisance. They cry and keep every-body upset, and you never get your waistline back again. I'd never want one," Jessie said.

"I would," Bernie said on a long, happy sigh.

"Good luck with that, in your physical condition," Jessie said sarcastically.

"If I could have a child, with my blood pressure, there's no reason Bernie couldn't have one with her limitations."

Bernie smiled at her. "Thanks."

"Not a chance I'd take," Jessie muttered.

"Thank you for your input, Miss Tennison, and how about that call I asked you to make half an hour ago to the DA in Bexar County on the Ramsey matter?" Kemp asked shortly.

Jessie flustered. "Oh. Sorry. I forgot. I'll get him for you right now, Mr. Kemp!"

Kemp gave her an angry glance, smiled at the other women and went back into his office.

Bernie went to lunch at Barbara's Café and there was Mikey, holding down a table for them. He got up as she joined him, after she'd given her order and paid for it.

"I could have gotten the tab, honey," he said.

"I can pay for my own stuff," she teased. "But thanks for the thought."

His hand slid over hers and held it tight. "You don't look so good. Bad morning?"

"Sort of," she said. "But it's improving already," she added with a loving glance at his handsome face.

He grinned. "That's better. I like it when you're happy."

"I usually am." She didn't mention the confrontation with Jessie or the woman's harsh words. She pushed them to the back of her mind while she and Mikey had nice pieces of roast beef with perfect mashed potatoes and gravy and home-cooked green beans.

"This is so good," she sighed. "I love to cook, but it's hard for me to stand for long periods of time. Still, I used to do it when I lived at home with my parents."

"We were going to talk last night," he mused.

She flushed.

He laughed sensuously. "We didn't do a whole lot of talking, though, did we, baby," he whispered. "It's hard to think of things like that when I'm with you. I just go nuts when I touch you."

"I go nuts, too," she whispered back, and her face colored even more as she looked at his mouth and re-called the havoc it could create suckling at her breast. She caught her breath just with the memory of how it had felt.

"Oh, this won't do," Mikey said, and shifted uncom-fortably. "We'd better not think too much about last night. Especially in a roomful of people."

She laughed softly.

He laughed, too.

"What sweet memories we're making, honey," he murmured as he forced himself to go back to his roast beef. "And we'll make plenty more, I promise you."

"You still have your shadow, I see," she replied under

her breath, glancing out the front window at the black sedan parked there.

"They're being careful. After all, one guy almost got by them." He made a face. "It makes me wish I'd made fewer enemies along the way. This isn't the first time I've had somebody come after me over territory."

She was looking at him with open curiosity.

"What is it?" he asked.

"Nothing much. Just… Well, there's a coin-shaped depression in your back," she began. "I felt it last night."

"Noticed, did you?" He wasn't offended. He just smiled. "Yeah, I caught a bullet there when I was overseas in the Middle East. Punctured my lung and almost killed me, but I survived."

"I'm so glad you did," she said demurely, and she was unspeakably grateful that it had happened in a combat zone and not as a result of conflict with gangsters. He spoke of that world as if he knew it very well. Certainly he had to, if he was mixed up with a Mafia don whom he was protecting. It made her just a little uneasy. She didn't know much about organized crime. What she'd seen in movies and read in books was unlikely to be a mirror of the real thing. That word Mikey had used, *omertà*, she'd seen it in print somewhere. She couldn't recall where. She was going to do a search on Google when she got home that night, just to see if she could find the connection. No need to tell Mikey. She looked at him with hungry eyes that she couldn't help. He was becoming the most important thing in her life.

But what if Jessie was right? Mikey was rich and sophisticated. Yes, he liked going out with her and kissing her, but that wasn't a future. She knew some gangsters married, but most of them seemed to just live together. Or so she thought. And she couldn't do that.

It would break her heart if Mikey didn't feel the same way she did. If he was only playing with her, she was going to die.

"Hey, what's wrong?" he asked. "You look tragic."

She forced a smile. "It's been a long morning, that's all," she said brightly. "Lots of people breaking the law. Of course, that's not a bad thing for us."

"Not at all." He looked up and his dark eyes sparked.

Bernie followed his gaze and there was Jessie, just picking up a salad and coffee at the checkout. It was on a tray, which meant she wasn't leaving.

"The bubonic plague has arrived," Mikey muttered.

"Well, hi there, Bernie. I didn't know you were coming here for lunch. And Mikey, how's it going with you?" she added, almost purring.

He looked up at her with cold eyes and took a minute to answer. "We're having a private conversation, if you don't mind."

Jessie shrugged. "Well, excuse me, I'm sure," she drawled. She went to a table nearby, at the window, and put down her food.

Bernie was crestfallen. She'd hoped to have a nice quiet lunch with Mikey, but Jessie was already staring at them. Cooking up plots. Bernie was certain that the woman was searching for ways to split her from Mikey, because Mikey was rich and Jessie wanted him.

"Don't look like that," Mikey said, smiling at her. "She's trying to upset you. Don't let her."

"She really likes you," Bernie said, almost choking on the words.

"It isn't mutual."

The way he looked at her sent all her fears flying away. She smiled slowly. So did he. The rest of the world faded away until there were just the two of them.

They didn't look in Jessie's direction at all. She glared at both of them the whole time. She didn't stop even when they were walking out of the café.

"If looks could kill," Bernie said on a heavy sigh when they were back on the street.

"Why doesn't Kemp fire her?" he asked abruptly.

"I think he'd like to, but he has to have a reason that will hold up in court."

"Lawyers," he muttered.

She laughed. "You sound like one of the men we prosecuted for theft. He was sure that lawyers were all bound for a fiery end."

His hand caught hers. "I've gone my rounds with prosecutors," he mused as they walked toward her office.

"You have?" she asked, curious.

He looked down at her solemnly. "We really are going to have to have a talk," he told her. "There are things about me that you need to know."

She drew in a long breath. "There are things about me you need to know, too."

"Come over for lunch Sunday," he invited. "Paulie said Sari was going to ask you, anyway. We can walk down through the woods and talk without people watching us all the time."

"Would you be safe if we did that?" she worried. "I mean, snipers love deserted places, don't they?"

He chuckled. "The one who's watching me surely does," he pointed out.

"Oh! I forgot."

He grinned. "I'm glad. I don't want you upset. I can take care of myself, honey. I've been in worse jams than this. I'll tell you about it, Sunday." He paused and turned toward her. "You think you can live with my past. I'm not sure you can. But I'll leave the decision up to you."

"You undervalue yourself," she said, searching his dark eyes. "I said it wouldn't matter. I meant it."

He smiled and touched her cheek gently. "You think it wouldn't," he said sadly. "That may not be the case."

"You can tell me Sunday."

"And there you both are again," Jessie said from behind them.

"Yeah," Mikey said, glaring at her.

She made a face and went past them into the office, slamming the door behind her.

"Sore loser," he muttered after her.

Bernie smiled. It made her feel good that Mikey preferred her to the beautiful woman who'd just gone past them. She felt valued.

"Idiot," he whispered. "You're worth ten of a woman like that." His head jerked toward the office. "She's anybody's. She'll play up to a man for what he's got, nothing else. Women like that are after hard cash, not love."

"I don't care about money," Bernie said.

"I know that. It's one of your best traits, and you've got a lot of them."

"Me?" she laughed. "I'm just ordinary." She drew in a breath. "You know, I have flares in the winter," she began. "I spend a lot of time in bed…"

He put his forefinger over her lips. "That won't matter, either. You nursed me through one of the worst headaches I've ever had. If you get down, I'll take care of you," he added huskily.

Tears stung her eyes. She lowered them to his broad chest.

"Don't cry," he whispered. "People will think I'm being mean to you."

She laughed. "Sorry. It's just that I've never really had anybody take care of me, not since my father died."

"I don't want to be your dad," he pointed out. He frowned. "You know, Bernie, I'm a lot older than you."

"Bosh," she mused, looking up into his face. "You'll never be old. Not to me."

His breath caught in his throat. He looked around. Cars everywhere. People on the sidewalks. Her boss, coming toward them.

"Oh, damn," he said under his breath.

Her eyebrows arched. "What?"

"Bernie, I want to kiss you so badly that it hurts and we're surrounded by people. Damned people!"

She grinned up at him. "There's Sunday," she teased.

He pursed his lips. His dark eyes twinkled. "Yeah. There's Sunday."

"Lunchtime's almost over, Bernie," Kemp teased as he came up beside them. "Back to boring routine."

"It's never boring, Mr. Kemp," she said, and meant it. "Tedious and maddening, but never boring!"

He grinned, nodded to Mikey, and went inside the building.

"I'd better go in. When?" she asked. "Sunday, I mean."

"About eleven suit you?"

She nodded. "That sounds great."

"I won't see you for a couple of days," he said. "I've got some people to see up in San Antonio. Santi and I have a room reserved for it. But I'll be here to pick you up Sunday, okay? And tell Mrs. Brown not to rent out my room while I'm gone!"

"I will, but she never would. She thinks you're terrific. So do the other boarders." She lowered her eyes to his chest. "So do I."

He bent and brushed a kiss over her forehead. "I think you're terrific, too, kid," he whispered. "Now go to work before I wrestle you down in the grass over there and do what I'm aching to do!"

Her breath caught. "It's in public view!"

"So would we be, and they'd be snapping pictures for the local paper, too," he assured her. "See you Sunday, honey. Be careful. Don't go out at night for any reason at all. You're being watched, but don't take chances. I couldn't live if anything happened to you." He touched her cheek and walked away before she could get the words out that she'd wanted to say.

No matter, she told herself. She could recite them on Sunday.

Jessie was wary of Sari and Glory, so she kept her hot words to herself. But just before quitting time, she stopped by Bernie when the other women were getting their coats and leaned close.

"You think he's hooked? You just wait," she threatened softly. "There's never been a man I couldn't get!"

And before Bernie could say a word, she was out the door and gone.

Bernie was agonizing over what she was going to have to tell Mikey on Sunday. She knew that he had a past, and she was sure she could live with whatever it was. But she wasn't so sure that he could live, not only with her disability issues, but with what had happened in her family. It was so horrible that she never spoke of it. Only a few people in Jacobsville knew. Her father was a good man, a kind man, who was wonderful to his daughter. But her grandfather had been a different story. He'd been notorious, in fact, and the story was so gruesome that it was fodder for the tabloids for the better part of a month.

None of that was Bernie's fault. She'd only been involved because he was part of her family, but it stung just the same. She felt dirty because of it. There had been survivors who were outraged. Her father had been targeted by one. Only the quick arrival of the sheriff's department had saved Bernie and her dad, because the man had been armed. She couldn't even blame him. The grief must have been horrible. But her father was no more responsible for it than Bernie was. It was just that the survivors couldn't get to the people responsible, so they went after the people who were left.

That had eventually blown over. Tempers cooled,

people went back to church and remembered that part of their religious faith was the very difficult tenet of forgiveness for even the most horrible crimes. Bernie and her dad moved from Floresville back to Jacobsville, and distance helped. But that didn't mean that Bernie might not be a target in the future from some other relative who was frustrated by not having a means of vengeance.

She'd have to tell Mikey that. She'd also have to make him understand about her illness. There was no cure for rheumatoid arthritis. There were many treatments, most of which worked, but the most useful were beyond Bernie's pocket. Even with them, she would still have flares, days when she couldn't work at all. And because the drugs required worked at lowering her immune system to fight the RA, she was more disposed to illness than healthy people. She had bad lungs and often had respiratory infections. Mikey had to understand that just an occasional flare was the least of her health issues.

If he still wanted her after all that, well, it would make him a man in a million. Her family's notoriety was going to make things more complicated.

But it might work out, she told herself. They might actually be able to make it work, if they could keep Jessie at bay. She was an odd sort of person, very narcissistic and pretty horrible. She didn't feel compassion and she had an acid tongue. What in the world was she doing in a small town like Jacobsville when she was obviously more suited to big cities? It was a puzzle.

There was a cold rain on Friday afternoon just as Bernie was getting ready to go home. She hadn't worn a raincoat or brought an umbrella, and it was pouring outside. Even in south Texas, it could get pretty cold in autumn.

"Let me drop you off at your boardinghouse, Bernie," Sari offered. "You'll get soaked going home and you'll be sick."

"Yes, you have to stay well or Mikey won't be able to take you anyplace, will he, sweetie?" Jessie purred as she passed them outside, her umbrella raised.

"One day," Sari said with venom, and glared at the other woman.

Jessie made a harrumphing sound in her throat and went on down the street to where her car was parked. Strangely, it was an expensive foreign one. How could she afford that on what she made as a stenographer and receptionist for the local DA, Sari wondered.

"You should have a car," Sari chided gently as the limousine driver started off down the street with his two passengers in back.

"They break down," Bernie said with a smile. "I can't afford to run one. And I can mostly walk to work, except when I'm having flares. Then I get a cab."

"You can always ride with me," Sari said. "Anytime you need to."

"Thanks," Bernie said. "But I do okay."

Sari laughed and shook her head. "Honestly, you're the hardest person to do anything for."

"I guess so. Sorry."

"It's not a bad trait. Jessie would do anything for someone with money," she added harshly. "That woman makes my blood boil."

"Mikey can't stand her," Bernie said with a wicked little smile.

Sari laughed. "So he said. I guess he's seen that sort so much in his life that he hasn't got any interest in them anymore."

"He said that he was a bad man," Bernie mentioned.

"Some bad, some good, like all of us."

Bernie looked at her warmly. "I told him it wouldn't matter, whatever he'd done."

"That's like you," Sari replied. She studied the other woman quietly. "He'll tell you the truth. I know about it from Paul. He and Mikey both had hard lives as children. They grew up with people who weren't good role models. Mikey went the wrong way. I think he's trying to leave that behind him now. But…" She hesitated, noticing how Bernie hung on every word. "But he'll have to tell you the rest. And you'll have to make a choice." She paused. She didn't want to say it. "That choice may be harder than you think right now."

Bernie drew in a long breath. "It's too late for choices," she said softly. "He's my whole world, Sari. He's…everything."

Sari smiled. "Paul is mine. I understand. It's just… Well, Mikey will explain it to you," she finished.

Bernie studied her hands, poised on her purse in her lap. "He's mixed up somehow with organized crime, I think," she said without noting Sari's sudden alertness. "I watched *The Godfather*, so I sort of know about that stuff."

She didn't know anything, not a thing, about the harshness and the blood and the savagery with which

Mikey's associates did and could act. Sari didn't want to enlighten her, though. It was going to be up to Mikey. If Bernie truly loved him, they'd find a way to make it work.

"Paul says he's never seen Mikey so happy," Sari said, instead of voicing her thoughts.

Bernie beamed. "I've never been so happy, not in all my life." She looked at Sari. "You know all about my family, about what happened. Will Mikey be able to handle it? I mean, there are people who went after Daddy, when he was alive, because of what my grandfather did."

"Nobody's ever come after you, and nobody ever will. If they even try, we'll sic Mr. Kemp on them. He'll handle it. Okay?"

Bernie let out the breath she'd been holding. "Okay."

"And Mikey's the last person who'll blame you for something someone in your family did," she added.

"I was notorious for a while," Bernie said hesitantly.

"Only for a while, and never after you moved here with your dad," Sari added.

"I suppose so." She lowered her face. "I don't want Mikey to be ashamed of me."

"As if that would ever happen! Honestly, Bernie!" she laughed. "He's crazy about you. It won't matter."

Bernie smiled. "Okay."

"And the past doesn't matter. For either one of you."

"If I stay sick all the time, it may," Bernie voiced her other fear. "I've got a weak immune system already, and the medicines I have to take for RA make it even weaker. I get sick a lot, especially in cold weather."

"It won't matter," she said firmly. "Besides, Mikey could afford those outrageously expensive medicines that they think might help you," she added with a smile.

"As if I'd let him do that," Bernie began.

"Under certain circumstances, you would," Sari drawled, and laughed at the expression on her coworker's face. "Life is sweet. You're just finding that out."

"It's never been sweeter, in fact."

"So live one day at a time," Sari counseled, "and let tomorrow take care of itself."

"That sounds easy. It's not."

"Nothing is easy. But we get by. Right?"

"Right."

"And if Jessie makes one more snide remark about how unhealthy you are, I'm going to encourage Olivia to pour coffee on her head!"

"Oh, don't suggest that—Olivia would do it on a dare," Bernie laughed uproariously.

"I heard about the coffee incident after I got back from vacation this summer," Sari said mischievously. "Nobody had made coffee. Agent Murdock came to see the boss on a case, and he made coffee just for himself and turned off the pot. Olivia went to get herself a cup. It was barely lukewarm by then, but she thought she'd drink it anyway. She took a sip, spat it out, glared at Murdock, who was flushed by then, and she poured the whole carafe right over his head and his suit. Lucky it wasn't hot!"

"Mr. Kemp came out of his office to usher Agent Murdock in," Bernie recalled, laughing so hard she almost choked. "And when he saw Olivia with the empty pot and the full cup in Agent Murdock's hand, he put his hand over his mouth and went right back into his office and closed the door. I swear, he laughed for five minutes."

"What did Agent Murdock do?"

Bernie whistled. "He got up, in the ruins of his suit, stared at Olivia for a minute, and then poured the contents of his own coffee cup over her head."

"And?" Sari prompted.

"He walked out the door in a huff and she went home to change. We're still laughing about it. Except that when Agent Murdock comes through the door, they both pretend that the other one is invisible. It makes things interesting."

Sari just grinned.

Chapter Ten

Sunday morning, Mikey came by to pick up Bernie at Mrs. Brown's boardinghouse. He was preoccupied at first, frowning.

"What's wrong?" she asked gently. "Can I help?"

He turned toward her and smiled slowly, oblivious to Santi's quick and amused glance in the rearview mirror from the front seat. "There's that sweet compassion that I've hardly had in my whole life," he said. "You really are one in a million, kid."

She flushed. "So are you. But can I help?"

"You can listen, when we get to Paulie's house," he said. He glanced in the front seat. "And you can have the day off until I call you to take us home, Santi," he added with a grin. "You might go take in a movie."

"Not a bad idea, boss," Santi said with a big smile. "Thanks!"

He shrugged. "I'm not a bad guy."

Santi made a sarcastic noise, but Mikey ignored him. They got out at the front door of Paul's house, and Santi raised a hand and waved as he drove off.

Mikey held Bernie's hand tight in his and put his finger on the doorbell.

Before he could push it, the door opened. Sari and Paul welcomed them in.

"We have lunch," Sari announced. "Mandy made a macaroni and ginger and chicken salad, and sliced some fruit to go with it."

"That sounds wonderful," Bernie said.

"It does. Nobody cooks like Mandy," Mikey said.

"I heard that," Mandy called from the kitchen. "Come on in. I've almost got everything on the table."

She did. The place settings were immaculate, like the white linen napkins. Mikey pulled out a chair for Bernie and then one for himself.

Mandy came back in with a basket of blueberry muffins and put them on the table. "Who wants coffee?"

Every hand went up.

Mandy laughed. "That's what I figured," she mused. "Coming right up."

Bernie was a little self-conscious at first. She wasn't used to mansions and elaborate dining room place settings, and this was her first real meal with the Fiores. But the conversation and Mikey's attention thawed her out in no time at all.

"This is delicious," Bernie commented as she savored a bite of the chicken dish.

"We like it as a light meal," Sari said. "Neither of us likes anything heavy in the middle of the day. Or in the evening, for that matter."

"No wonder you're both so slender," Bernie teased.

"People in law enforcement have to be fast," Paul chuckled. "I had to run down a counterfeiter just last week," he added. "If I overeat, I lose my edge."

Mikey grinned at him. "Not likely," he commented. "You do okay, cousin."

"Sari says Jessie is giving you two a hard time," Paul noted.

Mikey's lip pulled down. "She's persistent, I'll give her that. But she has the appeal of a skunk on acid. Know what I mean?"

Paul laughed. "I do."

"Besides," Mikey said, his eyes on Bernie, "I have other interests."

Bernie beamed and almost spilled her coffee. Her heart was going so fast that it shook her blouse. Mikey noticed that and flashed her a wicked smile.

After lunch, Mikey took Bernie's hand and led her down the wooded path that eventually ended at the stables where the Grayling racehorses lived in luxury.

"I love it here," Bernie said, looking around at the leafless trees next to tall fir trees that were still green. "Fir trees are awesome."

"Yeah, they are," he agreed. "Out west, we've got Colorado blue spruce that go right up into the sky."

"Are they really blue, or is that just a description that stuck?"

"They're really blue," he replied. He stopped walking and turned to her. "Next time I go to Vegas, you can come with me. We'll go by way of Wyoming and have a look at Yellowstone and Old Faithful. It's a sight you'll never forget."

She hesitated.

He noticed that. "I have plans," he said softly. "First, I have to take the heat off Tony and get him out of the mess he's in. He's family, you see?" he asked, scowling. "It's loyalty. You take a solemn vow. You fulfill it. If you don't, there are terrible penalties. Nobody ever sells out anybody in his family. If he does, the penalty is unspeakable." He didn't add that he'd participated in such retribution. He had to confess as much as he could to her, but there were things he had to keep to himself.

She looked up at him with her heart in her eyes. "It won't matter," she said stubbornly.

He touched her cheek with the tips of his fingers. "Bernie, I've been involved with the mob since I was old enough to carry a piece. I've done things..." He hesitated. It had never really bothered him before. Now it was hard to reconcile what he'd done with what he wanted to do now. He drew in a breath. "You've watched *The Godfather* movies, haven't you?"

"Oh, yes. They're great movies," she said.

"You remember about the horse's head being in bed with the producer who wouldn't give the outfit's singer a job?"

She nodded.

"And the way Michael's older brother was murdered, a hit organized by a rival family?"

She felt cold chills down her spine. "Yes," she said huskily. "I remember that, too."

"Well, that was glossed-over stuff," he said flatly. "Family hits are just plain gore. You don't know what happened to Paulie, do you?"

She just shook her head.

"He had a wife and a little girl, before he came down here to work for old man Grayling as a security expert," he said. "Paulie was the only person in our whole family who went straight. He worked with the FBI in Jersey, and he shut down one of the minor crime bosses. He felt great about it. But when he went home that night, his wife and his little girl had been done with a shotgun."

Bernie put a hand to her mouth. "Oh, the poor man!" she exclaimed, shocked.

"He took years getting over it," he said. "Eventually, he fell in love with Sari, but he got cold feet and made some excuse to quit. It was three years before he came back. In the meantime, Sari's father had beaten the girls to within an inch of their lives. Sari blamed Paul and had nothing to do with him when he worked out of the FBI office in San Antonio. But she was in a hurricane down in the Bahamas. Paul thought she was dead, but he and Mandy went to bring her home. She turned up alive and they were married the same week. Paulie never got over losing his family, though. He blamed himself for pushing the crime boss too hard and going after his whole organization."

"What happened to the man who killed his first family?" she asked.

His face grew hard. "I knew a guy who was inside," he said shortly. "I took care of it."

She felt the blood drain out of her face. "You...?"

"I took care of it," he repeated quietly. "Yes. I have that kind of power. I worked my way up through the organization for years, to get to where I am now. I own one of the biggest casinos in Vegas and I'm filthy rich. I was arrested once on a murder charge, but I had witnesses swear I was nowhere near the scene of the crime. They had no real evidence, so they dropped the case."

She moved to a big oak tree and leaned back against it. This was news she hadn't anticipated, and it was shocking. She looked up into cold dark eyes.

"I'm so sorry, honey. I didn't want to have to confess how bad a man I am. But you had to know," he said. Inside, he was churning like storm clouds. He hadn't wanted to tell her these things, but he couldn't offer her a future without making her aware of the past. "There's more," he told her. "A lot more. But this is enough for now."

Her lips parted on a long breath. She looked at him helplessly. She loved him. He was a criminal. He would probably never give up that life. He'd told her graphically what the family he belonged to would do if they were betrayed.

"Omertà," she whispered heavily.

He moved closer. "Yeah. Omertà," he replied. "It's the code we live by. Or die by, if we betray anybody in our family. They don't just kill you. They kill everybody you love. It's like erasing your whole life."

She leaned her head back against the hard bark of the tree and just looked at him. She didn't understand what he wanted from her, why he was telling her something so personal.

"So that's the secret I keep," he said. "It's bad. It's horrible. But it's a part of my life that you have to understand if we go forward together. So. What secrets are you keeping?" he added in a tender voice.

She took a deep breath. "My grandfather owned a little store over in Floresville. He and my grandmother ran it. We noticed that Granddaddy was forgetful, and sometimes he had rages, when he just went wild over something he saw on television, or something a politician said. We overlooked it because we thought it was just the product of normal aging."

He moved closer. "But it wasn't?"

"It wasn't. One day, he was listening to what a politician said about the economy and new regulations that were going to go into effect. Granddaddy started yelling that those people needed to be killed, slaughtered."

She hesitated, then plowed ahead without looking at him. "Maybe he would have calmed down, but the mayor was in his store buying some hardware, and he and Granddaddy got into an argument about politics. They were completely opposite in their views. The mayor tried to calm my grandfather down, and he thought he had. My grandmother chided him for being so violent over just stupid politics. She said he needed to lie down for a while. Granddaddy didn't argue with her. He went out from behind the counter without a word. My grandmother was relieved, she thought he was over his anger. Not five minutes later, he came back into the front of the store with an automatic pistol." She swallowed hard. "He killed my grandmother and the mayor, and then he turned the gun on three customers and killed them, too. The survivors screamed and ran out of the store. A local policeman heard the screams and went into the store with his pistol drawn. Granddaddy shot him dead the minute he walked into the store. The police called in the SWAT team from San Antonio. Granddaddy was holed up in the store, and he wouldn't come out and give up his gun." She sighed. "Long story short, the SWAT team went in and shot my grandfather. He died on the way to the hospital. My mother was so ashamed and sick at what her father had done, so grieved at the loss of her mother and the forthcoming fury of the townspeople, that she locked herself in the bathroom and slashed her own throat with a razor blade. We thought she was taking a bath." Her eyes closed. "By the time we realized something was wrong and Daddy got the door open, it was much too late. She died."

"Oh, God," he said. "You poor kid!"

She bit her lower lip. "Daddy sold the house and moved us here. It was horrible, the aftermath. We were hated by so many people who lost loved ones that day. I didn't blame them, you know, but Daddy and I had nothing to do with what happened. Nothing at all."

He moved forward and pulled her into his arms, folding her close, rocking her while she cried. "And

I thought I'd had a hard life," he whispered at her ear. "Baby, I wish I'd known you then. Nobody would ever have hurt you!"

She pressed close, resting her wet cheek over his heart. "I thought you might not want anything else to do with me when you knew about what happened."

"Dopey girl," he murmured, and laughed softly. "I'm hooked. Haven't you noticed? Who do I hang around with all the time? Who do I take to movies and into rooms where we do naughty things together?"

She laughed through her tears. "Me, I guess."

"You." He drew in a long, slow breath. His arms tightened. "I pledged allegiance to Tony. I have to fulfill my vows. I can't let him die, whatever I have to do to save him."

"Family is more important than your own life, isn't it?"

"Yes." His breath was warm at her ear. "I'm mixed up in this in a bad way. I can't make commitments right now. But when it's over, when I clear Tony…"

She didn't move. Her eyes closed. "I told you," she whispered. "I meant it. It won't matter."

"God!" His mouth moved over hers and he kissed her with subdued passion, with pure hunger. He hadn't imagined that she could live with the things he'd done, that she could still want him after she knew them. She was an extraordinary woman. "Bernie," he said unsteadily, "you're the very breath in my body!"

She couldn't even find words to express what she felt, so she kissed him with her whole heart, her arms stealing up around his neck, her mouth answering his with the same hungry passion that he was showing her.

He groaned and his hands ran up and down her sides, his thumbs pressing under her breasts.

"Ahem."

Mikey lifted his head and stared at Bernie blankly. "What did you say?"

"I didn't say anything," she began.

"Ahem." It came again. Mikey frowned and felt around his lapel. There was a device that had been placed there in San Antonio. He glowered at it.

"Yes?" Mikey asked abruptly.

"I have a bead on you and quite frankly if you don't break that up, I'm going to have to leave you defenseless and go get several drinks of hard liquor."

Mikey's teeth ground together. "Damn it, Billings," he muttered.

"A lot of drinks," Billings continued. "Maybe a whole damned fifth. It's been a long dry spell and I have to watch you. Get it? Watch you."

Mikey drew a long breath and stared at Bernie with amused regret. "Okay. We'll go look at the horses."

"Good idea. Blakely's in there. You can drive him nuts!" There was a click and the device went silent.

Bernie was flushed and embarrassed.

"Hey," Mikey said, pushing back the unruly long, blond hair from her face. "Billings is right. This isn't the time or place."

"Did he hear all we said?" she worried.

"Not likely. He doesn't eavesdrop. I guess we were getting pretty heated, huh?" He laughed. "Okay. Let's behave." He caught her fingers and entangled them with his. "Let's go look at the pretty horses."

She laughed. Life was sweet. He didn't mind her past. She didn't mind his. This was a relationship with a future. She'd never been so certain of anything.

They wandered through the stables. There was a man in charge of the thoroughbreds. He explained them to Bernie.

"They're descended from three stallions imported into England in the seventeenth and eighteenth centuries, the beginning of their line. We won the Kentucky Derby with this fellow," he said, smiling as he approached the big stall where the racehorse lived. "He has his own pasture and he's at stud. We get fabulous amounts of money from his colts. He's a grand old fellow."

Bernie looked at him with awe. He was grand, elegant and handsome, and he knew it, too. "He's gorgeous," she said.

The stable manager chuckled. "We think so, too. He has a colt that was born just two months ago. It's down here."

He led them down the paved aisle to another stall, where a handsome young thoroughbred was playing with a big ball.

"Horses play?" Bernie exclaimed.

The manager laughed. "Of course. They're like puppies or toddlers at this age. When they hit adolescence, or the horse equivalent, that's when the problems start.

Right now, they're just children and it's a whole new world for them."

Bernie just watched the colt play, fascinated. "I've never been around horses much," she confessed. "We had a small ranch in Floresville where my people had a few head of beef cattle. There were a few horses for the cowboys, but I never rode one. I was afraid of them."

"Never let a horse know that," the manager told her. "They'll take advantage."

"I'm not likely to be put on a horse anytime soon," she assured him.

"If you ever did want to ride, we have a fifteen-year-old gelding, very gentle, who would be perfect for you. If you ever did," he added.

Mikey chuckled and pressed her fingers with his. "There may come a day," he said with a gentle smile at Bernie, who returned it.

"There may," she said.

They went back to the house.

"You're back soon," Sari commented.

"Yeah," Mikey said with a rueful smile. "Billings is a wet blanket."

"Chet Billings? You saw him?" she asked.

"No. We heard him. He's got this device on me," he added, indicating the electronic thing on his lapel.

"Oh. He talked to you?"

"He threatened to get drunk is what he did." Mikey looked at Bernie and sighed. "I guess there's no real privacy left on earth."

"Yes, there is. The conservatory is very nice, very

quiet and it has a door. However," she added mischievously, "not being stupid, I'll call you when supper is ready and I'll probably open the door to do it."

Mikey sighed. "Speak loudly, okay?" he teased.

Sari laughed. "Very loudly." She gave them a knowing look and went back into the kitchen, where she and Mandy were sharing coffee. "Do you want coffee?" she called over her shoulder.

"Later," Mikey said. "When supper's ready. Thanks, Sari," he added.

"I wasn't always married," Sari replied, and grinned.

Mikey took off the lapel pen, put it on a table in the hall and drew Bernie into the room with him. He closed the door behind him and, as an afterthought, locked it.

"Just so you know," he said as he pulled her gently into his arms, "we're big on innocence. Some people might call us reactionary, but we respect our women and we don't dishonor them. You get what I mean?"

He was telling her that he wouldn't let it go too far. She smiled. "I guess you know all about me."

His mouth brushed hers. "I know that you're an innocent, Bernie," he whispered. "It excites me and maddens me, all at once."

"Maddens you?"

"Obstacles are frustrating," he mused. He kissed her with slow, hungry brushes of his mouth, feeling hers follow it helplessly. "But we'll muddle through. When things get too hot, and they might, all you have to do is remind me that I promised not to let things go too far."

She laughed. "Okay."

He smiled as he kissed her again. "You make me hungry for things I never wanted before," he murmured as he maneuvered her onto the cushy sofa and came down beside her. "A home, a family, roots," he whispered. He had her blouse off and her bra unsnapped in seconds. "Belonging," he murmured as his mouth opened over her taut nipple and suddenly suckled her, hard.

She came right off the sofa, a tiny, shocked cry pulsing out of her throat, a sound she'd never heard from it before.

"Shh," he whispered gruffly. "They'll hear."

She bit her lower lip and pulled his head closer, her fingers spearing through his thick, wavy black hair as his mouth made magic on her body.

"Glory!" she moaned. "Mikey, do it harder," she whispered frantically. "Harder!"

"I'll hurt you," he groaned.

"No. You won't. Please…!"

He took all of her firm breast into his mouth and his tongue worked on the nipple until she was writhing wildly under the sudden heavy press of his body.

One big hand was under her hip, grinding her against the growing hardness of him, letting her feel his need. It was desperate.

She felt guilty. She was inciting him, and they couldn't be intimate. She remembered suddenly what he'd told her about heavy petting, that he could have the clothes out of the way and be inside her in less time than it would take to react.

She thought about feeling him inside her, and she shivered with the sudden need.

Her nails bit into the back of his head as she held it closer, arching so that he could feed more easily on her breast. She shivered rhythmically as he suckled her, harder and harder. All at once she arched and sobbed and felt a shaft of pleasure pierce her that was beyond anything she'd ever dreamed. She convulsed, shuddered, flew up into the clouds and exploded.

Then she cried, embarrassed. He cuddled her close, denying his starved body the release it begged for. "It's all right," he whispered. "It's natural, baby. It's all right."

"It really is? Natural, I mean?" she whispered brokenly.

He laughed softly. "That only happens to one woman in a hundred," he said. "Maybe one in a thousand. I've never seen it happen to a woman I was with." His mouth brushed over hers. "God, what a thrill it was! You've never felt it, have you?"

"Not...until now," she managed.

He drew in a rough breath. "I'm better than I thought I was," he teased.

She laughed. "You're better than I thought you were, and that's saying something."

He lifted his head and looked down at her bare breasts. "You know that you belong to me, don't you?" he asked, and met her eyes with his. They were solemn. "You're mine, Bernie."

She melted into the sofa under the hard, sweet pressure of his body. "Yes. I know it."

He moved over her, his body pressing her down. He fought his shirt out of the way so that his muscular hair-roughened chest was rubbing against her bare breasts. He shivered.

She did, too. "If you want to," she said unsteadily, "I will."

"Right here?" he asked huskily.

"Right here."

"You don't know how much I want to," he bit off.

She moved her hips just a tiny bit. "Oh, yes, I do," she said, feeling him swell even more.

"Baby," he whispered. He moved between her legs and pushed up, so that he was intimately pressed against the heart of her.

She sobbed, because it was beyond anything she'd felt before. Her legs moved apart, inviting him.

"It would have to be quick," he said gruffly. "Very quick. And it will probably hurt."

"I don't…care," she said unsteadily.

He kissed her softly, and his hand went under the band of her slacks, under her briefs. She caught his wrist, embarrassed.

He lifted his head. "You have to let me do this," he whispered, his voice shaken. "I have to know how careful I need to be with you. Okay?"

She bit her lip. "I've never…"

"I know that. But you belong to me."

She let her body relax, let the hardness of him fit against her so that it was heaven to feel. "Yes," she said, her voice tender, her eyes wide and rapt on his taut face.

His hand smoothed over her belly and he thought

of a baby who would look like her or like himself. He had something to use, but he didn't want to use it. And he didn't want to take her here in a rush, the way he'd taken women in his youth. She would need time, lots of time, and he couldn't give it to her if they went too far.

His fingers moved down. She hesitated and tightened as he suddenly began to probe where she was most a woman. She bit her lip hard enough to draw blood as he explored her intimately. Even loving him as she did, it was hard to give up control to another person.

He whispered, almost groaning as he drew his fingers back and smoothed them over her stomach, "It will hurt like hell, and I'm not sure I could even get through the barrier, you understand?"

"Oh!" She winced.

"Sorry." He rolled over onto his side and pulled her into his arms, grinding her breasts into his chest. "No, I'm sorry. I never meant to take it this far." His arms contracted. "God, Bernie, I want to get you pregnant so badly…!"

He kissed her shocked mouth and groaned again as he pushed her hips closer to his. "I want you. I want to go inside you, so deep, so hard, that you'll shoot up like a rocket!"

She flushed under the pressure of his hard mouth, moaning as she felt him move her rhythmically against his hips. "I'm so sorry…"

He managed a husky laugh. "Think of it as a chastity belt. It will keep me in line until we can make things legal."

She hid her face against his throat. Make it legal.

Could he mean that he wanted to marry her? She was so entranced that she didn't even hear footsteps in the hall.

Neither did Mikey, who was kissing her as if he couldn't manage to stop.

The hard, insistent knock on the door and the rattling of the locked doorknob broke them apart.

"Supper!" Sari called.

Mikey laughed. "Okay! We'll be right there."

"I have a master key, you know. It fits all the locks," Sari threatened.

Bernie went beet-red. Mikey just chuckled. "We're behaving, starting right now!"

There was a laugh outside the door. "Fair warning. Five minutes and I unlock the door."

"Got it!" Mikey called.

Footsteps retreated.

Mikey took one long, last look at Bernie's half-nude body and groaned. "I hate dressing you," he muttered, as he refastened her bra and pulled her blouse down.

"I hate dressing you, too," she teased as she buttoned his shirt again. "I love the way you look undressed."

"Yeah. I feel exactly the same way about you."

"You're not upset by what I told you?" she asked, worried.

He cocked his head and stared at her. "I've done things almost as bad as your grandfather," he said flatly. "I can't sit in judgment on somebody else. Not my business. But now that you know what my business is," he added quietly, "you have to decide if you can live with it. There's no way I'll give it up. I can't. It's for life."

She was beginning to realize that even though he

ran an honest gaming hotel in Las Vegas, he was firmly entrenched with a group that routinely broke the law. He could go to prison in certain circumstances. She'd have to be in the company of people who thought of crime as a way of life, an occupation. She'd be the outsider. Would the women in his organization hate her? And what about the women he'd had before her? Would they be around? Would they be like Jessie and make her life miserable?

"Deep thoughts, huh?" he asked quietly.

"Very deep." She drew in a breath. "Mikey, I'm not like you. I don't even jaywalk. My great-grandfather was a United States Marshal. I have a cousin who's a Texas Ranger. Law enforcement runs through my whole family."

"I see," he said heavily. "You don't think you could handle it."

"No!" She went close to him. "I'd be the outsider. The freak. They wouldn't accept me."

"Baloney," he mused. He smiled as he tangled his fingers in her hair. "You have no idea how much they'd accept you. They'd go places with you, protect you if you needed protection. They'd sit with you when you were sick, when you have flares. It's another whole world, baby. One you've never seen. It's violent, yes. But the people are just like anybody else. The women are a close-knit group, because there's always some danger involved that the men have to handle." He winced at her expression. "I don't know any other way of life, Bernie," he concluded. "I can't change what I am, what

I do." He shrugged. "I don't want to. If that's selfish, I'm selfish."

She pressed herself close to him, sliding her arms around him. "I can try," she whispered.

His heart jumped. It lifted as if a dark cloud had dissipated in the sunlight. His arms tightened around her. "That's all I ask," he said. "That's all I want."

She smiled and closed her eyes.

There was a click and the door opened. Sari looked in with pursed lips when they turned toward her. She chuckled. "I warned you," she said, lifting the key to show them. "Supper."

Mikey grinned. "We're right behind you."

"Yes," Bernie agreed.

Mikey linked her fingers with his and the two of them looked, to Sari, like two halves of a whole. She had no doubt that there would be a wedding in the future.

Bernie clung to his hand and smiled. She looked up at Mikey with wonder, with adoration.

He saw that look and it made him feel a foot taller. His fingers contracted gently around hers. She tightened her own grip. She'd never known such wonder, such joy. It spilled out around her like sunshine. She smiled. So did Mikey. They both knew where this was leading, now more than ever.

Chapter Eleven

Supper was as uproarious as lunch had been. Paul had a dozen stories of things that had happened to him in the course of his duties. Foremost among those stories was the one he'd heard from Sari about agent Murdock. He recited it for Mikey and chuckled at his cousin's amusement.

"I like Olivia," Mikey said. "She seems very nice."

"She is," Bernie agreed. "Mr. Kemp hired her so that there would be another paralegal in the office on the days I can't work," she added, and felt uncomfortable talking about her limitations.

"You do very well, considering your obstacles," Sari told her. "We don't think of you as handicapped, you know," she added. "You have a disability. Lots of people have them. Look at poor Glory. She had dangerously high blood pressure and a light heart attack. But she overcame that to work here, where she and her husband and little boy live."

"I'd love a little boy," Mikey said, glancing at Bernie, who flushed. "Or a little girl. I'll bet little girls are sweet."

Bernie laughed. "I was never sweet," she teased. "I got into so much trouble when I was small. The worst time was when I climbed into the corncrib and couldn't get out, and a king snake decided to come in with me. He was huge. Over six feet long. I was terrified. But he didn't strike at me or even threaten me. He just stretched out on the corn and looked at me."

"Probably hunting rodents," Sari remarked. "They love corn."

"Probably," Bernie agreed. "All in all, he was a very polite snake. He didn't even seem bothered when Daddy came to find me and lifted me out of the corncrib."

"He might also have just eaten a few rats and was feeling lazy," Paul chuckled.

"Equally possible," Bernie laughed.

"Well, I've got briefs to read," Sari said.

"And I've got cases to work," Paul added as they both got to their feet. "You two can watch movies or just sit in the conservatory and watch the plants grow. You're both always welcome. Anytime."

"Thanks, Paul," Bernie said.

Mikey echoed the sentiment.

They were left with Mandy, who started to clear away the dishes. "You two want coffee?" she asked with a warm smile.

"Not for me," Mikey said. "I don't sleep good. It keeps me awake."

"Me, too," Bernie said.

Mikey stood up and helped Bernie out of her chair. "I think we'll go watch Sari's plants grow for a while, if you don't mind."

"Help yourselves," she said with a knowing grin.

Mikey led Bernie into the conservatory and locked the door.

"Nobody's likely to try it, but who knows?" Mikey teased. He took Bernie into his arms and kissed her hungrily. "Dessert," he whispered. "Sweeter than cake."

"Sweeter than honey," she agreed on a moan.

He picked her up and sat down with her in his lap, kissing her all the while.

She didn't protest his hands under her blouse. He was so familiar to her now, so dear, that she welcomed anything he did.

He knew that, and it kept him honest. He didn't want to take advantage of an attraction she couldn't help. She was very innocent. It made his head spin, that lack of sophistication. He loved it.

He eased her blouse and bra down to her waist and unbuttoned his shirt, pulling her hungrily inside it.

"Oh, glory," she choked when she felt thick, soft hair and warm muscles against her bare breasts. Her face sank into his throat while he caressed her.

"We're good together," he whispered. "Better than I dreamed. God, I want you!"

Her arms tightened around his neck. "I want you, too," she whispered back.

His hands smoothed over her hard-tipped breasts. "We've talked around it," he said after a minute. "But not any particulars." His hands moved her away and he looked at her breasts with possession and appreciation. "You're beautiful like this, Bernie. It makes me hungry just to hold you. But this goes to my head like whiskey."

She arched backward, her body demanding, hungry, ignoring her mind's attempt to be sensible.

"This what you want, sweetheart?" he whispered, and his mouth swallowed up one small, taut breast almost whole.

She moaned and shivered.

"I thought so." His voice was rough, but his mouth was tender as he worked at the hard nipple slowly, tenderly, with a growing suction that very soon made her go stiff and then suddenly burst with pleasure that made her whole body convulse in his arms.

"God, I love this," he groaned against her breast. "I love that I can make you go off like a rocket when I suckle you!"

Her nails dug into him. It was a little embarrassing, but she was too exhausted with pleasure, with satisfaction, to protest. She shivered and clung to him in the aftermath. "I never felt anything like it in my whole life," she said brokenly. "It embarrasses me…"

His arms contracted. "Don't you dare be ashamed of something so beautiful," he whispered at her ear. "No two people ever belonged to each other more than we do right this minute, Bernie."

She swallowed, hard. "Do you feel that, too?"

He chuckled and turned her just a little, so that her

hips were pressed to that part of him that was male and very hard. "Do you feel this?"

"Mikey!" she protested.

"A man can't fake that, honey," he said at her ear. "It's as honest as the way you react when I put my mouth on you." He drew back and looked down at her with pure possession. "There's nobody in the world like you."

She reached up and touched his cheek. "Or like you," she said solemnly.

He bent his dark head and smoothed his mouth over her breast tenderly. He drew in a breath. "We need to talk."

"We are."

"We need to talk when we're both dressed," he said with a droll smile.

"Oh."

He put her clothes back on and buttoned his shirt. When they were calmer, he drew her onto the love seat and sat holding her hand.

"Bernie, I'm not proud of what I'm about to tell you. But there's more about me that you need to know." He drew in a breath. "My family has belonged to what's known to outsiders as La Cosa Nostra for three generations. My father died working for them. I've been with Tony Garza since I was sixteen. I don't know any other way of life."

"You mean, you work outside the law," she said very calmly.

"That's exactly what I mean." He studied her face. She was a little pale, but she wasn't trying to get away from him. "We're like normal people. We pay our taxes, go to church, work for charitable causes, all that stuff. We just earn our living in ways that aren't conven-tional."

"I told you that I watched *The Godfather* movies," she said.

He brushed her disheveled hair back from her face. "That was a sanitized version of what really goes on," he said after a minute. "I won't, I can't, tell you how brutal it can be. You don't ever quit. And you don't rat out your associates. There are deadly penalties for that. Remember what I told you about Paulie's family?"

She just nodded. Her eyes were sketching his hard face as if she were painting it.

"I could go to jail one day," he persisted. "I could die."

"A meteor could land on the boardinghouse and take us all out," she said matter-of-factly. "Nobody is ever guaranteed even one more day."

He just looked at her.

"I'm not Italian," she said. "Would that make me an outsider?"

He smiled slowly. "The wives come from all sorts of backgrounds," he said, and noticed her flush at the word. "Some are American. Some are Italian and Span-ish, even Polish. But they have one thing in common and that's family. We all belong to each other. If you shared that life with me," he said, "you'd be part of it. You'd never be an outsider. And if anything happened, anything at all, you'd be taken care of as long as you live. That's how it works."

She bit her lower lip. She drew in a breath. "Mikey,

I won't get any better," she began. "There's no cure for what I have. They can control it with medicine, although I can't afford the kind that might make it easier. But they can't stop it. Eventually, I'll end up with twisted hands and feet, and even if I can walk with a cane at first, there's a good chance that one day I'll be in a wheelchair." She said it without a plea for pity. She just stated it as a fact.

He tilted her chin up. "I can live with your limitations. Can you live with my profession?"

She just nodded. She didn't say a word. She didn't have to.

He wrapped her up in his arms and just rocked her slowly, his face in her throat. They sat that way for a long time until there was a brief tap and the sound of a key in the lock.

Sari peered around the door and burst out laughing. "And I was afraid I'd have to run for my life when I opened this door…"

Mikey and Bernie both laughed.

Mikey got up and drew her up beside him. "We were talking about the future," he said, smiling. "It looks pretty sweet."

"Pretty sweet, indeed," Bernie said with a long sigh as she looked up at him.

"I'd better get her home," Mikey said. "She has to work tomorrow."

"I know. So do I," Sari wailed.

"There, there," Bernie comforted her. "But there's always next weekend!"

They all laughed.

* * *

Mikey took her back to the boardinghouse and left her at her door with a discreet kiss on her forehead because Mrs. Brown was lurking.

"It was a lovely day. Thank you," Bernie said.

"It was one of many to come," he replied. He smiled at her with his heart in his eyes. "See you in the morning, kid. Sweet dreams."

"Oh, they'll be sweet, all right," she whispered, and then flushed.

He wrinkled his nose at her and winked.

She watched him all the way down the hall before she went back into her room and closed the door.

Work was difficult. Bernie's happiness lit her up like a Christmas tree, and it showed. Olivia teased her. But Jessie watched and smoldered. She was furious that a plain little country girl like Bernie, one who was likely to end up living on disability, had attracted a man who could buy half a county with pocket change. Mikey was sophisticated, handsome and loaded. Jessie wanted him, and she couldn't get to first base. He avoided her like the plague when he was in town.

There had to be some way she could get him out of Bernie's life so that she had a chance with him. Being rude and unpleasant didn't do any good. But if she could play one of them against the other while pretending to turn over a new leaf... Well, that was a promising idea. She began to plot ways to accomplish it.

Her first step was to stop being abrasive to the other women in the office. She toned down her bad attitude and took on her share of the work instead of avoiding it. She offered to bring coffee to Olivia and Bernie when they were swamped with paperwork, and she even brought lunch back for them once.

Everyone was surprised, even Mr. Kemp, who actually praised Jessie for her changed attitude.

Nothing had changed at all except that Jessie was playing a new game. But she smiled and did her best to look humble. She even apologized for the way she'd behaved before. It was hard being a city girl in a small Texas town, she explained to the other women. She'd always had to fight to get ahead, where she'd come from, and it was difficult to stop. But she wanted to fit in. She was going to try harder. The other women in the office, suspecting nothing, warmed to her.

And Jessie just smiled to herself. So far so good, she thought. She even lost her fear of being fired, which she couldn't afford just now. She had a job to do. So she smiled and answered the phone and stopped flirting with rich men.

Bernie mentioned the changed attitude to Mikey on one of their dates, and he laughed. Bernie, he commented, was rubbing off on the other woman. He was happy to see it. So the next time he came across Jessie in the courthouse, where he'd gone with Paul to talk to a judge, he smiled and was pleasant to her.

Several days later, there was a complication. Bernie was walking back to the boardinghouse from work, after refusing a ride from Glory, and a car ran off the road, up onto the curb, and missed her by a few feet.

It sped away while she was getting back onto her feet. She was badly shaken. She picked up her pocketbook and her cane, and stood shivering while she tried to catch her breath. Had it been a car that just lost control, or was it deliberate? She worried the question all the way home.

She'd have told Mikey, but he was out of town on business. He'd mentioned at the boardinghouse that he had to meet with one of the deputy marshals in San Antonio, but he'd be back in time for a date they'd arranged for Saturday. He and Bernie had planned a sightseeing trip to San Antonio because they had plenty of chaperones. Bernie had always wanted to go through the Alamo, but there had never been time since she'd been an adult. Now she looked forward to seeing that part of Texas history with the love of her life.

Mikey picked her up in the limo, with Santi at the wheel, just after she got off work at one o'clock on Saturday. She was wearing a beige sweater and skirt with flats and a cane that matched her outfit.

"Color coordination, huh?" Mikey teased as he helped her into the back seat and climbed in beside her.

"I like things to match," she teased.

He indicated the beige suit he was wearing with a white shirt and a brown paisley tie. "And so we do," he laughed.

She grinned. "We do, indeed."

"I wanted to see the Alamo when I was here last time, when Merrie was in trouble. But I never had the time. You Texans are pretty proud of it, aren't you?"

She nodded. "We really are."

He sighed. "I don't know much about history, even in Jersey," he commented. "Well, maybe one sort of history, but it's not told in polite company," he chuckled.

"I won't ask," she returned, smiling up at him.

"You haven't carried the cane lately, until today," he pointed out. "Having a flare?"

"Well, not really. I had a fall the other day on my way home from work."

He scowled. "A fall?"

She nodded. She bit her lower lip. She hadn't wanted to mention it. "A driver lost control of his car and it came up on the curb where I was walking. It missed me by several feet," she added.

"What sort of car?" he asked with barely concealed anger.

She blinked. "That's the thing, I really didn't have time to notice. I fell and, while I was getting up, it sped away."

"Big car, small?"

She frowned. "Medium."

"What color?"

She tried to remember what it had looked like. "I think it was dark. Not black, but not a colored car, like blue or red or anything."

He looked troubled. He pulled out his cell phone and texted a message to someone. She couldn't tell who.

"I don't think it was deliberate, Mikey," she added softly. "I mean, it didn't come right at me."

"Warnings don't," he said curtly. He typed some more.

Her heart jumped. He was thinking it might be his

enemy. But she was thinking it might be an enemy of her family, someone who'd tracked down the one surviving member and tried to avenge a loved one. It wouldn't be the first time it had happened. That worried her.

He put down the phone. "I wish you'd told me sooner," he said. His big hand reached out and touched her long hair lightly. "I couldn't bear it if anything happened to you, Bernie."

She beamed.

He caught her hand in his and held it tight. He leaned back against the seat, clearly concerned. "I sent a text to Paulie. Did you tell Sari about it?"

"No," she said. "She's been in court all week and then she had to go and depose a witness in an assault case she's prosecuting. And honestly, we've been pretty busy at work all week, too."

He was weighing it in his mind. He knew Cotillo was after him, that the man could also target Bernie. But it wasn't the way Cotillo did business. He'd already sent a cleaner after Mikey. That was how he handled threats. Aiming a car at a woman and missing her by several feet, that wasn't the way a man used to violence did business.

Bernie's hand in his tightened. "Maybe it was just an accident," she said. "People do lose control of their cars for all sorts of reasons."

"Yeah. They do. But it's suspicious."

She leaned her head on his shoulder and laughed. "That's you. Suspicious."

He kissed the top of her head. "I've spent my whole

life being suspicious. It's why I'm still alive, kid," he teased.

"I suppose so." She looked up into his eyes. "It could be somebody from my own past, from my family's past, still hunting vengeance, you know. Daddy was almost killed once for it."

"How many years ago was that?" he asked.

"Well, quite a few," she recalled.

"It's more likely that it's somebody connected to me," he said. "But in any case, the feds will hash it out." He slid an arm around her shoulders. "Your coworker Jessie has changed," he commented. "Even Paulie said Sari's talking about it." He glanced down at her. "Is she pretending?"

She laughed. "You really are suspicious. She said that it was hard to come from the city and get used to a small town, that she was used to having to be on her guard with people."

"Did she say what city?"

She shook her head. "She came down here from San Antonio. But she's originally from somewhere up north, I think, like her friend Billie who works at the courthouse. They room together."

He frowned. He hadn't considered that the two of them were both from up north. "Have they been here a long time?"

"Not really. Jessie's only been here a few weeks. I believe she and her friend moved from San Antonio together. Billie knew somebody at the courthouse who wanted a temporary secretary after his got sick. They know the cook at Barbara's, too—he's from New Jersey."

Mikey felt his heart stop and start again. He hadn't been asking the right questions. Neither had Paulie. What if the two women and the cook were part of Cotillo's bunch? If nothing else, the timing was right. He was going to suggest to Paulie that they get somebody to keep an eye on those three as well. It was too convenient to be a coincidence.

"You're worried," she said, breaking into his thoughts.

He smiled at her. "Nothing major," he said. "Just thinking. We're going to see the Alamo. No worries for today, at least. Okay?"

She grinned. "Okay!"

They walked around the old fort like tourists, holding hands and watching leaves drift down out of the trees.

"It's going to be Halloween next week," he pointed out.

She grinned at him. "Are we going trick-or-treating, then?"

He burst out laughing. "Oh, that would be one for the books, wouldn't it?"

"I used to go when I was a little girl," she recalled. "Mom and Dad would drive me up to some of the nice neighborhoods in San Antonio door-to-door so that I could get candy. We had only a couple of close neighbors, and they didn't celebrate it at all."

"Paulie and I went with a bunch of the guys from our neighborhood," Mikey recalled. "This one house, a little old lady always invited us in for hot chocolate. It was a hoot. She'd been a Hollywood agent in her younger days. She could tell some stories!"

"I'll bet!"

"I imagine kids in Jacobsville have a great time at Halloween. And the other holidays."

"They do. Christmas is the best time, though. They stretch garlands of holly and lights all over the streets and across them. There are Christmas trees everywhere, and the local toy store has trains running in the window." She sighed. "It's just magic."

He chuckled. His hand tightened on hers. "Grandma always made Christmas special for me and Paulie," he said. "Of course, we had to go with her to midnight mass every Christmas Eve and it went on for a couple of hours. You know how kids are. We squirmed and suffered, but we didn't dare complain. She was scary for a tiny little old lady," he added.

She smiled. "I know what you mean." Her eyes were sad. "My grandmother was so sweet. She was always baking for people who had family die and sitting with sick people. She was wonderful. My grandfather was violent and dangerous. Daddy said he'd been in trouble with the law a lot when he was a young man. But I never thought he'd do something so terrible."

"Listen, kid, lots of people do terrible things they never planned. Kids get on drugs and kill people. Old people get dementia and kill people. Alcoholics get behind the wheels of cars and kill people. I don't think most of them go out with the idea that they'll do harm. It just happens."

"I've never used drugs," she said.

He laughed softly. "Why am I not surprised?"

She leaned her head against his arm. "I'm predictable."

"Very. I love it," he whispered.

She drew in a long breath. "I've never been so happy in my whole life."

"Neither have I, baby," he said gently.

She looked up at him and he looked back, and the world vanished.

It took a car horn out in the street to snap them back to reality, and they both laughed.

They walked through the dark halls of the Alamo, paused at the door to the Long Barracks, looked at the graffiti on the walls where the last stand had been held. They were solemn as they filed into the gift shop for souvenirs.

"It's a sad history," she commented.

"Most history's sad," he returned. "Life is violent."

"I suppose it is."

"What would you like?" he teased, indicating the gifts in the glass display case. "Come on. Be daring. Pick out something outrageous."

She looked up at him, searching his dark eyes. She looked down into the shelves and when the saleslady came over, she indicated a pretty inlaid turquoise ring."

Mikey's hand tightened on hers. "Yes," he said under his breath.

The saleslady handed it to her and she started to try it on her right hand, but Mikey stopped her and slid it onto her left ring finger, his eyes holding hers. It was a perfect fit.

"We'll take it," Mikey said.

The saleslady took the credit card he handed her while Bernie touched the pretty ring.

"You can think of it as an engagement ring until we can do the thing right," he whispered at her forehead.

She caught her breath and fought tears as she looked up into hungry dark eyes.

"An engagement ring?" she asked.

"I can't let you go," he said quietly. "I'd have no life left. Whatever happens."

She bit her lower lip. "Whatever happens, Mikey," she whispered huskily.

And just that simply, they were engaged.

Mrs. Brown cried when she saw the ring and heard the story. "It's a lovely ring!" she said.

"Not a diamond just yet," Mikey chuckled, "but it's standing in for one. I have to text Paulie and tell him." He bent and kissed Bernie's cheek. "I have to go up to San Antonio tomorrow, but we'll do this again next weekend, okay?"

"Okay," she said softly.

"I'll see you at breakfast in the morning, honey. You sleep well."

She reached up and kissed his own cheek. "You, too."

He laughed. "I doubt I'll sleep a wink." He grinned, smiled at Mrs. Brown, and went along to his room.

"Congratulations," Mrs. Brown said.

Bernie hugged her. "I'm so happy!" she exclaimed. And then the tears did, finally, fall.

Bernie showed her ring off at work. Olivia was overjoyed, so was Glory. And when Sari saw it, she just hugged Bernie.

"He's never been the sort of man who wanted to settle down and get serious about anyone," Sari told Bernie. "But I can see why he wants that with you."

"Me and my limitations," Bernie said with a sigh. "He could have any woman he wanted, you know. Somebody young and beautiful and, well, whole."

"Oh, you'll be fine," Jessie said, and she even smiled. "Men don't think about obstacles, you know. They just plow right ahead when they want something. Congrats," she added.

"Thanks," Bernie replied.

Jessie noticed that nobody thought she was the least bit insincere. Which worked to her advantage.

Later in the day, Billie alerted her to the fact that Mikey was at the courthouse with his cousin Paul, talking to a man in a black suit.

"I'm going to lunch early so I'll be here when all of you leave, is that all right?" Jessie asked them.

"Sure," Glory said.

"I won't be long," she added, and smiled again. They were so gullible, she thought smugly as she left. Nobody suspected a thing.

Mikey was by himself while Paul and the man in the suit went into an office nearby. Jessie walked up to him.

"Hi," she said breezily. "How's it going? We heard about the engagement. Congratulations!"

He grinned. "Thanks."

She sighed. "I know you'll be happy with her." She made a face. "It's just, she was talking about your past, you know? I couldn't help but overhear."

He felt his face go taut. "About my past?"

"She's such a straight arrow," she continued. "It's not surprising that she'd be upset when she knew your family had ties to organized crime. She said she gave her word and she'd keep it, but she didn't know how she was going to live with a man who was accused of murder, a man who lived with other men who killed people without guilt." She smiled sadly. "I'm really sorry. I guess I shouldn't have mentioned it…"

"No, it's okay," he said. "Really."

"She'd never tell you herself," Jessie added. "She's so sweet." She grimaced. "It will be hard for her to get used to another way of life. But, hey, she's young. She'll adjust, right?"

"Right," he said, but he didn't look convinced.

She glanced at her watch. "Oops, I'll be late getting back. I dropped by to see what Billie wanted for lunch. I'm bringing it to her." She smiled at him. "I've got two uncles who worked for a local crime boss in New York," she said. She shrugged. "I don't have a problem with it. But some people, you know, they don't quite understand the life. See you."

"Yeah. See you."

She walked toward Billie's office, feeling proud. She'd just put the first stick in the spokes of his relationship with Bernie. She had him off balance. Now it was just a matter of keeping him that way for some people she and Billie knew.

The next step was to talk to Bernie and make a similar confession to her about Mikey. Funny how easy it was to make them believe things about each other. But she knew people like Mikey. He'd never ask Bernie directly if she'd said such things because he wouldn't really want to know. He'd be afraid to hurt her feelings by accusing her of it, and of course she'd deny it—because it wasn't true. But he'd have doubts. Big doubts. Jessie was going to make them even bigger.

Chapter Twelve

Mikey went back to San Antonio with Paulie to talk to the feds, and he was morose. Could Bernie feel that way about his lifestyle and not be willing to tell him? She'd certainly been shocked when he'd told her about the man who'd killed Paulie's family. Well, he hadn't confessed that he'd ordered the hit—although he had. What he'd told her was enough to shock her, even without that. Had he been too truthful? Maybe he should have waited until they knew each other much better before he confessed just how full of violence and turmoil his life had been.

"Sari ever have a problem with your past?" he asked his cousin, who was driving them in a Bucar, the designation of a bureau vehicle used by the FBI.

Paul frowned. "Well, she wasn't overjoyed, if that's

what you mean. She's an assistant district attorney, you know. A real straight arrow. I guess it bothered her some, but she loved me enough not to let it matter. Why? Is Bernie having second thoughts? She told Sari the two of you just got engaged."

"We did. But I told her a lot of it," Mikey said quietly. "She's got violence in her own past, something tragic. But hers was the result of an unbalanced relative. I'm not unbalanced. I've been a bad boy, Paulie. I'm not sure she can make a life with me, the way she is."

"You should talk to her."

"And say what? That I'll change? That I'll go straight and sell out my family? Fat chance, and you know why. You get in this racket for life. Nobody gets out except feet first."

"Marcus Carrera did," he was reminded.

"Yeah, Carrera. Well, he was a big fish and people were scared to death of him. Sure he got out. He always made his own rules. I'm not Carrera. I'm a small fry, compared to him."

"You own a casino in Vegas," Paul reminded him drily. "You drive a Rolls back home. You've got millions in overseas banks. And people are scared of you, too, kiddo."

"No kidding?"

"No kidding."

One corner of his mouth pulled down. "Well, that won't matter much if I turn my back on the outfit."

"Sadly, no, it won't. Hey, there's always the witness protection program," Paul teased.

"I noticed how well that worked out for the guy who

squealed on the big bosses. He got hit right in protective custody, now, didn't he?" Mikey chuckled.

"He did."

"You don't get out. Hell, I don't want to get out," Mikey muttered. "It's the only life I've ever known, from the time we were kids. I like being part of a big family. I like the style and the cachet."

"Will Bernie like it? She's more of a butterflies and wildflowers girl than she is a showgirl."

"Yeah. I know that. But she's so sweet, Paulie," he replied heavily. "She's the sweetest human being I've ever known. And I don't think I can give her up, unless she wants me to. Even then, I don't know how I'd go on without her. It's only been a few weeks and I'm lonely when I'm not with her."

"It was that way with me when I was mooning over Sari and thinking how hopeless it all was. She was worth two hundred million, and I worked for wages."

"You're still working for wages," Mikey pointed out.

"I'm not a sit-at-home type of guy. I love my job." He glanced at Mikey. "So what are you going to do?"

"Rock along until I'm sure she can cope. Then I'm getting her to the nearest justice of the peace before she changes her mind," he chuckled.

Bernie, meanwhile, was still basking in the glory of her first proposal and looking forward to years of happiness with Mikey.

The others were getting ready to go to lunch. Bernie got to her feet a little unsteadily and picked up her cane.

"Rough day, huh?" Jessie asked in a gentle tone.

"Just a little," Bernie confessed. "I had a bad fall on my way home the other day. A car went out of control and almost hit me."

"Gosh, here in Jacobsville? People need to learn to drive!" Jessie muttered.

"Just what I was thinking."

"Bernie, we'll wait for you outside," Glory called as they went out the door.

"Be right there," she said, reaching for her purse.

"Mikey was in the courthouse when I went to take Billie her lunch," Jessie said. She made a face. "I really shouldn't tell you what I overheard him say to his cousin."

Bernie's heart dropped in her chest. "What?" she asked, and sounded a little breathless with worry.

Jessie sighed. "He told his cousin that he was worried about what you'd be like in a few years, because his grandmother had what you've got, and she was twisted like tree roots and almost helpless. He said that it was going to be hard to live with somebody who was sick so much. But that he'd made a promise and he was going to keep it. He said he was going to marry you because he gave his word. But that it was going to be like pulling teeth. He was used to women who could keep up with the pace. He went all over the world on trips for his family, vacationed in foreign countries. He didn't know how you'd manage the travel. It was hard for a healthy woman, but you'd never keep up. He said," she added with sad eyes, "that he'd rushed in because he was infatuated with you, and then it was too late to turn back after he'd thought about the difficulties."

"I see." Bernie's heart was beating like a drum. She felt sick inside.

"I knew I shouldn't have told you," Jessie groaned. "I'm sorry. But I thought you should know. I mean, he'd never tell you himself."

"Of course, he wouldn't."

"Please don't tell him I told you," Jessie pleaded. "I don't want to make an enemy of him. He gets even with people. You don't know how dangerous he is," she added. "I come from up north. I've heard things about him. He scares people. Even bad people." She laughed hollowly. "I don't want to end up floating down a river…"

Bernie felt sick inside. Even Mikey had hinted at something of the sort, that he had power in his organization. She remembered what he'd said about taking care of the man who'd killed Paul's first wife and his child. It chilled her. "No, of course I won't tell."

"Thanks. I'm truly sorry. I know you're crazy about him."

Bernie managed a smile. She didn't answer. She went out onto the street with her coworkers and pretended that nothing at all had happened. But she was devastated.

Jessie smiled to herself. She was going to reap rich rewards for her little acts of "kindness." Throwing Mikey off balance had been the first step. Now she had Bernie doubting. The next thing was going to happen just as they'd planned it. And soon.

They spent all too much time in the Jacobs County courthouse, Mikey was thinking as he waited for Paulie to come out of an office where he was comparing notes with a contact in the probate judge's office.

He was staring at a plaque on the wall, denoting the building of the courthouse almost sixty years ago, and the names of the men on the county commission who'd authorized the construction. Farther down the wall were portraits of judges, many long gone. He was bored out of his mind.

"Fancy seeing you here again," Jessie said with a smile. She was carrying a box with food and a cup of coffee in it. "I came to bring lunch to poor Billie. She hurt her foot and she can't walk far."

"How're you doing?" he asked, and smiled, because she really did seem to have changed in the past week or so.

She shrugged. "Can't complain. It's just hard to get used to these Texans," she laughed. "They aren't like people up north."

"Nobody's like people up north. Where you from?"

She hesitated. "Upstate New York originally. You?"

"Jersey," he said. He grinned. "Doesn't the accent give it away?"

"It does, sort of." She cocked her head and studied him. "I've heard of your family. You were an underboss to Tony Garza, weren't you? Shame about him. He was a decent guy."

"He still is," Mikey said.

"I'm truly sorry that Bernie has such a hard time with your lifestyle..." She stopped and gritted her teeth. "Didn't mean to say that," she added quickly.

He scowled. "What did you mean?"

"Well, it's just," she hesitated. "Bernie doesn't understand the world you come from and she's afraid of it."

He felt his heart sinking. "She told you that?" he asked suspiciously.

"Of course not. She'd never talk to me about you," she said. "I told you about it before, remember? I heard her talking to Olivia, the other paralegal in our office. She said she was crazy about you, but that she wasn't sure she could cope with the way you made your living. She said she'd never fit in with a bunch of, well, criminals."

He could barely get words out. The pain went all the way through him. He'd wondered about the way Bernie accepted what he was, that she said it wouldn't matter. But she was a girl who'd never cheated in anything. She had a tragic past that predisposed her to loving the police. After all, they'd saved her and her father from a potential killer after the tragedy her grandfather had caused.

Apparently he hadn't been thinking straight at all. Rather, he'd been thinking with his heart instead of his brain. Bernie wasn't like him. They had different backgrounds, and she didn't understand the forces that honed his family into a criminal element over the years. The scandals of the Kennedy era, the unmasking of the five families, the scattering of bosses had been a wholesale offensive against organized crime. And it had largely succeeded. There were still bosses like Tony, who commanded power, but there was no more real commission that met and decided on who got hit, who had which territory, which politicians to support. Now the bosses were largely autonomous until they crossed the line. Nobody liked drawing attention to the outfit that was left, and people who did it got punished. Mostly, the days of wiping out a man's relatives to make a point were over. But there were still renegades who paid insults back with blood. Cotillo was one of those. That would never really end so long as there were power-mad people in the loop.

"I'm sorry," Jessie was saying. "I shouldn't have said anything."

"It isn't anything I wasn't already thinking," he confessed.

"You live in the fast lane. Fast cars, fast women, easy money," she said. "Bernie likes band concerts in the park and watching television in her room." Her mouth twisted. "Not a good mix."

"No." He wished he could forget what she'd told him about Bernie, the other day and now. But he knew it was true. He'd seen the way Bernie had reacted when he described his life to her. She'd said she could cope, that it wouldn't matter. It would matter.

"Please don't tell Bernie I said anything to you," she said softly. "I'd hate to have her mad at me now that we're getting along so well."

"I won't mention it to her," he said absently, and he was thinking that there was no way he could discuss it with Bernie without putting her on the defensive, making her ashamed of her feelings. He couldn't blame her. His lifestyle would be hard for any woman unless she came from a similar background. He'd been living in a dream. It was a sweet dream. But it wasn't real.

"I'd better get Billie's lunch to her. Nice seeing you." She walked away with a smile. It wouldn't do to lay it on with a trowel.

Paul came out of the probate judge's office with a worried look. He fell in beside Mikey and they walked outside. "Harvey," he said, referring to his contact inside, "told me that Billie and Jessie at Sari's office came down here at the same time. It's a little too cozy for coincidence."

"You think they're Cotillo's?" Mikey asked.

"They could be. We're going to do a thorough background search on all of them. What about that car that barely missed Bernie? Did she tell you anything about it?"

He shook his head and stuck his hands in his slacks pockets. "Only that it was a dark sedan. It happened too fast." He glanced at Paul. "Do you know about Bernie's grandfather and what he did?"

Paul nodded. "Tragic thing to happen to a child. There was a serious attempt on her father's life not long after it happened, by a member of a victim's family. He's doing time."

"She said it might have been somebody like that, trying to scare her." Mikey frowned. "It's not Cotillo's style, you know? He has people hit if he has a problem with them, like he tried to hit Tony and me. He doesn't make threats."

"Neither do you," Paul mused.

"Hey, I am what I am." He strolled along beside Paul. "I've been having second thoughts about this engagement," he confessed.

"What?" Paul stopped in the middle of the sidewalk. "But you're crazy about Bernie. She's crazy about you!"

Mikey took a breath and smiled cynically. "She likes small towns and band concerts, Paulie. She's never been in trouble with the law in her life. How's she going to like jetsetting, mixing with celebrities and crooks, wearing designer clothes, traveling around the world with me when I've got people to meet? How's she going to feel if I ever get arrested for something?"

Paul took a deep breath of his own. "I don't know. I don't live in that world. I never did."

"Well, I do. I have to." He grimaced. "And there's her health to consider. I remember our grandmother. She got twisted like a tree in a hurricane. She was in bed most of the time at the end. She got upset and she had flares, remember that? Bernie would be stressed-out all the time. It would affect her health."

"You've done a lot of thinking," Paul said. He wasn't saying anything, but his tone was full of curiosity and suspicion.

"Yeah. She's the sweetest woman I've ever known. I'd like her to stay that way. Involved with me for life? It would…kill something in her."

Paul didn't speak. He knew that Mikey's lifestyle involved stress. But he'd never seen Mikey involved with any woman to the extent he was involved with Bernie. He thought that love would resolve all those issues. Mikey clearly didn't.

"What are you going to do?" Paul asked.

"Ease off. Just a little at a time, so it doesn't look like I'm shooting her out of my life." He smiled sadly. "I want her to be happy. I can't give her the sort of life she deserves."

"You, being unselfish. Call the journalists," Paul drawled.

Mikey chuckled. "Out of character, isn't it?" he agreed.

Paul threw an arm around him. "Not anymore, it isn't, cuz," he said quietly. "But I'm sorry for both of you."

"Me, too," Mikey said. His eyes were solemn. "Me, too."

Mikey and Bernie were subdued at supper at Mrs. Brown's. Neither spoke much although they went through the motions of participating in the conversation.

But afterward, when Bernie started toward her room, Mikey stopped her.

"Listen," he began quietly, "I've been thinking—"

"Me, too," she interrupted.

She looked as uncomfortable as he did.

He shoved his hands into his pockets and felt his heart breaking inside him. He wanted to say something, but what could he say? His life wasn't butterflies and roses. And, realistically, she wasn't the sort of woman who could adjust to partying and casinos and jet travel and organized crime. It was impossible, but he hadn't realized it until Jessie told him what Bernie had said.

He looked down at her tenderly. She was so unworldly. It would be like her not to want to hurt his feelings or make him feel bad about what his world was like.

She was thinking the same thing about him, that he didn't want to hurt her feelings by admitting that he couldn't live with a woman who might be an invalid one day, a woman who could barely keep up with him on a slow walk in the woods. He needed somebody vibrant and healthy, who could thrive in his company, not a woman who would limit his activities.

"It might be an idea to cool it, just for a little while,"

Mikey said finally. "I've got people working on that car that almost hit you. We'll find out who it was."

"Probably somebody drunk who misjudged the curb," she replied with a faint smile. "It's a small town. Odd things happen here."

His dark eyes seemed even darker as they searched her light ones. "I've never enjoyed anything more than this time with you."

"Me, either," she confessed, and tried not to show that she was dying inside.

"But we need to give each other a little space. Just for now," he added quickly so it didn't sound like he was trying to dump her. He couldn't bear to hurt her feelings.

She nodded. "It's a good idea." She fingered the ring that stood in place of an engagement ring. She started to take it off.

His big hand went over both of hers. "No," he said, and sounded choked. "You keep that. You keep it forever. Think of me when you wear it."

She looked up, fighting tears. "I'll never forget you. No matter what."

"Yeah. It's like that with me, too." He hesitated. "Santi doesn't like having me apart from him at night, the way things are going."

Her eyes widened with worry. "They haven't sent somebody else after you…?" she asked almost frantically.

He almost bit his lip through. That soft concern made him hate himself. "No," he lied quickly. Some quick thinking by Paulie and the feds had saved him, already. "It's just that he thinks a bodyguard should stay with the boss, and he can't live in the room with me here.

So…well, I'm moving over to the motel, and Santi and I can have adjoining rooms."

Her heart sank. She'd gotten used to seeing him at the table when they had meals, in the hallway, everywhere. "That's probably a good idea," she said softly. She looked up. "You take care of yourself, okay?"

His big hand touched her cheek. "You do that, too. Don't go out alone after dark. Be aware of your surroundings."

"I always do that. Well, almost always," she amended. "But the car came out of nowhere. I didn't even hear it coming."

That wasn't surprising. Most newer model cars had quiet engines. It still bothered him that it didn't sound like an accident. Paul was checking. If there was anything sinister, he'd find it.

"So," Mikey said. "I'll see you around."

She forced a smile. "Yes. Well, goodbye."

She went into her room, resisting the urge to look behind her. She closed the door and let the tears fall silently. It was the biggest pain of her life, almost as bad as knowing what her grandfather had done, losing her sweet grandmother and the community where she'd grown up. It was like losing a loved one.

Outside the door, Mikey was feeling something similar. But he had to do it. If he stayed here, seeing her every day, he'd go nuts. He couldn't keep away from her, not unless he distanced himself from her. It was the hardest thing he'd ever done in his life. It was the only thing he could do. Bernie couldn't live with the man he was. He didn't blame her. It was just that she was the only woman he'd ever wanted to live with him.

He let out a weary breath and went into his room to pack.

"You moved out of the boardinghouse," Paul remarked a week later, when Mikey was having supper with him and Sari while Mandy bustled around in the kitchen making a cake.

"Yeah," Mikey said. He moved his cup around in the saucer. "Santi kept harping on it. He said he couldn't protect me if he was several blocks away. I finally listened."

Paul, remembering an earlier conversation, knew what the truth was. Mikey was distancing himself from Bernie, removing temptation.

Sari glanced at Mikey's lowered head and started to speak, but a sharp jerk of the head from Paul silenced her. Instead, she started talking about a reality show she and Paul had been watching lately.

After Mikey went back to his motel, Sari questioned Paul about his odd behavior.

"He's doing it for her own good," Paul said on a sigh. "He thinks she couldn't cope with his lifestyle. You know, Isabel, it's not the same life as this one. Not at all. He's in constant company with people who break the law. He travels in high social circles just the same, rubs elbows with movie stars and politicians and gamblers. He couldn't settle down here if his life depended on it—well, except briefly, like he's having to do now. But Bernie would never fit into that sort of world."

Sari met his eyes and nodded sadly. "But she was so

happy," she said softly. "Bright as the sun. She almost radiated with it. And now she's so quiet we hardly know she's around. She never jokes and smiles anymore."

"Neither does my cousin," Paul said. He pulled her close. "You and I came from different worlds, but we worked it out, because we loved one another. You can tell how Mikey and Bernie feel about each other just by looking at them. Why couldn't they work it out, too?"

"I don't know," she said with a sigh. She laid her head against his broad chest. "What about the sudden residents? Any new intel on them?"

"Not a lot," he confessed. "Jessie and her friend Billie are both from New York originally. They do have mob ties, but not to Cotillo or Tony Garza. Their connections aren't apparent, but we're trying to run them down. There's still a family that operates in New York, even covertly, but it's fragmented and the boss is in prison."

"He can still run it from prison. It's not even hard."

"True. He has an underboss holding power for him. Jessie may have something to do with him. That wouldn't necessarily mean she or the boss favored Cotillo. He's an outsider and he does a bloody business. You know how well that goes over in mob circles. They don't like attention. Cotillo's getting them a lot of it."

"Wouldn't it be lovely if somebody in one of the old outfit families decided to take Cotillo out of the equation?" she asked on a sigh. "Shame on me. I work for the court system. I should be ashamed."

"Yes, you bad girl." He kissed her hungrily. "You need to be severely reprimanded. Come right over here and I'll do my best."

She laughed as he tugged her down onto the bed. "Oh, this is a reprimand I'm going to love," she teased.

He chuckled as he started to remove her gown. "You bet, you're going to love it!"

The driver of the car that almost hit Bernie was a local businessman who'd had three drinks too many out at Shea's Bar and misjudged the curb, just as Bernie had figured. He turned himself in to Cash Grier with many apologies and Cash got him into rehab.

Bernie listened to Cash's explanation in the office a couple of weeks after Mikey had moved out of the boardinghouse.

"I thought it was something like that," she said quietly. "I mean, if people in organized crime want to hurt you, they just kill you, don't they?"

"More or less." They were alone in the office. It was just after lunch and the other women hadn't returned. "What about you and Mikey? I thought that was going to be permanent."

She flushed. "I'm not healthy," she said. "His grandmother had what I've got. She was an invalid, bedridden, when she was old. I'm likely to end up in that condition a lot sooner." She fought down panic at the thought that she might not even be able to work. She was far too proud to ask for government relief, even though she might one day be forced into it.

"There are new drugs," he pointed out.

She smiled sadly. "Chief Grier, the sort you're talking about costs over a thousand dollars a month. They do have programs to help people afford them, but it isn't that much of a reduction."

He grimaced.

"I get by. My rheumatologist has me on a regimen of medicines that mostly take care of the pain. I have flares, days when I can't get out of bed, and I have to use a cane from time to time. But there are lots of people worse off. Look at Glory in my office, and what she had to go through in her life. She still limps from time to time because her hip was broken long ago and it has arthritis in it, and her blood pressure is controlled but still subject to spikes. She lives with it. I live with my problems."

"But you don't think Mikey could?" he fished, his eyes piercing hers.

She toyed with a pen on her desk. "He was overheard telling his cousin that he wasn't sure that he could." She looked up. "Don't you dare repeat that, ever. It would hurt his feelings. He can't help what he thinks. He lives with glitzy people, rides in limousines, travels all over the world. I'm lucky if I can get from work to my boardinghouse without falling over my feet. How would I fit into that sort of lifestyle? I'd be a sparrow among peacocks, if you see what I mean."

He did see. But she was a sweet, kind woman. "If he loves you, it won't matter."

"That's the thing, though," she continued. "He said it would be better if we sort of let things cool off. And he's probably right. He has enough problems right now. They won't kill him, will they?" she asked, and looked agonized by the thought.

"He has powerful friends," he replied. "Marcus Carrera is one of them. Carrera runs a legitimate operation in the Bahamas, but he wasn't always a good guy, and his reputation still strikes fear in people who knew him back in the day." He chuckled. "He's got Tony Garza so surrounded by experienced mercs that only a suicidal maniac would try to get to him."

"Sari said that Mr. Garza gave her sister away at her wedding to that Wyoming rancher," Bernie said.

"He did. He's not what he seems." He cocked his head and studied her. "Neither is Mikey. His reputation is fearsome. But he's not as bad as people think he is."

"He was arrested once, though," she said.

He nodded. "And charged with attempted murder. But the charges were dropped," he reminded her. "Nobody's ever been able to bring him to trial on a major crime. For a man who operates outside the law, he's amazingly conventional."

She smiled sadly. "He's amazing, period," she said softly. "I'll never forget him." As she spoke, she twisted the turquoise-and-silver ring he'd given her. She wore it on her right hand, though, not her left. She didn't want it to get back to him that she considered herself engaged, not when he was backing away.

Cash muttered something about men being fools, smiled, and left her.

"What in the hell is wrong with you?" Cash asked Mikey when he saw him with Paul at Barbara's Café one day at lunch.

Mikey's eyebrows raised. "Excuse me?"

"You have almost as much money in foreign banks as I do," Cash said as he joined them for coffee and pie. "You could easily afford the newest treatments for rheumatoid arthritis, whatever they cost."

Mikey stared at him. "I don't have arthritis."

"Bernie does."

Mikey averted his eyes. "I know."

"She wouldn't let him, though," Paul said, and he was giving Cash expression cues that asked him to cool it. "She's too proud."

"Besides that, we're not… Well, we're not an item anymore," Mikey added. "She has her life, I have mine."

"Yes, but she…" Cash continued, ignoring Paul.

Before he could finish the sentence, Jessie came in the door, spotted Mikey and came right to the table, smiling.

"Don't forget, you're taking me to Don Alfonso's for supper, right?" she asked.

Mikey chuckled. "You bet, doll. Santi and I will pick you up about five."

"I thought maybe you could drive us both and leave Santi at home," she said with a husky laugh.

"Sorry. Santi drives, I don't."

"Well, okay. It doesn't matter. I'll be ready on time. Hi, Chief Grier. Mr. Fiore," she added, a little unsettled when Paul just glared at her without speaking. "See you later."

She went to the counter to pick up her order. Paul glared at Mikey with much more venom than he'd shown the gorgeous, well-dressed woman waiting for her order.

"She doesn't mind riding around with a criminal," Mikey said sarcastically. "She loves casinos and fancy restaurants and she's classy enough to take to ritzy gatherings. So?"

"You're about to ruin your life," Paul said curtly. "What if Bernie finds out? Jessie works in the office with her, for God's sake!"

"I told you," Mikey said, averting his eyes. "Bernie and I are no longer an item. I can date any woman I like. Jessie's not so bad."

But Paul was thinking that Jessie was every bit as bad as she seemed. She was rubbing Bernie's nose in the fact that she had Mikey's attention. Not only that, she was pressuring Mikey to be alone with her, without Santi. That was suspicious. Very suspicious. He glanced at a taciturn Cash Grier and had the impression that the police chief was thinking the same thing.

"I need a night on the town, anyway," Mikey said as he finished his pie and washed it down with coffee. "I've been vegetating down here in cowboy town."

"You watch your step," Paul said shortly. "Don't forget that Cotillo may have people here that we don't even know about."

"Surely you don't think Jessie's one of them?" Mikey drawled. "You checked her out and found no connections to any of Cotillo's people."

"Yeah, I checked out our last limo driver, too, and he almost got Merrie killed because the perp had connections I didn't ferret out," he was reminded.

"I can handle myself," Mikey reminded him curtly.

"You'd better have a concealed carry permit if you walk around with a weapon in my town," Cash told him humorously, but with a cold glint in his eyes.

"I got one the second day I was in town, for your information," Mikey said smugly. "I know you, Grier. No way I'm stepping out of line around here!"

Cash just chuckled.

Paul cornered him after Grier left, while they were waiting on the sidewalk for Santi to collect Mikey.

"This is going to ruin any chance you have of getting back together with Bernie," he told his cousin. "You know that, right?"

Mikey's eyes were hollow with pain. "She can't live with a crook, Paulie," he said shortly. "That's what she said."

Paul's lower jaw fell. "She said that to you?"

"Of course, she didn't say it to me! She wouldn't hurt my feelings for anything. But she was overheard saying it," he added, and flushed, remembering who'd told him. "There's Santi. I gotta go. See you around, cuz."

"Watch your back!" Paul called after him.

Mikey waved and climbed into the limo.

Paul stood watching it pull away from the curb. Something Mikey had said piqued his curiosity. He was going to speak to Sari about it when he got home.

Chapter Thirteen

Sari was going over a brief when Paul walked into the study and closed the door.

"What's up?" she asked, because he looked worried.

"Did Bernie say anything to you about having an issue with Mikey's background?" he asked curiously.

"No," she replied. She grimaced. "But she doesn't really discuss Mikey with me," she added. "I guess she thinks I might tell him what she said." She put down the pencil she was using to edit the document she was working on. "Why?"

"He said she told somebody that she couldn't live with a man who made his living outside the law, with a criminal," he replied. "Would she tell somebody at work something so personal?" he persisted.

She frowned. "Well, I don't really think so. Bernie's

a very private person. She's not the kind to blurt out intimate details of her life to people she works with. It's not the way she is. And there's not really anybody else she might tell, either. She has no close friends."

"That's what I thought. Mikey has the impression that she can't live with his past."

"I know that's not true," Sari said gently. "She loves him."

One side of his mouth pulled down. "I tried to tell him that. He wouldn't listen. He's destroying any chance that he could get back together with Bernie."

"How?"

"He's taking your coworker Jessie out on the town in San Antonio tonight," he said through his teeth.

"Oh, no!"

"I tried to warn him. It will ruin everything. But he wouldn't listen. He's convinced that he's so bad, only a bad woman would ever want him."

"What an idiot. Even if he is your cousin."

"Hey, no argument from me. I said the same thing, to his face."

"It will kill Bernie if she finds out."

He laughed coldly. "If? Jessie will tell the world tomorrow. I don't doubt she'll embroider it into something even more than it is."

"Jessie." Sari made a rough sound. "She was our worst nightmare for weeks. Then overnight she turned into a caring, worrying coworker who did everything she could to make things easier for us."

"And all an act," Paul said. "I can see right through her. I wish Mikey could."

"I didn't. Neither did Bernie or Glory or Olivia," Sari said.

"I've spent my life with people who bend the truth. I'm good at recognizing phonies."

"Poor Bernie."

"Poor Mikey, when he finally realizes he's been had," Paul said flatly. "I'm checking out an acquaintance of Jessie's in Upstate New York. I have a suspicion that she didn't just happen down here with her friend Billie."

"What about the cook from New Jersey who's working in Barbara's Café?"

He laughed. "I'll tell you about that," he said. "It's a hoot." And he did tell her.

"Now, this is my kind of place," Jessie said as they were seated in the five-star restaurant.

"Mine, too," Mikey said, but without any real enthusiasm. He studied the gorgeous woman across from him with only vague interest. She was wearing a couture cocktail dress with diamond earrings, necklace, bracelet and several rings. All diamonds. The best quality and set in 18 karat gold. He knew, because he'd spent a fortune on them for various women over the years. He was curious about how she afforded that kind of jewelry on a receptionist's salary.

Even as he had the thought, he felt cold chills inside. He was carrying. He had a snub .38 in a pancake holster behind his back, and a hidden gun in an ankle holster. He never went anywhere without being armed. Would he need to be? Santi was at the next table, apparently oblivious, but watching.

Odd, how he suddenly remembered that if the family ordered a hit on you, they sent your best friend to do it. He was warned that if he didn't, somebody else would, and he'd end up as dead as the intended victim. His blood ran cold as he stared at Santi.

But his bodyguard just grinned at him and went to work on a huge plate of spaghetti. He was getting paranoid, Mikey considered, just like his old man.

He remembered his father with loathing. The man had been a dirty jobs soldier for the underboss in New Jersey, the one who'd preceded Tony Garza. Mikey's dad had killed men over and over again, never felt the least remorse, and spent his life at a local bar where the outfit hung out. Mikey rarely saw him, and if he ever did, his father treated him like a disease. He hated Mikey and made no secret of the fact that he thought the kid was some other man's son. Mikey's mother, long dead, had an affair, he'd told the boy one day, and Mikey was the result. It was to get even with him for something he'd done to her. So Mikey had no real family at all until his maternal grandmother, Paulie's grandmother, too, took both boys in and raised them. The old lady was Greek. She still spoke the old language. Mikey and Paulie had been schooled in Italian by the other kids and the families they associated with, but their grandmother taught them Greek, as well. Mikey could even read in it. Not a lot of people knew that. He kept his intelligence hidden; it gave him an advantage if his colleagues thought he was stupid.

"How was it you heard what Bernie said in the office?" he asked out of the blue.

Jessie's hand, which was holding her wineglass, jerked, but she recovered quickly. "Oh, she and Olivia didn't know I was there," she replied. "I'd just come out of Mr. Kemp's office and they were in the hallway."

"I see." He didn't know Bernie well, but it seemed unlike her to confide something so personal to an office worker, even one she was close to. She was, like him, a very private person.

"This place is nice," she said, changing the subject. She smiled at him alluringly. "You know, I have the use of a friend's apartment here in town," Her voice changed to a throaty purr. "We could be all alone there."

Mikey just stared at her. His dark eyes were cold, as cold as they'd ever been when he had another man at gunpoint. "Really?"

His glare disconcerted her. "You know, Bernie won't change her mind, and she'll never tell you what she really thinks of you," she said.

He cocked his head. "You're trying too hard."

"Excuse me?"

He just laughed, but it had a hollow sound. He was just beginning to believe he'd been had. And he was out with this jeweled barracuda, who would go back to the office Monday and tell Bernie all about this date, probably with some embroidering. He took a big sip of his Chianti and cursed himself silently through the rest of the meal.

"Oh, it was the most wonderful date!" Jessie enthused to the other women, including Bernie, the following Monday. "Mikey made me feel like a princess! And we went to this apartment a friend loans me..." She stopped when Bernie's face went white. "I'm so sorry, that was cruel," she added in a conciliatory tone. "But you know how he feels about you, honey."

"She knows what you told her," Olivia replied, her eyes narrow and suspicious.

"Odd, how you knew something so personal," Sari added her own comment to the discussion. "I mean, Mikey isn't the sort to discuss personal things with Paul, even in private, and Paul's the only person he's really close to."

Jessie looked uncomfortable. "It was just a comment he made—he didn't seem to think it was very personal."

Mr. Kemp's door flew open and he looked livid. "Miss Tennison!"

Jessie actually jumped. "Yes, sir?"

"Come into my office, please," he said icily.

Jessie collected herself quickly and forced a smile. "Yes, sir, at once." She jumped up and headed toward him without looking back.

"Don't you believe her," Sari told Bernie firmly. "Mikey never told Paul anything about you, not ever, in private. He would never blurt out something like that in a public place."

Bernie wasn't comforted. She forced a smile. "I could never keep up with him, don't you see?" she asked softly. "He lives in the fast lane. Some days, I can't even get out of bed. He'd get tired of it. I don't like bars and flashy places. I've never even owned an evening gown." She cocked her head and smiled at Sari. "The people in his circle would think he'd lost his mind if they ever got a look at me, and you know it."

Sari wasn't convinced. "Bernie, if somebody loves you, things like disabilities and things they've done in the past—none of it matters at all."

Bernie's green eyes were sad. "I believed that, once. But he took her out on the town," she added, indicating the door behind which Jessie was closeted with Mr. Kemp. "And he slept with her. It's over. I'm going to get on with my life. It's obvious that he's gotten on with his."

And she went back to work.

Jessie came out of Mr. Kemp's office with an absolute snarl on her face. "I'm fired," she said icily. "Just because I told that old man on the phone that Mr. Kemp didn't want to talk to him and not to go to court because I thought it was canceled that day!"

"What old man?" Olivia asked.

"Oh, some rancher named Regan."

Olivia's eyebrows arched. "Ted Regan?"

"Yes, I think that was it," Jessie muttered. She started pulling things out of desk drawers.

"Old man Regan," Sari told her, "is worth millions. He owns the second biggest ranch in Jacobs County, and properties all over the country. He's also a prime witness in a case we're prosecuting." She pursed her lips. "Or he was. I'm assuming Mr. Kemp lost the case, if you told Ted not to show up. Judge Drew was presiding and he didn't want to try the case to begin with."

Jessie just ground her teeth. "Well, it doesn't matter now, I'm fired," she muttered. She looked up and noted the pleased expressions on all the faces except Bernie's. Bernie wouldn't even look at her. "It's just as well," she commented. "I've done what I came to do. Aren't you the gullible bunch? I put on an act and all of you bought it. You pitiful little small-town people, you'll never know what life is all about."

"It's about family," Glory Ramirez said.

"It's all about family," Sari agreed. "Something you'll never understand."

"The only family I care about is the one I take orders from," Jessie muttered absently, and then looked up and flushed as she realized what she'd said. "My dad, I mean," she corrected, "and he's not from some little Texas town!"

But Sari picked up on what she'd said at once and hid her suspicions. She went back to work, ignoring Jessie.

"Well, so long," Jessie said as she carried the cardboard box with her things in it to the door. She turned and stared at Bernie. "I'll tell Mikey you said hello, Bernie," she purred. "After all, we're going to be seeing a lot of each other. I know his world and I love it. Unlike you, I don't mind being seen with him and his criminal friends," she drawled sarcastically.

Bernie felt shocked. "What do you mean?"

Jessie had slipped again. She shrugged. "Nothing at all. Goodbye."

She went out the door and closed it behind her.

Bernie didn't say a word. She brooded, though. Mikey was already involved with that vicious woman, but perhaps he liked that sort of person. Maybe he was frustrated because he'd wanted Bernie and she wasn't the sort to sleep around. But it still hurt to think of him in bed with Jessie. It hurt terribly.

"She was lying," Sari said gently.

Bernie looked up. Her eyes were sad and wise. "No, she wasn't," she said quietly. "And like I said, it doesn't matter. We were mismatched from the start. Opposites attract, don't they say, but the divorce rate for marriages like that is pretty dismal. I'd better get back to work."

Sari didn't say any more, but she was livid.

"Mikey did what?" Paul Fiore asked at supper, his fork poised in midair.

"He slept with Jessie," Sari said angrily.

He whistled, aware of Mandy's curious stare. "Well, damn, that's the end of it all."

"I know." Sari picked at her food. "Jessie was poison. I'm glad Mr. Kemp fired her. It was all an act, that sweetness and light attitude."

"No surprise, there."

"She let something slip when we were talking about families and how they mattered," Sari continued. "She said the only family she cared about was the one she took orders from."

Paul dropped the fork. "Families. Like Cotillo's."

"Maybe," Sari replied, watching him retrieve the utensil from the floor and carry it to the sink before he got another and returned to the table. "Don't you have somebody checking her out?"

"I do. I'll call him after we finish eating. Damn the

luck! If she's involved with Cotillo, then her friend Billie may be, too. It's been right under our noses."

"What about that cook at Barbara's?" Mandy asked as she refilled coffee cups. She made a face at Sari. "And you should be drinking milk, not caffeine!"

Sari flushed. "Mandy..."

Mandy was grinning.

Paul, caught unaware, looked at Mandy's twinkling eyes and his own darted to his wife, looking flushed and guilty.

"Okay, spit it out," he told Sari. "What's going on that I don't know about?"

She cleared her throat and glared at Mandy. "I was going to tell you later."

"Tell me now," he persisted.

She drew in a breath. "I'm pregnant."

Paul sat very still for just a minute, then he rose, picked her up in his arms, and kissed her and kissed her, whooping in between at the top of his lungs.

Mandy pursed her lips. "Well," she said to nobody in particular, "I guess it's no secret that he's happy about it."

Bernie went home to a lonely apartment, her heart down in her shoes. Mikey was sleeping with that rat, Jessie. Mikey was a rat, too, she told herself. He'd taken her in, pretended to care about her, then backed off because she had an incurable disease.

If he'd been that concerned about her illness, why hadn't he stopped seeing her in the beginning? Why had he spent almost every day with her? Why had he bought her a ring and then asked her to marry him?

None of it made sense, unless he'd truly thought he could make it work and then decided he couldn't live with her limitations. She felt miserable. She couldn't help what was wrong with her. She couldn't cure it. Maybe she could have adjusted to travel, to his friends, to flashy places, if she'd been given the chance. But what did it matter now? She would never get over the fact that he'd promised to marry her and then cheated on her with another woman. She had too much pride.

"Are you out of your mind?" Paul demanded of Mikey the next day when they were having a quick lunch at the house.

Mikey blinked. "Excuse me?"

"Sleeping with Jessie. My God!"

Mikey's lips fell open. "Sleeping… Good Lord, do I look crazy to you? I wouldn't touch her with a pole!"

"You took her out on the town, didn't you?" he persisted.

Mikey grimaced. "I was feeling pretty low. I needed to feel like a man again."

"Great job."

"Bernie didn't want me!" he burst out. "She said she couldn't live with a man who'd been a criminal most of his life!"

"She told you this, huh?" Paul asked.

Mikey sighed. "No. She'd never want to hurt my feelings like that. She told somebody else and she was overheard."

"Let me guess—by Jessie."

Mikey scowled. "What?"

"Jessie told Bernie that you went with her to an apartment in San Antonio."

Mikey grimaced. He could only imagine how much that had hurt Bernie. He was hurting from her rejection, but it wounded him to think he'd caused her even more pain.

"She let something else slip. She has a 'family' that she takes orders from."

Mikey lost color. "Hell!"

"I've got a man digging hard into her past. He's hit a couple of dead ends, but he thinks he's onto something. I should have an answer today," Paul told him.

"You think she's on Cotillo's payroll."

"I think she might be," Paul replied. "Think about it. She and Billie are as out of place here as roaches in a ritzy hotel. So why are they here? Maybe to watch you and report on your movements to a third party."

"Like a cleaner," Mikey said, referring to a contract killer.

"Maybe. It depends on which family she has ties to. Cotillo's not the only man in the game. He has enemies. She's from New York. Cotillo's moving on Tony Garza in Jersey. Suppose another boss has Cotillo in his sights and wants to know if you're protected before he orders a hit."

Mikey toyed with his coffee cup. "That's a possibility."

"Cotillo's drawn a lot of attention to himself and to the outfit in general with this takeover thing. He's harking back to the mob wars in the past, which were bloody and public and ended in the congressional hearings that tore the Five Families apart. They can't really afford to make themselves too visible even today. Cotillo's a threat to them as well as to you and Tony. They might decide to act."

"If Jessie was lining up a hit, she had a perfect opportunity while we were at the restaurant," Mikey said. "Santi was at another table. Of course, I was watching the door. I know how hits go down."

"Which is why I don't think her boss is Cotillo."

Mikey drew in a long breath. "That might be." He looked into the coffee cup at the thick black liquid. "Bernie will never forgive me. I don't guess it matters. She didn't want me to begin with."

"Or so Jessie told you. She likes rich men. Kemp already called her down about it at least once. Of course, he fired her this morning."

"What?"

"She mouthed off to Ted Regan, of all people, and told him court had been canceled. Since she was calling from the DA's office, he believed her. He didn't show up and the case was thrown out of court. Kemp was livid."

"I guess so. She'll get another job, I guess."

"She and Billie left town late this afternoon," Paul replied. "I got that from Mandy. She knows everything that goes on in this town. But I'm sure Jessie will keep in touch with you," he added sarcastically. "I mean, since you're dating her and all."

"You don't understand," he burst out. "I lost everything! Bernie couldn't live with what I am, and I don't know how I'm going to live without her! Jessie kept asking if we could get a meal somewhere and I said yes. I know I shouldn't have done it. I was so damned low I didn't care about how it would look."

"Jessie is poison," Paul said. "I'd bet real money that she told Bernie some tale about you, as well, to the tune of your not being able to live with a woman who might be an invalid later on."

Mikey was very still. He just stared at his cousin.

"Think about it. She told you that Bernie hated your past. Maybe she told Bernie that you hated her disease."

"Dear God," Mikey said huskily, and buried his face in his hands. "Oh, God, what am I going to do?"

"Talk to Bernie."

Mikey removed his hands from his face and drank the coffee. "Sure. I'm going to walk into the office, and she's going to throw me out headfirst, or the verbal equivalent. She thinks I slept with damned Jessie. She'll hate me."

"Sari hated me, too, when I first came back here." Paul grinned. "Remember what I did when she wouldn't speak to me?"

"Everybody in Jacobsville remembers," Mikey chuckled. "They even talked about it at the boarding-house and it was three years ago."

"Whatever works," he commented pointedly.

Mikey drew in a breath. "I'll think about it."

"Meanwhile, I have news."

"About Cotillo?"

Paul chuckled. "Not yet. About Sari."

Mikey's eyebrows arched.

"She's pregnant," Paul said, and smiled from ear to ear.

"Damn, that's great! Absolutely great!" Mikey burst out. "I'm happy for you."

"It's the nicest surprise," Paul confessed. "We've been trying for a long time, but, well, nothing happened and I thought maybe we couldn't have kids. It wouldn't have mattered. I love her so much. I'd rather have her and no kids than the biggest family in the country with any other woman."

"I know how that feels." Mikey put his cup down. "I wanted them with Bernie. Never with anybody else. Even with her limitations, she could carry a child. I asked a doctor." He flushed. "There are medicines she can't afford that I could have bought for her, and they would have helped. She could have private duty nurses, anything she needed. I'd have…taken care of her." He stopped, choking up.

"It isn't too late."

Mikey looked up, with the saddest expression Paul had ever seen. "Yes, it is, Paulie. It's too late. And I did it to myself, by not telling her what Jessie said and giving her a chance to tell me what she felt."

"We all make mistakes."

"Even you aren't in my class, cousin," Mikey said. He leaned back in the chair. "At least you're having that happy ending people dream about," he added with an affectionate smile. "You got lucky."

"I wish you had, too."

Mikey shrugged. "Let's just hope that Cotillo doesn't."

* * *

They were prophetic words. A day later, the story broke on all the major news networks. A New Jersey mob figure named Anthony Cotillo was found dead in his apartment of apparently natural causes. A friend said that the man had no apparent health problems and that it came as a shock to his associates.

"Can they detect an air embolism?" Mikey mused. "It doesn't matter—they'll have people in the coroner's office to make sure that doesn't go into the report."

Paul sighed. "Well, it's a novel way to take care of an interloper without getting the government all stirred up," he agreed. "No mess, no blood trail, no nothing. But I wonder who hit him?"

Mikey smiled. "Marcus Carrera has many friends from the old days," he pointed out. "Some of them owe him really big favors."

Paul's eyebrows arched.

"Really big," Mikey emphasized. And he smiled.

Tony Garza came home to New Jersey amid promises from an obscure New York outfit family that the loose association of bosses, the one that had existed since the Five Families were scattered by pressure from the feds, had no problem with him. They assured him that no more problems were expected, and that they had several people making sure of it. The message was clear—Carrera might not be a mob figure any longer, since he'd gone straight, but he was still a power to contend with in the States. A lot of people were afraid of him. Tony was going to be safe.

"So I guess I'll go home now," Mikey said sadly, when he was having supper with Paul and Sari. "I'll come back for the christening, though," he teased.

"Wrong church," Paul teased. "We're Methodist. Although, Reverend Blair does have a sort of christening ceremony, but not like the one you're thinking of."

"We can pretend. I'll come anyway." He toyed with his food. "So I guess Jessie and Billie worked for the New York boss."

"I guess so," Paul said.

"Carrera was a terror when he was younger," Mikey remarked with a smile. "You could just say his name ten years ago and people would start running for the door."

"It shocked everybody when he went legit," Paul said. "Even the feds. Now he's got a wife and two sons and he's the happiest man on earth."

"Families are nice," Mikey said absently.

"You should get married and have one," Sari said firmly.

"Chance would be a fine thing."

"You never know," she replied. "Strange things happen when you least expect them."

He smiled at her. "They do, don't they? What do you guys want, a boy or a girl?"

"Either," Paul said.

"Both," Sari said, and grinned.

"No twins on our side of the family, cousin," he told Paul.

"But there are loads on my side," Sari laughed. "Distant cousins, but at least three sets of twins among them."

"Son of a gun! You could have your whole family in one year."

Paul laughed. "Who knows?" he teased, and he looked at his wife with eyes that absolutely ate her. She looked back at him the same way.

Mikey felt more alone than he ever had in his whole life. Much more, although he was happy for his cousin. But he was leaving town. His heart would stay here, with that sad little woman who lived in Mrs. Brown's boardinghouse. She'd never forgive him for Jessie. He knew it without asking. It was the worst mistake of his life, and he couldn't fix it. Nobody could.

He packed his bags and Santi packed his. His heart was breaking. Bernie was the light of his life and he was leaving her behind. He hadn't felt so low since the death of his grandmother, and the murder of Paulie's wife and little girl. He felt the grief like a living thing.

"Where we going, boss," Santi asked. "Vegas or Jersey?"

"Vegas," Mikey said without missing a beat. "I need a diversion. A big, bright, flashy, glitzy diversion."

"Vegas is a nice place," Santi said. He grinned. "Lots of glitzy girls there."

"You're welcome to all you can find," his boss replied glumly. "You can have my share, too."

"That's nice," Santi replied.

They packed their things into the convertible. Mikey went to the office and took care of the bill. Santi was waiting just outside the door in the limousine as he came out.

Mikey put himself into the back seat and leaned against it wearily as Santi pulled out into traffic. It was early morning, so they'd probably hit the work traffic on the way to the airport. He didn't care. Santi had been a wheelman for Mikey in earlier times. He was still a great driver.

"Do me a favor," Mikey said suddenly.

"Sure, boss. What?"

"Drive through town. Past the courthouse."

Santi didn't say anything. He just smiled.

The women who worked in Kemp's office were just filing in. There was Glory Ramirez and Sari Fiore. Olivia was ahead of them all. And there, behind them, in an old tweed coat, walking slowly with a cane, was Bernie.

"Slow down, okay?" Mikey asked, sounding half out of breath as he watched Bernie's slow progress to the door. She was hurting. It was a cold, rainy day, and he imagined she was having one of her flares.

He remembered her sitting up with him when he'd had the migraine. He remembered carrying her into the boardinghouse the day they'd met, when she had fallen in front of the car and he thought she was playing him. It seemed so long ago.

She made her way into the building, not looking behind her. She'd screwed her beautiful blond hair up into a bun. She looked tired and in pain, worn-out. He grimaced as he watched her disappear into the office. The door closed behind her.

Mikey felt the loss of connection like a blow to his chest.

"We leaving now, boss?" he asked Mikey.

There was a hesitation, only a very brief one. "Yeah," Mikey said finally. He slumped a little. "Yeah, we're leaving. Let's get to the airport."

"Sure thing," Santi said, and sped up past the office building, leaving it and Bernie behind, perhaps forever.

Chapter Fourteen

Bernie, never a late sleeper, woke very early the next morning. She couldn't get what Sari had said out of her mind. Suppose Jessie had told lies to both her and Mikey? She had been too shy to speak to him about something so intimate, and he would probably have been reluctant to say anything to Bernie about her supposed distaste for his background.

Jessie had been putting on an act. Why? The woman was patently out of place in Jacobsville, which led to a worrying conclusion. What if she was a lookout for that man who was trying to have Mikey killed? It really bothered her.

She got up and dressed, aching and barely able to walk for the pain and stiffness. After a few minutes, she felt better, but she'd still need the cane, even on level ground. Rheumatoid arthritis flares were painful and fatiguing. She took her medicines regularly, but they'd begun to be less effective, as many drugs became over the years. She recalled the wonder shot that was used to control it, but even with a large discount, she'd never be able to afford the monthly expense. It might have made a difference in her quality of life. Days like this, cold and rainy, were agony to people who lived with arthritis.

She didn't tell the other women that she'd walked to work, because they'd have fussed. Any one of them would gladly have offered her a ride, but she wanted to be independent. It wasn't good to lean on people. Her father had always said that they had to take care of their own problems and not advertise them to the world. It was a burden that honorable people shared. She smiled, remembering the wonderful man who'd raised her. She missed him.

"You're just on time," Sari Fiore teased, smiling.

"I'm always on time," Bernie replied with a small laugh. "I wouldn't want Mr. Kemp to fire me."

"No danger of that, as long as you don't tell Ted Regan that court's been dismissed," Olivia said, tongue in cheek.

They all laughed as they filed into the office.

Bernie was the last one inside. She almost stumbled going in, but she regained her footing quickly, holding on to the doorknob. The back of her neck tingled. Odd, she thought, that feeling. But it was probably nothing. She ignored it and went on inside the building.

* * *

Sari was pregnant. It was happy news, and the whole office went wild when they knew. Even Mr. Kemp congratulated her, grinning from ear to ear.

"You'll find that babies are addictive," he teased. "Which is why we have another one on the way, too."

"That's wonderful," Sari said, smiling. "I know Violet's over the moon. Are the twins coping with your toddler?"

"The twins?" Bernie asked curiously.

"He has two Siamese cats," Sari explained. "He made them mad one day and they tag-teamed biting his ankles and ran under heavy furniture afterward."

Mr. Kemp chuckled. "They've calmed down. Well, a little. Violet learned early that they like salmon, so she keeps cans of it handy."

They all laughed. Bernie was thinking about children. She'd wanted one so badly with Mikey. Just as well, she realized, that she'd never been intimate with him, considering the way things had turned out.

In his world of glitzy women and casinos, he probably had a procession of beautiful women at his beck and call. Including Jessie.

But she remembered that Sari had told her Mikey was no longer in danger; nor was his boss, Tony Garza. Apparently a group of bosses had decided that Cotillo was calling too much attention to certain underworld figures, and he'd been taken out of the equation. It was called "natural causes," but Sari said it wasn't at all, that the mob knew how to cause sudden death that looked natural.

That was Mikey's world. Death. Violence. Glitter. Of course, she was well out of it. Her health wouldn't have allowed her to endure the stresses of his profession, much less the strenuous lifestyle he enjoyed.

But she missed him terribly. It had sent her into days of depression when she knew he was gone. He'd left without even bothering to say goodbye. But what, she reasoned, could he have said? That he couldn't live with a disabled woman, that he preferred her sexy coworker, that Jessie was great in bed? All those things? It would have tormented her forever. No. It was better the way it had happened—a quick ending, as painless as possible. It was over.

Now all she had to do was adjust to her new reality. Maybe one day she could look back and remember a handsome, dashing man who'd taken her places and kissed her as if he'd have died for her mouth, who'd seemed to love her. Maybe she could recall just the joy of being with him, without remembering how it had ended. It would be a pretty memory, tied up with ribbon and tucked away in a scrapbook.

Mikey watched people come and go in the casino with hardly any interest at all. Beside him, Tony Garza, who was breaking his California trip with a stop in Las Vegas to see Mikey, was sipping a whiskey highball.

"They ever find out who hit Cotillo?" Mikey asked.

"No. And they never will. The New York family arranged it all. Cotillo was about to point the finger at one of their underbosses. It would have devastated the family. So they sent Jack the Mackerel and Billy Tenspot

down to visit Cotillo. They had a guy in the coroner's
office swear it was a natural death."

"What about Cotillo's family?" Mikey persisted.

"Running scared. It wasn't that big, and most of them
tried to talk Cotillo out of biting off more than he could
chew. The New York boss even spoke to him personally
and told him how it was. He didn't listen."

"Terminal error," Mikey commented.

"Very." He sighed. "At least we're off the hook. I
owe you, Mikey. Big-time. You ever need a favor, you
know where to find me."

Mikey shrugged. "No sweat. You'd have done it for
me, boss."

Tony chuckled. "Yeah. I would have." He paused.
"What's this about some Texas girl you got involved
with?"

Mikey's face closed up. "Closed chapter," he said
tautly.

"I got a good look at Texas women when I gave Merrie Grayling away at her wedding," he reminded Mikey.
"They're good people."

"She was. But she couldn't live with my profession."

"I heard you couldn't live with her maybe being an
invalid one day."

Mikey turned. His eyes glittered. "I never said that,"
he replied. "Never! It wouldn't have mattered to me
if she couldn't even walk. I'd have carried her—" He
broke off, averting his eyes.

Tony laid a big hand on his shoulder. "Jessie Tennison belongs to the New York boss. She's his mistress,"
he continued. "She made trouble for you because it's

what she does. Nobody likes her, and one day the wife is going to complain loudly enough that the boss will have to do something about her. Something unpleasant. She's making her own sad future and she doesn't even know it."

"I won't mourn her," Mikey said.

"Your cousin said she carried tales to both of you," he said. "She lied and you both believed her."

Mikey's face hardened. "Bernie told me herself that she was always on the right side of the law."

"And you told her that it didn't matter that she might become disabled one day, yes?"

Mikey's teeth clenched. "For all the good it did me."

"It's your life, *paisan*," he continued. "But you've been moping around here like a lost soul ever since I walked in the door, when we should both be celebrating. If I were you, I'd go back to Texas and talk to the woman. Really talk to her."

Mikey grimaced. "I took Jessie out on the town. I know, it was stupid. I was feeling low because of what I'd heard, what Jessie told me that Bernie said about my past. I wanted to feel better, so I took her up to San Antonio for supper. She told Bernie I slept with her. It's a lie, but Bernie had every reason to believe her. So even if I wanted to go back and talk it out, she'd never trust me again. She'd probably shut the door in my face."

"There are these things called roses," Tony mused. "Women go nuts over them. I know my late wife did. Chocolates. Greeting cards. I went through all those things while I was courting her." His eyes were wistful with memories. "She didn't even like me at first, but I wore her down. I was a bad man, too, Mikey, and her dad was a cop, but it didn't matter. She had leukemia," he added softly. "I took care of her when she had relapses, right up until the last one that took her out. I never minded. She knew it. We loved each other. None of the small stuff mattered. Love kept us together in spite of the difficulties we faced."

Mikey hadn't said anything. He just listened. "That's a lot like me and Bernie," he said after a minute.

"Yeah. How about that?"

Mikey took a deep breath. "I'll think about it." He glanced at the boss. "Roses, huh?"

"Might send yellow ones," Tony suggested. "Isn't there some song about yellow roses and Texas?"

Mikey actually laughed. It was the first time he had since he'd left Jacobsville.

It was the middle of the afternoon when the florist brought them in. Judy, who owned the flower shop, came herself, grinning from ear to ear as she carried them straight to a shocked Bernie at her desk and placed them on it.

"Oh!" Bernie's hand went to her throat. She couldn't believe what she was seeing. There must have been three dozen yellow roses in the arrangement, along with flowers of every single color, and greenery highlighting it all.

"I know, it's closer to Thanksgiving than spring," Judy laughed, "but the man said yellow roses, so that's what you get."

"The man?" Bernie was dumbfounded. Her coworkers were grinning from ear to ear.

"Read the card," Judy suggested, indicating it on a plastic stand inside the arrangement.

Bernie pulled it out with hands that held a faint trembling. She opened the envelope. The card only said, "Miss you terribly. Can you forgive?" And it was signed "Mikey."

Tears were rolling down her cheeks. She read the card again, just to be sure that she wasn't seeing things.

"Well?" Sari prompted. "What does it say? Who's it from? Or should we just guess?" she added with a grin.

"Mikey," Bernie said in a husky tone. "The flowers are from Mikey!"

"Doesn't he do things in a big way?" Olivia mused, studying the huge arrangement. "Amazing that your back didn't break under the weight, Judy," she teased the florist.

"I have liniment," Judy chuckled.

"They're so beautiful," Bernie said, caressing a petal on one of the roses, most of which were in bloom.

"I guess he thinks you are, too, sweetheart, because let me tell you, I could almost retire on what this arrangement cost," Judy laughed.

Bernie struggled to her feet and hugged the florist. "You always do the most beautiful arrangements, but this one is extraordinary."

"Thanks." Judy hugged her back.

Mr. Kemp came out of his office, stopped dead, and gaped at the arrangement that took up most of Bernie's desk. "Did somebody die?" he asked.

They all burst out laughing. Kemp grinned.

"Mikey, huh?" he asked Bernie, who flushed. "I figured he'd work it out sooner or later. Okay, people, back to work."

"Yes, sir," they chorused.

Bernie and Judy moved her beautiful floral arrangement to a side table so that the desk was clear, but all day Bernie's eyes went to it, and she felt as if she could walk on clouds.

Paul and Sari Fiore drove her home so that Paul could carry the arrangement inside for her. It was very heavy.

"Right there, if you don't mind," Bernie said, indicating the cleared-off part of her chest of drawers. "It's so beautiful!"

"Good thing that Judy makes arrangements that don't have a loud scent," Sari teased, "or you'd smother in here from the fumes."

"Oh, I wouldn't even mind." Bernie sighed. "Nobody ever sent me flowers in my whole life," she added softly.

Paul and Sari exchanged glances. It was obvious that Mikey's peace offering had struck pay dirt.

He phoned Paul that night.

"Well?" he asked. "Did she donate them to the hospital or her church?" he prompted, and sounded worried.

"No. She cried," Paul said. "Then Sari and I brought her home so I could carry them inside for her. God, Mikey, did you buy out a florist? I never knew there were that many yellow roses in the whole damned state," he added, chuckling.

"I wanted to make an impression," Mikey replied.

There was a smile in his voice. "So she liked them, huh?"

"She loved them."

There was a sigh. "In that case, Santi and I might come down for a visit in a week or so. Just to get the lay of the land."

"I think that would be a very good idea," Paul replied.

Bernie was walking home late in the afternoon, wrapped in a coat against the chill, using her cane because it was rainy and her footing wasn't good.

A big, black limousine pulled up beside her and the window rolled down while her heart almost beat her to death.

"Now, don't fall under the wheels this time, okay?" said a man with a New Jersey accent.

Bernie laughed. "Hi," she said softly.

The door opened. Mikey got out, leaving Santi behind the wheel. He stuck his hands in his pockets and moved close to Bernie. His dark eyes searched her wan face in the late-afternoon dimness. They were intent, as if he was looking at something almost out of a fantasy.

"You look good," he said. "A little worn. You've lost weight, I think."

"Just a little," she confessed. Her eyes went over his lean face. "You look worn, too."

"I never slept with Jessie," he blurted out. "I like to stick to my own species."

She laughed in spite of herself.

"I did a dumb thing," he muttered. "I should have

known that you wouldn't pour your heart out to somebody in a public place."

She grimaced. "I should have known the same thing
about you."

He drew in a breath and smiled. "So. Suppose we
start over? Hi. My name's Mikey. I sometimes break
the law, but I'll try to restrict myself to jaywalking for
the rest of my life if you'll take a chance on me."

Her heart leaped. "Hi. My name's Bernadette, but everybody calls me Bernie. I never break the law, but I'd
take a chance on you no matter what you did for a living."

His lips parted on a husky breath. "Oh, baby," he said
in a rough whisper. "God, I've missed you...!"

She would have told him the same thing, but he had
her up in his arms and was kissing her as if there was
no tomorrow. Her arms were around his neck, her cane
was on the sidewalk somewhere getting wet. She was
kissing him back.

Long minutes went by. The rain was coming down
in buckets and they were both soaked. Finally Santi got
out of the car and stopped beside them, coughing loudly.

Mikey drew back, shivering a little with the overwhelming hunger he felt for Bernie. He looked at Santi
blankly. "What? You got a cold?"

"Boss, it's raining. Really raining. You know?"

Mikey blinked. Santi's hair was plastered to his head
and face. He scowled and looked down at Bernie. Her
hair was plastered to her head and face, too. He laughed
out loud. "Damn. So it is! I guess we should find a dry
place, huh?"

"I guess," Santi mused. He opened the car door.

"But I'm wet," Bernie wailed.

"The seats are leather, honey, they'll dry. Santi, find her cane, would you?"

"You bet!"

Santi closed the door.

"Now," Mikey murmured, drawing her close. "Where were we...?"

They were married in the courthouse, in the office of the justice of the peace. Bernie wore a winter-white coatdress and carried a bouquet of white roses. She had on a little saucy white hat that had a veil, and Mikey lifted it as he kissed her for the first time as Mrs. Michael Fiore.

Sari and Paul were their witnesses, and Tony Garza came down with his entourage for the wedding. In fact, Marcus Carrera and his Delia, and their little boys, also came to town for the event.

"I owe you a lot," Mikey told Marcus.

The big man waved away the thanks. "No sweat," he chuckled. "But if you come across a bolt of antique cloth, you know where to mail it, right?" he teased.

Mikey clapped him on the back. "You bet I do."

The honeymoon was in Jamaica, in Montego Bay, where they swam and acted like tourists. Well, at least, after the first night they were together.

"You don't need to worry about a thing," Mikey whispered to her as he undressed her very slowly and eased her under the covers.

She shivered a little at the first contact with his nude

body, but he kissed her and caressed her until she didn't care what he did as long as he didn't stop.

He carried her from one breathless plateau to another, from one side of the bed to the other, for what seemed hours before he finally moved over her with intent. She was so sensitized by then that she barely felt the little flash of pain that hallmarked his slow penetration of her welcoming body.

She was aching for him, so hungry that she knew nothing, saw nothing, except his face above her as the passion grew and grew and grew and finally exploded into pleasure beyond anything she'd ever dreamed.

"Oh, my goodness," she moaned as they finally moved apart. She shifted her hips and the exquisite sensations went on and on.

He chuckled, drawing her to his side. "It's addictive."

"Very!"

He pulled her onto him and looked up into her soft eyes. "I've never missed anyone the way I missed you. I was just ashamed to even call you, after what I did."

She bent and kissed him tenderly. "We both believed lies because we were insecure."

"But no more."

"Not ever," she agreed.

"There's still the matter of the little unlawful things," he said, grimacing. "But I've got a legitimate casino now, and two of the biggest mob bosses in history in my corner. So if I want to move out into the world, so long as I don't betray any secrets, I can leave the old life behind. Not that I'll give up my house in Jersey. You'll like it," he added softly. "It's old, but it's got character."

"I'll love anywhere you live," she said simply. "And I'll cope, however I have to." Her pale eyes met his dark ones. "I love you."

He hugged her close. "I love you, too, baby. And don't you dare think I mind about the cane and the days you have flares, or if you get sick. I can afford nurses, anything you need. But I'll take care of you myself," he added, lifting his head, and his eyes adored her. "Because you're the most important thing in the whole world."

"So are you to me," she whispered, and kissed him.

"Listen, I spoke to your doctor," he said. "Louise Coltrain said there are medicines you can inject, that will make your quality of life a hundred times better."

"Yes, but they're so expensive—"

"I could fund the treasury of a small country, honey," he interrupted. "It will be money well spent, especially when the kids come along. You won't need to try and keep up with me," he chuckled. "I'll carry you, if I need to. But you *will* need to keep up with our kids…"

She laughed with pure delight. "Are we having several?"

He grinned. "However many you want. And I'll learn to change diapers and give bottles, just so you know."

"We can do it together," she said softly.

"We'll do everything together," he replied quietly. "As long as we live. Yes?"

She bent and kissed him hungrily. "As long as we live." And they did.

* * * * *

MILLS & BOON

Coming next month

THEIR ROYAL BABY GIFT
Kandy Shepherd

The woman's wet dress clung to her body making no secret of her curves. She was a scandal in the making.

He grabbed a striped towel from a stack on a nearby lounger and threw it around her shoulders, another one around himself. "Keep your head down and walk as quickly as you can," he said.

She attempted a faster pace but stumbled and he had to put his arm around her to keep her upright. He scarcely broke his stride to pick up the phone she'd dropped when she'd fallen.

"Are you hurt?"

"Only…only my pride."

"Are you staying at this hotel?"

She shook her head and wet strands flew around her face, sending droplets of water on him. "I…I only came here for lunch. My hotel is in the older part of town."

"I'm in the penthouse here. There's a private elevator down to my suite. I'll take you there."

"Please." She was still shivering, and her eyes didn't look quite focused.

He had to get her—and himself—out of here. Edward kept his arm around Ms Mermaid as he ushered her to the discreet private elevator. If people didn't recognise him, a scandal could be averted.

Within minutes they were in the expansive suite where he was living while his Singapore house was being gutted and refurbished. He slammed the door behind them and slumped in relief. No one with a camera could follow him here. He turned back into the room. Then realised he had swapped one problem for another. Standing opposite him, dripping water on the marble floor of his hotel suite was a beautiful stranger—and her presence here could so easily be misconstrued.

"Thank you," she said. "I could have drowned." Her eyes were huge, her lush mouth trembled. Hair wet and dripping, makeup smudged around her eyes she was breathtakingly lovely. A red-blooded male, no matter how chivalrous, could not fail to feel a stirring of attraction. "I…I can't swim, not enough to save myself. But you…you saved me."

Continue reading
THEIR ROYAL BABY GIFT
Kandy Shepherd

Available next month
www.millsandboon.co.uk

COMING SOON!

We really hope you enjoyed reading this book.
If you're looking for more romance, be sure to
head to the shops when new books are
available on

Thursday 15th
October

Within minutes they were in the expansive suite where he was living while his Singapore house was being gutted and refurbished. He slammed the door behind them and slumped in relief. No one with a camera could follow him here. He turned back into the room. Then realised he had swapped one problem for another. Standing opposite him, dripping water on the marble floor of his hotel suite was a beautiful stranger—and her presence here could so easily be misconstrued.

"Thank you," she said. "I could have drowned." Her eyes were huge, her lush mouth trembled. Hair wet and dripping, makeup smudged around her eyes she was breathtakingly lovely. A red-blooded male, no matter how chivalrous, could not fail to feel a stirring of attraction. "I…I can't swim, not enough to save myself. But you…you saved me."

Continue reading
THEIR ROYAL BABY GIFT
Kandy Shepherd

Available next month
www.millsandboon.co.uk

COMING SOON!

We really hope you enjoyed reading this book.
If you're looking for more romance, be sure to
head to the shops when new books are
available on

Thursday 15th October

LET'S TALK
Romance

For exclusive extracts, competitions
and special offers, find us online:

- facebook.com/millsandboon
- @MillsandBoon
- @MillsandBoonUK

Get in touch on 01413 063232

JOIN US ON SOCIAL MEDIA!

Stay up to date with our latest releases, author
news and gossip, special offers and discounts, and
all the behind-the-scenes action
from Mills & Boon...

 millsandboon

 millsandboonuk

 millsandboon

might just be true love...